# FOUR
# YEARS
# LATER

a novel

emma
doherty

Cover by Murphy Rae at www.murphyrae.net
Editing by www.murphyrae.net
Proofread by Caitlin with Editing by C. Marie
Formatted by Stacey at www.champagneformats.com

*Four Years Later* can be read as a standalone, but to get a true idea of Becca and Ryan's history and to see how they got together, you'll want to check out *Four Doors Down* first.

# DEDICATION

This book is dedicated to all those people who feel
unable to speak out

# CHAPTER 1

*Becca*

WALK THROUGH THE ARRIVALS GATE, DODGING people who are strolling along leisurely. I'm dragging my carry-on along behind me; I only brought hand luggage because I didn't want to waste a single second when I got off the plane. My eyes dart around, trying to spot him through the thick crowd. I quickly scan and dismiss every person that isn't him, and it takes almost a minute before I spot the familiar figure. He's leaning against a wall to the right, his arms crossed over his chest and his gaze locked on me. My face breaks out in a huge smile, and my heart swells just at the sight of him. I've been counting down the days until I see him, and now, when he's only maybe thirty feet away from me, I'm frozen in place, happy just to watch him, to soak him in. He raises an eyebrow, and a cocky smirk crosses his face as he stares straight back at me. My feet kick into motion and I make my way over to him. His gaze never leaves me; it rakes up and down my body, making me blush like a schoolgirl. I stop in front of him and can't wipe the humongous grin off my face.

"Hey," he says. His stunning blue eyes twinkle as he looks into mine.

"Hey," I say right back, my heart swelling with happiness.

We stare at each other for a couple of seconds, soaking each other in. It's the first time we've seen each other in two months. It's the longest we've ever gone, and it felt like a lifetime. His gaze flickers to my lips, and with reflexes quicker than I can comprehend, he steps forward and scoops me up in his arms, pulling me tightly against his body and spinning me around. I laugh with delight, hugging him back until he silences me with a kiss so passionate I lose my breath and have to pull back.

"I missed you," he tells me, smiling against my mouth.

"I missed you too," I say, leaning my forehead against his and staring into the eyes I've been dreaming about for weeks. He squeezes me again and picks me up off the ground. I start to laugh again, but then he shuts me up with another kiss.

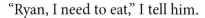

"Ryan, I need to eat," I tell him.

I'm sprawled out, facedown in his bed, trying to stop my yawn. We got back to his house three hours ago and didn't even stop to see who else was home. We headed straight upstairs, and we've spent the whole time in his bed. He shifts next to me, and the next thing I know, he's hooking his right arm under my neck and turning my body so I'm facing him.

He pulls me up against him so my head rests in the crook of his neck and my arm stretches across his stomach, skimming over the solid muscles of his abs. He starts to trace small circles on my arm with his fingers, and it's both relaxing and exciting at the same time. I sigh, completely content and happy to finally be with him.

"Did you think any more about what we talked about?" he asks.

I freeze and try to stifle a sigh. I'm not ready to have this conversation yet; it'll only lead to a fight, and I just want to enjoy being together.

"Becca?"

I lean back and prop myself up on my elbows so I can see him. His blue eyes stare back into mine with such hope, I feel terrible that I'm about to crush him. "I can't transfer, Ryan." I see the flash of annoyance in his eyes so I rush on. "I love being at Southern U. I have friends there, my classes are there. We just have to get through the rest of this year, then we'll have the whole summer, and then it's only one more year 'til we graduate."

"That's more than eighteen months, Becca."

"It'll fly by, you know it will. We've already done more than two years."

He sighs. "Please, Becca. I'd do it for you if I could."

*If I could*—that's the thing. Ryan has a football scholarship at California State, and is on the fast track to make it to the NFL—something I never thought would happen. Ryan can't leave Cal State, even if he wanted to. If someone is going to make the sacrifice and move, it has to be me. It's something we both know. We also both know I don't want to.

I shake my head slightly and look away from him. I hate making him upset, but being at Southern U is my thing. It's my thing away from him, and I kinda love it. I love living in Texas. It's somewhere so completely different from the California town I grew up in; it's new and exciting, and I'm not ready to give it up yet. I know people laughed when we said we were going to stay together through college while living in different states, but we've made it work; only now, Ryan's starting to lose patience.

"Please don't be mad. It's just one more year." That's not true; it's closer to two years, and we both know it.

He sighs but doesn't look at me. His whole body has gone tense and I bite my lip, knowing how upset he is, even if he's not willing to say it. He thinks I'm not willing to make the sacrifice for him, that I don't care enough to move here for him, but that's just not true. I just like being something other than Ryan Jackson's girlfriend, but I can't say that to him.

I dip my head and kiss him on the mouth; he doesn't respond. I kiss him again. I don't stop giving him big, wet, sloppy kisses. He tries to move his head away but I turn with him, not letting him get away from me, keeping my mouth attached to his, moving with him. Finally he gives in. Finally he starts to laugh and starts kissing me back, and they soon stop being wet and sloppy and turn to passion and hunger. I breathe an internal sigh of relief that he's not going to stay mad at me. I don't stop kissing him though, not when I've been apart from him for so long, and not when I want to prove how much I love him and how much I want him—because I do. I love Ryan Jackson with a passion that shocks me. He kisses me back, and before I know it, he's flipped me over and is towering above me, grinning down at me.

"Dinner?" I ask, smiling.

His eyes are heavy with lust, and he dips down and plants another kiss on my mouth, his hand slipping under the bedsheets. I know I'm not leaving this bed any time soon.

# CHAPTER 2

*Becca*

W E ENTER THE FRAT HOUSE TOGETHER, AND although Ryan tries to hold on to my hand, he's immediately swept up by people greeting him, slapping him on the back, and wanting to talk to him. He looks back at me apologetically, but I just smile back and wave a hand, letting him know it's fine. I'm used to people wanting Ryan's attention; he's always been crazy popular, and this is his domain, his college, where he's the football star. Of course he's going to attract attention.

I step farther into the party, into a huge side room where people are already dancing over by the windows on a make-shift dance floor. My eyes dart past all the people dancing, laughing, and holding red cups and shot glasses as I try to find who I'm looking for. I can't help but smile when I spot him. Jake stands over by the wall, chatting with a guy I don't recognize. He looks pretty animated and is throwing his arms about, gesticulating dramatically for effect. I start to walk over to him, but someone else gets to him first. A petite blonde girl steps in front of me, pulls his face down to hers, and starts sucking at his mouth. I pull up short and can't help the smirk that crosses my face. *Wow, making out is actually gross from this close up.* She looks like she's trying to taste what he had for dinner. I wait for them to finish, but when they show no sign of stopping, I clear my throat loudly. They break away at the interruption, and when Jake spots me, a huge grin breaks out on his face. He quickly steps forward and grabs me in a tight hug, picking me up off the ground. *Someone has definitely had a few drinks tonight.*

"Was wondering when you'd show up!" he tells me, tousling my hair as I scowl in irritation—well, mock irritation. It's impossible for me to stay mad at Jake for long.

"Um, Jake!" his make-out partner snaps, clearly annoyed I've distracted him.

"Heather, Becca. Becca, Heather," Jake introduces us, waving a hand between us.

She eyes me suspiciously, and I raise an eyebrow at her. "How do you know each other?"

Ah, she thinks there's something between us. I nearly snort out loud at the mere thought of it.

"Becca's an old friend from way back. From grade school," he tells her.

That doesn't seem to appease her. "What are you doing here?"

"Visiting."

"Who?" She glances at Jake questioningly.

I can't resist. "My boyfriend," I tell her, flicking my eyes

7

over to Jake and wrapping my arms around his waist.

Her eyes widen in fury before Jake is pushing me away from him and rolling his eyes.

"Ryan," Jake clarifies. He turns to me, and he can't hide his smirk of amusement. "You are such a shit, McKenzie."

"Wait!"

We both turn back to her. Her eyes have widened in surprise, but she's no longer staring at me with hostility.

"Ryan who?"

I frown. Surely if she's dating Jake, she'd know who Ryan is—they're practically inseparable.

"Jackson," I clarify. "Do you know him?"

"Know him?" she practically squeals, her face lighting up with excitement. "Everyone knows Ryan! Oh my God, you're really Ryan's girlfriend?" Her demeanor has completely changed.

"I take full credit for getting them together," Jake informs her, which earns him an eye roll from me.

"Oh my God! It's so nice to meet you," she tells me, stepping toward me and apparently completely forgetting that she hated me a minute ago. "I've wanted to meet you for so long. Everyone's dying to know who's managed to catch Ryan and keep him so hooked."

I take a step back from her, flashing a questioning look at Jake. He looks at Heather uneasily. This is weird. I mean, *seriously?* She makes it sound like I'm some mystical creature who is never around and doesn't really exist. I visit as much as I can, but when I'm here, Ryan and I would rather spend the time together, just the two of us. So, it is pretty rare that I come to a party with him, but I am around, and I know most of his close circle here. And 'keep him so hooked'? As if we're not just a normal couple who love each other and are happy together? Why does she care so much about my damn business?

"You are so lucky! Seriously, Ryan is so into you. Like, he could get with anyone, and girls are always hitting on him. Like, seriously hot girls who would do anything, and he doesn't even care!" I cock an eyebrow at her. *Is this supposed to be reassuring?* "I mean, seriously, girls will do anything to just talk to him, but he doesn't even care. He loves you so much. And you are way prettier than Kelly said you were!" Okay, this does annoy me. "Like, you're actually really, really pretty," she continues.

Jake clears his throat awkwardly while I try not to glare. "Okay, I think maybe we should get you some water," he tells Heather and steers her away, smiling apologetically at me. "Ignore her," he mouths over his shoulder at me, but I'm pissed off now. *Why is some random girl I've never even met so interested in my relationship?*

I turn to try to spot Ryan, and I swear my blood stars boiling instantly, because sure enough, there she is—Kelly Taylor, creeping up on Ryan.

Kelly Taylor has been hanging around Ryan since he first got to Cal State and they were in the same dorms. She's a major football groupie who's hooked up with over half the team, but it's Ryan she's been intent on since the start—he's the prize in her eyes. I'm sure she's convinced she's perfect for him or some other nonsense. Every time I see her, I want to slap her smug face. It's annoying that she's actually really good-looking, and God, does she know it. She's delusional if she thinks

I can't see through the fake smiles she gives me whenever I visit. She wants Ryan badly, and I'm pretty sure she's made that clear to him. I trust Ryan completely, but I wouldn't trust her as far as I could throw her. She's forever tagging him in pictures on Facebook and Instagram. Usually she's draped all over him, pouting like a Kardashian, and while he's never touching her or doing anything to raise suspicion, it still pisses me off.

*Oh my God!* She actually reaches out and strokes his arm before Ryan awkwardly pulls it away. It's as though she can feel my eyes on her, because she turns and spots me watching them, my arms crossed over my chest. She frowns at me, obviously unaware that I was here, and then nods slightly, says something to Ryan, and walks away. Ryan turns to me and looks confused while I glare, then he smirks at me, probably happy that I'm jealous. He strolls over to me and stops just in front of me with a cocky smile playing on his lips.

I glare back at him. "Having fun over there?"

A low chuckle leaves his mouth and his eyes gleam. "You're jealous."

"I'm not jealous!" I snap in annoyance.

His grin gets bigger. "Yes you are."

"No, I'm not, and if I were jealous, it certainly wouldn't be of Kelly Taylor," I say with disdain.

A pleased smile crosses his face. I roll my eyes and tell him I'm going to get a drink, turning to walk away from him, but he reaches out and tugs me back against him. His arm wraps around my waist, and his mouth finds my ear. "I love that you're jealous," he whispers.

And I know that he does. I know sometimes he feels like

he's more into this relationship than I am, which is absolutely not the case, but I think it boosts his ego when he sees me jealous.

I shrug away from him and attempt to walk off, but he just starts laughing and tugs me around so I'm facing him. He reaches down to my waist and picks me up, hauling me over his shoulder so my ass is in the air.

I'm mortified. "Put me down now!" I demand, grateful that I'm wearing my usual jeans and not a skirt.

He laughs in return and starts making his way through the room. "Make way!" he calls. "My hot-as-fuck girlfriend is in town, and we need to sit down." I try to struggle free, but he just slaps my ass, and I can't help but laugh.

He stops over by a couple of sofas that are pushed together and repositions me so that when he sits down, I find myself in his lap with my back against his chest. I try to straighten my hair, feeling completely flustered, and then I turn and shove him. He simply grins at me wildly.

"Idiot," I mutter, smiling at him. I go to move off his knee, but his arms clamp around me, pulling me tighter against his chest, and I know he won't let me leave. I don't really care; this is the best seat in the house, and I love being this close to him.

A low chuckle across from me turns my attention back to my surroundings, and I realize Ryan has sat us down next to Jason, Dean, and Marty (who might just be the nicest guy in the world); they're Ryan's teammates and they all live together, along with Jake. "Should have known you were in town, Becca." Dean winks at me. "He hasn't answered any of my texts since Thursday."

Jason starts to laugh. "Dude, he's been walking around

with his head in the clouds all week, you should have known he was about to get laid." I scowl at him, and Ryan reaches out and slaps him across the head, making them all laugh harder. I roll my eyes at them and look away. Of course they know Ryan and I have sex, but they don't need to broadcast it to the entire party.

I look over and see Kelly scowling from her place in the corner. She's standing with a few other girls who are also looking at me in disdain. Her eyes lock with mine, and I know this is driving her crazy. She wants Ryan so badly; she's not even bothering to hide it anymore. The last couple of times I've been here, I've noticed it more and more. I'm almost tempted to plant one on Ryan right now, just to piss her off, but I think better of it. I don't have to prove myself to her. In fact, girls like her make me sick. The thing about Ryan and his teammates is, they are big deals on this campus, however crazy that might seem. They are at the top of their game in college football. If they make it to the NFL, they'll have more money than they could possibly imagine, and there are certain girls in colleges all across the country (mine included) that see this as a huge selling point. That, combined with the fact that most of the guys on the team are friendly, funny, and good-looking, means they get some serious female attention. These girls want them badly and will do almost anything to get them. Given the fact that Ryan is also drop-dead gorgeous and probably one of the most charismatic guys I've ever met, it's easy to see why I don't like Kelly Taylor and the other girls that are lining up to take my place.

"Becca?" I turn and see Hayley Walsh smiling at me. "I didn't know you were in town this weekend."

I return her smile as she sits down on one of the sofas. Her boyfriend, Max, stands behind her and nods at Jake when he too wanders over.

Hayley is the only other serious girlfriend that I know on the football team. She followed Max to Cal State, and they live together now. Although a bit excitable and preppy, she's actually a sweet girl I've come to really like. She always makes me feel welcome whenever I visit. I know Ryan's teammates found it crazy when they first heard that Ryan and I were together despite living so far apart, and I know they initially encouraged him to live the single-college-guy party lifestyle, but they soon understood we were unbreakable. Now, they just treat me as one of their own.

"How are you?" I ask. "Enjoying your last year at college?"

Hayley beams at me. "Yeah! Graduation will be here before we know it."

I grin. "Scary times."

"Nah, it's exciting. Just annoying that we can't make plans until we know where we'll be next year."

"You don't know?" I ask, surprised. I know I have no clue about what I want to do after graduation, but I'm hoping that in a year's time, I'll at least have considered some options.

"Of course not. I'm hoping for the West Coast, but it really depends on Max," she says, gesturing behind her.

I raise my eyebrows in confusion.

"You know, where he gets drafted, where he'll be based?" she continues.

"You're going with him?" Now I get it—she can't make plans until she knows where he'll be. "Wow, I didn't realize," I continue, smiling at them both while she looks at me like I'm crazy. I feel Ryan stiffen around me.

"Yes, I'm going with him," she tells me, a frown on her face, like it's the most obvious thing in the world.

"But what if you guys end up in the middle of nowhere? What will you do for work?"

"Well, I don't know yet." She laughs at the expression on my face.

"You don't know yet?" Isn't the whole point of college to study hard and then get a job in your area of interest?

"No, I'll figure something out."

"Wow." I'm impressed. Hayley's told me before how much she loves living in California, so I'm amazed she'd willingly move somewhere she knows nothing about. "Doesn't that bother you?"

"I don't know why you're surprised about this. I want to go, to support him," she says, awkwardly glancing behind me at Ryan.

"But," I continue, trying not to make Max feel uncomfortable even though I do think this is crazy. "Don't you think—"

She cuts me off. "I'll do whatever. Work wherever. I probably won't even have to work, and we might start a family in the next few years."

*Wow.* This is news to me, although she's right—it probably shouldn't be. It just seems crazy to me that you would put your own life and plans on hold to follow your boyfriend to the middle of nowhere and just be there waiting for him when he comes home. What about her hopes and dreams? And a baby, already? She's only twenty-one, twenty-two at the very oldest.

"Unbelievable," Ryan mutters behind me. I turn to look at him, but he grabs me by the hips, shoves me to the side, and stalks toward the kitchen, leaving me behind.

I look around in surprise. His friends are either looking awkwardly away or looking at me like I'm stupid. "What?" I ask. I turn to Jake. "What did I do?"

He rolls his eyes at me in frustration. "Use your brain, Becca." When I just stare back at him blankly, he gestures after Ryan. "Well, follow him then."

I send Hayley one last confused glance and follow after Ryan. I catch up with him in the kitchen and see that he's grabbed a beer. When I reach out to grab his hand, he turns to me, and his face is thunderous.

"What's wrong?" I ask.

"Are you fucking kidding me, Becca?" he demands, his voice low and angry. He looks furious. "It hadn't even occurred to you that we might have to live somewhere completely random if I get drafted?"

*Um, no.* I hadn't thought about it all.

"Have you even thought about where you'll live and what you'll do after you finish college?"

"Well, no. Not really. You know I want to be on the East Coast." My roommate is from New York, and after hearing her talk about it over the last couple of years, I've been desperate to move there after college.

"But what if that's not where I'm playing?"

"Well, it's not an issue yet, so there's no point in worrying about it, right?"

His eyes narrow, searching my eyes. I look away awkwardly.

"Jesus Becca, you haven't even thought about what we'll do after we graduate?" I stare back at him, openmouthed. "Has it even entered your brain that I might want you to move with me?"

*Oh crap.* "Yes."

"Don't lie to me," he snaps. He knows me too well. "For fuck's sake, what is the point of all this then? You won't transfer to be with me now. You're not even thinking about us being together when we graduate. What the fuck is the point of this long-distance crap if there's not even going to be an end to it?"

My jaw falls open in disbelief, and he turns and walks away in annoyance. I watch him stalk out of the kitchen for a few seconds before my brain kicks in and I hurry after him, reaching out and grabbing his arm. "Wait," I say quietly.

He sighs but reluctantly turns to face me. I tug on his hand and pull him out into the hallway, aware that we've garnered a few curious looks now that we're back in the huge living room. The last thing I want is his friends witnessing this fight, and I definitely don't want Kelly Taylor to see it. He allows me to pull him into a dark corner where we have some privacy.

"What the hell was that?" I demand, my own voice sharp with anger. "If you don't want to be with me Ryan, just tell me."

His jaw clenches, and I can practically feel the anger radiating off him in waves.

"You think I don't want to be with you?" he demands. "Becca, all I want is to be with you. I hate this long-distance shit. I thought I'd get used to it, but all I want is to see you.

16

Every single day. That's all I want. That's all I've ever wanted, but I have to stay here and play football, and then you tell me that when this is all over, when neither of us are tied to a college anymore and we can both be together, you haven't even thought about moving to be with me?"

*Oh shit.* He's right. A wave of guilt floods me as I realize how this must look. Ryan always considers me in every decision he makes, and I don't always remember to consider him. Like when I decided to go to Southern U after he'd already accepted his scholarship. My right hand reaches out to his left, and I lace my fingers through his.

"I'm sorry, okay? I wasn't thinking. That was stupid."

He sighs and looks past me, but I can tell I've placated him slightly. I tug on his hand, pulling his attention back to me.

"You're right. Long-distance is shit, but we make it work because we're us. We're Becca and Ryan, and we're always going to be together. Nothing is ever going to change that."

He still doesn't look at me, but his body has started to relax ever so slightly.

"It's you and me, Ryan. Always will be." I tug on his hand again, and he finally looks down at me. "When it comes to leaving college and you getting drafted, we'll make it work, right? Everything will work out just fine," I tell him.

He gives me a reluctant nod, and I smirk back up at him. "I love you, Jackson," I tell him—and I do. I love Ryan Jackson more than I ever thought possible. As far as I'm concerned, he's the best person in the world, and I still get butterflies when I see him. Sometimes, I just need my brain to engage a little more so I realize how things might look from

17

his perspective.

His eyes soften. "I love you too, McKenzie." I know he means it; he knew it before I did.

I stand on my tiptoes and press my lips to his. He responds, pulling me into him. I deepen the kiss, putting everything I have into it, trying to prove to him how much I feel for him, how much I love him. He kisses me right back, and suddenly I'm backed up against the wall with Ryan's hands roaming all over me. I pull away, breathless, and he's smirking down at me, blatant lust in his eyes. I'm pretty sure they reflect the look in my own.

"Wanna get out of here?" I ask, even though I already know the answer.

He gives me a look that makes my stomach flip and takes my hand, pulling me out of our private corner. He strides ahead, cutting through the large front room. We pass his friends by the sofas, but Ryan doesn't even slow down, just shouts "We're out!" over his shoulder at them. I catch them smirking at us, clearly realizing we've made up. Kelly and her friends scowl at me as Ryan pulls me into the backyard and then onto a back road. We get back to his room in record time, and all arguments are completely forgotten.

# CHAPTER 3

*Becca*

"SO, DID YOU AND RYAN MAKE UP LAST NIGHT?" I glance over to Jake, who's walking down the street next to me. "Yeah." I smirk. "And this morning."

Jake immediately pulls a face and shoves me away from him, muttering, "It's like thinking of your parents doing it." I laugh. I know it must have been weird for Jake when we first got together. He went from barely seeing us together to us being inseparable, but he's never once said anything about it or moaned about losing Ryan's attention. I know he was the biggest supporter of us getting together, and to be honest, Jake is with us all the time. It's like we're the Three Musketeers, and I love it.

"I'm starving," Jake announces, and I nod in agreement. Ryan had to get up early for practice this morning, so we're on our way to campus to meet him for lunch. Jake got a walk-on slot on the Cal State Warriors' team his freshman year, but he busted his knee up in practice one day and doesn't play anymore. He still hangs out with the team a lot though, and he has a part-time coaching role with the coaching staff. He was considering becoming a physical therapist, but has since decided he wants to be a lawyer. He still enjoys working with the team a couple times a week, and I get the impression he enjoys the perks that come with being associated with the team, AKA the girls. He's been filling me in on his latest girl drama (Heather's not the only one on the scene), and it makes me even more grateful I've got Ryan and will never have to deal with the single life. I'm exhausted just hearing about it, although I have a feeling not everyone's single life is quite as exciting as Jake's.

"Did he tell you he wants me to move here?"

Jake glances sideways at me. "Yeah." Of course he knows; Ryan pretty much tells him everything. "Are you gonna do it?"

I sigh, stop, and turn to face him. He stops walking and looks at me. "I can't. I mean, Cal State's great and all, and I miss him so much, but I can't. I love it at Southern U and…" I pause and say the one thing that's stopping me from moving here above all else. "I can't just be Ryan's girlfriend, you know? I mean, I love him, but I've got to be something more than just Ryan Jackson's girlfriend."

Jake smiles down at me. "I get it, Becca." And I know that he does. A lesser person than Jake might be envious of Ryan's success and the way his life always seems to work out perfectly, how he seems to always get everything he wants, how everyone adores him—but not Jake. Ryan is Jake's best friend in the world; they've been inseparable for years, and I know he doesn't resent Ryan's success. He's as proud of him as I am, and Ryan would do anything for Jake, too. I honestly think Ryan would have cried if Jake went to a different college. I joke with him sometimes that Jake's the true love of his life, and I'm pretty sure Jake benefits from his status. I'm certain Ryan makes an excellent wingman for him, and anyone who talks to Jake for more than five minutes knows he matches Ryan in personality and charisma. They make quite the duo.

"Is he upset?"

I let out a loud sigh and shrug my shoulders. I know Ryan's upset that I won't move here, but I need to do this for me. Jake leans over and nudges me with his shoulder. "He just misses you, that's all."

"I know. I miss him too. It's like he thinks it's easy for me being away from him."

"He knows deep down that it's tough for you too. He just wishes you were here."

I shrug my shoulders. I wish we could be together too, but not here, not at Cal State, where it's all about Ryan, and I'd just be walking around in his shadow.

Jake grins at me. "It would be awesome if you were here though."

I roll my eyes. "Yeah, right. I'd just cramp your style." He laughs and shoves me into the hedge on the side of the road. He nearly falls over laughing when I right myself and have to pick leaves out of my hair. I flip him my middle finger, and he drapes his arm around me as we hit the campus.

"So your mom set me up to work at her office again next summer," he says.

"That's awesome." Jake interned with my mom last summer and fell in love with it. He reminds me a lot of her, actually, wanting to make a difference for those who need it. I think he'll make a great lawyer.

"And she's arranged for me to do a couple weeks with a friend of hers who works in one of the big firms in the city, so I can see both sides of it." I nod. There's a lot of money to be made in law, but not if you do legal aid like my mom. It's good that he'll see both sides of the world of law, but he won't go into private practice though—I just know it.

"You really like it, huh?"

He nods. "Yeah. I just feel like it's where I want to be. I want to be able to make a difference, at least in a small way, and this is a way to do it, y'know? I'm passionate about it."

I don't know. I've not had that feeling about a career yet, and I know that's part of the reason Ryan doesn't understand why I won't transfer here. When I first started at Southern U, I was all set on making a career out of my passion for art, but after a couple of months, I changed majors. I hated having someone dissect and criticize every little project I worked on. It stopped being fun for me. Then I decided to give English literature a go, as well as keeping up my other options, but that didn't work out either. Now I'm doing humanities, which doesn't seem to hold my interest. I guess it's not hard to see why Ryan sees it as me messing around at Southern U, changing my mind, yet I still won't transfer here, where he's actually carving out a career for himself—one that will have us both set up for life. The thing is, I don't care about that. I mean, I'm ridiculously proud of him and all he's achieved here, and the day he gets drafted and his dreams come true, I'll be the happiest person in the world. But, I'm my own person, and I have my own hopes and dreams. I just haven't quite figured them out yet. I want my independence. No way do I want to rely on Ryan for anything.

Jake notices my silence. "You'll figure it out, McKenzie. No rush."

He's right. There is no rush for me to figure out my life, no matter what Ryan and my parents might think.

I turn to go right, but Jake's arm stops me as he rolls his eyes and leads me in the opposite direction. Even after over two years of visiting Ryan here, I'm still pretty lousy at finding my way around, but I do stop when I see a convenience store on the left that I recognize.

"Hold up," I tell him before disappearing inside. Last time I was here, I found some awesome greeting cards that my roommate, Tina, loved, and I promised I'd get her some more the next time I came here. It takes a couple minutes for me to locate the cards, and by the time I've picked out a couple and lined up to pay, I've pretty much been inside for a solid ten minutes.

I walk through the shop door, expecting to see Jake waiting for me, and stop dead when I see Kelly Taylor talking to him with her minions. One of the girls has her arms wrapped around him, and another is flipping her hair. Jake definitely doesn't look like he minds the attention. I stand with my arms crossed and wait for him to notice me, but he seems to be listening to whatever crap Kelly is spewing. I take a step forward so I'm within earshot, and that's when I hear what she's saying—Ryan this, Ryan that. "Ryan loved it when I made those cookies last week, and I was going to bring some more around tonight…I know he's taking that economics class I took last year, so I can help him study…My parents have a place down near the beach that we can all party at after the game on Saturday, I just know Ryan will love the view." Yada, yada, yada—bullshit, bullshit, bullshit. My blood boils and I snap. It might have taken me a couple years to do it, but Kelly Taylor is about to hear what I think of her.

"He doesn't want your cookies, Kelly," I say loudly and clearly. She flinches at the unexpected noise and whirls around to see me. Her face immediately lifts into a sneer, which she tries to mask before I see it. Too late. I know exactly what she thinks about me and the inconvenience of me being here. I've never felt the need to call her on it before, but I'll be damned if I let her get away with this shit. "And he doesn't need your help studying," I continue, glancing at her friends to make sure they're listening too. "And I can promise you he does not give a shit about your parents' place on the beach." I step forward so that we're really close. "*My* boyfriend doesn't need a thing from you, so I think it's best if you run along now and stay the hell away from him."

I'm fuming, actually fuming. Who the hell does this girl think she is, chasing blatantly after *my* boyfriend? And using Jake, *my* friend, to do it. I'm not usually the confrontational type, and I hate getting dragged into petty drama, but this is not okay. I am not going to let her chase my boyfriend as if I don't exist. I won't let her think she actually stands a chance. I'd rather swim in acid.

She doesn't even have the decency to look embarrassed about being caught drooling over him. She just looks down her nose at me and flips her hair over her shoulder. "I didn't realize you were still here," she tells me with disdain.

"Yes, I'm still here." I match her snooty tone with my own voice, dripping with disgust, and take a step closer to her. "And even if I wasn't, Ryan would still be my boyfriend, just like he will be next week." I take another step toward her. "Next month." And another. "Next year." I'm directly in front of her now, with hardly any space between us, and I stare into her eyes, not backing down for a second or caring that she's an inch or two taller than me. "Just like he has been for the last three years." A sneer crosses my face as I look at her in disgust. "You can't touch us, Kelly." It sounds like it's a challenge, but it's not. It's a fact. Nothing can touch my relationship with Ryan. "No matter how hard you try, you can't get near us." I pause slightly, making sure she's taking in every word I say, because I mean them. "Now stay the hell away from *my* boyfriend."

I'm breathing heavily by the end of my rant, and I meant every word. I should have told her this years ago when I first met her and she looked me up and down in disgust, like she couldn't believe Ryan would pick someone like me, someone who's more comfortable in flats than heels and doesn't spend two hours a day applying my makeup and styling my hair. I've known she's wanted him for years, just like she's known I've known she's wanted him for years, but this is the first time I've felt the need to come out and say it, and I feel better for it. *I mean, seriously? Who the hell does she think she is?*

"Boom!" Jake shouts loudly, grinning at me. He steps toward me and slings his arm around my shoulder, pulling me away from her. "You got told!" he exclaims to Kelly. I'm a bit surprised at this, and I realize he must not like her either.

That makes me wonder why he doesn't like her, what she's like when I'm not around, because Jake likes everybody. Kelly shoots him an irritated look but doesn't say anything. I'm guessing she knows if she wants to stay on Ryan's good side, she can't piss his best friend off. I go to open my mouth again, but Jake pulls me away and starts walking in the opposite direction. "That was fucking hilarious, McKenzie."

I look back over my shoulder. Kelly's watching us with her hands on her hips. I suddenly have the urge to rip every single one of her hair extensions out of her head and claw at her contoured face.

"Is she like that all the time?" I demand.

Jake just smirks at me.

"Jake!" I demand, pulling him to a stop. I'm pissed—really pissed. I knew she was into him, but not like this, not where she's showing up at his place and inviting him to her parents' house. It doesn't matter that I know he wouldn't go and that he doesn't give a crap about her; I had no idea she was being so blatant about it.

"Oh, come on, Becca. Ryan doesn't see past you, you know that. He never has."

"But is she seriously all over him all the time?"

Jake just rolls his eyes.

"I'm being serious here. He never told me she's there all the time."

Jake laughs. "That's because he never notices her. He couldn't give a crap where she is. Ever."

I glare back at him. I can't believe he didn't tell me there was a skank actively going after my boyfriend. I'm almost as mad at him as I am at Ryan. "You should have told me!" I'm so pissed off, I'm actually close to stomping my foot on the floor.

He rolls his eyes and pushes my shoulder playfully. "You're giving her way too much credit here, Becca. She hangs around the team. A few of the guys keep her around because she's good for rounding up girls, and she brings them food. That's it."

I exhale noisily out of my nose. I don't care what he says, they still should have told me. Even if the truth does just make her look as pathetic as I've always known her to be, I still would have liked to know.

Jake grins at me. "You know what Ryan does when she's there? When any of those girls are there? Or any girls in general, for that matter?" I cross my arms and glare at him. If Jake Edmondson thinks I can't see straight through him, he's dumber than I thought he was. Jake just laughs in my face. "He talks about you! Like, the whole time. 'My girlfriend's so funny, she's so clever. Becca is so beautiful.'" His voice goes high pitched, like he's imitating a little girl. Despite myself, I let out a smile. "'I'm so lucky to have her, I love her so much.'" He pauses and winks at me. "Honestly, as someone who's known you since you picked your scabby knees and then dared me to eat it, it's pretty nauseating."

I shove him away from me but start to laugh regardless. I have never been able to stay mad at Jake for long, and deep down I know he's telling the truth. I know Ryan loves me; it's just unnerving when you realize how actively someone is chasing your boyfriend.

A loud whistle rips across the stretch of grass beside us. "Yo, Edmondson!"

27

We both turn to face the direction of the shout and see three guys walking toward us. Even if they weren't wearing Warrior t-shirts and carrying large sports bags, it's pretty obvious from the sheer size of them that they're football players. Their eyes move to me as they approach, and they subtly flick their gazes up and down my body in that way that tells me they're used to being able to look at any girl they want. I don't quite resist the urge to roll my eyes at them.

The tallest one, a black guy I recognize as one of the linebackers, smiles cockily and then turns to Jake. "This your girl, Edmondson?"

Jake immediately pulls a face. "Ugh, gross. No." My arm flies out and smacks him in the stomach before he even has time to finish his sentence. He smirks over at me. "This is Becca, Ryan's girlfriend."

This seems to interest him even more, because his eyes immediately snap to me, assessing me with curiosity. "You're Jacko's girlfriend?" I nod my head and smile at him. "You're the one he turns down all the pretty girls for?" My smile immediately turns into a frown. He looks me up and down again. "I can see why now."

The guy next to him, an equally tall mixed-race dude with stunning green eyes, reaches up to the first guy's head and pushes him away. "Shut up, man!" He turns to me and grins. "Hey, Becca. Ignore Henry. We don't let him out much. It's good to see you." I smile back at him. Evan Princely is the defense captain of the Warriors, and he and Ryan are great friends. Together, they captain the team. I've met him a couple times after games and at the odd party here and there.

"Hey," Henry says good-naturedly. "I'm just happy to

finally meet Golden Boy's girl."

I shake my head at him, but I do allow a small smile to slip free. There's something I like about him. He reminds me of a friendly giant.

"Yo, Henry!" Ryan shouts from behind us. "Stay away from my girlfriend."

I glance behind me and see Ryan walking over, flanked by Jason and Marty. I can't help but smile just at the sight of him. His hair is still damp from the shower, and his cheeks are slightly flushed from exercise. He looks like the hottest thing I've ever seen, and my stomach actually flips at the sight of him. For me, no one else even comes close.

He grins back at me as he approaches and drops his bag by Jake's feet. Just when I think he's about to stop, he takes a step closer to me and plants his mouth on mine. I'm completely taken by surprise as he cradles my jaw. This works in his favor as my lips part in surprise, and he slips his tongue into my mouth, ignoring the catcalls from his friends as he wraps his arms around my body and hauls me against him. He literally sweeps me off my feet.

"Get a room," someone shouts; I think it's Jake.

Ryan breaks away, smiling against my mouth. "Gladly," he whispers before giving me a quick peck and then pulling me against his side while I try to catch my breath. I'm feeling a bit flustered.

"First we eat," he tells me. "Then we get a room." I slap him in the stomach as his friends burst out laughing, but I don't really mind. If I'm completely honest, I want to get a room too.

He starts walking over to a building on the far right of

29

the square, pulling me with him. He smirks down at me, giving me a wink. I know exactly what's going through his mind right now, and I actually blush, which makes his grin even wider. He laughs as he looks behind him. "You guys coming?"

# CHAPTER 4

*Becca*

"**B**ECCA WENT ALL POSSESSIVE GIRLFRIEND ON Kelly before," Jake tells Ryan. "It was hilarious."

Ryan's face breaks into a huge grin. I knew he'd like that. "Oh yeah?"

I raise my eyebrows at him. "I didn't realize how well acquainted she was with you," I tell him sarcastically.

Ryan scrunches his face up, confused. "What?"

"She brings you food, Ryan!"

"What? No. She brings over stuff for Jase. I just eat it."

I glance over at Jason, who is pointedly trying not to look at me. I get the feeling he knows full well Kelly's not bringing that stuff over for him, even if Ryan does believe it, but there's no point in calling him out over it. Even if I asked him now, he wouldn't sell Ryan out.

I roll my eyes and turn back to my pile of fries just as a wave of noise hits us. Evan and a bunch of the others from the team cross the courtyard toward us. I look around, but there's no spare room. I'm sitting between Ryan and Jake, Jason's on the other side of Jake, and Marty is opposite us. I expect them to go to the long table at the back where there's more space, but no, apparently space is no object when you're the superstar team of college football. They plonk their stuff down on the floor next to us, go over to the long table, actually pick it up, and bring it back over to us. They stick it on the end and then pull a bunch of chairs around us. Suddenly I'm not just sitting at a table with four guys that I know really well; now there are at least twenty guys from the football team all around us, and I'm a little overwhelmed. Then the girls come, like moths to a flame, and even though I glare daggers at her, Kelly's among them. She and her crew flounce over to join us, all pouty lips and glossy hair. I have no idea what her friends are like, and I know I'm judging them because of her, but I wish they'd go away. They don't. Each of the girls obviously has her hookup planned, and all four of them go and either wrap their arms around the guy they're sleeping with or sit on their knee. Kelly's eye catches mine, and she actually smiles at me. It's the fakest smile I've ever seen, and I want to slap her. I can't believe how blatant she's being. I feel a nudge from my left and glance over to see Jake smiling at me. He doesn't say anything, but his eyes have a warning in them. He's telling me not to let her wind me up. I nod in return, but I don't feel comfortable.

"You need a seat, Kel?" My head snaps to Ryan. *Kel? KEL!* Kelly's the only one standing off to the side. There are no spare seats that she can pull over, and I feel like that means she should just leave. Apparently Ryan doesn't feel the same. "You can have Becca's."

I glower at him. *What the hell is he talking about? I'm not having this.* Kelly practically preens in Ryan's direction, giving me a sly look. I put my drink down in disgust. I'm ready to get up and leave them all to it when Ryan turns and looks at me. He reaches out, grips my upper arm, and before I know it, he's tugged me out of my seat, turned me around, and pulled me down onto his knee. Then he grabs the seat I was in and pulls it away from the table and behind him. Before I can even blink, Jake moves his chair closer to Ryan and me, so that even if she wanted to, she couldn't sit anywhere near us. Jason shifts over too so that he's closer to Jake, and just like that, there's no room over here. I catch her jaw falling open in surprise, and her eyes harden before I dismiss her from my sight. Jake turns and winks at me, and Ryan squeezes my knee as Marty and Jason smirk over in Kelly's direction. All of them know exactly what Ryan did there, and I practically beam in delight. I know it's petty, and I know she can't touch us, but she was bothering me, and in one quick movement, Ryan showed me just how little he thought of her. Plus, Jake backed him up. I love my boys.

"Damn, boy." Henry's lazy Southern drawl makes me look up at him. He's way over on the other side of the table, but his eyes are trained on us. "You whipped!"

Ryan chuckles behind me and pulls me to him so that my whole back is pressed against his chest. "Hell yes I am," Ryan says, resting his head on my shoulder. I can feel him smile against my cheek. I love that he does this. I love that he doesn't ever try to downplay our relationship or act like he doesn't care. He's always affectionate with me no matter who's around.

Henry chuckles and turns his gaze to me, a big smile on his face. "Y'know, you're kinda famous on the team."

"Oh yeah?"

"Yeah. Your man never shuts up about you. When we first got here, your boy got a lot of attention. One night, this smoking hot senior spent all night trying to get with him, and he just kept showing her pictures of you on his phone."

I burst out laughing. Don't get me wrong, I don't like that some girl was hitting on him, but I know he's telling the truth about the pictures. I've heard he's done that before.

"You guys been together long?"

I nod. "Three years."

"The best three years," Ryan whispers in my ear, and I smile in response. They have been the best. I genuinely don't think I've ever been happier than I've been since we got together. I feel like I can't remember a time when we were apart.

"How'd you guys meet?" Evan asks. I glance around and see that no one's having individual conversations anymore. They're all listening to us.

"We've always known each other," I tell Evan, not looking at anyone else. I hate having this many people looking at me, and I hope I haven't gone red. "Our parents are neighbors and friends. We grew up together."

"So love at first sight then, huh?" Henry asks. He genuinely seems interested.

Jake snorts next to me, and I turn to scowl at him. Ryan starts chuckling behind me. "Not exactly," Ryan explains. "We had a falling out in middle school, and Becca ignored me after that, and through most of high school."

Jake starts laughing too. "Yeah, Ryan was in love with her

34

for years, and Becca was too dumb to notice."

"Hey!" I throw a fry at his head, which just makes him laugh harder as the rest of the table snickers. I roll my eyes and turn back to Henry. "It just took me a little longer to figure it out is all."

Henry smirks and glances at Ryan. "She make you work, boy?"

I can feel Ryan grinning against my cheek. "Oh yeah. Getting Becca was harder than it'd be to get Trump to kiss Marty's Mexican ass!"

The whole table erupts in laughter, and I join in. I don't like thinking of those days and the way I used to ignore him, but when I turn around to look at him, his eyes are shining, and he wraps his arms around me even tighter. "Worth every second of the wait, baby," he tells me, kissing me on the cheek.

I turn back around, and Kelly is positively glaring at me. I just smirk back at her. The more she sees us together and hears about our history, the more she'll realize she's wasting her time.

"You guys are like seriously in love, huh?" Henry continues. He's still watching us; he seems to find us fascinating.

"She's the one, man," Ryan tells him, not caring at all that he's announcing it to almost thirty people, most of whom are his teammates.

I start to shift uncomfortably in his lap, wanting the conversation to move on. Jake notices. "Don't worry about him, Becca," he tells me, shooting Henry a smirk. "Couples are like a different species to him 'cause he never goes back to the same girl twice."

"Just spreading the love, Edmondson." He winks at me

and points to his chest. "It'd be a crime to keep all of this to myself." I burst out laughing along with the half the table. The other half groan at him, and it sets them all off, talking about their various relationships and conquests. I'm soon in fits of laughter just from listening to them.

"You okay?" Ryan whispers in my ear. He adjusts his right hand so his thumb can brush under the hem of my t-shirt and stroke the side of my hip. I cast him a backward glance, but he just stares back innocently at me. I know what he's doing. He's done with the conversation around here and is thinking about the room we were going to get after we eat.

I raise an eyebrow at him and place my hand on his roaming one. I'm not about to let him feel me up in front of all his friends. He chuckles and then repeats his question. "Seriously, are you okay?"

He's asking if I'm okay being around this many people I don't know; crowds sometimes make me uncomfortable. I nod my head in answer to his question. It's actually really nice seeing this side of his life. Usually I just see his roommates, but it's good to see the rest of the team and see how close they all are. I knew his team was one of the best in the country, but it's nice to see how well they all mesh when they're off the field.

"You staying for the game on Saturday, Becca?" I turn away from Ryan and look at Evan, who's lounging back in his seat, watching us.

I shake my head. "My flight's later today."

"Where you go to school?" Henry asks.

I brace myself for the response I know I'll get. "Southern U."

The predictable boos ring out around me, but they're good-natured, at least from my side of the table. It's not a surprise to most people where I go to school.

"You're a King?"

I shrug. "I go to school there. They've got a great arts program." One I don't use anymore. I don't glance back at Ryan when I say this. I don't want him to start in on me about transferring again.

"But you root for the Kings?"

Jake starts laughing next to me. "Becca barely watches Ryan's games, let alone another team's."

"Shut up!" I tell him, throwing another fry at his head. That's a touchy subject for Ryan. I texted him last year to congratulate him on a win, when in fact they'd lost the game in the last five minutes. He was not impressed that I hadn't watched the whole game. Now I make sure I know the result before I text him. "I watch all Ryan's games."

"So you see that bitch, Mulligan, around campus?" He's referring to the quarterback of my college team. I shake my head, even though that's not strictly true. I definitely know who he is, and I see him way more often than I'd like, but considering I can't stand the guy, seeing him once every couple months is too much. I avoid the football team at all costs. A few of the guys I've met are okay, but that is so not my scene. If it weren't for Ryan, I don't think I'd ever speak to a football player. "He still crying over coming second to your man all the time?"

Ryan starts to laugh. He knows he's a better player than Mulligan, and he also knows that Mulligan hates him. It all comes down to jealousy. He's trashed Ryan in the media a bunch of times, and the couple times they've played each other, he's always talked shit about Ryan before the game, saying he'll crumble under the pressure, saying he just gets lucky and there's no real skill there. Ryan's beaten him both times. I don't really get football or player rivalry, but Ryan's one of the best in the country and therefore has a lot of opposing players jealous of him. I know Ryan doesn't like Mulligan, but not enough to bitch about him. He's not even on Ryan's radar. Clearly he doesn't see the guy as a threat.

"Stay." The word is whispered quietly into my ear.

I frown and glance behind me to look at Ryan.

"Stay," he repeats quietly.

My face softens. "I can't. You know I can't."

"Just for this week."

"I have classes. I can't miss them."

"You can get notes later. Please, Becca. Just this once."

This is unlike him. I know he hates us being apart, but he doesn't ever ask me to stay longer than planned. He knows this is just the way it is for now.

"Ryan—"

"It hasn't been enough time, Becca." The intensity of his voice shocks me. "I can't wait another couple months to see you again."

I stare back at him. His eyes are on me, and though he has a smile playing on his lips, it looks forced. His eyes are practically pleading.

"It's Thanksgiving in six weeks and I'll be back for that, and then you guys play Southern U right after that."

"It's too long, Becca."

"But my flights are booked," I say feebly. "I don't have

enough clothes here."

"We can change your flights and I'll buy you as many clothes as you want."

I sigh. "I don't need your money, Ryan."

"Please, Becca. Just this once."

"Ryan—"

"Becca, please." He squeezes my thigh as though trying to reiterate his point. I glance away from his gaze, confused. Part of me is annoyed at him for putting me on the spot like this, but then the other part of me knows he wouldn't ask me unless he really wanted me to stay. I look sideways, and I see Jake sitting very still, as is Jason beside him. I know they're listening. Then I look across the table and see the conversation has died down slightly. I thought Ryan was being quiet, but I'm pretty sure Jake's not the only one listening to our conversation. I catch Kelly's eye from across the table and suddenly I don't care about her, or any of the girls hanging around him, or any of the rest the team. This is about us. Ryan wants me to stay, and if I'm honest with myself, I want to stay too. I love my boyfriend and I miss him.

"Okay," I agree with a smile. "I'll stay."

His whole face lights up, and he leans in and drops a quick kiss on my mouth as Henry breathes an exaggerated sigh of relief from across the table. "Thank God for that. I was not looking forward to dealing with his moody ass the rest of the week."

Ryan just grins back at him and flips him the finger. I glance sideways at Jake, who winks at me. "I knew you'd cave," he tells me, and I just shrug. If caving means spending more time with my boyfriend, then so be it. I'll cave more often.

Before I know it, Ryan's standing up, and I have little choice but to topple off his knee and stand as well. "Let's go change your flights," he tells me as he wraps an arm around my shoulder and pulls me into him. I hook an arm around his waist and nod in agreement. "And get that room," he whispers in my ear.

He picks up his bag, throws it over his shoulder, says goodbye to the rest of the guys, and leads me away. I realize I'm beaming like an idiot, just like he is, because I'm happy—I get another week with my boyfriend.

# CHAPTER 5

AFTER MY LAST LECTURE OF THE DAY, I MAKE MY way outside and cross the student quad, where people are milling about. I'm trying really hard not to think about Ryan. It's always crappy the first couple days after I've left him. It's like I remember how much I miss him and then have to retrain myself on how to be without him again, how to make do with FaceTime and messages. This time it's worse than usual since we spent over a week together.

A loud whistle rips across the quad, but I don't even glance around until I hear laughter and a loud shout. "Becca! Wait up!"

I turn around, annoyed, but instantly break into a smile when I see Mason Blackwell sitting on the benches. Mason is one of Ryan's best friends from high school, and although I avoided him like the plague for most of my teenage years, he's actually a really nice guy. Ryan and I spend a lot of time with him when we're back home. Mason and I randomly ended up at the same college, but we rarely see each other. He's on the football team, and although he's the first to admit he doesn't get much game time, his good looks and easy personality ensure he's usually surrounded by football groupies.

"Sup, Mase," I say, walking toward him. He's with Bernie Matthews, one of the stars of the football team, and as far as I can tell, Mason's best friend in college.

He pulls me into a quick hug, and Bernie offers me his signature lazy grin, waving a hand in my direction. Mason points to the guy sitting with them. "This is Liam, redshirt freshman, wide receiver. He's going to the big time," he tells me.

I smile politely, pretending to be interested.

Liam turns beet red, which is unfortunate since his hair is Carrot-Top ginger, and now his skin tone is almost matching it. "Nice to meet you," he mumbles, not looking directly at me. I look at Mason questioningly. "He's shy," he explains, causing Liam to go an even deeper shade of red.

"Did you go to Ryan's for a full week?" Mason asks.

I nod.

"You have fun?"

I smirk. Yeah, we had lots of fun. Mason rolls his eyes, probably guessing what I'm thinking. "Is Jake still whoring it up around campus?" he asks.

"Oh yeah, he's giving you a run for your money."

"I resent that," he tells me, mock insulted. His grin fades slightly and he nods at someone over my shoulder. I turn and let out a sigh of irritation when I see Robbie Mulligan approaching.

Robbie Mulligan is rich, arrogant, and also incredibly good-looking. He's always surrounded by girls trying to catch his attention and other members of the football team, along with just general tagalongs who want to be near someone of his wealth and status. Something about him makes me incredibly uneasy; maybe it's the way his smile never reaches his eyes and the way he looks at people, like he owns them and is better than everyone. Basically, the guy is a complete and utter asshole.

He approaches with his harem and greets Mason, Bernie, and Liam with a fist bump before turning to me. "Rebecca McKenzie...how's the hottest girl on campus doing?"

I sigh loudly and ignore the sniggers from his friends. Mason is smirking at me, waiting for my response; he knows the way this is going to go, the way it always goes. "Are we really going to go through this again?" I ask.

He grins, raking his eyes up and down my body in a way that makes me want to simultaneously shudder and slap him. "Just giving you a compliment."

*Okay, here we go.* "I am not the best-looking girl on campus, Robbie," I tell him. "In fact, I'm probably not even close to being the best-looking girl on campus. I am, however, Ryan Jackson's girlfriend."

That's what it really comes down to. Robbie Mulligan is one of the best quarterbacks in all of college football. He has this whole football-adoring college at his feet. He's destined to go pro and have a stellar career, but there's one person who is just slightly better than him—Ryan. Ever since he found out Ryan and I were dating, Robbie's been creeping around me, convinced he can get with me, solely so he could screw

Ryan over. I had hoped he'd be bored of it by now since I've told him to get lost more times than I can count, but no such luck. I know his precious ego hates the rejection, but he still keeps sniffing around.

"You know I saw some pictures of you online." I frown at this; my social media is private. "You were wearing some little cut-off shorts." My eyes narrow. I know the picture he's talking about—it was a sunny day, and I had a pair of shorts on with a baggy t-shirt. There's nothing sexual at all about that picture. "They'd look fucking awesome on my bedroom floor, McKenzie."

"Not even if you were the last man on earth, Mulligan," I tell him for what feels like the millionth time.

"Oh yeah?" He thinks I'm joking, thinks I'm playing some twisted game of hard-to-get…for the last two and a half years. He makes me sick.

"It will never happen."

"You need a real man, McKenzie."

I'm getting irritated. "I have a real man."

"That pussy." At his crude words, I feel Mason come and stand next to me. Mulligan's pushing it now. Mason knows I can handle myself against Robbie, but if I ever said the word, he'd step in and back me up. They may be teammates, but Mason won't have Mulligan talking about Ryan like that. Mulligan keeps going regardless. "That pussy wouldn't know how to keep someone like you satisfied."

I narrow my eyes. "Oh, Ryan kept me satisfied all week long."

"You'll give in one day, McKenzie," he tells me.

"And one day you might have as many passing yards as

Ryan," I snap back, taunting him. His ego deserves a little bruising. Anger flashes through his eyes, and his jaw clenches in annoyance as the group laughs at my barbs. The thing is, I don't even think he likes me. He prefers girls who giggle at his lame jokes and hang off his every word. He only wants me because I'm with Ryan.

"Your boy's a bust. He can't handle the pressure."

"I don't see your Heisman nomination anywhere." Ryan got nominated last year. He didn't win, but he should have. Robbie wasn't even nominated.

"He got sacked three times in last week's game."

"You know he never even mentions your name," I tell him, stepping toward him. He's riling me up, but I don't care. I'm ready to shut him up. "I doubt he even knows it. You're not even a blip on his radar, Mulligan. That's how little he thinks of you."

I can see his eyes flash in front of me. "We'll see if you're still saying that next month." The two teams will play then. Cal State won last year, but it was really close.

I roll my eyes, bored of the conversation, and glance around at his friends; I think most of them are on the team too. I suddenly have the urge to shut Mulligan up once and for all. "You know, I feel sorry for you guys," I tell them. I send a quick glance in Robbie's direction to make sure he's listening. "I mean, you're pretty good, but imagine how good you'd be if you had a decent quarterback."

Mason snorts back a laugh. Bernie doesn't even bother to hide his amusement; he openly laughs out loud, and I can see Robbie tense in front of me. This team is different from Ryan's. They are divided; it's more offense and defense. I know

Mason can't stand Mulligan, and I doubt many of the defensive players would argue with him. "Maybe I should get Ryan to transfer here, huh?" I threaten, enjoying the look on Robbie's face. There's not a chance Ryan would ever transfer here, but Robbie doesn't need to know that. I glance around the rest of the team. "Imagine how good you'd be then, eh? With Ryan Jackson as your quarterback?"

Robbie's eyes harden and he looks like he's about ready to explode at me for mocking his place on the team right in front of him. "If you knew anything about football, you'd know he can't do that—unless he wants to sit on the bench for a year."

"Lucky you, huh?" A smirk crosses my whole face. "He'd take your spot right from under your feet."

"Fucking bi—"

He steps toward me, but Mason gets there first, blocking his way to me. He'd never touch me, I know that, but I've riled him more than I ever have before. I start laughing behind Mason and look around him to see Robbie's usual control completely gone.

"You're too easy, Mulligan," I tell him while grinning at Mason and Bernie. They look like they're enjoying the show. I don't usually push him so far, but he should know better than to talk about Ryan like that in front of me.

"You've got a big mouth, McKenzie. Maybe if you stopped running it and used it for sucking—"

Mason shoves him so fast Robbie doesn't have time to brace himself, and he goes flying. "Don't talk to her like that, man." Bernie steps up next to him; they're a unit. A couple of Robbie's friends step beside him to back him up, and I roll my eyes at the unnecessary drama. This won't end in a fight, and we all know it. Yeah, Mason and Robbie don't like each other, but Robbie's still the quarterback, and Mason knows he can't go there. On the other side, Robbie is well aware that Bernie would back Mason without question, and Matthews is one of the best players on the team, maybe even *the* best—although his ego would never let him admit it. The team needs him. I shake my head at Mason—I don't need his help handling Robbie's bullshit; I'm used to it. Mason doesn't say anything back to me, but I see his shoulders relax just slightly.

"See you later, Mason," I say, giving him a wink. I turn back to Robbie with a full-on grin on my face. "Bye Robbie. Enjoy it over there in Ryan's shadow."

# CHAPTER 6

*Becca*

"**S**TOP DOING THAT," TINA SAYS, YANKING MY hand away from the hem of my skirt, which I'm trying to pull down, wishing it had a couple extra inches on it. "You look so hot. A ton of guys are checking you out," she tells me smugly, like it's a personal compliment to her since she picked out my outfit. I do as she says, mainly because there's not much I can do but try to ignore the appreciative glances we're getting.

Tina and I have been roommates since we were freshmen. You would have thought that by now I would know she doesn't take no for an answer, yet somehow I'm still surprised that I've let her talk me into coming to a frat party, something I would never usually agree to. When I announced I was ready to leave our apartment, Tina marched me into her room and insisted I get changed. She actually refused to leave until I did, which is how I ended up wearing her tiny leather skirt, which fits way more snugly than I'd like and ends at mid-thigh. She matched it with a black crop top, and although it keeps my chest covered with its high neckline, there's about an inch of my stomach showing.

Despite the outfit and my initial discomfort, we've had a fun evening. We started off by going to watch one of her friends sing in one of the clubs downtown, and she turned out to be an awesome singer. Also, the club didn't card, so we were able to have a couple cocktails while we were watching. After a while, I was starting to feel the effects of the alcohol, was having fun and had stopped feeling self-conscious in my outfit. I was ready to head home when Tina got a text about this party and insisted we stop by on the way back to our apartment.

I really don't go to many frat parties. I went a couple times with Tina when we were freshmen and decided it wasn't my scene, and I've barely been to any Southern U frat parties since. I go to more with Ryan at Cal State than I've ever gone to at Southern U.

This particular party seems like a wild one. The music is so loud I can barely hear Tina, and it's completely packed, wall-to-wall students everywhere. When my eyes stray to the sofas, I see more than one couple getting completely inde-cent. I pull a face and turn away to follow Tina. I guess this is what happens when you show up after the party's been in full swing for a couple hours. We weave our way through the crowds, trying to find her friends. Tina's way more active in the Southern U party scene than I am, and as she tugs me by the hand through the crowd, I know she's definitely partied here before and knows which direction to head in. My eyes scan the crowds, seeing if I recognize anyone. I spot a girl who was in one of my classes sophomore year, but Tina pulls me into the kitchen, where it's marginally quieter and we actually have a little more space. I lean forward to tell her about the live sex exhibition I was seconds away from witnessing, but my thoughts stay stuck on my tongue as I spot some of the football team by the doors leading to the backyard. My face turns into a scowl. "You didn't tell me this was a team party," I groan.

She grins back at me. "'Cause I knew you wouldn't come if I did!" she explains cheerfully. "Besides, I am not against hooking up with someone from the team, and I can't do that if I never see them, can I?"

I roll my eyes and follow her farther into the room. Tina had a thing for hooking up with football players when we were freshmen, but then she started dating musicians, and I thought she'd gotten over it. Apparently I was wrong. I spot Mason by a large table in the middle of the room, which is loaded with every type of alcohol you can imagine. He glances our way, and surprise briefly crosses his face when he sees me, followed by a massive grin.

"Rebecca McKenzie, to what do we owe the honor?"

I roll my eyes at him as I make my way over.

"Seriously, we don't see you at our parties very often."

"Yeah, well, didn't have much of a choice," I say, glaring at Tina, who winks at Mason flirtatiously. I doubt anything would happen between them though; they've been there before, a couple years ago.

Mason's gaze drops to my outfit. "Does Ryan know you're wearing that?" he asks.

"Shut up," I snap. He grins harder.

"Hey, just good to know you actually have legs," he tells me jokingly. I narrow my eyes and step up next to him, shoving him with my shoulder as I do. Maybe this party wasn't such a bad idea after all; I haven't hung out with Mason in ages.

"Daaamn, McKenzie!" My eyes drift past Mason as Bernie walks up behind him and claps his hand on Mason's shoulder, his eyes fixed on my body.

"Eyes up here, Matthews!" I tell him.

He lifts his head and gives me a smile—the one that makes girls all over campus drool all over him. "Can't help it, McKenzie. You look fucking good."

I shake my head but can feel myself blushing. Don't get me wrong, I know I don't look horrible or anything, but it still feels weird to get compliments.

"Dude, keep on looking at her like that, and Ryan will beat your ass the next time he's in town," Mason tells him, handing him a shot glass. Bernie laughs good-naturedly and winks, knocking back the shot and wrapping his arm around the blonde girl who's followed him over. She's giving me a dirty look, so I avert my gaze. It's impossible not to like Bernie; it's just a shame he indulges all the groupies that hang around the team.

Mason grabs a couple more plastic shot glasses and starts pouring tequila into them. He looks up at Tina and me. "You game?"

*Ah, fuck it.* I've got that buzz from drinking earlier in the night and a couple more might make this party more bearable, and it is Saturday night.

51

I nod and lick my hand before holding it out for him to dump some salt on. Tina does the same. He holds out the shot glasses and points out the lime he's already chopped up. He gives us the nod, and all three of us lick the salt, down the tequila, and then bite into the lime wedges. I'm wincing from the burn of the alcohol but accept a second shot from Mason regardless. I don't know what it is about tequila shots that I like; I think it's the routine.

Mason whistles as I bite down into the lime for the second time, and he holds his hand up to give me a high-five. I grin and slap it. Mason starts hunting around, trying to find us a couple glasses for regular drinks, and my eyes scan the room, taking in all the girls who are here trying to capture the attention of the football team. Tina and I are getting some dirty looks just because we're interacting with Mason and Bernie, which makes me smirk. I really don't get the big deal with football players. I genuinely wouldn't give a shit if Ryan never threw a ball again. What's wrong with just being with a guy because of who they are? I'm about to announce my theory on football groupies to Tina when she leans her body into mine.

"Robbie Mulligan hasn't stopped staring at you since you got here," she whispers.

I pause and turn to see where she's looking. Sure enough, there's Robbie Mulligan, all six-feet plus of him, wearing a crisp white t-shirt and black jeans. It really is a shame he's such an asshole; those good looks are a complete waste on him. He's standing in the far corner, surrounded by a group of guys—some look like football players, and others look like your typical frat boys. Of course, there are also girls over there, lots and lots of girls. They're all laughing and joking around him, but he's not paying them any attention. His gaze is focused solely on me. Our eyes lock, and he holds my gaze for a moment before he pointedly runs his eyes up and down my body. It takes everything I have not to shudder. I refuse to give him the satisfaction of knowing he can bother me at all. When his eyes meet mine again, he cocks an eyebrow at me, almost daring me to approach him, but I quickly turn away, feeling very uncomfortable. I haven't seen him since our argument a couple weeks ago. I saw him walking toward the food court one day and rapidly changed directions, and if I'd known he was going to be here, I definitely would not have come.

I accept another drink from Mason and down it quickly. I make small talk with Bernie and his blonde girl while Mason tells me all about his academic woes. Basically, he's been partying too hard, and now he needs to get his grades up or he'll be dropped from the team. I'm telling him to suck it up and actually study when Tina hears a song she loves and pulls me into another room where a makeshift dance floor has been made.

Usually I'd be the last person on the dance floor, but the alcohol I've had mixed with Tina's energy loosens me up. Her energy is infectious, and soon I'm laughing along with her, jumping up and down and singing along to the music. Unlike a lot of the other girls on the dance floor, there's nothing sexy about the way we're moving. We're having fun and laughing at ourselves as we drunkenly dance like idiots.

Mason and Bernie join us, twirling us around very ungracefully. Mason even attempts to dip me back like they do in the movies, and he nearly drops me on the floor. Because Mason and Bernie are on the floor, it suddenly gets crazy busy. Not only do the girls come out, but half their teammates do as well. It's one big, hot, sweaty mess with all of us jumping up and down and banging into each other. Tina's beaming at me, and I can't help but grin back. Turns out, the party is pretty fun after all. I hardly ever get to party with Mason. He and his friends make me laugh, and when Mason attempts to breakdance, I almost fall over with laughter when Bernie starts beatboxing (unsuccessfully) next to him. Tina has to pull me over to the side so I don't get crushed by everyone crowding in to watch the Bernie-and-Mason show. I'm grinning at Tina, knowing my face is probably all red and sweaty, and she laughs back at me. "I told you it would be fun."

Suddenly the beat switches, and a slower song comes on. A guy who was dancing near Tina earlier appears at her side and takes her hand. I see Tina bite her lip, and her face lights up as she lets him lead her back into the middle of the dance floor. She smiles at me over her shoulder, and I wonder what I've missed. She clearly likes the guy, I can tell, and I watch with interest as he pulls her into his arms and starts to sway to the music. I suddenly miss Ryan—like I really, really miss him. Not for the first time this week, I wonder if it really is worth being this far away from him. Sure, I love Southern U and I love all my friends here, but I love him more. Spending so much time with him when I visited has made me realize that maybe he's right; maybe after this year, I could consider transferring. The truth is, nobody makes me happier than Ryan, so why fight it?

I take one last look at Tina and see that Mason and

Bernie have also found willing partners and are dancing slowly with them; in fact, Bernie's partner looks like she's grinding all over him. They'll probably head out soon and find some privacy. I decide to go call Ryan. I know he's already home; he went for a few drinks earlier in the evening, but I think he was tired from practice and decided to have an early night. I decide to give Tina a bit of time with this new guy and chat with Ryan before he goes to sleep. I'm just about to turn around and leave the floor when a hand grips my hip, pulling me back into a hard body. I don't know what it is that makes me do it—probably the alcohol, probably being surrounded by so many couples who look so happy, probably the fact that I'm really missing Ryan—but I allow myself to lean back into the body, just for a second, enjoying the feel of arms around me before I abruptly remember it's not Ryan. I quickly start to move away, but the grip on my hip tightens and the opposite arm wraps around my waist, pressing me back.

A face leans over my shoulder and hot breath hits my neck. "Just go with it," is whispered in my ear. Robbie Mulligan—of course.

His words immediately sober me up. I stiffen in his arms and scramble to push his hands off me, stepping away in irritation. I can't believe I let him hold me, even if it was just for a minute. My skin crawls knowing he touched me, and I can't stand the smug look in his eyes as I turn to face him. He didn't miss the fact that just for a few seconds, I didn't push him off me. The arrogant asshole probably thinks I knew it was him all along, thinks I actually enjoyed it. "Do not touch me again," I hiss then walk away, ignoring the smug look in his eyes.

---◆---

My thighs are aching by the time I reach the third floor of the frat house. The drinks I'd downed earlier in the night were pressing against my bladder and the bathrooms on the first floor had a ridiculously long line, so I headed upstairs to try to find an available bathroom. I couldn't even find the bathroom on the second floor; I tried a couple doors, but when I accidently walked in on a girl kneeling down in front of a guy, I quickly closed the door and rushed away. That's when I noticed that there was a third floor, and I quickly walked upstairs, praying my bladder would hold out until I found a bathroom.

The music is deafening, even up here, and that's when I remember walking past several speakers on the way up here; the music is booming out on every floor of the party. I glance around the hallway I'm on. It's pretty narrow and cramped up here, and there are only two doors on either side of the hallway. At the end, there's an open door, and I practically squeal with glee when I realize it's a vacant bathroom. I hurry over to it, stumbling slightly in my drunken state, and slam the door shut behind me.

After I've seen to business, I check out my reflection in the mirror. My face is flushed from all the dancing, and my eyes are wide from the alcohol I've had. Bits of my hair have started to fall from the messy ponytail I threw it in, and my eyeliner is smudged. I bend down to grab my purse, and when I stumble again, I vow not to drink any more tonight and instead stick to water. In fact, I might just go home. I'll see if Tina's ready, and if she's not, I'll just get an Uber on my own. I grab my phone from my bag and call Ryan. He doesn't answer, which means he's probably asleep, so instead I send him a sappy text, telling him how much I miss him, which is really just telling him how drunk I am. I never get sappy with him unless I've had a drink, and he's well aware of that.

I grab some tissue and wipe under my eyes, getting rid of the black smudges, then pull my hair out of its messy ponytail and retie it. I give myself one last onceover in the mirror, satisfied that I don't look quite so disheveled, and turn to leave the bathroom.

I freeze in irritation at the sight that greets me when I open the door.

Robbie freaking Mulligan.

He's leaning against the wall, his eyes fixed on me like he owns the damn place.

I scowl at him but his eyes zero in on my stomach, and when I glance down I see that my top has ridden up slightly and is showing a couple more inches of my stomach than I intended. I quickly pull it down, and that's when he looks up at me. I don't like the look on his face; it's predatory, and I'm not in the mood for it.

"Did you follow me up here?" I demand.

He doesn't answer, just stares back at me, his eyes flicking over my body, always coming back to my face before they start to look me over again.

"Robbie!" I demand. "Did you follow me up here?"

He finally stops his perusal of my body. "What do you think?" he asks quietly.

"That's fucking creepy, do you know that?!" I tell him.

Again, he doesn't answer, so I roll my eyes and step

forward to go past him, but he pushes himself off the wall and steps in front of me.

"You look beautiful, McKenzie."

I scowl at him. It's probably the nicest thing he's ever said to me. Usually it's all about how hot I am or how much he wants to fuck me, how good he'd be in bed if we ever hooked up, never a straight-up compliment. That's fine with me, because I don't want one from him. The last thing I want is for Robbie Mulligan to think I'm beautiful.

"Go away," I tell him.

He takes a step toward me. "Did you wear that for me?" My mouth gapes open at the sheer audacity of him, and he smirks at my reaction. The guy's unbelievable. "Oh, come on. Don't play hard to get, Becca. Everyone knew this was a football party. Why'd you think it's so busy?"

"Your ego is insane, do you know that?"

His gaze drops to my body again. "Did you wear that for me?" he asks again, his voice low.

I can't even be bothered to argue with him. I should tell him I had no idea about this party and just came along with Tina at the last minute. I should tell him I wouldn't even file a fingernail for him. I should tell him the mere sight of him disgusts me, but I don't. I've told him variations of all these things before, but it never does any good. He never listens, and I'm over trying to get through his thick skull. He can think whatever he wants; I have better things to do with my time.

I go to walk past him, but the alcohol has made me unsteady and I stagger a bit. Robbie takes that opportunity to reach out and grab me. Usually I'd be grateful for somebody stopping me from falling, but not him; I don't want him touching me. I try to step back from him, but he doesn't let go. His right hand slides around my waist, and his left hand firmly grips my hip. I glance down at our bodies, which are only inches apart, unsure how he's managed to get me into this position so swiftly, and then he gives a quick tug so I'm pressed up against him.

My face jerks up to his, and he's smirking down at me. I send him the dirtiest look I can muster then bring both my hands to his chest and push myself away from him. "Get off me."

He doesn't budge at all; if anything, he wraps his arm tighter around my waist and pulls me against him. I'm mortified when I feel him hard against my stomach.

"Jesus, Robbie! Get the fuck off me," I demand again, pushing him away from me, but he doesn't move an inch. The muscles of his chest under my hands barely shift as I try my hardest to get away.

He chuckles to himself, but it's not soft and gentle; it's mocking and insulting, like he knows he's stronger than me and there's nothing I can do to make him move.

I lean my upper body back, hating that it's pushing my lower body against him just ever so slightly.

"Get. Off me. Now," I demand through gritted teeth.

He chuckles down at me and I open my mouth, ready to fucking scream in his face if I have to, when he quickly lowers his head and captures my mouth with his. I'm so surprised, I just freeze, just for a couple seconds as I feel his tongue force its way into my mouth and start to sweep across my own. I can taste the liquor on his tongue and his breath in my nose. It tastes like he drank a whole bottle of liquor. Then it's like a light goes on in my head, and I realize *Robbie fucking Mulligan is kissing me!* I rip my mouth away from him and reach up to slap him across the face, but his reflexes are too quick—he grips my wrist in his hand and forces it back down beside my body. I go to slap him with my other hand, but he catches that too and again forces it down beside me.

"You bastard," I snarl at him, contempt clear in my voice. I'm suddenly desperate to brush my teeth, desperate to get the taste of him out of my mouth. "How dare you do that to me?"

He just smirks back down at me, his grip on my wrists tightening even more. "You enjoyed that."

"If you ever do that to me again, I swear I'll bite your tongue off."

Mulligan lets out a humorless laugh and pushes me up against the wall. He's so quick, I'm pressed against it before I even know what's happening. "I've been waiting years to do that," he tells me.

"Get your hands off me right now," I demand. I go to raise my right knee, aiming to kick him in the groin, but his body is pressed up against me, forcing his weight onto me and stopping me from being able to move.

"Don't you think it's about time you stopped playing hard to get?"

My mouth falls open in disbelief, and he takes the opportunity to attack my mouth again, pressing up against me, sweeping his tongue into my mouth. I try to move my head to the side, try to get his lips off me, but his head turns with mine, pressing painfully against me, stopping me from breaking the contact. Then, when my brain finally snaps into action, I try to bite down on his tongue, his lips, anything, but he's pushed his mouth so hard against me that I can't close it. When he finally breaks away, we're both breathless, and my mouth feels swollen from the rough kisses. I again try to push him off me, but he holds my arms firmly down by my side, his grip so tight I swear he could snap them in two if he wanted to.

"GET OFF ME. RIGHT NOW!" I scream in his face and it sounds loud to my ears, but the noise from the speakers drowns out most of it. I have never been so angry in my entire life. How dare he think he can touch me like this?

"You want this," he hisses down at me.

"No, I fucking don't," I hiss back at him, venom dripping from my words, and when I look up at his face, I don't just feel angry—I feel uneasy. His brown eyes have turned practically black, and there isn't a hint of warmth in them. They're cold and determined.

"Robbie, please," I start, using a different tactic. "Tina's waiting for me downstairs. So's Mason. I have to go." I try to turn and walk away, but his grip on me doesn't loosen. If anything, it gets tighter. "Robbie, please," I say again. "They'll be looking for me."

"They're not looking for you," he tells me, and I realize he's probably right. Mason was dancing with whatever girl he grabbed on the dance floor, and Tina was with that guy she was all smitten over.

We stare at each other for a minute, and I realize my heart is beating loudly in my chest, only it's not from excitement or adrenalin. He looks down at me, not saying a word, and then suddenly, it's like he's made up his mind. He hauls my body against his, reaches to his left, and opens the door I hadn't even realized was beside me. He pushes it open and shoves me ahead of him, into the room. I whirl around just as he's locking the door behind me.

My eyes dart to the door and then back up to his face. "What are you doing?" My voice is quieter than it was outside. I don't understand how this has happened, how I've ended up in a locked bedroom on the top floor of a frat house when there's a raging party going on downstairs. My butt bangs into something, and I realize I've been backing away from him without knowing it, subconsciously trying to put some distance against us. I glance down to see what it is—a desk—but that's a mistake, because it means I've taken my eyes off him. When I glance up, he's striding toward me.

"No," I start, shaking my head as he gets closer. "No!"

He's on me in a second. He grips my hips, picks me up, and sets me on the desk behind me.

"Robbie, no," I say again. For the first time, real panic is setting in on me. *What is he doing? How is this happening? How have I gotten myself into this situation? This can't be happening. This cannot be happening.*

*I need to calm down. I'm panicking. I'm exaggerating. He just wants to make out, and eventually he's going to get it through his thick skull that I'd rather tear out my own eyes than do that.*

"You want this," he hisses, grabbing hold of both my hands—which are trying to push him away—and forcing them behind my back. Before I have time to think, he's on my neck, planting wet, messy kisses there as I try to move back from him. I try so hard, but he's strong. He's so, so strong, and I'm genuinely scared about where this might lead. *No! He isn't about to do what I think he's going to do. There's no way he's about to do that.*

"Robbie, please. Please stop." My body is trying to move away from him, jerking away from his touch, but I realize he's so much bigger than me as his body looms down on me.

"You need to stop playing hard to get, Becca," he mutters against my neck. He lets go of one of my wrists and grips my left breast in his hand, squeezing it painfully. *Shit, shit, shit. Robbie Mulligan is touching me. Robbie Mulligan is touching my body.*

"Robbie! Don't tou—stop! Please, please just stop." My voice has gotten quieter as I squirm, trying to get away from him as I realize that he might not stop. I push that thought away. *No. No, he's just drunk and he wants some action, that's all.* I happen to be the girl that's here, but he'll snap out of it in a minute. He'll stop any second now and back off.

"You want this," he says against my neck again, and his teeth drag painfully against my shoulder, biting at the skin. "I know you want this," he repeats over and over, like it's his mantra, like he actually believes it.

He lets go of my other wrist, and I feel a moment of relief as I reach out and push him away from me, but it's short-lived. He doesn't move an inch; his body is made up of muscle after muscle, and I'm reminded of when Ryan pins me down—never painfully, never to hurt me, but when he does, I know I can't get away, and Robbie has the same build as Ryan. The difference is that I never want to get away from Ryan. Robbie's hands go to my skirt, and to my horror, he starts to push it up over my thighs. "No," I whisper. "Robbie, no, no, no. Please stop. Please don't do this."

He doesn't stop; he doesn't even halt. When I look up at his face, his eyes are so focused on my legs and getting the skirt up that I'm genuinely terrified about how this is going to end. I reach up for his face and push it away, thinking that at least I can do that; at least I can move his head, and it might snap some sense into him. He just moves his head out of my reach, and when it comes back, I rake my index finger down his cheek, digging the nail into his skin. He hisses in pain, and when he finally drags his eyes away from my legs, I'm horrified by what I see in them. It's not the look I've seen when he's tried to rile me in class or around campus; it's not even the determined look he had outside in the hallway. No, now there's nothing there at all, just cold, passive, dark eyes that have already made up their mind.

Tears well in my own eyes, and he roughly grips my ass and pulls me up slightly, pushing the skirt up so it sits around my hips. My legs are kicking at him, but it doesn't do any good. He doesn't stop, and I am so weak, I can't get him away from me. I can't stop this.

"Please don't do this," I whisper over and over. "Please don't, please don't, please don't."

His fingers reach for my knees, and they dig so painfully into my flesh that I gasp out loud as he starts to pry them open. I try to get them locked together, twisting my ankles together, doing everything I can to stop my legs from opening to him, but it doesn't work. I can't do anything. I'm utterly defenseless against him as his hands inch farther and farther up the inside of my thighs, forcing me to open to him, digging into the soft flesh there. I'm in so much shock I don't even feel it. Even though it must hurt, even though I know it does, even though I know his fingers are digging so hard they must be leaving bruises on my pale flesh, I don't feel it. It's like I've left my body and am watching this scene from above—that's how utterly insane this is to me right now.

"That's it," he whispers against my neck. "Stop fighting it." I realize my legs are now just limply open, no longer trying desperately to stay closed. I know I can't fight him, I know he's going to do this, but tears still drip down my face as his fingers go to the zipper on his jeans, unzip them, and pull down his underwear. I don't look. I can't look at him. My eyes stray to his chest, his arms, the rest of the room, anywhere but his penis, which is hard and ready. My hands still try to push him away, my arms still grapple with him, and my voice still repeats the words I've been saying again and again and again.

"Don't. Please don't, Robbie. Please don't." I'm begging now. My voice is desperate, broken, but somehow I know he can't hear me. He's not even listening to me. Robbie is in his own head, and he's decided that he's doing this. There's nothing I can do to stop it.

He reaches out behind me and grips my ass. His hands are on the bare skin of my butt, dipping under the fabric of my underwear, and the tears start coming harder now. This is really happening. Robbie Mulligan is touching me, touching me intimately, and there's nothing I can do about it. His grip tightens on my butt, and he hauls my body forward, my open legs making it easy for him to step in and rest his hips against me.

I'm shaking my head now. "No, no, no, no. Don't, don't

do this. Please, please don't do this."

He either doesn't hear me or he doesn't care. He gives no indication at all that he's heard me, and I want to throw up. I actually feel my stomach churning, and I want to throw up.

"This is what you want," he tells me, but I have a feeling it's really what he's telling himself, which makes me think he can hear me after all. "This is what you've always wanted."

With that he reaches between us, shoves my underwear to the side, and roughly drags a finger down my most intimate area—an area that is bone dry from horror and fear and disgust. He thrusts forward, entering me with one big, painful, agonizing thrust.

I'm sobbing now, full-on messy sobs, as he thrusts into me again and again. I stop fighting him at this point. I just want it to be over. I want it to stop, and if that means he has to finish, then so be it; I just want it to be over as quickly as possible. A loud, guttural sob escapes from my throat with every painful thrust, and finally, after what feels like a lifetime, with a groan of his own, he stills against me, holding my body against his, resting his head on my shoulder.

He stays like that for almost a minute, a whole minute where I don't breathe in fear of what he'll do next. *Please tell me it's over. Please tell me it's done.* Then he stands up, pulls out of me, and turns away, tucking himself back into his jeans. I slump against the cold wall behind me, all energy completely drained. My mind flashes back over the last ten minutes, wondering how this happened, how something so horrible could happen to me, could happen so suddenly. I reach up to wipe the tears from my face and close my legs, trying to ignore the screaming pain from my lower body, which has just been violated, has just been attacked…my body, which couldn't stop his assault.

By the time I've managed to pull myself together, the loud, shaking sobs have finally stopped. I wipe the tears from my face with a hand that is shaking so hard, it takes three attempts for me to get it anywhere near my tear-soaked cheeks. I think Robbie's left, but when I look toward the door, he's standing there, watching me impassively like nothing's even happened, like he didn't just destroy my life.

I stare back at him, and he's the one who looks away first.

"Come on, Becca," he says quietly. "You can't stay in here."

For some reason his words make sense to me. I can't stay in here. I can't stay in here where he did this terrible thing to me. I need to go. I need to go home and lock the door behind me. I need to get into my own bed and pray this was all just a terrible dream and none of it really happened.

I push myself off the table and pull down my skirt, which miraculously doesn't even seem to have a single rip in it. I tug on my top, trying to pull that down too. I hate the thought that so much skin is on show, hate that this outfit could have given him ideas and gave him easier access to my body. I stumble toward the door where he waits for me, only this time I'm not stumbling from the alcohol—I've never felt so sober in my life. I'm stumbling because my legs seems to have forgotten how to work, and I'm shaking so hard, it's difficult to put one foot in front of the other.

He opens the door as I approach and I shrink away from him, desperate not to be anywhere near him, certain I'll die if he ever touches me again. I hear the door close behind me and pray he's stayed in there, but then I feel him behind me, feel his big, powerful, unyielding presence, and I know he's only a step away. This knowledge propels me forward, and I walk as quickly as I can to the stairs.

"Whoa!" Two hands reach out to steady me, and I flinch away in horror, desperate not to have anyone touch me.

"Becca? Becca, are you okay?" Two pairs of wide hazel eyes stare back at me, and I look up to see the freshman red-head Mason introduced me to. *Lennon? Leroy? Liam? Liam.* I think Liam was his name, and right now he's looking down at me in concern. "Becca?" His voice is gentler this time.

"She's fine." Robbie's firm voice comes from behind me. He's far, far too close, and I see Liam's eyes flash behind me in surprise before coming back to me, concern etched all over his face.

"Becca?" His voice is soft and so, so sweet. It makes me want to cry all over again. "Should I get Mason? He's just downstairs."

"She's fine, Coppell," Robbie repeats coldly. "Stay out of our goddamn business."

I see his eyes widen in surprise as he takes in Robbie's words and their implication. Then his gaze sweeps over me. He must see the skirt that isn't quite in place, the top that is slightly askew, the hair that is completely disheveled and fall-ing down around my face, but his face doesn't morph into a smirk like I expect it to—no, his eyes narrow in concern, and he takes a step closer to me. I flinch away yet again. "Are you okay? What happened?"

"Coppell." Robbie's voice has a warning it in.

"What happened to your face, man?"

I hear his words and look to Robbie in confusion. I see

the small scratch I managed to make on his cheek when I was trying to get him to stop.

"I have to go," I manage to whisper, and it's true—I have to get as far away from here as possible. I turn and run as quickly down the stairs as my platform shoes will allow me, practically tripping in my haste to get away. I burst out the front door, down the steps, and turn to the nearest bush. With a loud retch, I bend at the waist and empty the contents of my stomach all over the ground behind it.

# CHAPTER 7

*Becca*

I DON'T GET OUT OF BED THE NEXT DAY; I JUST LIE THERE in the sweatpants and t-shirt I changed into after I showered last night. As soon as I got home, I scrubbed myself red and raw to try to get the feel of him off of me, but I still feel dirty, still feel violated. Now I'm just staring up at the ceiling. I turned my phone off and haven't left my room all day. I didn't respond to Tina when she called through my door, asking where I went last night. I didn't respond when she shouted through a second time, telling me she was going out for lunch and asking if I wanted to join her. And I didn't respond when she returned a couple hours later and asked if she could come in and talk to me. I've just lain here all day, going over last night's events again and again in my head and thinking about how if I just hadn't gone to the bathroom, none of this would have happened.

There's hammering on the door to our apartment which

is located just off the main college campus and houses a bunch of students. The hammering continues, but I don't move. I have no intention of facing anyone today, not until I figure this out. Not until I figure out what to do next.

The next thing I know, the door to my room is being slammed open so hard it ricochets back off the wall. I turn my head to see Ryan in my doorway. He's breathing heavily, and his face is flushed and all hard lines. I sit up quickly in a panic, wincing slightly at the pain from below my waist.

"Wh-What…? What are you doing here?" My voice is shaking.

"Is it true?" he demands.

I start to cry—the very sight of him makes me sob. All I want is for him to come over and wrap his arms around me and tell me it's all going to be okay.

"I guess that's my answer then," he says bitterly.

I start to shake. *How could he possibly know?* I haven't told anyone what happened last night.

"How did—" I pause and take a deep breath, trying to pull my emotions together. "How did you know?"

He pulls his phone out of his pocket and presses some buttons before forcing it into my hands. I stare in horror at the picture on the screen. It's from last night, of when Robbie was kissing me, only you can't see that I'm trying to get away. You can't see that I'm disgusted. It just looks like our lips are connected and we're kissing.

"Scroll along, Becca. There's more," he tells me sharply.

I flip through the pictures and see there's more: one of us on the dance floor with his arms wrapped around me from be-hind, another of us supposedly making out, and then—worst

71

of all—us emerging from the bedroom. His jeans are unbuckled, and I'm pulling my skirt down with one arm and tugging at my top with another. My face isn't toward the camera, so you can't see the horror I know was there on my face, and because it's a picture, you can't see me shaking in terror.

"How did you get these?" I whisper.

"I woke up to those pictures this morning. He couldn't wait to share the news."

I start to sob harder and move my hand to cover my mouth.

"How could you, Becca?" he asks, his voice cracking. "How could you do that to me? To us?"

He thinks I slept with Robbie—that's what it looks like from the pictures. I shake my head and open my mouth to tell him what really happened, how I would never cheat on him, how I love him with all my heart, but the words won't come out.

"You're nothing to him, you know that?" he shouts angrily in my face, the hurt gone from his voice, replaced by pure rage. "He fucked you to get to me! That's how fucking stupid you are!"

He steps forward and roughly grabs his phone from my hands before turning and leaving the room.

It takes me a minute to react. It's only when I hear the front door slam shut that I move. "Ryan, wait!" I call, scrambling out of my bed and following him out of my room, through the apartment, and down the hall.

He's marching quickly down the hallway, and I have to run to catch up. When I reach for his hand to pull him back, he brushes me off. When I try again, he shoves me off him so hard, it sends me flying into the wall.

"Ryan please!" I beg, suddenly realizing how bad this is. He thinks I slept with Robbie Mulligan. He doesn't know what really happened, and although the last thing I want to do right now is relive last night, I know I have to tell him. "Ryan, stop."

He continues down the hall, ignoring me, and exits the building. I hurry to catch up to him, desperate to make him listen to me, desperate not to lose him. The tears are falling freely down my face. People by the entrance look at us curiously, but I don't care. All I can think about is getting him to stop, getting him to stay with me.

I try to pull him back, but again he just shoves me off him, and this time I stagger away, almost falling over. I start to cry harder.

He strides toward the main quad on campus with purpose, clearly looking for someone. With a feeling of dread, I realize he's probably looking for Robbie. He gets there ahead of me, and my prayers that Robbie won't be there are unanswered. I reach the center of the quad just as Ryan spots the football team sitting on the benches outside the campus gym. He rushes toward them without a second thought, pulls a surprised Robbie off his seat, and starts punching him in the face again and again.

I rush forward to stop him, but I don't know what to do. Ryan's relentless, hitting him repeatedly, and it takes Robbie's teammates a minute to react as they watch the scene in shock.

"Ryan, please, please stop," I beg as Robbie's teammates finally pull Ryan off of him. It takes three of them to get him away from Robbie. Thankfully Mason is there and pulls Ryan away before any of the others can go after him.

"I will fucking kill you," Ryan screams at Robbie while Mason holds him back. Bernie goes to stand in front of Ryan, giving me a quizzical look. They don't know what's going on; I can tell by their faces they have no clue.

Robbie puts his hand to his face then pulls it down and sees blood. Ryan got him pretty good; his nose is gushing blood, and his eye is already turning purple. Robbie glances over at me briefly, and I expect him to look ashamed. I expect him to admit what happened, to explain to Ryan that I didn't want it, that I didn't do what he thinks I did, but then I watch in horror as Robbie's face morphs into a smirk.

"She was good, Jackson," he taunts Ryan. "She was real good."

My world stops as I realize what he's implying. He's letting them all think we had sex. He's not telling my boyfriend, the love of my life, the truth about what happened, how I didn't betray him. Everything moves in slow motion as Ryan lunges forward again, and I feel like I can't breathe.

"Best I ever had." Robbie's words startle me back to attention, but he's not looking at me. His eyes stay focused on Ryan, and suddenly last night makes sense. Robbie hates Ryan—really, really hates him. The thought of Ryan being better than him has been eating away at him for years; the fact that other people think Ryan is better than him drives him insane—insane enough to assault his girlfriend just to make him think I cheated, just to hurt him. That's how much of a sick fuck he is.

Mason looks between Robbie and me in shock, and I can see the exact moment understanding dawns on him. He looks at me in disgust. "You didn't..." he says, shaking his head in disbelief, still pulling at Ryan. Bernie joins him, and it's taking both of them to hold Ryan back.

I'm shaking all over now, and I don't know what to do. I don't know how to get Ryan to listen to me, how to fix this. "Ryan, please," I beg again.

He looks over at me like he's just remembered I'm here, and he stops fighting against Mason's hold. He glares at me with such contempt and fury that I actually think my knees might give way. "We're done," he tells me flatly, no emotion in his voice.

My whole world grinds to a halt. "No," I say desperately, shaking my head. "No. You don't understand. You don't understand what happened. We can talk. I can explain. Please, just listen to me."

He pushes away from Mason and whirls to face me, stalking forward until he's just inches from me. He looms down on me, and it's so similar to how Robbie was yesterday, so aggressive, I actually shrink away from him. He doesn't notice; he's too angry. His eyes are wild as he points down at me. "Do you know how many girls I could have had, Becca?" he asks me harshly. "Do you know how many girls I could have fucked?"

I just stare back at him, begging him with my eyes not to do this, not to break up with me.

"No, actually, that's bullshit," he continues. "I fucked my way around Cal State. I had every girl there."

I shake my head at his words, fresh tears falling. "That's not true."

He shrugs and laughs bitterly. "Maybe, maybe not—how would you know?"

"Ryan—"

"No." He cuts me off and gives me one last look, a look filled with hatred and venom and everything I never thought he could feel for me, then turns and walks off. Mason looks at me in disgust and then follows after Ryan.

"Ryan, w-wait!" I shout, my voice cracking with emotion as I start to follow him. *This cannot be happening. I can't let this happen.*

He turns and glares at me, his eyes wild. "DO NOT FOLLOW ME!" he bellows, and it freezes me to the spot as he turns around and walks away. I stand there, watching him leave and feel helpless, completely and utterly helpless.

The rest of the football team are all watching me with a mixture of contempt, indifference, and amusement, like this has been tonight's entertainment. Bernie looks shocked, glancing back and forth between Robbie and me like he's trying to process what he's heard. Even though he's the defensive end and one of Robbie's teammates, I know he has a similar opinion of Robbie to Mason. His eyes find mine, and a wave of sympathy crosses his face. I must look terrible. I know I feel it. Nothing has ever hurt this bad in my life—not even last night. He takes a step toward me, but the young redhead from last night beats him to it. He gently touches my arm, and again I flinch at the contact, causing his eyes to widen in alarm.

"Becca, are you okay? What happened last night?"

I shake my head, fresh tears falling, not even hearing his words as I stare after Ryan as he walks away. Mason turns around to look back at me briefly, but Ryan doesn't look back once. I turn to face the football team. Half of them are still looking at me, and the other half are looking at Robbie, who's managed to find some tissue and has it held up to his nose, trying to stop the bleeding. I stare at him, and he eventually looks my way. Again, I expect him to do the right thing, to admit what happened, but he doesn't. He just stares back at me, his gaze hard as he watches me seconds after my life has fallen apart.

I feel a presence at my side and turn to see Tina there, concern etched on her face. She must have followed us out of the apartment and witnessed the whole thing. She gently takes my arm and turns me so we can go back home. She walks quickly and with purpose, striding through the watching crowd, leading me home, away from the people who are all watching and judging me, the people who saw my complete humiliation, who now think I'm a cheating tramp, who just witnessed my heart getting shattered into a thousand pieces.

# CHAPTER 8

## Ryan

I KICK THE FRONT DOOR SHUT BEHIND ME, AND IT slams so hard into the frame I swear it rattles the walls of the house. I hitch up the paper bag I'm holding higher in my arms and make my way into the kitchen. My roommates, Jason and Marty, sit around the table, and Evan is hanging out by the counter. They all turn as I walk in.

"Dude, where you been? I've been calling you all day."

"Coach is pissed," Evan tells me. "We were supposed to meet him at two."

I don't respond. I just drop the bag of liquor bottles on to the counter. I don't give a single fuck about anything right now. The only thing that exists in my brain at the moment is Becca and Mulligan, together. I threw up when Mason took me back to his place, and just the thought of her with him makes me want to do it again. Mason wanted me to stay there, to calm down and get myself together, but I just wanted him to take me to the airport. I couldn't stand the thought of being so close to her. All I wanted to do was put as many miles between us as possible, and I got the next flight out of there. Because of the time difference and the hours I had to wait for an available flight at the airport—during which Mason sat next to me, trying to make me feel better and not act like he's as bewildered as I am by the turn of events—I've been gone for over twenty-four hours. I left the house without a word after seeing those pictures when I woke up yesterday morning, and I've ignored all calls and messages. Now it's late afternoon, and I'm determined to forget.

"Dude, what the fuck?" This from Marty. They're all staring at me, and I realize my hands are clenched so tightly into fists that my knuckles are white. "What happened?"

I ignore them. The only thing I want to do right now is forget, and the only way for me to do that is to drink. I reach into one of the bags and pull out a bottle of Jack Daniel's. I unscrew the top and take a long hard sip straight from the bottle, enjoying the burn as it hits the back of my throat. I straighten up and see Evan's eyes widen at me. It's unlike me to drink in the middle of the day, but I need to forget. I need to not picture his hands all over her, kissing her, touching her. I take another long swig, swallowing more this time, and only stop drinking when my eyes start to water.

"What the hell are you doing, man? We got practice tomorrow." Evan looks confused as I continue to pace up and down in the kitchen.

I grab another bottle out of the bag and slide it down the counter to Evan. "Either drink or get out," I tell him. Evan looks at Jason as if he might have an answer.

"Actually, fuck it, yeah," I say, thinking out loud. I pull my phone from my pocket and type out a message. I hit send, and it goes to everyone in my phonebook—everyone except her.

Their phones beep from around the room, and they look down at the message. I've just sent my entire contacts list a message saying we're partying, right now.

"What's going on?" Marty asks just as Dean walks into the kitchen. "Jake's been freaking out all day, but won't say why."

"Hey, man. Where you been?" Dean asks. He pulls out his phone and reads my message. His eyes widen in surprise, and he looks at me pacing. The rest of the guys stare at me in confusion. "How many people did you send that to?" he asks.

"Everyone," I tell him as his head snaps to Marty and Jason in question. They just shrug back at him. I need to forget. I need to not think about it. I need to end myself tonight, and this is the only way I can think to do it. "Time for you boys to show me the crazy, single college life you all keep talking about."

A silence settles over them as they realize this must have something to do with Becca. They look from me to each other, completely lost as to what's going on. I look at Marty. "Can that dude you know get me two kegs?"

He stares at me for a second, and then nods his head slowly.

"Get all the girls here that you can. Anyone, I don't care. Just get some girls here." Becca's not the only one who can find someone else. If she can fuck someone else without a second thought for me, then I can do the same. She didn't give a damn about everything we mean to each other, didn't think about everything we've been through, our entire fucking history, which spans our whole lives. She fucked Robbie Mulligan, the guy who hates me more than anything, at a goddamn party. That just shows exactly what she really thinks of me. I've always worried deep down that she doesn't feel the same for me as I feel for her, but I accepted that, because I knew she loved me, and I knew nobody in this whole world could be more deeply in love with someone than I was with Becca McKenzie. It's just not possible. I've been so stupid. So, so stupid. Believing her bullshit about loving her life at Southern U too much and not wanting to transfer here because it doesn't feel right. Her and Mulligan have probably been at it for months. They've probably been laughing at me for fucking *months* while I've been over here pining after her, thinking she loved me just as much as I loved her.

"Dude, what happened?" Evan asks quietly, stepping in front of me and bracing his hands on my shoulders. I just shake my head back at him. I can't even bring myself to say the words. If I say the words, it makes them real. I lean back against the counter and close my eyes, instantly picturing her with him. He's kissing her, touching her, stripping her. Blind rage takes over. I throw the bottle in my hand as hard as I can against the wall of the kitchen and watch as it smashes into a thousand pieces.

There's stunned silence around me, and I'm breathing heavily. It feels like I can't breathe. I can't breathe knowing she did this to me, knowing she betrayed me like this. *How could she do this? How could she do this to me? To us?* We weren't supposed to be like other couples. We were different.

"Ryan?" I turn to see Jake's entered the kitchen, and he's watching me cautiously. Seeing him calms me down, but only slightly. He steps toward me, and I suddenly snap out of it. I head back to the counter and pull another bottle out of my bag. I bought enough for me to forget my problems—hell, I bought enough for us all to forget. Jake clears his throat. "You okay?"

"You speak to Mason?" I ask him.

He nods. "It doesn't make sense, Ryan. She wouldn't—"

"She did."

"Did she admit it?"

"She didn't deny it."

He shakes his head. "There's gotta be an explan—"

"She fucking did it, Jake."

"Seriously, what the fuck happened?" Jason demands loudly. "Is Becca okay?"

I let out a bitter laugh. *Is Becca okay?* I don't give a fuck if Becca is okay or not. I hope she's not. I hope she's fucking miserable, because whatever she's feeling right now, it's not even a fraction of the pain I'm going through.

Jake holds out his phone. "How many people did you send that message to?"

"Everyone in my contacts."

He sighs. "You wanna talk?"

I hold up my bottle. "I wanna do this."

"Ryan—"

"I don't wanna hear it, Jake."

"She's blowing up my phone," Jake tells me just as I look down at my own phone and see that she's calling me again. She's been calling me constantly. I push it away. There's no way I'm ever speaking to her again. "You need to talk to her."

"Leave it, Jake."

"Ryan—"

"I mean it, Jake," I shout, my voice loud in the silence of the kitchen. "You need to fucking leave it."

Jake bites his lip while looking down at the bottle on the counter. He looks back up at me, and I know he's worried. I know he thinks I need to talk about this and that getting drunk isn't the answer, but he doesn't push me on it; he lets me do it my way. He doesn't say a word as he steps forward and unscrews one of the bottles, takes a long swig, and winces as it goes down. He looks back at me. "I guess we're drinking then."

"What the hell is—"

"Becca fucked Robbie Mulligan, okay?" I snap, spinning around to face Jason. I watch as shock takes over his features. "Becca had sex with Robbie Mulligan. Last night."

There's complete silence at my words. No one moves an inch as I stand there and tell them what she's done to me. Marty starts shaking his head in disbelief. "She wouldn't."

"She did."

Marty opens his mouth and then closes it. There isn't really much you can say to that. "Dude, I'm sorry."

"So, yes, I'm fucking partying tonight."

"Bro." Evan's face says it all.

"Yup," I answer, nodding my head bitterly. "And then he sent me the pictures to prove it." I pause, trying to shake the pictures out of my mind, but it's like they're imprinted on my brain. "He sent me the pictures to prove he fucked my girl." It still doesn't feel real to me. How did this happened? Only two days ago, everything was perfect. Now, my life has exploded. Becca McKenzie isn't my girlfriend anymore. Becca McKenzie isn't in my life anymore. How can something so big happen so fast? I want nothing more than to forget the last twenty-four hours. I pick my bottle up and sit down at the table, watching as one by one, my friends all pick up a bottle and sit down next to me. People start arriving pretty shortly afterward, and it's not long before it gets out of control. I see the curious glances I'm getting from the team, and I know word's gotten out about the reason I insisted on the party. The girls show up too, but I don't even look at them. I don't give a fuck about anything but the bottle of Jack in my hand. Jake stays next to me the whole time, and it only takes an hour after everyone arrives before I'm so drunk I can't even think straight—which is exactly what I was hoping for.

# CHAPTER 9

*Becca*

I MET ROBBIE MULLIGAN IN MY FIRST WEEK OF college, and it's not an exaggeration to say I instantly disliked him. I was late for my first class of the year. I'd set out in plenty of time to get there but had gotten lost and ended up on the wrong side of campus. I was only about five minutes late when I finally found the lecture hall, but I had visions of everyone turning to stare at me and the professor humiliating me in front of everyone for being late.

The doors were already closed when I got there, and I was just contemplating walking away when another girl came rushing up next to me. She looked at the door. "Shit, we're late."

I nodded at her, biting my lip. I was never opposed to ditching in high school, but I didn't want to start out on the wrong foot at college.

She looked at me for a minute, trying to decide what to

do. "We should just go in," she decided and pushed the door open. I followed her in, and we both froze just inside the doorway. The lecture room was packed completely full, and my stomach flipped as every head in the room turned to look at us.

"Hello." We both turned to see a tall blonde woman at the center of the room. She had wide black-framed glasses sitting on her nose and she peered down at us. "I'm Professor Smithson."

"Hi," I managed to squeak.

"I'm so sorry we're late," the girl next to me said sincerely. I glanced to my side and saw she had long black hair and an olive complexion. She was about my height, and just a quick glance at her told me she had curves to die for. "You know how it is, first day and all that."

I pressed my mouth together while Professor Smithson looked at us. Suddenly, her face broke into a huge smile, and I knew she wasn't the ogre I feared. "I'll let you off, as it's the first day." She turned to face the rest of the class. "For future reference, if you're late from now on, don't bother coming in. Just get the notes off me later." She looked back at us, her eyes twinkling. "Now, come over here and tell me your names. I have a seating chart so I know who you all are."

The girl next to me gave me a wink and stepped up to the professor, stating that her name was Maddy Richards. Professor Smithson pointed her toward the back, and I saw there was an empty seat three rows from the back, second seat in. Then she pointed out mine, and I barely managed not to groan when I saw it was halfway up the steps, right in the middle of the row. I forced a smile at the professor, knowing

I couldn't exactly request to sit somewhere else when I didn't know her and had just arrived late for my first class. I quickly followed Maddy up the steps and smiled apologetically at the girl on the end as she stood to let me in. Everyone else stood too, some giving me sympathetic smiles, some just flat-out ignoring me. I was almost at my seat when I had to stop for a second. A tall, broad, dark-haired guy stood just next to my seat, only he didn't step back against his chair like everyone else had. No, he just held his ground. I paused for a second, waiting for him to move, but he didn't do anything but smirk back at me. I glanced to the front of the room and saw Professor Smithson waiting patiently for me to take my seat so she could begin. I was holding everyone up now. I looked at him once more and he didn't move, so I had very little choice but to squeeze by him. The entire back of my body brushed against his front as I passed, and I swear I felt his right hand reach out slightly to cop a feel of my ass. I dropped into my seat, jaw tense, feeling pissed off. Professor Smithson began the lecture, and I turned and glared at him. He was already looking at me and gave me a wink. My lip curled in disgust, and I turned to face the front of the room, refusing to look at him again.

At the end of the lecture, I waited for him to stand up before I did. I pretended I was busy on my phone, and I waited until he exited the row before I got up and filed out in the opposite direction, staying as far away from him as possible. He reached the front of the room before me, and I saw him greet a couple guys who had been waiting for him at the door. Finally, he turned and walked out of the room.

"I'm Maddy Richards." I looked up to see the girl who

was late with me standing on my right.

"Becca McKenzie," I told her, returning her smile.

"Dammit, why can't my last name start with an M," she said, and I screwed my faced up, confused. "McKenzie, Mulligan."

"What?"

"You know who that guy was, right?"

I hitched my bag farther up on my shoulder. "I don't know what you're talking about."

She stopped dead and turned to face me, completely disregarding the fact that she was now making all the students behind us file around her. She waved her hand down the hallway to the main exit. "That fine specimen of a man is Robbie Mulligan."

"Who?"

She waved again. "The guy you were sitting next to is Robbie 'I have the best abs in the world' Mulligan." I stared blankly back at her. She shook her head at me in disbelief. "He's the quarterback of the college football team? The Southern U Kings? He redshirted last year, but he's starting this year."

"Oh." That didn't mean he wasn't an ass. "Well, if he's a sophomore, why's he with us in English lit?"

She looked at me like I was crazy. "Who cares? The dude is beautiful." I pulled a face. Sure, he was good-looking, but he wasn't my type. Messy brown hair, piercing blue eyes, and a cocky smile were the only things I'd thought about in months.

"Seriously? You don't know who he is? He's rich too. His daddy owns most of the state."

I rolled my eyes. I couldn't care less about money, and I

knew I was fortunate to say that. My parents both earn good livings, and my grandfather left my dad a good inheritance, so I've never known what it's like to struggle. Regardless, rich entitled pigs like Robbie Mulligan flat-out do not interest me.

"The guy with the brown hair? He's a jerk. Did you see him not move out of my way?"

She smirked at me. "He can make me squeeze past him any time."

I groaned and she laughed. It was the start of our friendship.

After that I always made sure I got to class early. First impressions stick with me, and I just didn't like the dude. I could tell he thought way too much of himself. He walked into the room and looked around to make sure people were noticing him. He nodded at the guys and flirted with the girls, patting their asses as he walked past them. The sheer arrogance and entitlement of the guy made me feel sick, and we didn't really speak to each other. I think it was obvious to him that I disliked him, but he seemed to enjoy it, and it pissed me off that he always found an excuse to touch me, which just made my skin crawl. If my arm was leaning on the armrest, he'd put his arm right next to it so our skin was touching. He'd spread his legs wide in his seat so his right leg would be touching my left, and I'd end up shifting so far to my right-hand side, I swear the girl who sat next to me must have thought I was coming on to her.

◆

It was a couple weeks into the semester when I was in the

cafeteria on the main campus with Maddy after class. My roommate Tina had joined us, and I could already tell Tina and Maddy were kindred spirits. They were both outgoing and bubbly, and strangely enough, I loved being around them.

We'd just picked up our food, and I was staring down at the sad-looking beef burrito I'd decided to risk when Maddy piped up. "That is where we need to sit."

I glanced in the direction she was looking –there was a huge group of guys near the back of the cafeteria, taking up a whole bunch of tables.

"Hell yes," Tina agreed, looking excited. I looked at her and raised an eyebrow. She rolled her eyes. "It's the football team. I swear you don't know anything, Becca."

"We can't sit over there," I told them, taking in the scene in front of me. "Let's not feed their egos any more than necessary. Their heads are already so big, I'm surprised they fit in the door."

Tina laughed but completely ignored me and stepped closer to them.

Maddy glanced sideways at me. "As long as they fit in my bed, I don't care." Despite myself, I burst out laughing. I was starting to realize she had no shame.

She grinned back at me and started walking toward them. "Wait," I hissed at them. "There isn't even space over there." There really wasn't. Their table was jam-packed, and all the tables surrounding them were full too—mainly of girls who were glancing over in their direction with interest, which made me want to sit on the other side of the cafeteria even more. It kind of reminded me of high school, where the popular guys were the football players, but on a way bigger scale. Southern U was a massive football school; I knew that before I came. It was why Ryan was considering coming here, but I don't think I fully understood just how worshipped the guys on the team were. I barely noticed or thought about it, but Tina and Maddy had mentioned it a few times, and looking over at that table and all the people around them, I knew they hadn't been exaggerating.

Maddy led the way, swaying her hips like a pro, slowing down as she approached their table, hoping someone noticed her. Tina did the same, and I swear I saw her stick her chest a little farther out. I almost burst out laughing just at the sight of them. No one even looked up, and they slowed down in disappointment and glanced over at me. I cocked my head toward the empty tables on the other side of the cafeteria, and Maddy sighed and nodded her head in agreement. We were almost clear of the table when I heard a familiar voice.

"Yo, McKenzie!"

I froze in irritation but then kept going, pretending I hadn't heard anything, but Tina and Maddy stopped immediately and turned to face the table.

Laughter rang out. "Don't try pulling that shit, McKenzie. I know you heard me." I rolled my eyes and turned to see Mason Blackwell grinning at me. I smiled back at him—I couldn't help it; Mason's smile was kind of infectious. "Get over here," he told me, cocking his head.

I shook my head but walked over regardless.

"You know Mason Blackwell?" Maddy hissed in my ear. God knows how she knew his name, surely not just because he was on the football team—*right?* She and Tina were right behind me, and I knew they'd be wondering why I didn't mention I knew Mason when they spoke about the team.

Mason stood as I approached, taking the tray from my hand and wrapping me in a big hug, even lifting me up off the floor. "Where you been hiding, McKenzie?"

"Away from you," I answered with a smirk as he dropped back into his seat. I had avoided Mason for most of high school. He was one of the most popular guys there, and I always thought he looked down on me. I couldn't have been more wrong. He was one of the nicest guys I knew, and one of Ryan's best friends. The more I hung out with him, the more I liked him, and now I considered him one of my best friends too. I knew we were both coming to Southern U together, but I hadn't had time to see him yet. I knew he was on the team and would be busy with practice and all that.

He gave me a lazy grin and then turned his attention to Tina and Maddy. "Who're your friends?"

I narrowed my eyes playfully, suddenly realizing why he was so keen on getting me over here. "Keep your eyes to yourself, Blackwell."

"Hey, just being friendly."

I raised an eyebrow. "I've seen your friendly." Mason had been, and still was, a total player. I'd seen more than one girl get burned by him.

He chuckled at me, and before I could stop her, Maddy stepped forward.

"I'm Maddy, this is Tina."

Mason winked at me and then formally shook their hands. I knew he was trying to determine whether or not he had a chance with them. I'd have said it was pretty likely, from my viewpoint.

"How do you know Becca?" Tina asked him.

"School. All the way back to middle school," Mason replied. "And you?"

Tina points at herself. "Roommate." She points at Maddy. "They're in the same class."

Mason flashed them a cocky smirk, and I may as well not have been there. Clearly they were not as keen on keeping their virtue from Mason Blackwell as I was of protecting it from him.

"Who's your friend, Blackwell?"

I turned to see a big guy sitting opposite him. He was looking at me in that way all football players seem to look at girls, like they have a right to, but he had an easy smile and his eyes were twinkling. I later found out he was Bernie Matthews, and I rarely saw Mason at college without him.

"Don't waste your time, man," Mason told him. "She's locked down. Practically married." I flipped him the finger as he grinned at me. "Oh, come on. I bet you've already spoken to him twice today, and it's not even dinnertime."

Three times actually. What could I say? We missed each other.

"You've got a boyfriend?"

I looked up and noticed for the first time that Robbie Mulligan was sitting farther down the table.

"Yes," I told him coldly.

"So why do you keep eye-fucking me every time I see you?"

My jaw fell open in disbelief. "ARE YOU FUCKING INSANE?" I exploded. The people who hadn't been listening certainly were now. "You have got to be the most delusional—"

I stopped abruptly as he burst out laughing. "I'm kidding, I'm kidding," he said, holding his hands up in a surrender. "Got you to talk to me though, didn't I?" My eyes narrowed as I heard chuckles from around us, and I glanced at Mason, who was looking at Robbie with a strange look on his face. I recognized that look; he was not a fan of Robbie's, I could tell. "Feel free to eye-fuck me any time though." Robbie continued looking me up and down appreciatively, and I wanted to punch him. "And it doesn't have to stop with the eyes." *What an asshole!*

I turned to Mason. "Your friend's a dick."

Mason didn't say anything, but the look he gave me told me he agreed.

"How do you guys know each other?" Mason asked, looking between me and Robbie.

"We have English lit together."

"Yup," Robbie agreed. "Four hours a week I get to sit next to the lovely Rebecca McKenzie."

I scowled at him. "Dude," Mason said, sounding like he was joking, but I could hear the warning in his voice. "Seriously, her boyfriend is one of my best friends."

He rolled his eyes and dropped his arm around the girl on his right, brushing his hand just above her cleavage. *Ugh,* I thought. *What a pig!* "Clearly, I have options," he said, indicating the girl with his head.

"So, why didn't your boyfriend follow you here?" Bernie asked.

I shrugged. Actually, it was me who didn't follow Ryan to Cal State, which is what he wanted. He could have come to Southern U. He got offered a scholarship, but Cal State had a better football program. I didn't think this was the best group of guys to explain every detail to.

"He got another offer."

"He got a scholarship?"

I nodded.

"To where?"

"Cal State."

They perked up with interest. Cal State was a big rival of Southern U, but they knew it was an elite sports college and respected anyone who went there.

"He's an athlete?" Mulligan asked, suddenly interested.

Mason smirked at me and I grinned back. We both knew they'd probably know who Ryan was.

"Yup."

"What sport?"

I glanced at Bernie.

"Football."

They were all listening now. "What position?" This was from one of the older guys down the table; all athletes took an interest in their rivals.

I turned to look Robbie in the eye. "Quarterback."

The table erupted in noise.

"Damn! Your boyfriend is Ryan Jackson?"

"Did you see that touchdown he made in the state final?"

"Is he starting or redshirting?"

"That boy can run!"

"Man, I wanted him here so bad."

"Coach nearly cried when he declared Cal State."

"We'd be unbeatable with him."

"He'd have been perfect to take over from Sampson."

I watched Robbie's face as his teammates salivated over Ryan. I'd always heard how good Ryan was at football, but it wasn't until we got together that I realized he was a unique talent and had been heavily recruited by a bunch of colleges. I even visited some with him, and it was when we came to Southern U that I fell in love with the school. Something about the lush greenery and the welcoming locals made me want to come. By then I could tell Ryan was leaning toward Cal State, and I didn't want him to make a decision based on what I thought, so I just stayed quiet and let him choose on his own. He kept asking me where I wanted to go, and up until then, I hadn't really had a preference, but the campus visit had changed my mind. I think deep down, he thought I'd go where he went, but I was never going to follow him somewhere I didn't want to be. I applied for Southern U and got in, but I didn't tell him until after he declared Cal State. I wanted him to do whatever was best for him and whatever would make him happy. I didn't want him to make a decision based on my choice. The day I told him, it was like I'd punched him in the face. I would never forget the hurt that crossed his face. He didn't talk to me for a week, and I genuinely thought we were over. It was the worst week of my life. The thought of us being over broke me in two, but whenever I tried to talk to him, he'd just walk away from me. When he eventually did show up at my house, he started talking about seeing if he'd be able to switch to Southern U, said it might still be possible, but I told him to stay at Cal State. He'd looked at me, heartbroken, and that's when I'd realized he thought that meant I wanted us to break up. Eventually I convinced him that separate colleges didn't mean a breakup, and we went back to normal. It was still a sore point with him, but I'd known we could make it work.

Bernie turned to me with a big grin on his face. "You couldn't get him to come here, huh?"

I shrugged. I wanted Ryan to go where he wanted to. There was no way I wanted my choice to affect his future.

Suddenly the table seemed to remember Robbie, who was seething with anger and watching me with narrowed eyes. I got the feeling he knew I enjoyed that.

"Well, hey, you better tell your boy to watch out, 'cause we got Mulligan now, and he's gonna show your man up."

"Yeah," one of the older guys down at the end piped up. "We don't need him anyway. Mulligan's gonna tear it up."

"We got this. Cal State ain't seeing no title this year."

I grinned at them. It was all fairly good-natured, but it was always good to hear how highly thought of Ryan was. I was really proud of him.

"Yeah, yeah." I laughed. "We'll see."

Mason shifted so there was space next to him on the bench. "You sitting?" he asked me. I shook my head even as Tina and Maddy stepped forward.

"We're good," I told him, sending them a look. I did not want to spend my lunch break discussing football. "I'll leave you all to plan Ryan's demise."

The guys who were still listening chuckled, and I took one last look at Robbie, who was glaring at me like he wanted to kill me. Then I turned and walked away, with Tina and Maddy grumbling about how I'd just ruined their chances.

I kinda thought that would end Robbie's interest with me. I was hoping I'd pissed him off so much he'd think I was a bitch and be done with me. It didn't work. If anything, it made him more interested, like he had to prove he could have me now that he knew I was with Ryan, one of his rivals. It got to the point where I ended up asking Professor Smithson if I could move seats, making up a lie about my eyesight. After freshman year, I didn't have any classes with him, and I rarely saw him around campus. When I showed up at Mason's birthday one year, I stayed for one drink and then left because of the way he was looking at me. Robbie Mulligan had done nothing but piss me off my whole college career, but I never, ever would have dreamed he'd do what he did.

# CHAPTER 10

*Becca*

I GLANCE UP FROM MY LAPTOP WHEN TINA WALKS through the door. She sets her purse and books on the table and takes in my appearance. I look a mess. I know I do. I'm wearing an old sweatshirt of Ryan's and some black leggings that have holes in them. I haven't washed my hair in days, and when I did briefly glance in the mirror earlier today, I noticed black bags underneath my eyes.

"Have you been outside today?" she asks.

I shake my head. "Ryan changed his status on Facebook to single," I tell her. My voice is quiet, like if I don't say it too loudly, then it won't be real.

She nods her head. "I saw that."

"Did you see the comments beneath it?"

Sympathy crosses her face, and I know she has. "Don't read that stuff, Becca. People are stupid, and they don't know what they're talking about."

I glance back at my screen and hit the refresh button again. There have been seventeen more likes on his newly single status since I last checked twenty minutes ago. Ryan changed his status to single three hours ago, and he's had over three hundred likes. I didn't even realize he knew that many people on Facebook. The comments range from "She's not worth it" to "Good riddance to the slut." Some girls even told him to give them a call now that he's free. Most of the comments are from people I don't know, and I'm pretty sure Ryan doesn't really know them either, but a few of his teammates— and even Hayley Walsh, whom I considered a friend—have liked his status. A tear leaks from my eye, and I hastily wipe it away. I feel like all I've done in days is cry.

"I'm sorry, Becca."

I look back at her and see the same concern that's been written all over her face since she found out. "It's okay," I lie. None of this is okay.

She stares at me for a minute, opens her mouth to say something, and then closes it again. After another minute, she finally says whatever it is she wants to. "I have to ask you something." My heartrate speeds up ever so slightly as I nod in her direction. I've been waiting for this. Tina has been amazing since the weekend. She's listened to me, held me while I cried, and let me repeat over and over again that Ryan is wrong and that we're not over, but she's never asked me what happened, why I did it. She hasn't questioned me, and for some reason I can't quite work out, I haven't told her the truth. I haven't told her or Maddy, who showed up here the night Ryan broke my heart by dumping me without even asking my side of the story. Maddy's been AWOL for the last few months since she got a new boyfriend, and I guess that proves just how quickly gossip gets out—unless Tina called her. I didn't notice if she did or didn't; I just locked myself in my room and cried and cried.

Tina clears her throat, and I realize my mind has drifted off again. That keeps happening to me too. "When I got in last night, you were already asleep, and I came in to check on you." I nod. I haven't really slept since the weekend, and last night I just wanted to escape, so I took a couple sleeping pills and slept a solid ten hours. I was hoping it was going to make me feel better. It didn't. "You were pretty restless, and you'd kicked your covers off in your sleep." She pauses and takes a look around the room before turning back to me. I'm not sure where this is going. "The shirt you were wearing had ridden up, and you had bruises on the tops of your thighs, and on the insides of them."

My heart starts beating harder in my chest. She wasn't supposed to know about them—the finger-shaped bruises Robbie left on my inner thighs as he dug his fingers in and pried my legs open.

"Where did they come from, Becca?"

I shrug my shoulders. "I'm clumsy."

"Are you sure you have nothing to tell me? What happened that night?"

I'm still trying to work that out myself. I have no idea how it happened, how it escalated so quickly. "There's nothing to tell."

"You can't stand Robbie Mulligan. You've never looked at him twice. It doesn't make sense."

None of it makes sense. None at all. If only I hadn't gone

to that party. If only I hadn't drank so much. If only I wasn't wearing that stupid outfit. If only I hadn't gone to the bathroom. If only. If I hadn't done even a couple of those things, my life wouldn't be in pieces.

"I just had a moment of stupidity, that's all." I'm still trying to figure out what's best. This lie that I slept with Robbie seems to have taken hold, and I don't know what to do now. I don't how to tell her what really happened. I don't know how to tell anyone.

"Becca–"

"Please, leave it." My voice is firm and allows for no arguments. Her face falls, but she doesn't challenge me again. I do not want to talk about this, not now. I still need to figure out what to do.

"I tried calling Ryan again," I tell her, changing the subject back to the only thing I want to think about—Ryan. If I think about Ryan, then I don't think about Robbie. "But this time it didn't go to voicemail. It didn't even ring. He's blocked my number."

Sympathy crosses her face. "I'm so sorry, Becca."

"Jake won't answer the phone either. He won't speak to me, and I don't have anyone else's number over there." I've been trying desperately to get in touch with Ryan over the last couple days, but it's been pointless. My phone log tells me I've called him 216 times in four days, and he hasn't answered once. A thought suddenly occurs to me. "Can I use your phone?"

She opens her mouth to say something but then stops. She reaches into her purse, pulls out her cell, and hands it over to me. I can tell by her face she doesn't think this is a good idea, but she's trying to help me any way she can.

I dial Ryan's number into her cell and hold it to my ear. He picks up after four rings.

"Hello?" I'm actually surprised to hear his voice. He actually picked up.

"Ryan, we need to talk, I can—" He ends the call before I can even finish my sentence. I try to call him back, but he doesn't answer.

"He hung up," I tell Tina, and my voice cracks as I say it. She nods her head at me, her face full of concern. "Let me try Jake," I say, quickly dialing his number.

The phone rings for longer this time, and I'm about to hang up when he answers.

"Becca? Look, I'm with Ryan. I know it's you."

"Jake, please, just get him to speak to me."

"Becca, you need to stop calling. Just leave it for a bit, yeah?" He hangs up before I can say anything else. When I try to call back, he sends me to voicemail. One of my best friends in the world is refusing to talk to me.

I glance up at Tina. "He won't talk to me either." She nods and sits beside me. I hand her back her phone.

"I'm sorry, Becca."

I nod and turn back to my laptop, staring at it blankly.

"I should just go see him," I say, suddenly sitting up straighter. I don't know why I didn't think of this before.

Tina's eyes widen in surprise, and she starts shaking her head. "Becca, no. I don't think that's a good idea. You need to give him some time."

"No. If he won't take my calls, then I'll just go to his house, and then he'll have to talk to me," I say, jumping up from my seat. I go to my room, pull down my carry-on, and start throwing some clothes into it. This is ridiculous. Of course Ryan won't speak to me; he thinks I slept with one of his rivals. All I have to do is tell him the truth. It'll hurt, and I don't want to relive that horrible night again, but then at least he'll know, and we can work out how to deal with this together. Ryan will know what to do. Ryan will fix this. He'll be able to make me feel better and protect me, just like he's always done.

"How will you even pay for it?" she asks.

"I'll put it on my credit card," I say without hesitation. Ryan and I have always budgeted for our flights to see each other, and we can't usually afford more than one trip in a semester. I know my credit card is only there for emergencies, but this is definitely an emergency.

"Becca, please. Think about it tonight, yeah? If you still want to go tomorrow, that's fine, but I don't think you should make any snap decisions."

I glance up at her. "I need to see him, Tina."

"But it's late. Please think about it. You might not be able to get a flight tonight."

"So I'll go tomorrow then instead."

She sighs. "I just don't want you to be upset."

I zip up my carry-on, strip off my leggings, and pull on a pair of jeans. "I'm going," I tell her. "Now, are you going to give me a ride to the airport or should I get an Uber?"

The cab I jumped in at the airport pulls up outside Ryan's

house the next morning, a few blocks away from campus. It's a nice house, which they actually keep fairly tidy, and I know they enjoy the independence of having their own place.

I walk up the steps, clutching the small carry-on I brought with me. I'm suddenly terrified of what he's going to say to me, but I need to do this. I need to explain, and he deserves to know the truth. I knock on the door, trying hard to keep my emotions in check. A minute passes, and then the door is opened by Jason.

Surprise crosses his face when he sees me, and then the corners of his mouth turn up in a sneer. He obviously knows all about our breakup. Jason and I always got along, but I guess he's another one that hates me now.

I take a deep breath. "I'm here to see Ryan." I cringe when I hear my voice shake.

He shakes his head at me. "He doesn't want to see you."

He goes to close the door, but I step into the doorway, blocking it. "I'm not going until I see him." My words are confident, but my voice is shaking.

Jason cocks an eyebrow at me and then smirks. "Well, by all means then. I believe he's in his room," he tells me, a smug flash in his eye.

I nod and edge past him into the house. A quick sweep of the room tells me they had a party last night. A few people are walking around with trash bags, picking up empty beer bottles and garbage. I keep my eyes down and don't look at them, even though I can feel their stares. I guess Ryan's not kept our breakup—or the reasons he believes caused it—a secret.

"Becca?" I glance up at the familiar voice, and Jake is standing in the threshold between the kitchen and the TV room, his eyes wide in disbelief. "You shouldn't be here," he tells me.

I just shake my head and walk to the stairs. "I need to speak to him, Jake," I say quickly, running up the stairs and ignoring his call for me to wait.

I head down the hallway and quickly knock on the door to Ryan's room before swinging it open.

I stop dead in my tracks, and whatever small piece that was left of my heart breaks into pieces.

Two pairs of eyes stare back at me.

Ryan's not alone.

Kelly Taylor is on her back, and Ryan is above her in the missionary position. His sheets are covering their bodies, sparing me the gory details, but it's pretty obvious I've just walked in on them having sex. This is why Jason looked so smug about sending me to Ryan's room.

I feel like I'm going to throw up. My right hand flies to my mouth, and my whole body starts trembling. *Ryan is with another girl. Ryan is having sex with another girl. Right now. Right in front of me. And that other girl is Kelly Taylor.* I feel like my heart is breaking all over again, and all the air leaves my body. Tears spring to my eyes and start dripping down my face as he stares back at me.

"No," I whisper, so quietly I doubt he can hear me. "No."

Ryan stares back at me for another moment, his jaw tense. He bites down on his lip and turns back to Kelly. She reaches up and strokes his cheek, not giving a fuck that I'm here, and for one terrifying, heartbreaking minute, I think he's going to continue. I think he's going to continue having sex with her right in front of me, but he doesn't. He rolls off her onto his back and stares up at the ceiling.

"Ryan…" My voice sounds as broken as my heart feels.

He doesn't look at me. "Go away, Becca. You need to go away."

"Ryan—"

"I don't want anything to do with you anymore, Becca. I never want to see you again."

An arm reaches out from the side of me and slams the door shut, and I turn to see Jake standing next to me. *I never want to see you again.* The words repeat over and over in my brain and a sob escapes. Ryan's already moved on. He's already moved on to the next girl, a girl he knows I can't stand, like I'm nothing—like I'm worse than nothing—and I just saw it. I just witnessed him having sex with that girl.

"Becca." Jake sounds tired next to me.

I back away from Ryan's bedroom door in horror, feeling like I've entered the Twilight Zone, and I keep going until I bang into the wall of the hallway behind me. I sink to the floor and start crying uncontrollably on the floor, my entire body trembling.

The music in Ryan's room suddenly goes up in volume, and I know Ryan's turned it up to block out my sobs. He doesn't care that my world just ended in front of him.

Jake sighs. "I told you not to come up here," he tells me while I just sit on the floor, my body racked with sobs. I feel like what was left of my world has just been blown apart. He had sex with somebody else. He's done with me. I came here to tell him what really happened, and instead I find that he's moved on and never wants to speak to me again. *This cannot be happening. This cannot be happening to me…* After a couple of minutes, Jake holds out his hand to me. "Come on, I'll drive you to the airport."

I don't stop crying the whole way to the airport. Jake doesn't say anything to me. Not a single thing. Usually I can't shut him up. I've known him since I was a little kid, and now he can't even stand to look at me. He sits rigidly in his seat, and I realize that not only is my relationship with Ryan over, but probably my friendship with Jake too. Jake pulls into the drop-off area at the airport, slamming hard on the breaks. I lurch forward in my seat, the seatbelt digging into my chest.

"I am so fucking mad at you, Becca!" he explodes.

I jump in my seat at the sudden noise but just nod my head in response.

"I mean, were you drunk? Was that it?" I glance over at him, and he's staring at me, looking genuinely confused. "Mason said you had a few drinks," he continues, like he's trying to find a reason for me why I would sleep with Robbie, to explain it. I nod my head. "I mean, do you re-member doing it, or were you just completely out of it?"

My memory flashes back to that night. I remember Mulligan's hands all over me, remember him trapping my hands behind me, remember him prying my legs open and the sharp pain when he entered me. The utter inability to stop him. The utter inability to defend myself. No, I definitely remember it.

"I mean, you know Ryan couldn't have been more in love with you, right? You know you were his whole world, don't you?"

I nod my head. He's my whole world too. It's not possible for me to be any more in love with him—and it's not past tense with me.

"The thing you two had doesn't come around very often." He sounds so angry it makes me wince. "And you've just thrown it away with Robbie fucking Mulligan."

Fresh tears fall at Robbie's name. I can't cope with thinking about him. Not now. Not after what I've just witnessed. At this moment in time, I feel like if I think about Robbie as well, I'll physically die. I was going to. I was going to face it and tell Ryan, but that was before. Right now all I can think about is losing Ryan. I can't think about what Robbie did to me too. I refuse to.

Jake sighs. "Do you get that you've broken his heart?"

I turn away to look out the window. He certainly didn't look heartbroken when I saw him. I, on the other hand, feel as though he's stomped on my heart.

Jake's voice is sharp. "You've fucked everything up, you know that?"

*HE FUCKING RAPED ME!* I want to scream it at him, but instead a fresh wave of tears hits me at the memory of Ryan's face when I walked in on them. It was blank. Completely blank to me. Completely indifferent.

"Becca!" Jake's voice is sharp, and there's no sympathy there. "Are you even listening to me?"

I nod and turn back to him, wiping away my tears. "Well, we're even now, right? Ryan got with Kelly, so that's payback for Robbie Mulligan. We can go back to normal now, right?" I sound desperate, even to my own ears.

Jake looks at me in disgust and shakes his head. "Ryan is fucking Kelly to try to forget about you, and he's single. You were with him for years, and then you fucked his biggest rival. You're nowhere close to being even."

"It should never have happened," I tell him.

"Mulligan's pressing charges," Jake tells me suddenly.

My heart sinks. "Wh-What?" I stammer.

"Against Ryan. For assault. He just found out last night. The guy fucks his girlfriend, sends him pictures to prove it, then when Ryan rightly beats the shit out of him, he decides to press charges so he can ruin Ryan's career as well as his personal life." He pauses, and I can tell Jake is genuinely furious. He's devastated for his friend, and he blames me for letting this happen. "That's the guy you picked, Becca. That's the guy you chose."

"I didn't choose him, Jake! I would never choose anyone over Ryan."

"But you did, Becca. Even if it was just for fifteen minutes, you chose Mulligan over Ryan."

I feel like laughing at that. Jake thinks I chose Robbie over Ryan for fifteen minutes. I feel like screaming that those fifteen minutes were the worst of my life. That I would do anything in this world to change them, and that unless I focus on Ryan, they play over and over again on a loop in my head, and all the horror and all the helplessness floods my body until I can't breathe. But I don't. I don't tell Jake any of that.

"I love him, Jake."

Jake shakes his head at me, his upper lip pulling into a sneer. He can barely even stand to look at me.

"Jake, please talk to him for me? Make him listen to me,

yeah? Get him to call me?" I beg him.

Jake shakes his head at me. "I can't, Becca. He's my best friend. I need to be there for him."

"But I'm your friend too, Jake," I plead, my voice cracking.

He looks at me, and I see the Jake I've known for years, my good friend who has always been there for me, only now I know he sees me differently. Now I know he'll never see me the same way again. All because of something I can't tell him about, something I couldn't control. For a second, he looks genuinely upset. "I can't be your friend right now, Becca."

I stare back at him, searching his eyes for an ounce of sympathy, an ounce of anything but the resolve I see there. He shakes his head again, and I know he's picked Ryan. He's on Ryan's side, and that means cutting me out.

I nod my head slowly and reach down for my carry-on, and then I exit the car and walk into the departure area, realizing I wasn't quite at rock bottom before I flew to California.

But I am now.

# CHAPTER 11

## Ryan

'M SITTING AT THE KITCHEN TABLE WITH MY HEAD IN my hands. My head is pounding. This is the worst hangover I think I've ever had. I drank way too much last night, and I have a meeting with Coach in an hour. I should be showering and trying to get my head in the game. I know he's pissed at me, but I can't get the look on Becca's face out of my head.

The bench opposite me creaks, and I look up to see Dean sitting down. He looks fine, no signs of a hangover. He's even wearing gym clothes, and judging by the gleam of sweat coming off his body, I'm guessing he's already been for a run this morning. He passes over a cup of coffee, and I gratefully accept and take a large sip before wincing in pain when it scalds my tongue.

Dean chuckles and passes me a bottle of water. I down half of it immediately.

"Why are you okay?"

He shrugs. "Didn't go as hard as you. I don't think any-one did."

I scowl at him, but he's right. I've barely stopped drinking since I found out about Becca and Robbie. I'm just topping up at this stage. It's the only thing that helps me forget. I check my phone, looking to see what time it is and swipe away the unopened messages on my phone. Most of them are from girls. They're like fucking piranhas now that they know I'm single. I've been getting all kinds of suggestive messages and straight-up offers from random girls offering to help me get over Becca, and it makes me sick about how quickly all this has gotten out. I must look fucking pathetic.

"Did I hear that Becca was here?"

I glance at him and then look away. I'm more ashamed about what Becca saw than I'd like to admit. I can't believe she saw me with Kelly, and I hate that I care. I shouldn't give a fuck what Becca thinks after what she's done, but I can't get the im-age of her face when she saw us in my bed out of my mind. I know it's bad. I didn't know what to do when she showed up, I just froze. I just froze and let her take in the scene in front of her so she'd have no doubt about what was going on.

As soon as the door slammed shut, I knew how low it was. I'd stooped to her level by having sex with somebody else, except I didn't physically see her having sex with Mulligan. The truth is, if I'd seen that, it would have destroyed me, which in that moment is what I wanted to do to Becca. When I heard her crying outside, I swear it squeezed my heart—but she did this to us, not me, and I don't care what she's feeling. It couldn't be half as bad as what I'm feeling.

The front door slams, and Jake appears in the kitchen. He

looks tired.

He opens his mouth to say something, but then closes it again and joins us at the table. Marty wanders in too, stuffing a protein bar down his throat.

"Where's Kelly?" Jake finally asks.

"She left half an hour ago." As soon as I heard Becca and Jake's footsteps walking away from my bedroom, I got up, went to my window, and watched Jake drive Becca away. When I turned back to Kelly in my bed, who was not even bothering to cover herself and looked so fucking pleased with herself, I felt dirty, and guilty—so, *so* guilty. I sank into a chair, staring at the ground for twenty minutes while Kelly rambled on. I told her I had things to do, and even though she tried distracting me with a blow job, I just wanted her to leave. She finally took the hint, telling me she'd call me later. I was gonna have to figure out a way of telling her it was a one-time thing.

"You couldn't have picked someone else?"

My eyes flare, and I turn to glare at him. "What's that supposed to mean?" I know what it means. It means that out of all the girls I could have chosen to rebound with, it didn't have to be Kelly, the one girl I know Becca can't stand. The thing is, that's why I picked her. If I'm totally honest, I did it to hurt Becca. I just never thought she'd physically see it.

Jake doesn't back down. "Did you have to tell her you didn't want anything to do with her the second she sees you pull out of Kelly fucking Taylor? That's fucking cruel, Ry."

"Dude," Dean admonishes, shaking his head. He obviously agrees with Jake.

"I didn't know she was going to walk in, did I? What was

she even doing here? Who let her up to my room?"

"We couldn't stop her! She was a nervous fucking wreck, ran right upstairs to get to you, and then she sees you balls deeps in a girl you know she hates."

"I didn't know she was here!"

"Couldn't you have at least talked to her? Just for a minute?"

"Whose fucking side are you on?" I demand of Jake. I can feel myself getting angrier. He has no right to question me. Becca did this.

"Yours," he snaps back instantly. "Of course I'm on your side."

There's silence, and then Marty clears his throat. "Is she okay?" Marty asks Jake quietly. He gives me a guilty look, like he shouldn't be asking the question, but Marty's the nicest guy I know. He hates to see anyone upset. "She didn't look good."

Jake shakes his head. "No. She's not okay." He sighs. "She didn't stop crying the whole way to the airport." He turns to look at me. "She's devastated, Ryan."

"Good," I say without conviction. No matter how much I don't want to admit it, I hate the thought of her being upset. Whenever I've seen Becca cry, I've just wanted to fix it and make it better, ever since we were little kids.

"Yeah," Jason says, echoing my sentiment. "Bitch fucking deserves it."

Both mine and Jake's eyes snap to him, and his eyes widen when he realizes he's crossed a line. I won't have anyone talk about her like that.

"Don't call her that," Jake demands sharply.

Jason holds his hands up. "Sorry man." He looks over at

me. "I'm just pissed for you, dude."

I nod and look away.

"She didn't know about the charges."

I look back at Jake but don't say anything. It makes no difference if she knows or not. I cannot believe Mulligan's pressing charges. I thought it was a joke when the police rolled up at practice yesterday morning and—in front of everyone—told Coach they needed to talk to me down at the station in relation to assault charges pressed by Mulligan. I'd nearly passed out. I couldn't believe it, could not fucking believe the nerve of that guy. I mean, he destroys my life by sleeping with the only girl I've ever loved, and then when I send a couple punches his way, he calls the cops. I hated him even more in that moment. The whole team went silent as I stepped forward. They didn't put cuffs on me or anything, but they did escort me to the car as I tried to listen to everything Coach was telling me in my ear. He told me not to say anything until he got me a lawyer, said he was going to follow me in his car and would be right behind me. I have never felt so much shame as I did riding in the back of that police car to the station.

When I got there, they put me in a room until a lawyer came. The college sent him, and I knew they would have gotten the best money could buy. I'm not stupid; I know it's not because they care about me. It's because I'm the team's quarterback. They've invested too much money in advertising me to the whole country, and they need me to get out of this without damaging my reputation. The lawyer even told me in private that the public relations team could spin this in my favor, make it look like I was just exacting revenge on the enemy after a heartless girl broke my heart. I felt sick about what happened becoming common knowledge, but I shut up, just wanting to get out of there. I made a statement, and they released me on bail, which the college paid, but I couldn't play football until they investigated further, and the college had to cooperate with the police. I'd gone home to find most of the team hanging out at my house. They were relieved when I walked in, but I didn't want to talk about it. I'd had my mom on the phone, nearly in tears over the whole thing. She told me she was going to speak to Sarah McKenzie, Becca's mom, so she could understand the legal side of it and asked if I wanted Sarah to come down there and handle my case, so I could have someone I knew by my side. That's when I told her Becca and I had broken up, something I hadn't wanted to tell her before because I couldn't handle the fallout, and Becca clearly hadn't told her parents either. She was shocked into silence, and then when she asked me why, I told her the truth: because Becca had slept with Mulligan, and that's why I assaulted him. Then I ended the call before she could react. I didn't want to deal with her being upset and her endless questions.

I just wanted to forget, so the boys helped me, just like they have been doing all week. The girls came, just like they always do, and when Kelly came sidling up to me, just like she'd been doing ever since she heard about me and Becca, I didn't resist her. This time I kissed her like I gave a shit, right in front of everyone, showing everyone at that damn party that Becca didn't have any hold over me, and then I took her up to my room, not caring who saw. I could feel Jake's eyes boring into me the whole time, but I didn't look at him. I didn't care. Becca fucking created this mess, and now I was going to do whatever I could to make myself feel better—even if that was just doing something I knew would break Becca in two.

I push my chair back and turn to leave, not looking back at any of them. I do not want to talk about it.

# CHAPTER 12

*Becca*

I TAKE A DEEP BREATH AND LOOK UP AT ROBBIE Mulligan's townhouse. It's huge, with large bay windows that are all lit up. Every light in the place seems to be on. It's where he lives with a bunch of his teammates. I think it's a house a booster owns, and they get free rent—not that Robbie needs it. I only know the address because Tina's been to a couple parties here, and I've driven over to pick her up.

I reach out and knock on the door, ignoring the fact that my hand is trembling. The thought of seeing him chills me to the bone, but I need to do this. I wait for the door to open, my eyes darting around nervously. Finally, the door swings open, and I see one of Robbie's teammates standing there.

"Well, well, well," he says. "It's the woman of the hour."

I feel like I need to throw up. I don't know this guy's name, have never spoken to him before, yet he seems to know all about me.

I clear my throat. "Is Robbie here? I need to speak to him."

He smirks at me and throws the door open. "Come on in."

He turns and walks away before I have the chance to tell him I don't want to come into the house, that the only way I will speak to Robbie is outside, under the streetlights, on the suburban street, where people can hear me scream if I need help.

I hover on the doorstep, unmoving, but when it's clear the guy has already entered the next room, I have little choice but to follow. I slowly walk down the hall and stop at the end when I see it opens into a huge living room. The room is full of people from the team. They sit around, talking and drinking. There are a few girls in the room too, and everyone falls quiet when they see me standing in the doorway.

I scan the room quickly, and my heart sinks when I see Mason sitting in the corner, scowling over at me in disgust. I haven't seen him since Ryan dumped me on campus. He's been ignoring my calls too.

"Hey Becca," Bernie says to me. He's on Mason's right, giving me a sympathetic look. I realize how pathetic I must look to all of them right now. I'm wearing a shapeless gray sweater with old leggings, and my tangled hair is pulled back off my face, which doesn't have a scrap of makeup on it. The bags under my eyes seem to be getting darker by the day, and I know I'm paler than usual.

I nod at him in acknowledgement and then turn to Mason. He stares back at me like he doesn't even know me, like I haven't known him for years and he isn't one of my good friends. Like Jake, he's dismissed me from his life, and he doesn't want to know me anymore. "I just…I just need to speak to him for a few minutes," I tell Mason quietly, my voice stammering. "Then I'll never speak to him again. I promise."

Mason raises an eyebrow at me and shakes his head in disgust.

"Mason, I promise there's nothing going on. Please don't tell Ryan."

A sneer crosses his face. "Ryan wouldn't care anyway. He's done with you. From what I've heard, he's moved on already," he tells me cruelly.

I suck in a breath as I hear the muted snickers and laughter from around me. It's like he's punched me in the face. I know he's just sticking up for his childhood friend, but his words hurt and humiliate me—they were meant to. Bernie reaches out a hand and smacks Mason on the stomach, glaring at him in admonishment, but Mason doesn't even look at him. His angry gaze doesn't leave my face.

The guy who opened the door for me starts to laugh. "Hey Becca, I don't blame you for giving Mulligan a go. Ryan Jackson is Cal State scum."

Mason stands abruptly to square up to him. "Watch your mouth, Jones."

Jones steps up to Mason without a second thought, and suddenly Bernie's right behind Mason as a couple of other guys go to back up Jones. The divide between the offense and defense on this team is more evident than ever.

Liam jumps in front of Mason and pushes him back, trying to dissolve the obvious tension in the room. Liam turns to me. "There have been a few arguments on the team recently," he says tactfully. I know that means Mulligan and Mason have been at it, and as a result, so have their respective friends. If Mason and Mulligan are fighting, it means Bernie's sided with Mason, and if Bernie and Mulligan aren't in sync, it affects the whole team. "That's why we're all here. Coach's orders to do some team bonding."

I nod my head and look around, but I don't see Mulligan in the room. I stand there awkwardly until Jones takes pity on me. "Mulligan's in his room upstairs. Last door on the left."

I shake my head. There's no way on this earth I'm going up to his room. "I'm not going up there," I tell them, my voice barely above a whisper. "Could you tell him I'm here please? I'll be outside."

I turn and leave the room before they can respond. I'm suddenly desperate for air, feel like I can't breathe. I hate how they all look at me, judging me like they know me, like they know what I'm about, like I'm worthless. It makes me feel sick to my stomach.

I stand on the doorstep, trying to pull my emotions together, staring out across the street.

"Becca?" I jump out of my skin at his voice, and I turn to see Robbie Mulligan standing behind me. My mind immediately flashes back to Saturday night, and my throat tightens at the sight of him, but I stiffen my jaw and shake it off. I came here to do something, and I'm going to do it. If he even takes one step too close to me, I will scream down this whole fucking street. There's no loud music blocking me out now. I gaze back at him, unflinching, and he doesn't look as arrogant and cocky as he usually does. He looks uneasy and uncomfortable. I take a step away from him and walk down the steps, indicating for him to follow me down the path to the street. I don't want anyone from the house to overhear us.

He stops behind me, and I take a step back, putting as much distance between us as I can. He's standing under a streetlight, allowing me to get a good look at his appearance. He has two black eyes and scrapes down his left cheek. He also has a bandage covering his nose. Ryan did some serious damage. *Good.*

"What's up?" he asks, not quite meeting my eyes.

"You're pressing charges against Ryan?" I ask him.

He nods his head.

"I want you to drop them," I tell him.

He scoffs. "No fucking way. Look at my face. He broke my nose."

"I want you to drop the charges," I repeat, my voice surprisingly firm.

"I'm not gonna do that, Becca," he tells me, finally looking at me.

"Yes you will," I tell him, looking him straight in the eye. "Or I'll tell everyone what you did to me."

He shakes his head in disagreement, but I can see the worry that crosses his face. "We had sex, Becca. Don't make it into something it's not just because your boyfriend found out."

"I didn't want that, Robbie, and you know it. That wasn't sex. That was rape." Because that's what it was. Robbie raped me.

"Shut up, Becca. That's not what it was, and you know it."

"Wasn't it? The part where I pushed you away? The part where I tried to fight you off? The part where I begged you to stop?" Tears start sliding down my face, but I refuse to walk away.

"Look Becca—"

"No, Robbie," I interrupt him. "Tell yourself whatever you want, but we both know what you did to me."

"No one will believe you," he says vehemently, trying a different tactic. He's right. I'm pretty certain no one will believe me, but I'm not about to tell him that. "I'm Robbie Mulligan, I could have anyone, and they saw us on the dance floor together. They'll just think you're saying it because your boyfriend found out."

"Ex-boyfriend," I tell him bitterly. "You saw to that."

"You've led me on for years, Becca. You know that. You wanted it, and we both know it. Don't play hard to get and then get mad when it actually happens."

I scoff at his words. If he actually believes that, he's delusional. "That's not true, Robbie. I've had a boyfriend for years, and you wanted to get one over on Ryan. That's what it was. That's what it's always been, and you did it. Well done. This had nothing to do with me. It never has."

"I didn't—"

"You raped me." My voice is strong for the first time in days. Even if everything else in my world has been flipped on its head, I know this with absolute certainty.

"They won't believe you," he repeats, his voice angrier this time. He can sense how set I am on this.

I shrug my shoulders. "Maybe they won't." I'm not stupid. I know the drill. I know they'll all believe the star quarterback over a nobody like me, but I don't care. "But I'll still tell everyone anyway. I'll plaster it all over social media. I'll make an announcement outside your stadium. I'll print fucking fliers if I have to. Whatever it takes, I'll make sure everyone on this campus knows."

He looks at me warily, trying to size me up, to see if I'm serious. "You wouldn't," he finally decides.

"I would," I tell him, and this time my voice doesn't stammer. It doesn't sway. This time it's steady and sure, and I mean it. I would tell the whole fucking world if it stops Robbie ruining Ryan's career, and I don't care who hears it. That's the thing now—I've got nothing left to lose.

He stands, staring at me for a while, waiting to see if I'll cave, to see if I'll back down, but I just stare blankly back at him. He knows he's stuck. Even if they don't believe me, it'll still be out there. He can deny it all he wants and yeah, they'll believe him and turn on me and make my life miserable, but it'll still be out there in public. Somebody somewhere might believe me, and he doesn't want that.

"Fine," he spits out. "I'll drop the charges."

I nod my head and then turn to walk away, but he stops me.

"You know Becca, it doesn't have to be like this," he tells me. "I really do like you. We could go out sometime."

I look at him in disgust. "Why? So you can convince yourself that I wanted it? That you didn't force yourself on me?" I wait for his response, but he just scratches the back of his arm and looks past me down the road. I shake my head. "You stay away from me from now on, okay? Don't talk to me, don't talk about me, forget I was ever born. And if I ever find out you've done this to someone else, this deal is off. Charges or not, I'll go to the police."

He stares back at me, hatred flashing in his eyes, and I turn on my heel and walk away, desperate to put as much space between us as possible. As I walk to my car and open it with shaking hands, I don't feel a sense of relief that he is going to do as I ask. I feel empty. I feel broken. I feel like everything I've ever cared about is gone—and it is, in a way, because Ryan is everything I've ever cared about.

# CHAPTER 13

*Becca*

I 'M LYING ON MY BED, STARING AT THE CEILING, unable to get the image of Ryan and Kelly out of my head. I'm not even sure I want to. I want to stay attached to him, stay involved with him, even if that means thinking about him with someone else. I think about the way his body was pressed into hers, and I feel tears slide down my face.

It's what I deserve. I shouldn't have baited Robbie the way I have for years. I shouldn't have had so much to drink, and then I would have been more aware of the way he was looking at me and could have made sure I wasn't alone. I shouldn't have worn such a revealing outfit; that was a stupid thing to do. If I hadn't been wearing that dumb skirt and had been in my usual jeans, he wouldn't have been able to do it so easily. *This is all my fucking fault.*

There's a quiet knock on my bedroom door, and it slowly opens as I turn my head to face it. I expect to see Tina at the door, offering me some food or a drink, anything she can do to help me. She's always trying to help me, but it's not Tina this time. Sam, my best friend in the whole world, stands in the doorway, smiling at me sadly.

"Hey," she says quietly.

I sit up straight, surprised to see her. She's goes to college in Connecticut, and although it's only a few hours by plane, it's not often we see each other unless we're both back home during the holidays.

She walks into my room and sits down next to me on the bed.

"What are you doing here?" My voice cracks as I ask the question.

"Jake called me," she tells me. "He said he needed to be with his best friend right now, and that you could probably use having yours around."

"Did you hear about what happened?" I haven't told anyone from back home that Ryan and I have broken up, but I'm certain they all know about it. If it wasn't Ryan, it would be Jake or Mason who would have told all our friends, or they would see it on social media. Ryan is suddenly very single on social media. I've avoided all messages from friends from home, from anyone really; I just want to curl up in a ball and pretend none of it is happening.

She nods.

"Which part?" I ask. "The part where I had sex with someone else?" I nearly choke on the lie, but I've committed to it now. It was already set in place, and as long as Robbie drops the charges against Ryan, I'll stick with it. Sam sighs at my words and takes a step closer to me. "Or the part where I walked in on Ryan with someone else?"

"I'm so sorry, Becca," she tells me. She comes to sit down beside me, and I start to cry. Knowing Jake still cares enough about me to call Sam is such a relief—it means he doesn't completely hate me after all.

She wraps her arm around me, and I cry harder, full-on body-wrenching sobs. I cry over Robbie and what he did to me. I cry over losing Ryan and what he now thinks of me. I cry at Ryan moving on and the look he gave me in his room. I cry over Jake and Mason and all the other people from home and what they'll think of me now. And I cry because my best friend flew in to see me, to make sure I was okay.

"Shhh" She tries to soothe me, stroking my back and speaking in a hushed tone. "Shhh, it's going to be okay, Becca. Everything is going to be okay."

<hr>

Sam and I spend a quiet weekend together, and it's the best thing that could have happened to me. She doesn't ask me any questions about it, and she doesn't judge me. She's just there for me completely, even if that only means us sitting in silence while we pretend to watch TV. Sam knows me better than almost anyone. She understands how I work. She knows that when we go out to dinner Saturday night, I don't know what to say, so she jumps in with her plans for the summer—backpacking around Asia with her roommate. She knows when to give me a hug, like when we're walking back to the car and I start to cry, my body shaking with sobs when the reality of what has happened hits me yet again. She knows when to just

129

sit and listen while I ramble on and on about Ryan and how he doesn't really mean that it's over, how we can still work it out. She reminds me why I love her so much, and she and Tina make the first weekend without him just that little bit more bearable.

Sunday afternoon, Sam and I are finishing up the leftover spaghetti Tina made and watching old episodes of *Gossip Girl*.

"Have you spoken to him?" I ask Sam. I've wanted to ask her this for most of the weekend, but I didn't want to hear the answer. I'm only now feeling brave enough to ask the question.

She looks up at me and nods her head. "Only briefly. I called him to see how he was, but then when I mentioned you, he cut me off. He didn't want to talk about it."

"He really doesn't want to know me, does he?"

She sighs, and I can tell she's trying to find the right words to say. "He's really hurt, Becca."

I nod my head. She's right. I know she's right. I can't blame him for the way he feels. I'd probably feel be the same if I thought he did that to me. I just wish more than anything this wasn't happening. "Do you think you could try speaking to him for me?"

She stares at me for a few minutes. I know she thinks it's useless, but I have to ask. Finally, she nods her head. "I'll leave it for a couple weeks, and then I'll call him, okay? After he's had some time to cool down."

I nod my head and smile gratefully. Ryan likes Sam, respects her. He'll listen to her—I know he will.

"Can I use your laptop to check in for my flight?"

I nod my head and tell her where to find it. I pick up the

TV remote and start flipping through the channels, finally settling on an old romantic comedy with Julia Roberts.

I begin to watch the film and after a minute, I glance up to see Sam standing in the doorway to my room, staring at me. She's turned pale. "What's up?" I ask. She opens her mouth to say something but then snaps it shut again. "What is it?" I ask, putting the TV on mute and turning to give her my full attention.

"Why..." She pauses, shifts her gaze around the room, closes her eyes for a second, and then opens them. She takes a sharp breath and looks me straight in the eye. "Why have you been looking up rape counseling groups on your laptop?"

Time seems to stand still as she stares at me, her gaze unwavering. Her breathing is heavy, like she's trying to control herself, and I can't bear the swell of emotion I see in her eyes, so I break her gaze and look away.

"It's nothing. It wasn't for me," I tell her.

I stand up, grab our empty bowls off the floor, and take them over to the kitchen area.

"Becca?" I don't respond, but I can sense that she's moved to stand behind me. I put the bowls in the sink and turn the tap on to start rinsing them. "Becca?" she asks again, her voice quivering with emotion.

I pause, stopping my task. "Sam, it's nothing. Just leave it. Please."

She reaches out and touches my shoulder, and I actually flinch from the contact. I can't stand it when someone touches me unexpectedly anymore. She lets out a shaky breath at my reaction. "Becca, please. Talk to me."

I slowly turn around and face her; tears have started

forming in her eyes. I shrug my shoulders at her, completely lost as to what to say. How do you tell your best friend something like this?

"He raped you?" I look away. "Becca?" Her voice is rising in pitch, desperate. "Did Robbie Mulligan rape you?"

My eyes flicker over the whole room before finally working their way back to her face. Her eyes are focused on my face, and her whole body is at attention, like she's waiting for an attack. I slowly nod my head.

Her face crumbles, and she takes a step closer to me. I start to shake my head, stepping away from her. "No, no it's okay. It's my fault; I've always antagonized him, and I knew he'd always wanted to sleep with me. I should have known better, and I'd been drinking. I shouldn't have gone upstairs on my own, and you should have seen what I was wearing, Sam, my skirt was so short—"

"NO!" Sam firmly cuts my rambling off. She steps forward and places both her hands gently on my shoulders, staring into my eyes. "Did you say no?"

I nod my head as tears begin to form in my eyes.

"Did you tell him to stop?"

I nod again. Because I did. I begged and begged him to stop, but he wouldn't. I couldn't get him to stop, no matter what I said or did. He was too determined. Too strong. There was nothing I could do. The tears spill over, leaking down my cheeks, and she steps forward and hugs me fiercely. "This is not your fault, Becca. None of this is." She holds on to me for what feels like hours as I sob onto her shoulder, the relief that somebody finally knows the truth completely overwhelming.

———————◆———————

A couple hours later, I'm driving Sam to the airport. She'd offered to change her flight so she could stay another couple of days, but I dismissed the offer. As much as I want Sam to stay and keep me sane, I know I can't rely on her forever. I need to deal with this my way—I just haven't figured out what way that is yet. I told her I was okay. I could see the worry in her eyes, but she didn't fight me on it.

"Pull over, Becca."

I glance at her in surprise. We're still ten minutes from the airport, and we're already running late. "Sam, you'll miss your flight."

"Becca, seriously, pull over."

I do as she says and then turn to her expectantly.

"You need to go to the police."

I shake my head. I already told her I wouldn't be doing that.

"I mean it, Becca. This is serious. You can't let him get away with it."

"I can't go to the police, Sam."

"Why? I don't understand why you're protecting him."

My mouth curls in disgust. "I'm not protecting him! I hate him."

"Then why? Explain to me why you're not reporting him."

"Come on, Sam. You know the drill. No one would believe me."

"Of course they will."

A humorless laugh escapes my mouth. Yeah, in an ideal

world, everyone would believe me, and he would go to prison, and I could forget he ever existed—but this isn't an ideal world. This is a world where athletes all over this fucking country get away with assaulting women on a regular basis just because of how good they are at their sport, and why would I want to put myself through that? Have a lawyer rip my character apart, commenting on my clothes and how much I'd had to drink, so that even if someone did believe me, they wouldn't by the end, because that's what happens. You see it all the time on the news; I just never thought I'd be one of those statistics.

"Becca, they'll believe you. I know they will."

"He's Robbie Mulligan, Sam! He's the star quarterback of Southern University. Do you even know what that means?"

She bites her lip, and I know she doesn't. Sam has no clue what this state is like when it comes to football. She doesn't understand that football players are worshipped like heroes and that they get everything they want.

"Do you know how many people go watch him play football every week?" She doesn't respond. She probably doesn't know. Like me, Sam couldn't care less about football, but I've seen it firsthand with Ryan. I know exactly what it's like. "Eighty thousand people watch him throw a ball around a field."

"What does that have to do with anything?"

"It has everything to do with it. Eighty thousand people worship him. As far as people around here are concerned, he walks on water. He brings millions of dollars into this school just by being here. People travel for hours just to watch him play." I scoff; it's fucking ridiculous, but it's true. Robbie

Mulligan can do no wrong in these parts. They'd never believe me. Never. They'd just turn on me and make my life hell. "Did you know that? Did you know how much he's worshipped?" I pause, letting my words sink in. "And I just go here, go to class, and then go home. Who do you think they're gonna believe?"

"They'll believe the truth, Becca."

I roll my eyes and shake my head. "They won't care about the truth, Sam. They'll believe whatever he tells them." I know with absolute certainty, that's what will happen. No one, and I mean no one, will believe me.

"You have to report this."

"And even if that weren't enough, he's Robbie fucking Mulligan. His dad is one of the richest men in the state. His uncle is a freaking senator. Did you know that?" I laugh bitterly. "Do you honestly believe anything would happen if I reported him?"

"It's not right, Becca."

I sigh. "Besides, he pressed assault charges against Ryan. I told him I wouldn't report him if he dropped them."

Her jaw drops open. "Are you serious?"

I stare back at her, confused by the look of horror on her face.

"Becca, do you honestly think if Ryan knew the truth, he'd care about the assault charges?" I look away from her. I know she's right, but this is something I can do, something I can take ownership of. The fact that Robbie went along with it tells me he knows it was rape. He knows I didn't give consent, even if he'll never admit it.

"It wouldn't make a difference to Ryan anyway. He's

already moved on."

She shakes her head in irritation. "Ryan's hurting, Becca, that's what all this is, but you're the one who needs looking after right now, not him. You have to tell him."

"I can't, Sam. I just want to forget all about it."

"Seriously, Becca? Robbie Mulligan is dangerous. What if he does this to somebody else? You need to report it!"

"Sam, please!" I yell at her. "He's not going to do it to anyone else, I made sure of that. He only did it to me because I wound him up and he wanted to get back at Ryan." I know that's the truth. It was about showing me who was the most powerful and sticking it to Ryan at the same time. "I promise he won't ever do that again."

"How do you know?"

"Sam!" I'm getting exasperated now, and I'm starting to wish I'd never told her. Her knowing isn't helping me block it from my mind. "I just want to forget it ever happened, please."

She presses her mouth together, and I know she's trying to think carefully about what to say next. "You should tell Ryan the truth. You owe him that."

"I've tried! I've tried several times. That's why I went to see him. What am I supposed to do? He won't talk to me. He probably won't even believe me."

She looks at me in disbelief. "Ryan loves you, Becca. He always has. Of course he'll believe you."

"But he saw those pictures. It looks like it's true."

"What pictures?"

I shrug and explain how Ryan found out about Robbie and me to start with, about the photos he forced me to look at, that Robbie somehow sent to him. I don't even know how those photos were taken; I don't want to think about it.

"What the fuck?" She's livid. Totally livid. "Someone took pictures of you and didn't stop it?"

I sigh. "I don't know." I've been trying not to think about those pictures. I hate to think someone stood by and let it happen. "I can't think about it, Sam."

"We need to tell someone. We need to tell Ryan."

"He won't even talk to me, Sam."

"Because he thinks you cheated on him! You need to tell him the truth."

"I can't."

"You can, Becca. I'll come with you if you want me to. I can even tell him if it's too hard for you."

"It's too late, Sam. He's already moved on. He wants nothing to do with me."

"It's not too late! He's hurt and that's why he went with someone else, but if he knew the truth, Becca…" Her voice trails off, like it's paining her to think about it. "If Ryan knew the truth, he'd be here in a second. You need to tell him."

I close my eyes. I can't. Robbie's words have been ringing in my head. *They won't believe you.* He's right. They won't. I know it's true, and I can't stand the thought of people not believing me—especially Ryan. I don't know what I'd do if Ryan didn't believe me. "Sam—"

"Please, Becca. This is serious."

I shake my head. I've made up my mind. I told Robbie I wouldn't tell, and I won't. It's the only thing in this whole mess that I've been able to control. "If Ryan has to face assault charges, it could ruin his whole life. It might affect his chances of going pro."

"He won't care about any of that. You'd really rather he thought you betrayed him than know the truth?"

"Yes, Sam! I would. Do you really think he'd want me after this?" My voice cracks. "I'm damaged goods now." I hadn't realized it until now, but that's how I feel—like damaged goods. I'm useless. Completely useless.

"You are not damaged goods, Rebecca McKenzie!" she says fiercely, leaning over and gently gripping my shoulders. "You are my beautiful, funny, kind, sassy best friend who has had a horrendous experience, and I hate, HATE that this has happened to you, but this was not your fault, and you will get past this."

My eyes well up at her passionate words. "Please just let me do this my way?"

She sighs in frustration and runs her hands through her hair. She stares forward out the window, like she's trying to make up her mind about something. "Promise me you'll go to one of those counseling groups? Talk to a professional, someone who can help?"

I nod my head. "I will. I promise."

She swallows hard. "Have you…have you thought about getting tested?" She closes her eyes like she's physically in pain. "I'm guessing he didn't use anything."

I nod my head and look away, blinking back my tears. That's the only sensible thing I've managed to do since it happened. I went down to a walk-in clinic and took the morning-after pill the day after Ryan showed up here. I've been on the contraceptive pill for years, but I didn't want to risk even the smallest chance of pregnancy. While I was there, I had an STD test. I haven't got the results back yet, but I'm hoping everything comes back clean.

"I love you, Becca."

I smile at her, a genuine smile—probably my first since the attack. "I love you too, Sam." She reaches over and hugs me tightly, crushing me to her. I let her hold me for a couple minutes before pulling away. "We'd better go, or you're really going to miss your flight."

# CHAPTER 14

*Becca*

I'VE GOTTEN THIRTEEN MISSED CALLS FROM MY MOM and seven from my dad. They know about Ryan and me. They must. Usually if I miss a call, they'll just send me a quick message, but not this time. This time they just leave voicemails asking me to call them and keep trying to call me again and again. When I try to appease them with a text, telling them I'm spending the weekend with Sam, they don't let it go, and they keep trying to call. I can't bear the thought of them thinking I did what Ryan thinks I did. They love Ryan, have known him since he was a baby. I know they'll be so disappointed in me, so angry, but I'd rather that than they know the truth. I can't stand to think of them knowing that, and that's just how it's going to have to be. I'll have to deal with them thinking less of me and just go from there.

My phone rings again in my hand. I have to answer it, I just have to. It's almost time for Thanksgiving break, and although Tina's offered for me to go back to her place with her, I know I have to go back home. I want to go back home. If I'm home, it means Ryan's not too far away from me. He can't ignore me there. He's only four houses down from me there. He'll have to talk to me. He'll just have to.

"Hello?" I finally pick up the phone. My voice is quieter than normal—well, what was normal before that night with Robbie. Ever since then, it's been quiet, stilted, broken…a bit like me really.

"Becca? Honey? Are you there?"

"Yeah Mom," I reply after a pause. "I'm here."

She lets out a sigh, a sigh of relief, I think. "Oh honey, are you okay? I've been so worried about you."

Tears pool in my eyes. I feel like all I ever do these days is cry, but the concern in her voice just makes me realize how much I miss her, how much I wish she was here right now and could just wrap me up in a hug and tell me everything is going to be okay, just like she did when I was little—only she can't do that now. Now I'm twenty years old and have to deal with things on my own, and as much as I hate it, as much as I don't want it to be true, I honestly believe nothing will ever be the same again—I will never be the same again. "I'm okay," I manage to force out. It's a total lie; I've never been so far from okay in my whole life.

There's a pause, and I know she's trying to think of the best way to say it, to tell me she knows about Ryan and me. Finally she lets out a sigh. "Honey, why didn't you tell me about you and Ryan?"

Tell her what? That the boy she thinks of as a son believes I slept with his archrival, who then pressed assault charges because Ryan was so upset at me, he beat the crap out of said rival? That in actual fact, I didn't sleep with him, but that he raped me at a party, and now my whole world is in complete shambles? Yeah, I didn't really know how to have that conversation.

"How did you find out?" I ask her instead.

"Kathy told me."

I close my eyes at this. I hadn't really thought about Ryan's parents. I've been so wrapped up in just trying to make it through the days, I didn't think about what they would think of me. Ryan's mom is the kindest, sweetest woman on earth. She's the type who would do anything for me, who'd see something in the shops, and if she thought I'd like it, would just buy it for me, just because. And his dad, his loud, friendly, loving dad, who is genuinely interested in everything I do and just took it for granted that at any family event, I'd be there, because to him, I'm a part of their family—was a part of their family.

"Did she tell you why?"

She pauses again, for a second too long. "Honey, I don't believe it. I know there must be a mistake, an explanation." My heart squeezes at how eager she sounds, how much she trusts me and believes I could never do something like this, and I want to tell her she's right, tell her I didn't do what everyone thinks I did—but then I imagine her face if I did tell her the truth. The horror and desperation would overwhelm her, and I know it's better this way, to continue this lie I didn't start but has taken hold and gotten so big that sometimes even I question what really happened.

"It's true, Mom," I tell her. "I did it."

I hear her suck in a breath, but she doesn't say anything. I want to fill the silence with words, words to reassure her, words to reassure me, but I can't. I can't say anything. At this point, I have no words left.

"Are you seeing this new boy now?"

"No!" My voice is sharp, too sharp. "It was a mistake. A stupid, stupid mistake. I want to fix things with Ryan."

"Oh, Becca."

"He won't talk to me, Mom."

"Do you want me to come over there? I can get on a flight tonight."

I'm shaking my head, even though she can't see it. "No, no, it's okay. I'm fine."

"Honey—"

"Mom, seriously. I'll be home in a week anyway. I promise I'm fine."

"Actually, honey, that's one of the reasons I've been trying to get in touch with you. Your father and I were thinking it might be nice for us to come to you for Thanksgiving this year, and then we thought we could go on vacation for Christmas."

"What?" *No, no, no, that's not the plan.* I don't want them to come here. I want to go back to Maxwell, back to my house, back to the same street where Ryan lives, where he can't ignore me, where I can make him listen to me, back to where I can try to make things right between us.

"Yeah, we've already booked the flights to you and I've booked a great place where we can go for lunch." I hear her swallow down the line. "And you know how much your father loves Hawaii, so we were thinking we could go there for

Christmas and we saw a great deal, so we just thought, why not, and booked it."

"Mom—"

She cuts me off. "Honestly, honey. I think the break will be good for all of us. We could do with a change of scenery and a break in the sun to look forward to. Aunt Ruth is even looking into flights to see if they can come out and join us for a few days."

"Mom, what? I don't want you to come here. I want to go home."

"Becca—"

"And I can't go to Hawaii for Christmas break. I need to be back in Maxwell. I don't want to go to Hawaii."

"Why not?" She lets out a nervous laugh. "Who doesn't want to go to Hawaii?"

"Mom, I want to be at home. I need to be a home."

She sighs. "Honey, honestly, I think it's best if we get out of town, just for a couple weeks."

"But I need to see Ryan."

"Honey." She pauses. "Baby, I'm sorry. He doesn't want to see you."

All the air leaves my lungs at this admission. To hear that she knows something I don't and is willing to come out here and book a vacation to keep me away from there is like a punch to the gut.

"What's going on, Mom?"

"I just think it's best if we give the whole Jackson family a bit of space right now."

My stomach falls through the floor. The whole Jackson family? For the last three years, we've always spent

Thanksgiving and Christmas with the Jackson family, and while I wasn't exactly expecting that (I'm not delusional), I didn't think their feelings toward me would be so bad they'd want me out of the state.

"Have you spoken to Ryan?" I ask.

"No, honey. I haven't spoken to him."

"Has dad?" My dad's relationship with Ryan is great, and they have so much in common with football, and it's not unusual for them to speak on the phone every now and again.

"No." Her voice sounds sad.

"Then what? What happened?"

"Look, your father and Bill had a silly little argument the other day, and I think it's best if we all just give each other a bit of space."

My blood turns cold.

"Was it about me?"

She doesn't answer.

"Mom! Was it about me?"

"Yes, honey. It's nothing to worry about, and it'll blow over, but I don't want you to come back and have to deal with it."

His parents hate me. I should have been expecting this. They blame me—I mean, why wouldn't they? As far as they're concerned, this is all my fault, but I think of Ryan's parents as family, and it hurts. It hurts to think that my dad, someone who never argues with anyone, someone who is fun and outgoing and popular, felt the need to defend me, and somehow, that's ended up with them coming to me for Thanksgiving and us going away for Christmas.

"What happened, Mom?"

She sighs. "I think Ryan's taken the breakup badly. He's been drinking a lot, and he missed a practice, so his coach is mad at him. Then there's the assault charges. I know they've been dropped now, but Bill had a few things to say about it, and your father wouldn't stand for it."

"I'm so sorry," I whisper. The Jacksons are my parents' best friends, have been for years, and I hate the thought that I've affected their relationship. I'm not worth it; I'm really not worth it.

"Do not apologize, Becca." My mom's voice is firm. It's her lawyer voice, her no-arguing voice. "You are twenty years old, and people make mistakes."

"But I've ruined your friendship with them."

"I pick you, Becca. I pick you over everyone, every single time. You have absolutely nothing to be sorry about. I love you, honey, we both do. We are going to have a wonderful Thanksgiving together and a fabulous Christmas in the sun. I've already booked us a boat trip for Christmas Eve. We'll have a great time."

"Okay," I say in defeat. I'd been counting on going home and seeing Ryan, on making him listen to me, but maybe my mom's right. Maybe he needs some space. It's only been a couple weeks; maybe if I give him some time, he'll calm down and then will be ready to talk to me. I'm not going to tell him the truth; I'll never tell him about that, because as far as I'm concerned, that never happened. I want it to never have happened, and I'm going to do everything I can to forget it happened. Maybe when he's had some time, maybe when he's gotten it out of his system in a month or two, maybe he'll be willing to talk to me then. Maybe he'll be ready to give us another chance.

"I've booked your flight, honey. I've managed to find a direct one for you, straight to Hawaii. Your father and I get in a couple of hours before, and we'll meet you at the airport. What do you think?"

I listen to my mom ramble on the way she does when she's anxious, and I know things must be bad at home. The Jacksons must have made their feelings toward me perfectly clear, and I know now, more than ever, that things are never going to be the same again.

# CHAPTER 15

*Becca*

THANKSGIVING ISN'T GOOD. MY PARENTS STAY IN A nearby hotel but I barely want to leave my apartment. They try to take me to a bunch of restaurants and even get tickets for a couple of plays for us to go see, but I avoid everything they suggest. I lie and say I have a headache and my stomach hurts. It isn't exactly a lie; I really don't feel good. When I meet them for Thanksgiving dinner, I look at the plates and plates of delicious food and it makes me want to throw up. I force a couple mouthfuls down my throat before it closes up completely, and then I lie to them and tell them I ate some candy in my room before meeting them. My parents are trying so hard and I'm trying my hardest to act like everything's okay, but I don't think they believe me. I spend as much time as possible in my room, sleeping, dreaming, and torturing myself with thoughts of Ryan.

Stalking Ryan on social media has become my new

obsession. At first I was relieved to see he hadn't blocked me on Instagram, Facebook, and Snapchat. It was a way of seeing him, of feeling close to him, of staying connected with his world—but I soon realized it was a different kind of torture he was bestowing upon me. He's never been one for posting many pictures; he's more the type to get tagged in them, but not anymore. He's uploading more and more pictures of himself surrounded by girls, and they're all the same. The girls are hanging off him, all over him, desperate to be near him. Each time I see a picture, it's like a hammer to my heart, but I can't stop looking at them. Can't stop checking for updates from him. Can't stop torturing myself. It's never the same girl with him in a picture, and I suppose it's a relief that at least Ryan doesn't seem to be with Kelly. He seems to be with as many girls as possible, and they're all beautiful. Every single girl I see him with is gorgeous—but then that doesn't surprise me either. Ryan is the best-looking guy I know, and he's always been charismatic, always been able to get whoever he wanted. It's like now that he's back on the market, now that he's no longer chained down, three years' worth of girls have all swarmed at once.

There are even some girls I recognize from home. Thankfully I don't know most of them, but the ones from over Thanksgiving break are girls I recognize from high school, girls who were in my grade, the grade above, and the grade below. It's like we're back in high school, and Ryan's the most popular guy in school again and all the girls want him. Those girls aren't my friends, aren't people I've kept in touch with, but they have to have known we were together for years. Even so, one lazy smile from Ryan has rendered them his, and he seems to be having anyone he wants.

It hurts too just to see the normal pictures, the pictures of him and Jake, Katie and John, Mason and Jess, Bianca and Luke, all his old crowd from high school. When they post a picture of themselves at his Thanksgiving game, I immediately burst into tears. I was supposed to be there with them, and they now probably think as badly of me as Jake and Mason do. I've had missed calls from both Jess and Katie, but I can't bring myself to call them back; I can't face the pity and the disapproval or maybe just the plain disgust they want to send my way. The only person I'll respond to is Sam. My parents even said they'd pay for her flights if she wanted to join us for a couple days, but I didn't want that. I don't want Sam asking me about the counseling I've lied and told her I'm going to go to. I don't want her watching me, and I don't want her pity. I've decided I'm going to do it my way. I'm going to focus on Ryan, even if he won't speak to me. Because if I think about Ryan then I don't have to think about Robbie. I'm going to pretend that horrific night with Robbie never happened, and I'm going to get on with my life. Then when enough time has passed, once Ryan might actually be willing to talk to me again, then I'll see if he'd ever be willing to give us another shot. For now, it's enough just to see him on social media, even if it is killing me, even if part of me thinks he's putting these pictures and videos up just for me to see, so he can hurt me. I don't care. It's a piece of Ryan, and I find myself checking every few hours to see if something new has been uploaded.

After Thanksgiving, I try to act normal. I try to act like this is any other December where I'm looking forward to Christmas and focusing on my studies and pretend that my heart hasn't been shattered into a million pieces, but it's hard. It's really, really hard. I've lost the energy to do anything, and even when I do agree to meet Tina or Maddy out for dinner (never for drinks—I haven't had any alcohol since that night), I always make an excuse to leave early and pretend I don't notice the disappointment on their faces. I'm trying desperately to act like everything is normal, like Ryan isn't constantly on my mind, but it doesn't work.

It's the week after Thanksgiving break when Tina knocks on my door. "Someone here for you, Becca," she calls.

I look up in surprise. I wasn't expecting anyone, and I'm not exactly on the social scene at the moment. I walk into the front room and freeze when I see Jake. He looks up when I enter and gives me a small smile.

"Hey Becca."

Immediately tears spring to my eyes, and I have to bite my lip hard to stop them from falling. This is the first time I've seen him since he told me he couldn't be my friend anymore, and I've missed him. It's not on the same scale as Ryan of course, but Jake has been my friend forever, and I've missed him a lot. He sees my reaction and sighs. I think he's about to turn away from me in irritation when he steps forward and holds his arms out. It's all the invitation I need, and I fall into his arms, sobbing into his chest. He wraps his arms tightly around me, and I sag against him in relief. I thought he was done with me too, and it's a relief to know he's here, to know he doesn't completely hate me after all. Jake's been my friend since I was little. He's always been there for me, even before Ryan and I got together, and the thought of him hating me hurt.

"I was gonna ask how you are…" He trails off. It's kinda obvious from looking at me that I'm not doing too great. I look a total mess, and I know it.

I try to smile and shrug. "I'm okay."

He nods. "You've lost weight."

I shrug. I have dropped some weight over the last couple weeks, and I was slim anyway. I know my mom's worried about it, but there's not much I can do. I have no appetite.

"How was your Thanksgiving?"

I blink. "What? Oh, I just stayed here. My parents came to visit."

"I know that."

"You do?"

He rolls his eyes. "Of course we knew you weren't back home, Becca."

I suck in a breath. I want to know who told them, and what Ryan thought of me being out of town, and if he mentioned it at all, but I know he won't tell me.

"So how was it?"

I shrug. It was fine, but I was miserable the whole time. You could put me in freaking Disneyland right now, and I wouldn't be able to crack a smile.

"Did you have a good Thanksgiving?" I ask.

He stares back at me for a minute. He knows I'm not asking about his break. He knows I want to know about Ryan and what they were up to over the holiday. He sighs. "It was interesting."

I nod. He's not going to tell me anything about Ryan. He might be here now, but he's still definitely Team Ryan.

"Are you here for the game?" I ask him. I'd forgotten completely about Cal State playing Southern U this weekend until I was walking across campus this week and saw posters and fliers everywhere. It's the biggest game of the season, and when I picked up a flier and saw Robbie and Ryan's faces on the paper, I wanted to throw up.

"Yeah. We got in this morning."

"Is Ryan here?" I know he is—he's Cal State's quarterback—but I need clarification that he's in the same town as me.

Jake nods, his gaze leveling me. "Yeah, he's here."

"Does he know you're here now?"

Jake shakes his head. "I didn't tell him I was coming here, but I'm sure he'll figure it out."

I nod and look away. I hate the way he's looking at me, like I'm not one of his best friends, like I'm just some random girl who cheated on his best friend.

"How is he?" I ask eventually. I know he won't tell me anything, but I can't resist the urge to find out something about Ryan.

Jake shrugs. "He's doing all right." I nod my head. I don't know what I expected him to say; it's not like Jake's about to open up to me and tell me exactly how Ryan's feeling. "I mean, for someone whose girlfriend of three years slept with his biggest rival." It's like he's slapped me across the face. I blink back tears and look away from him; maybe he's not ready to be friends again after all. He lets out another long sigh. "Are you going to come to the game?"

I glance at him in surprise. That, I wasn't expecting. I'm pretty sure nobody from either team would be happy to see me there. "No."

"Not going to see your boyfriend?"

My brow creases in confusion, and my immediate thought is to tell him Ryan's not my boyfriend anymore, but the hard look on his face makes me stop.

"Do you mean Robbie?" I ask in disbelief. "We're not together. I haven't seen him in weeks." Six weeks and three days to be exact, since I told him to drop the charges or I'd tell everyone the truth about what happened.

Jake's gaze doesn't leave my face. He's studying me like he's trying to decide if I'm lying or not.

"He'll probably be playing tonight."

I pale at the thought of Ryan and Robbie being so close to each other. I don't know why I didn't consider that before. Jake must notice my reaction. "Don't worry, they won't be on the field at the same time, and Coach has the whole team on lockdown. We're all under orders to keep Ryan away from Mulligan on and off the field."

"Your coach knows what happened?"

Jake sighs. "Everyone knows, Becca."

*Oh God.* I'm mortified, actually mortified that everyone thinks I betrayed him like that.

"How'd you get him to drop the charges against Ryan?" My attention snaps back to him, and he's searching my face intensely. I look away from him, unsure how to answer. I hadn't thought about him working that out, realizing I had something to do with it, and now I don't know what to say. "I thought maybe you two had..." he continues, and then I get it—he thought I got Robbie to drop the charges because we were together now.

"I don't know why he dropped the charges. We're definitely not together though," I tell him firmly.

He stares at me for another minute and then nods his head, and I know he believes me.

"Ryan doesn't think we're together, does he?" I ask quickly, panic taking over. That's the last thing I want Ryan to think—if he even thinks about me at all.

Jake shrugs and doesn't answer my question. "You know it doesn't make sense, Becca. Mason told me Robbie's been chasing you since you were a freshman, and you never even looked twice at him. And I know you loved Ryan, Becca—any idiot could see that—so why would you throw it all away just for one fuck, only to never speak to the guy again?" He's watching me carefully, waiting for my reaction, and I just stare at a spot over his shoulder, terrified that I'll give something away and this will all blow up in my face again. I'm dealing with it the best I can, and right now, that involves me never thinking of Robbie Mulligan. "And Robbie Mulligan is an arrogant fucker, everyone in college football knows that. The guy will brag about the size of a freaking sandwich, yet Mason said he's not spoken at all about you since you showed up at his house one night. According to Mason, if anyone mentions it, he changes the subject."

I glance down at the floor. "I don't know, Jake. You'd have to ask him."

"He was all set on pressing charges against Ryan, then you show up at his house, speak to him for five minutes, and suddenly he's dropping them?"

"I don't know," I repeat.

He sighs in frustration. "Why'd you do it, Becca? I just don't get it."

I shrug, tears springing to my eyes again. When it's clear I've got no response, he nods quickly and turns to go.

"Do you hate me?" I ask quietly, thinking back to the way he was with me when I showed up at his house. The look on his face when he dropped me off at the airport. The way he's looking at me now, which shows he's clearly not ready to go back to how we used to be.

He stops, turns to face me, and gives me a sad smile. "No, Becca, of course I don't hate you." He sighs. "I could never hate you. I just wish it hadn't happened." *That makes two of us.* He stares at me for a minute, and I manage a small smile in reply and watch as he leaves. He closes the door behind him, and I stare at the pale wood without seeing it. I'm relieved he came here and relieved he doesn't hate me completely, but I'm desperately sorry my childhood friend has such a low opinion of me, desperately sorry that this is happening at all.

# CHAPTER 16

*Becca*

BEFORE ROBBIE MULLIGAN, I'D ONLY SLEPT WITH two people. Do I even count Robbie as a number? Does it count when it's not consensual?

For a long time, I regretted losing my virginity to Charlie, my asshole of an ex-boyfriend. As soon as I got with Ryan, I realized just how ridiculous my relationship with Charlie had been. I got swept up in the idea of him, but I didn't love him, no matter what I thought at the time. Then on a summer break from college, Ryan and I bumped into him at the mall.

Ryan was awkward as hell, but I realized it was actually good to see him. He was working full-time and still in the band I was so impressed with back in high school, and I realized he was harmless. Yeah, he'd hurt me, but we weren't in love. He hadn't scarred me for life, and at that point in my senior year, I had been crazy about him, so who cared if he was the first person I slept with? Big deal. I'd moved on to bigger and better things, but I could always look back and smile at the first boy who had made my stomach flip, even if it wasn't going to last forever.

When Ryan and I first got together back in high school, I think everyone just assumed we were sleeping together instantly. I mean, Ryan's pretty affectionate, and we were so wrapped up in each other and didn't care who saw it. I went from avoiding him at all costs to being with him constantly. The only time we weren't together was during classes or at lunch. At lunch, we tried to make an effort to stay seated at our own tables, but in reality, one of us usually ended up moving to be with the other by the end of lunch period. It wasn't that we were constantly making out—although that did definitely happen quite a bit—we just always wanted to be together. It was simple, really. We couldn't get enough of each other, and you know what? For me, everything was just better when Ryan was there.

We didn't sleep together though, not for months. For the first couple weeks, we were always making out whenever we had a spare moment alone together, and I had no doubt that he wanted me. He couldn't keep his hands off me, always pulling me into his side, wrapping his arms around me, holding my hand. His friends all teased him, telling him he was whipped, but he didn't care at all. He just wanted me with him wherever he was, and the feeling was mutual. For whatever reason, sex just didn't seem to happen. I'd hear my parents or his come home or we'd be distracted, knowing we had to be somewhere, but one night, when I knew we had time on our hands, I decided that was going to be the night. I made an effort with my hair and makeup, shaved my legs, and wore matching underwear. I was nervous. I mean, of course I was. It was a big step, but I knew without a shadow of a doubt that I wanted it.

We started watching a movie, and within minutes, we were making out, just like I knew we would be. Ten minutes later, we were clearly really into it, and it seemed like it was definitely going to happen, so I reached for his jeans and undid the button, but he grabbed my wrist and stopped me. He had his eyes closed but shook his head slightly. It wasn't happening.

I was absolutely mortified. I mean, come on, what seventeen-year-old boy turns down sex? And with the girl he professed that he loved?

I jumped off him right away and slammed down into the couch at the opposite end, straightening my top, which he'd had no problem shoving his hands under.

"What the hell, Ryan?"

He just looked at me. "What?" He looked like he needed to catch his breath.

"Am I not good enough or something?" I demanded.

"What?!" he said again, looking angry this time.

"I mean, come on, it's not like either of us have never done it before." He knew I'd slept with Charlie—in fact, I'm pretty sure that piece of information drove him insane—and I, along with the rest of the school, was well aware that Ryan was no virgin, yet he couldn't bring himself to do it with me? "Am I not as good as your other girls?"

He turned on me in a flash, suddenly right in my face, and I thought maybe I'd gone a little too far.

"You think I don't want to have sex with you?"

"Uh, yeah! It's been weeks, and I'm the only girl you seem to have a problem doing it with!"

"Are you fucking insane, Becca?"

I stood up, furious. "Well, I must be. Can't imagine why I would be upset when my boyfriend, the guy who's been with half the town, can't bring himself to have sex with me!" I turned and stormed out of his house, slamming the front door behind me before stalking to my house. I marched into my house, ignored my parents where they stood in the kitchen, and stomped up the stairs. I was beyond pissed off with him, but I was hurt too. I mean, what was wrong with me? Why didn't he want to have sex with me? I kicked my shoes off, threw them against the wall, and then flopped back on my bed, letting out an exasperated scream.

A throat was cleared at my open door and I turned to see my mom standing in the doorway. "Do I want to know?"

"No," I replied curtly, and she chuckled as she walked away. My parents had been pretty cool when Ryan and I started dating. I mean, they loved him, always had. My dad saw him as the son they never had, and he'd spent hours with Ryan and Ryan's dad, watching sports. Our moms were inseparable too. Even though I'd avoided Ryan for years, my parents saw him on a pretty regular basis. When I casually told them over breakfast that we'd started dating, they hadn't been surprised at all. My mom just told me she "knew I'd figure it out eventually," and when my jaw had fallen open in surprise, my dad had laughed and said, "The boy's been in love with you for years." I mean, they were still my parents and insisted the door to my room be left open when he was over, but the rule didn't really matter considering my parents worked a lot.

We were often in the house by ourselves.

I lay on my bed for maybe twenty minutes, getting more and more pissed off, then I heard the doorbell. I knew it was Ryan, but I didn't move as I heard my mom walk toward the door, let him in, and tell him I was upstairs.

"Hi." My eyes stayed glued to the ceiling, and I didn't say a word. I could hear his footsteps as he came closer, and he sat on the bed for a moment before lying down beside me. I still didn't look his way. He let out a long sigh. "Of course I want to have sex with you, Becca," he told me quietly. "I've dreamed about it for years."

My head finally turned to look at him, and my eyes caught his. "Then why aren't we?"

He held my gaze. "Because it needs to be special." He turned onto his side so he was facing me properly, and his left hand reached out and began tracing lazy circles on my arm. "I'm not gonna have sex with you for the first time on my parents' couch."

I don't think he knew quite what his touch was doing to me. "It will be special, Ryan. It's bound to be with us."

He shook his head and looked back in my eyes. "I want us to wait, Becca, until you're sure you're ready."

*What?* "I'm ready, Ryan. I promise you."

He sighed. "Your first time wasn't special." His jaw tensed while he spoke; I knew he hated thinking about me with Charlie. "Our first time will be."

"Ryan—"

"I mean it, Becca. I'm in no rush."

"Don't you miss sex?"

His eyes found mine again. "How could I miss anything

when I've got you?" I melted. Right then and there I melted, and all my arguments went out the window. "Our first times should have been with each other, and I'm gonna make sure that when the time's right, it's what you deserve."

I just looked back at him, overwhelmed (not for the first time) by how much I loved this boy. I had thought I loved Charlie, but that was just infatuation; it was nothing compared to what I felt with Ryan. Ryan and I just made sense, in a way that nothing had ever made sense before. We were meant to be together, and I knew we always would be. I leaned into him and kissed him, but not the raw, passionate kisses of half an hour earlier; this was slow and tender, and I poured all my feelings into it.

"That bedroom door had better be open!" my dad suddenly shouted from down the stairs, and we broke apart, laughing.

"Come on," Ryan said, sitting up and pulling me with him. "Let's go see what they're cooking." We went downstairs and hung out with my parents all night.

Of course we eventually did do it, and as clichéd as it sounds, it was on prom night.

I didn't even want to go to prom. Sam and I joked that we'd stay home, but Ryan was insistent that we went. He'd gotten all nostalgic about finishing high school and was insisting that we make the most of everything. I just laughed, knowing he'd probably be prom king, and I teased him, telling him he just wanted to wear the crown.

We actually had a really fun night; we let our parents take all the obligatory prom pictures they wanted, then we got in a limo with all our friends and hung out in a big group. When

Ryan won prom king, Jake and I sat in the back and laughed at him while he awkwardly danced with Katie (who got prom queen). After they'd gotten through the song, Ryan pulled me over to him, and Katie found John. He took the crown off his head, placed it on mine, and wrapped his arms around me. That was when I got my perfect high school moment, right there in his arms.

Then we all went to Katie's parents' beach house. Most of our class was there, and we had the best night of drinking, laughing, and appreciating everyone we'd spent the last four years with. When the sun was almost rising, he took my hand, led me out of the house, and we made the fifteen-minute walk down the beach to the hotel on the front. When we got there, there were rose petals on the bed. Ryan played some cheesy, romantic music, and I loved it all, but I loved him most of all. That's how we ended up having sex for the first time, almost six months after we started dating, and it was perfect. Absolutely perfect.

# CHAPTER 17

*Becca*

"**H**EY," I SAY, SURPRISED AS I WALK THROUGH the front door. I've been thinking of my conversation with Jake, wondering if I can maybe get him to talk to Ryan for me and see if he'll see me while he's in town, and I wasn't expecting Tina to be home. I take in Tina's sweatpants and baggy t-shirt and her stance against the kitchen counter. She looks like she's settled in for the night. "What are you doing here?" I ask, confused. "You're not going to the game?"

Tina is a diehard football fan. She lives and breathes Southern U Kings, and although she's no longer too bothered about hooking up with the players, she follows their results and never misses a game. Seriously, whenever we bump into Mason (especially if he's with one of his teammates), it's like I might as well not be there. They dissect every play, and I practically die of boredom. She was really excited when we met and she found out I was dating Ryan. She assumed I'd be crazy about football too and would want to attend all the games with her, so she was massively disappointed when she realized I only ever watched football when Ryan was playing.

"Nah," she replies nonchalantly. "Thought I'd miss it today."

I raise my eyebrows in surprise. The rivalry between Southern U and Cal State is one of the biggest in college football; it's practically the highlight of Division 1 football. This game is going to be huge, and there was no way Tina would ever miss it. "That's not like you," I tell her.

She shrugs. "I'd rather stay in with you. I downloaded a bunch of movies we can watch."

My eyes find hers, and she's staring at me earnestly. Something's not right here. Tina would never miss the game, and now not only does she want to skip it, she wants to watch a movie instead of watching it on TV. "What's going on?"

"Nothing."

"Why don't you want to go to the game?"

"I'd just rather be here, with you."

"With me?"

"Yeah." She lets out a nervous laugh. "What's wrong with that?"

"I wanna watch the game." I'm not gonna miss an opportunity to see Ryan, even if it is just in a football game. "I'm gonna pull it up on my laptop."

"No." Tina shakes her head. "Let's ditch the game and watch a movie."

"Tina! What is going on?"

She sighs. "I don't think you should watch it." There's

sympathy in her eyes.

"Why?" My voice is sharp.

She bites her lip and looks at the floor. "Did you not have any messages today?"

My heart starts to beat faster in my chest. "I left my phone here today." I've been studying in the library all afternoon. "I haven't seen anyone." Suddenly my mind flashes back to my walk home. It only takes ten minutes from the library, but I swear people were looking at me and whispering about me; I told myself I was being paranoid. I suddenly feel really uneasy. I drop my bag on the floor and walk quickly to my bedroom to snag my phone off my dresser where I left it by accident.

My heart skips a beat when I see twelve new messages and a bunch of missed calls. I quickly flick through a couple of them.

**Mom: Hey, honey. Just checking in…are you okay? Love you.**

Followed an hour later by another.

**Mom: Hey, I've tried calling you a couple times. Can you call me back? Don't worry about any of this nonsense. Love you.**

And then another a few minutes later.

**Mom: Honey, I'm getting a little worried. Honestly, you know how the media likes to twist things. Ignore it all. Love you.**

I lose my breath at the word *media*.

**Sam: Fuck them all.**

**Sam: This is such bullshit. I hate this.**

**Sam: I hope you're okay. I'm here if you need me. Call**

**me. Love you.**

And then it's Katie's turn.

**Katie: They don't know what they're talking about. They know nothing about you and Ryan. Don't let it get to you.**

My whole body goes cold.

**Tina: We're having a pizza and movie night. It'll be fun and we can drink to forget.**

I can't bear to read the rest of them, especially not when I see one from my dad. I turn to look at Tina, who is staring at me with worry plastered all over her face. "Wh-What is going on?" I manage to stammer out.

She lets out a long sigh. "Ryan did a press conference for the game tonight."

My blood runs cold. "What did he say?"

"The media knows all about your breakup and how Robbie was involved," she tells me quietly. "They know about the charges that were dropped, and now they're hamming it all up for the game. They kept asking him questions about you."

I swallow hard. "Did he answer them?"

She bites her lip. "Not many, but enough."

I feel like I've been slapped. On shaky legs, I go sit on my bed and open my laptop, which is on my bedside table. I pull up the webpage where I've always watched Ryan's games, and instantly, Robbie's face comes up on the screen. It makes me want to recoil and slam the screen shut in disgust, but I don't. I just sit there and watch the commentators talk through his stats and gush over his skills while he does his warm up. It makes me want to be sick, but I make myself watch it while

Tina hovers nervously nearby. The camera pans to the home team. Bernie is jogging up and down the field, concentration on his face, and then it pans back to Robbie, who seems to be staring at something in the distance. The camera pans to Ryan, and my stomach flips. He's staring too, and it's not hard to figure out who he's looking at. The anger radiates off him as he looks down the field, not even pretending to be warming up, just full-on staring at Robbie Mulligan. Someone claps him on the shoulder, and he finally breaks his stare.

The screen cuts back to the studio, and the commentators start to talk about tonight's game, discussing with glee what it will be like watching the two best quarterbacks in the division compete against each other in one of the biggest rivalries in college football. Then with a huge smile on his face, like this is all one big joke, one of the commentators says how it will be even better than usual because of the bad blood between Ryan and Robbie, which "rumor has it," is due to Robbie sleeping with Ryan's girlfriend. My whole body turns cold as a picture of me, *of me,* flashes up on the screen. It's from a game of his that I watched last year when I was visiting. His mom is on one side of me, and my cousin Jay is on the other. Ryan had just made a touchdown, and we were cheering and clapping when my face showed up on the giant replay screen, telling the whole crowd I was Ryan Jackson's girlfriend. I was mortified and immediately ducked my head. The screen switched back to Ryan, who was laughing and looking up at me in the stands, knowing full well I would have hated that. Now, almost a full year later, it's splashed up on TV in front of God knows how many people so they can put a face to the name of the girl who caused all the drama between Ryan and Robbie.

"Don't watch any more, Becca." I glance up at Tina, and she's shaking her head at me, her face covered in sympathy. She's seen it. She knows how bad this will be. "They don't know anything."

I swallow but turn back to the screen and watch as they announce that they're going to once again return to the Cal State press conference and see Ryan Jackson's response to the Robbie Mulligan rumors.

"Don't watch this, Becca," Tina tells me. She makes a move to grab the laptop away, but I move it out of her reach, and my eyes stay glued to the screen. I need to see this.

Ryan's face fills the screen. It's a close-up shot, and even after everything that's happened between us over the last couple months, even after he's successfully wiped me out of his life, the sight of him still gives me butterflies. He's so handsome, and it's easy to see why he's got legions of fans throughout the country. No one can deny how good-looking he is, but the people who know him best can tell instantly—I can tell instantly—that he's pissed right now. His jaw is hard, his eyes are cold, and you can see the tension in his face.

He's sitting at a table with the Cal State football banner on the wall behind it. Bill Campbell, his head coach, is on one side of him. Evan Priestly is on the other, and Arthur Henry is on the other side of Evan.

It takes me a minute to tune into what they're saying. It's hard for me to focus on anything except his face, but when I do listen, I know immediately what the reporters in the room are doing. Various reporters are throwing questions at them, and every single time, Coach Campbell, Evan, or Arthur jumps in and answers. Ryan doesn't say a word; he just sits there, glaring across the room, seemingly not paying attention to any of it.

Even when a reporter directs a question at Ryan specifically, the others answer, and it's apparent why they're doing it. The reporters are trying to get a reaction out of Ryan. They're out for blood when it comes to Mulligan.

"So, what do you think of Mulligan's game? His stats were pretty impressive at the end of last season."

"Overrated," Evan responds instantly. "He'll crack under pressure. The boy's got no game."

"But you can't deny his stats."

"He's not a concern," his coach says firmly. "We've got the best quarterback in the division sitting right here," he tells them, clamping a hand down on Ryan's shoulder. Ryan doesn't even glance his way.

"But there's no denying his skills. You've got to admire that, right?"

Arthur lets out a low, mocking laugh. "We don't talk about Robbie Mulligan. He ain't a concern."

There's a chuckle from the room of reporters. "Not a concern? He's the Southern U Kings starting quarterback."

Arthur just laughs again. "That boy bores us all to tears. Hell, we barely talk about him when we're watching tape. He ain't no threat to us."

"You can't deny he's one of the best players in the division."

"His daddy bought his place on that team, everyone knows it," Arthur replies, and there are gasps around the room. That's not true. Sure, Mulligan's father is a big alum at Southern U, but Robbie is good. He's got the starting QB spot because he's earned it. Arthur knows it, too; he's just intent on trashing Robbie as much as he can.

I can see their coach stiffen. He plasters a smile onto his face, but I know he won't be happy about that. The players at Cal State go through media training so they can be diplomatic and professional in interviews. Their coach insists on it. Very rarely does another player outright disrespect an opposing player; usually it's just mild digs disguised behind fake smiles, but not this time. Arthur's feelings on Mulligan are very clear, and you can hear the murmur run through the room as the reporters sense blood in the water.

"So you guys aren't fans?"

"No," Evan states with absolute authority. "The Cal State Warriors are not fans of Robbie Mulligan."

The reporters don't stop there. They ask more and more questions about Robbie, and Evan and Arthur keep insulting him again and again. This isn't how it's done, and if anyone had any doubts about the level of hostility that would be involved in this game, they certainly won't after this press conference.

"Becca." I turn, and Tina's there again, watching me. "Please, let's turn it off." It's coming up, it must be. Whatever she doesn't want me to see is coming up.

Arthur Henry is just telling the reporters how he feels sorry for any team Robbie Mulligan will get drafted to when Ryan sits up suddenly, like he's sick of just sitting there and listening quietly.

"Ask us about Bernie Matthews," Ryan says, cutting in with ice in his voice. "Ask us about someone we actually respect, someone who can actually play ball."

A buzz goes through the room as the reporters realize Ryan may actually be ready to talk.

"What do you think of Robbie as the opposing quarterback, Ryan?"

"I think the stats speak for themselves. Didn't I beat him in all of them last season?" He doesn't sound smug when he says it; he sounds flat. He's stating a fact.

Then they ask the question they've obviously been wanting to ask all along. "Can you tell us any more about the charges Mulligan brought against you last month?"

Ryan's response is immediate. "No comment."

"It was regarding you assaulting Robbie Mulligan, here on the Southern U campus. Can you tell us why?"

"No comment," Ryan repeats.

"Can we stick to the football?" his coach asks.

"Sources have said it was in relation to your ex-girlfriend, Rebecca McKenzie." I actually gasp in horror at being named like this.

Ryan visibly tenses, and you can tell his coach is getting pissed next to him. "I think we'll finish up there."

"It's alleged that Robbie engaged in a sexual encounter with your then girlfriend. It's easy to see why you might hold animosity toward the guy."

Ryan lets out a humorless laugh and squares his shoulders; it's the exact moment that I know he's going to say something. He's not just going to let that comment go. He turns to face the reporter who spoke to him. "Animosity? You think I hold animosity toward him?" He shakes his head in disgust and then pauses so he can make sure they're all listening. "I wouldn't spit on that fucker if he were on fire." He says it loud and clear. The swear word is bleeped out, but it's obvious what Ryan said, obvious what his feelings are toward Robbie.

Silence settles over the room, and it's an admission. It's an admission that what they've said is true, even if he hasn't said the words.

After a minute, another reporter clears their throat. "Sources say Rebecca—"

"Don't talk about Rebecca," he tells them. I know after all that's happened, it shouldn't matter, but the fact that he used my full name is just another example of how detached he's become from me. "She has nothing to do with me anymore. She means nothing to me." It's like a hammer through the heart. He'd have to know I'd see this. He'd have to know all our friends would see this. He's publically telling me and everyone listening that I mean nothing to him.

"Do you have a message for Robbie Mulligan before tonight's game?"

Ryan smirks. "Tell him I'll see him out there."

"I got something to say to him." The camera pans to Evan at his words. For someone who is usually so calm and relaxed, he looks pent up, like he's ready for a fight. "Tell that boy I'm looking forward to seeing him out there. Tell him my defense is ready for him." He smirks, as if thinking of a memory. "We been waiting for him for weeks." And I realize with dread that all Ryan's teammates have known about Robbie and me for weeks. They know what their rival did to their quarterback, and they've been waiting for the opportunity to get back at him. "He's gonna spend the game on his ass. He ain't gonna get up off that ground."

I see Ryan chuckle next to him, and even their coach is smirking.

Arthur starts to laugh too, a loud, mocking laugh that echoes around the room, so much so that I feel like I'm there in the room with them. "Tell that boy we coming for him," he tells the reporters, staring straight into the camera. "We gonna embarrass him in his own backyard."

Laughter rings out throughout the room, and the camera pans around. I see the rest of the Cal State team are in there too, standing in the back. I see all the familiar faces, Ryan's roommates, and Jake too. There's a smirk on his face as he joins in with the laughter. This isn't normal; usually it's just a select group of players who sit at the press desk. The rest of the team doesn't have to be there, but they've obviously shown up to support, and they're enjoying the laughter. Evan and Arthur are leading it while Ryan smirks next to them, like there's a joke among the teammates. Like they've thought this through. Like they're ready to make Mulligan pay. They want to make sure Robbie sees this beforehand. To make sure he knows they're coming for him. To make him nervous, to make him anxious going into the game. As the laughter rings out throughout the room, with all the players joining in on the mockery they're making of Mulligan, it doesn't sound like your usual laughter. It sounds like a war cry.

◆

"Don't cry, Becca," Tina whispers next to me as she reaches over and squeezes my knee. I feel tears drip down my cheeks, but I make no move to wipe them away. It's been a few minutes since she grabbed my laptop and closed it down. I've just been sitting here, trying to process what I've just seen. What everyone's just seen. What everyone will think of me now.

"Everyone will think I'm a cheating tramp," I whisper back, the reality of it hitting home. I remember the curious looks I got on the way home, and I now know why. The people who didn't know about what happened now will, and on this campus, where the football players are revered like gods, they'll all now know I slept with Robbie Mulligan behind my boyfriend's back. Because that's the lie I've gone with, but I didn't think it would go this far. I didn't think it would be televised for everyone to see. I close my eyes in despair. Everyone I care about will have seen it.

"No," she tells me earnestly, grabbing my hands and turning me to face her. "No. Nobody that knows you would ever think that."

I shake my head. She's wrong.

"Becca, come on, please stop crying. You made a mistake, that's all. Everyone does it. You have to stop torturing yourself over it."

"Everyone will have seen it."

"Fuck everyone," she tells me fiercely. "They obviously don't know you well if they believe it's as simple as what's just been shown on there. You're a good person, Becca. One mistake doesn't change that."

"I hate that I've hurt him like this."

"I know," she tells me kindly. "And he will get over it, Becca. It's just still too raw at the moment."

"You think he just needs more time?" I ask. Right now, I

175

feel like I could give him ten years and he'd still never forgive me.

Tina sighs. "I don't know, Becca."

"I know he's hurting."

"You know what, Becca?" Her voice has turned sharper. "So are you." I stare back at her in surprise, and she lets out a sigh of frustration. "I'm sorry, but I hate seeing you like this. He was with you for so long, and I know he's hurt, but he shouldn't just turn his back on you. He should at least listen to what you have to say."

"This is all my fault," I say. That's the thing I know for absolute certainty—because even though Robbie attacked me, it's still my fault because of what I wore and how much I drank and for leaving my friends. If I hadn't done those things, this would never have happened. "He doesn't have anything to apologize for."

Tina goes to say something but then snaps her mouth shut. She reaches over and squeezes my hand. "Come on, let's order a pizza and pick out what movie we want to watch."

I shake my head. "No," I tell her. "I want to watch the game. I want to watch Ryan destroy Mulligan."

The game is a complete write-off for Southern U. They're one of the best teams in the league, but Cal State completely destroys them, seventy to three.

Ryan plays the game of his life. Bernie Matthews and the rest of Southern U's defense can't get close to him. He manages to get all his throws away clearly and sets up touchdown after touchdown, never missing his target.

If Ryan's having the game of his life, Robbie is having the worst of his. He can't get a throw away. Every time he tries, Cal State's defense is on him with a rugged determination I've never seen from them before. It makes me realize I was right—this isn't just a game for them; this is their way of paying Mulligan back. He gets sacked more times in the first quarter than I've ever seen before, and every single time, the Cal State players stand over him, looking down at him on the ground. Usually when a player gets sacked, the defense will celebrate and move on, but not this time. They stand over him, not helping him up, not moving out of his way. They just stare down at him until someone from Robbie's team comes over and helps him up, pushing the Southern U players away. It's embarrassing to watch how easily Cal State beats them, but with every single hit Robbie takes, I just find myself feeling more and more grateful. *Good.* This is what Robbie cares about—being the star quarterback of a winning team. I'm glad he's being made to look like a fool. I'm glad something finally isn't going his way. I want him to suffer in any way he can.

You can see the frustration on the rest of Southern U's faces. They're humiliated too, and they're getting more and more worked up, but it's not helping them. They're still missing blocks and not getting close to Ryan. Even when they do get to him on the rare occasion where Ryan's teammate hasn't blocked him, Ryan always gets his throw away first. I can see how irritated Bernie Matthews is every time the camera goes to him. He's not used to being beaten like this, and there's nothing he can do to help his offense.

I sit and watch it all with a churning stomach, but I don't look away once. Not when they cut back to the commentators during the break of play, not when they laugh and joke about Ryan's game and how it's not a contest at all. Not when they cut to the crowd and I see Ryan's parents there, the camera focusing on them and the commenters pointing out who they are. They're obviously there for moral support, having thought this might be tough for him, but they were wrong. Ryan single-handedly destroys Mulligan, and it's impossible for me to look away from the screen. My eyes are glued to the game.

"Oh Jesus, let's turn it off," Tina mutters next to me.

I look over at her in surprise. I'd forgotten she was there, to be honest. I've been so engrossed in the game, but every time Ryan made a seemingly impossible pass, she's squeezed my arm reassuringly (which is pretty big of her considering she's a Kings fan all the way).

"What?" I ask, confused. There's no way I'm turning it off when there are only five minutes left and Ryan's still on the field. She purses her lips, looking back at the screen, and that's when I hear it. I've been so focused on not taking my eyes off Ryan, I've been tuning out the commentators, sick of hearing about the revenge Ryan is reaping on Robbie, but now the cameras are on the crowd. Clearly the spectators are sick of the beating their team is getting, and they've been getting more and more vocal about it, booing Ryan every time he touches the ball. They're not booing now; they're chanting—so loud it's echoing in my ears. When the camera goes to his parents in the crowd, the way Kathy Jackson is gripping her husband's hand makes me feel like my heart is breaking all over again. It kills me to know they're witnessing this.

"SHE WAS GOOD, SHE WAS GOOD, SHE WAS GOOD, SHE WAS GOOD," is being chanted at top volume from what seems like every corner of the stadium. The home fans are desperate to upset Ryan, to put him off his game, anything to punish him for the way he's emphatically beaten their team tonight.

The camera zooms back to Ryan, and even though he hasn't reacted, even though he still throws a perfect pass into the hands of his wide receiver, I know he must be able to hear them. I know how much this must humiliate him.

"SHE WAS GOOD, SHE WAS GOOD."

Tina goes to grab my laptop, but I stop her. I'm watching this whole game, no matter what is being chanted. She sighs in defeat, sits back, and squeezes my knee in a comforting gesture while I wipe the tears from my eyes.

Finally the game is over, and Ryan's team swarms him immediately. They're jumping on him, on each other. They're so hyped up, so celebratory, you'd think they'd just won the Super Bowl, but I have a feeling this means more to them than that would. This was a chance for them to show their support for their friend, their captain, their leader, and they did it.

Ryan pulls off his helmet, and he's grinning. He's happy that they've done it, but his eyes are scanning around, looking for someone. The crowd is now booing their team, making their feelings about the defeat known, and it's just as loud as the chant. Bernie Matthews approaches Ryan and shakes his hand quickly before moving away. Mason comes off the side-lines to do the same and then falls into step with him, talking

179

in his ear, trying to tell him something. Ryan's entire team is behind him, and the defense has joined them, as well as his offense. The team shakes hands with any of their opponents that offer, but they don't break stride with Ryan; they keep up with him.

Ryan is shaking his head at whatever Mason is saying to him, the camera zooming in on his face. He looks around, his eyes still scanning. The camera angle changes so that you can see where he's heading, and I realize he's heading over to the part of the field where Robbie's standing with his teammates, cradling his shoulder as though it's giving him pain.

My stomach drops as Ryan gets closer to him. Robbie looks up and wariness crosses his face, but he doesn't back away. He turns to face Ryan. Ryan gets closer, until he's right in front of him. Robbie's offense has appeared behind him, and Ryan leans in, a smirk on his face, and says something into his ear. The noise from the crowd is deafening as Robbie pulls back to look at Ryan, complete rage on his face. Ryan laughs in his face, and Robbie pulls his arm back and punches him. Ryan must expect it, because he manages to move his head back just in time. Then Ryan throws a punch of his own, landing it directly in Robbie's face. That's all it takes for the teams to go at each other, their emotions high from the adrenalin of the game. Suddenly it's an all-out fight, with half the team intent on hitting the opposing team, and the other half trying to pull them away and stop the fight.

It's angry, it's vicious, and when I see Ryan land another punch on Robbie, I close my eyes. This isn't the boy I know, the boy I've grown up with, the boy I've loved for three years. He's doing this because he's hurt. He's doing this because I was too dumb to see the signs; I was too dumb to watch what I was drinking and wandered off alone at a frat party. It's my fault Ryan's stooped so low as to start a brawl at a football game. Everything is my fucking fault.

This time when Tina grabs my laptop to close it, I let her.

# CHAPTER 18

## Becca

I'M LYING IN BED LONG AFTER THE GAME HAS finished, staring up at the ceiling. I keep thinking about the game over and over again. I think of Ryan's face throughout it all as the crowd taunted him about me, how that must have made him feel, the anger I could see on his face. I make a snap decision, one I promised myself I wouldn't make, and sit up and pull some clothes on. I grab my keys and quietly exit the apartment, hoping not to wake Tina. I get in my car, and within ten minutes, I'm pulling into the parking lot of the hotel where I know the Cal State team is staying. It's the same hotel they always stay in, only Ryan's never stayed here before. He's always stayed at my place, and I would drive him over in the morning to drop him off so he could start his journey home.

I park under a streetlight where I can see the entrance of the hotel, and I look down at my phone, debating what to do.

I can't call him. He's blocked my number, and he may have another one by now. I debate sending him a message over Facebook or Twitter, but I doubt he'd answer it. I could always call Jake and tell him I'm here, but I know he'll just tell me to go home. I have a feeling they'll have been partying hard; you could see the adrenalin running through the team and the euphoria on their faces when they beat Southern U. They did that for Ryan, and I know they'll be celebrating with him long into the night. I dread to think how they're all blowing off steam. I even consider walking in and asking the person at the desk to call up for him to see me, but I doubt they'll do it. They'll just mistake me for another groupie and tell me to leave. He might still be out at a bar; they might not have moved back to the hotel yet. So, in the end, I just sit there. After an hour, I realize it's pointless and I should probably leave, but something stops me. Knowing he's so close to me, knowing we're in the same town makes me stay in the car and not drive back to my apartment.

When I've been parked there for almost two hours, my eyes start to get heavy. I'm just about to drift off to sleep when I hear a high-pitched giggle in the darkness and some male voices shouting loudly. I turn my head and see a big group approaching the entrance to the hotel, and my breath catches when I see he's with them. He's surrounded, as always. Jason's shaking his shoulder and talking in his ear while Marty nods in agreement. Jake's with them too, but he's farther back in the group, talking to some girls who are with them. That's where Evan Priestly and Arthur Henry are too, with the girls.

They stop as a group outside the hotel and continue the conversation. Ryan's facing me, but his head's down as he focuses on whatever Jason is saying. They're loud, they're energetic, they're fun, and they look like they've had the best night of their lives. I can't tear my eyes away from them. One of the girls reaches for Arthur, and they're soon full-on making out like no one's watching. Then they disappear inside the hotel to catcalls and whistles. Some of the other girls attach themselves to the other players, but to my relief, Ryan just keeps listening to whatever Jason's saying to him and nodding in agreement.

I still don't know what to do, how to get his attention, but to be honest, in this moment, just seeing him relaxed and at ease with his friends is enough for me. Seeing him again does something to me after all the trauma of today. It gives me a certain sense of calm.

He says something back to Jason, and that's when he lifts his head. I know the exact moment he sees me, because his entire posture tenses up. I see his eyes drop slightly, and I know he's looking at my car plate to check that it's mine. His eyes come back up to my face, and I know he knows it's me. I can tell by the hard stance that's come over his body and the light that's left his face. Jason looks confused and follows his gaze, and I know he sees me too. I'm under a streetlight, visible to them. The disgust Jason has for me is written all over his face.

Ryan watches me for another minute and then reaches out and tugs one of the girls over to his side, never taking his eyes off me, and that's when the first sob comes out of my mouth. The second comes after I see him acknowledge my cry, nod at me like he's achieved his goal, and then bend his head down to kiss her. Regardless of the fact that he was with

Kelly the last time I saw him, despite the fact that this girl seemed to be totally separate from him a couple minutes ago and was talking to one of his teammates, he kisses her like he's stuck in a desert and she's the water he needs to survive. This garners the group's attention, and I can hear them laughing and looking at them in surprise, egging them on. The girl has no objections, and she wraps her arms around his neck and grinds herself into his body. After what feels like forever, he pulls away and looks back at me, like he wants clarification that I saw that, like he wants to know how much that hurt me. I'm sure one look at my face tells him exactly how much it hurt as tears stream freely down my cheeks. He then turns and leads her into the hotel.

My heart feels like it's breaking all over again. I never, ever thought he'd be so cruel. I never thought he'd hate me enough to do that to me. Not when I've sought him out, not after all this time. It's like our entire history—not just our relationship, but our entire friendship together—meant absolutely nothing to him.

The sliding doors close behind him, and I know that's it. I know he'll never give me another chance. I know we're done. There's no point in hoping anymore. It finally hits home that Ryan completely despises me. To him, I'm nothing. He wants nothing from me anymore. I don't even tell myself he's behaving like this because of today, because of the reaction of the Southern U fans and the humiliation he felt. No, I know Ryan wants nothing at all to do with me. I close my eyes as the realization hits and the despair overwhelms me. When I finally have the strength to open them again, I see that his friends and his teammates haven't moved; they're just watching me try not to fall apart. I wonder if they're thinking I'm going to get out of my car and march over there and cause a huge scene. I won't do that—I genuinely don't think my shaking legs would allow me to do that.

I watch them watch me, a mixture of wariness, contempt, and disgust on their faces. These people who, only two months ago, laughed and joked with me over lunch now look at me like I'm something they've stepped in, and I don't even blame them. I know their loyalty lies with Ryan, and they see this as me getting what I deserve for what they believe I did to him. I see a movement and I see Jake take a step toward me, and then another, but I just shake my head at him. I don't need to hear anything from him right now. I get it. I get the message from Ryan loud and clear, and I turn the key in the ignition and drive out of the parking lot. I drive away from them all, away from Ryan.

# CHAPTER 19

*Becca*

CHRISTMAS COMES AND GOES AND I BARELY notice I'm in Hawaii. I escape to my hotel room as much as possible and decline any offers to do anything even remotely interesting. I don't have the energy. All I want to do is be on my own, and even when some girls that are around my age ask me to go dancing with them, I decline, even though my mom is sitting there with her eyes boring into me, begging me to go with them. The rest of my junior year of college is pretty much a disaster. I just can't bring myself to care about anything. Nothing at all. I stop going to my classes, worried that if I go to campus I might see Robbie, or even Mason. I don't want to deal with either of them. At first I get my notes from classmates, asking them to email over what they have and picking up stuff online so I can get the work done. Then I stop doing that too. I submit work I know is substandard, but I just can't bring myself to care.

I say no to every single thing Tina asks me to do. A lesser person would give up on me, but not Tina. She comes in and updates me on her day, tells me her gossip and invites me out for dinner. Even when I say no to everything, she's still there, asking me what I'm up to, if I want to do anything. I'm so, so grateful to her for the pretense she's maintaining, acting like everything is normal and that I'm not falling apart. That I've not lost fourteen pounds because my appetite has permanently left me. That it's normal that I hardly ever leave the apartment. That when I do, I dress in clothes that absolutely drown me so I can look as unattractive as possible, because the last thing in the world I want is to ever look attractive to anyone again. Because if I had been a little heavier, a little spottier, if my hair had been a little greasier, maybe Robbie wouldn't have noticed me that first day in class, and then when he found out about Ryan and I dating, maybe he wouldn't have wanted to take what was his, just to piss him off. Maybe he would have laughed at Ryan and pitied him over me, and none of this would have ever happened.

It's only after one of my professors insists on a meeting that I eventually drag myself out of my apartment and head back to campus. I've been trying to stay up to date with work and don't think I've fallen too far behind, but the thought of having to see anyone but Tina is enough to make me want to stay inside, lock the door, and never speak to anyone again.

I'm walking home after my meeting with my head down, trying to get home as quickly as possible.

"Becca?"

I jump at the voice and the close proximity of it. I turn to my left and see Bernie Matthews leaning against the building there. A couple of his buddies surround him, and I'm pretty certain they're on the football team. My eyes quickly search them, but Robbie's not there. *Thank God.* I haven't seen him since that night when I told him to drop the charges, and as far as I'm concerned, that should be the last time I ever see him.

"He's not here," Bernie tells me, pushing away from the wall and walking over to me.

"Who?" I ask quietly, my eyes darting back to his friends. I can feel my heartbeat picking up slightly. They all make me nervous. They're all so tall and so strong. If they wanted to, they could do whatever they wanted to me, and I wouldn't be able to do a single thing about it.

"Mason," Bernie tells me. Of course he's talking about Mason; I should have known that. "He's at home feeling sorry for himself. He's hungover but has convinced himself he has the flu or something."

"Oh."

Bernie frowns slightly at me, and I realize it wasn't the response he was expecting. The old me would have rolled her eyes and called Mason a baby, or at least laughed at his explanation, but that was before...before Robbie destroyed my life.

"You okay, Becca?" he asks, his gaze sweeping over me. His voice is full of concern.

I nod my head and force a smile. "I'm good."

"I haven't seen you in months."

"Yeah." My voice is flat. "I've been really busy," I lie.

"He feels bad, you know." I'm completely lost as to what he's talking about, and I start edging away from him, wanting to get back to my apartment and away from his eyes, which seem to be looking at me just a little bit too intently. He steps in front of me, blocking my path, forcing me to take a step back, otherwise we'll be too close, and I can't stand the thought of having someone of a similar build to Robbie too close to me. "Mason," he clarifies.

"Why would he feel bad?"

Bernie scoffs. "Because of the way he spoke to you after you and Ryan split up. Because you're supposed to be his friend, and he hasn't seen you in months. Because he was a little bitch the last time he saw you? He should feel terrible."

*Oh...yeah.* I shrug my shoulders. Mason has every right to be annoyed with me. He thinks I betrayed his friend. He should despise me. I despise myself. "It doesn't matter, Bernie."

"Yo, Matthews!" He turns back to his friends, and I take this as my opportunity to move away from him.

"I've got to go," I tell him.

He turns back to me immediately and puts his hand on my arm, stopping me from leaving. My jaw tenses at the effort of not flinching away from his touch. I honestly don't know what is wrong with me anymore. This is Bernie, for Christ's sake, and we're in the middle of the campus green in broad daylight. Nothing is going to happen to me.

His eyes narrow on my face, and he turns back to his friends and waves them off, telling them he'll see them later. They send me curious looks, and I immediately drop my gaze to the ground. I hate what they must all think of me.

"I'm buying you lunch," he tells me.

My eyes widen. "No, no. Thank you, but I can't. I have plans."

"What plans?"

"Um." I can't think of anything off the top of my head, and Bernie smirks and raises an eyebrow at me. We both know I don't have other plans.

"Come on, let's go."

"No, Bernie, honestly, I can't."

He turns to look at me, his face deadly serious. "Becca." His voice is soft but firm. "I've been worried about you. I saw Tina a couple weeks ago, and she said you've barely left your apartment." I bristle at this; it's the truth, but I don't particularly want Tina going around telling people I'm now a complete loser. Bernie rolls his eyes at my reaction. "I cornered her and asked her about you. She would never say a bad word about you, but I wanted to know how you are and why I haven't seen you in forever."

"I'm fine," I insist. I don't know what his problem is. It's not like I saw him a whole lot anyway, only when he was with Mason.

"You're not fine, Becca." His eyes drop from my face to take in my body, and he actually grimaces before they come back up to my face. "You look like you haven't eaten a decent meal in months."

"I just haven't been hungry," I insist.

"Yeah?" he shoots back. "Haven't been wanting to sleep much either, if those bags under your eyes are anything to go by."

I scowl at him. I know I look like crap at the moment, but I don't care, and I don't know who Bernie thinks he is, talking to me like this. We're not even friends, not really. We're just two people who chat every now and again when

191

we see each other.

"You either let me take you out to lunch now, or I'll follow you back to your apartment and order pizza from there and then make you hang out with me all afternoon."

I sigh. As nice as Bernie is, I don't want him hanging around all afternoon, and I know he's stubborn enough to follow through with what he's said. "I don't want to stay on campus," I finally tell him with a sigh. "I don't want to see..." I let my sentence trail off. I'm sure it's pretty obvious who I don't want to see, and I don't want Bernie thinking he can just go eat with his football buddies and get me to join them. There might be the chance Robbie would come, and I never want to be near him or the football team again.

"I have my car," he tells me. "Let's go to that Italian place off the main strip in town. Their pizza is really good."

I stare at him for a minute, but his brown eyes are unwavering, and I have a feeling he's not going to let me get away with this. I sigh. The sooner I agree, the sooner I can get this over with. I nod my head in agreement and follow him down toward his car, and that's how I end up eating lunch with Bernie Matthews on a random Wednesday. He doesn't stop talking, which I appreciate because it means I don't have to say anything, but he doesn't talk about football, or Mason or Ryan or anything I can't stand to think about. He talks about Texas and travel, and I realize I like Bernie a whole lot. He's one of the good guys.

# CHAPTER 20

*Becca*

I GLANCE DOWN AT MY PHONE AND SEE A MISSED call from Sam and a text message from her asking me to call her. I frown and call her back. She answers after the third ring.

"Hi!"

"Hey, how are you?" I ask.

"Good, glad finals are finally out of the way."

"Yeah, me too." I don't want to think about how I did on my exams; that's something I'll deal with another time.

"How have you been coping? How's the counseling?"

I sigh. Every couple of days it seems like she messages me about how I am and how the counseling is going. The counseling I never followed up on. The counseling I've never even been to. She keeps offering to come see me, but I just want to forget, and because she knows the truth, it's harder to do that when she's around. "Sam—"

"I know, I know, you don't want to talk about it, but are you okay? I just need to know you're okay."

"Yes," I lie. "I'm okay." I don't remember what it's like to be okay anymore. "I promise you I'm okay."

"Good. So, I've had an idea."

"Yeah?"

"I think you should come to Asia with me for the summer."

I'm so surprised I can't think of a response. That was the last thing I was expecting.

"Becca? Did you hear me?"

"Yeah, but…no. I can't just go to Asia."

"Why not? What else are you going to do this summer?"

"I, I…" I trail off. Summers were mine and Ryan's time together. We'd planned to work for the first month or so and then head off in his car somewhere, just the two of us, for the rest of our time off. I hadn't really thought about what I wanted to do now. I figured I'd just head home, get a job working in a local diner or an office or something, and hope I would bump into Ryan occasionally, hope he'd at least talk to me.

"Becca." Sam's voice is gentle in my ear. "I really think this would be good for you. I know you probably want to head home and see Ryan, but I don't think you'll get the reaction you're hoping for."

My heartbeat quickens. "You've spoken to him?"

I can hear her sigh. "Yes. I called him a couple days ago, but the first thing he said to me was that if I was calling about you, he'd hang up on me. I'm sorry, Becca, I tried."

I let out a breath I hadn't even realized I'd been holding. "No, it's not your fault." Another thought occurs to me. "You didn't tell him, did you?" I can hear the panic in my voice.

"No, I didn't tell him. I promised you I wouldn't."

"Okay, good." I can hear her sigh of frustration at my response, and I know she thinks he should know, but she'd never go against my wishes. "I guess he still needs more time."

"Maybe," she agrees, but she doesn't sound convinced. "Look, Becca, I really think you should come away with me. I think it will be really good for you to get away from everything. You need a break. You've been through so much recently."

I frown. Sam's had this trip booked for months, but she's never once mentioned me coming with her. "But what about Hannah? Won't she mind?" Hannah is Sam's roommate whom she'd planned the trip with. Her boyfriend Chris is planning on joining them after a couple of weeks too.

"Not at all. You know Hannah really likes you, and it'll be really fun. I promise."

I shake my head. It might be fun, but it's not what I want to do. "Maybe next time," I tell her.

"No way. This is a great opportunity. You have to come with us."

"But, I don't…I don't have any money, Sam. I can't afford it." I don't even know why we're having this conversation. It's not even close to being a possibility.

"Well, I kinda already spoke to your mom, and she agreed with me that it was a great idea, and she transferred me the money for your flight. I've already bought it. You're booked on the same flight as me and Hannah."

My jaw falls open. "She did what?"

"She's worried about you, Becca. Really worried. She

knows something's up. Look, she told me you won't talk to her about your breakup with Ryan, said you just freeze whenever she brings it up."

My heart slams in my chest. I know my mom's worried about me. She keeps calling and messaging me constantly, and about a month ago, her and my dad flew out here to visit for a weekend. It wasn't a very successful visit. I had no energy, and I could just feel them watching me the whole time. My mom got upset at one point about how worried she was about me. I just lied and said I'd had food poisoning, which is why I'd lost all the weight. I don't think they believed me.

"What else did you say?" I ask nervously.

"I didn't tell her about Mulligan. You know I wouldn't do that to you, but you should tell her. She'd be able to help."

"I'm not gonna do that, Sam."

She sighs. "I know you won't. Look, the flights have been booked, and this is a once-in-a-lifetime experience, okay? We will have the best time, and you've always wanted to travel. It's really cheap when you get there, and your mom said she's gonna give you spending money too, so you really don't have to worry about a thing. I'll plan all our trips when we're there, and you can talk to me about anything, Becca, whatever you want. You know I'll be there for you."

I'm practically speechless. My whole summer's been thrown together without me knowing. Sam's right—I've always, always wanted to travel, but I never thought it would be like this, and I can't deny that I've been thinking to myself that when I'm home this summer, I'll definitely see Ryan. I mean, we live on the same street, and even though I'm sure he'll avoid me, he can't do that forever, right? Then again,

I'm such a complete mess right now, so drained and exhausted all the time; can I really take a summer full of rejections from him? Seeing him parade around with other girls while our friends look at me in disgust, knowing what I've done? Maybe they won't even want to be my friend anymore. Maybe they'll do what Mason and Jake have done and just drop me for Ryan. He was always ridiculously popular with everyone back home. There's no doubt everyone will hate me for what I've done. Can I really face a summer back home without Sam? A summer full of fresh heartbreak?

"Becca?" Sam's voice is cautious on the other end of the line. "What do you think?"

I take a deep breath. "I guess I'm going to Asia for the summer."

# CHAPTER 21

## *Ryan*

I PULL UP OUTSIDE JESSICA'S HOUSE AND TAKE IN ALL the cars that are parked along the street. I'm supposed to be at training camp already, but I delayed it because I wanted to come here. It's not to see Jess and the rest of our old crowd; it's because I know Becca's back in town, and even though I hate it, even though I can't stand that she still has this pull over me, I can't resist the urge to go to a party where there's a small chance she might come.

I get out of my car and make my way over to the sidewalk just as the passenger door opens and long, tanned legs step onto the sidewalk. My eyes pan up, and I've got to admit, Kelly's fucking gorgeous. She's wearing a dress that should be illegal. It's black and skintight, showing off every last curve of her body. She spent nearly two hours getting ready and it was definitely worth it. Her hair is curled and hanging down her back, and she has a full face of makeup on. She looks like a knockout, like something out of the Playboy Mansion, and I'm proud to have her on my arm. I know some people will have been laughing at me over what Becca did—I mean, seriously? Fucking my biggest rival? How low can you get?—but showing up with Kelly will show that I've moved on. Hopefully they'll see I've moved on to better things, and that's why it's good Kelly's here. I hate the thought that anyone's been pitying me or laughing at me.

Kelly's about as far as I could get from Becca. Not in terms of their looks—don't get me wrong, Kelly's body is good, but Becca's is insane, and she doesn't have to do a single thing to maintain it. She stuffs her face every chance she gets, yet never gains a pound. She's the perfect height, not too tall and not too short, and her curves might be more subtle than Kelly's, but they're the stuff I've dreamed about since I was twelve years old. Even now, as much as I hate it, Becca's still in my dreams. Where Becca and Kelly are complete opposites is in their style. Becca would have just shown up to Jess's wearing jeans and whatever clean top she could find, maybe thrown on a bit of makeup if she had time, but if it was a choice between getting ready and hanging out at the beach or chilling with friends, she would have chosen that without caring about what she looked like.

Kelly flips her hair over her shoulder and smirks at me, catching me checking her out. I don't think she'd be quite so happy if she knew my thoughts had strayed to Becca, something I try not to let happen, but which seems to be happening more and more.

Kelly takes a deep breath. "You ready?" she asks. She's nervous; she won't admit it, but she is. She knows the people here are some of my best friends in the world, and she wants to make a good impression because I care about them.

I nod and start walking toward the house. I hear her heels click against the sidewalk as she hurries to catch up to me. She reaches out and grabs my hand, lacing her fingers though mine and stepping into my side so that the left side of her body is rubbing up against my back. Usually I'd probably enjoy the feel of her beside me, but I can't. I can't because I might see Becca any minute, for the first time in nine months.

I open the door, and a wave of noise assaults us. Kelly grips my hand tighter, and I lead the way in. The house is packed; it looks like everyone from my class and the ones above and below mine are here. Jess has always thrown an end-of-summer party, for as long as I can remember. It used to be to send us back to high school, and now she does it when we're all heading back to college. It's gotten to be like a reunion too, since we don't get to see each other often enough anymore. I know Jake and the rest of the guys will be in the kitchen, so I lead the way through there, negotiating my way through the crowd, smiling and nodding at the people who shout my name. I can see them glancing past me at Kelly and giving me winks, letting me know they think she's hot. I turn around to make sure Kelly's okay, but I shouldn't have worried. She's totally loving the attention, preening like a peacock. I swear she's stuck her chest even farther out and is smiling coyly at any of the guys who are looking her way. I resist the urge to roll my eyes and quicken my pace. I'm ready for a drink.

We finally reach the kitchen, and I immediately see my old friend Katie Thompson. She's facing me and talking to her boyfriend, John, another good friend of mine, but her eyes dart to me when I enter the room, and her face breaks into a huge smile. I love Katie; she's one of those people I've known forever and can just be myself around. She doesn't care that I play football and might go pro, and it's the same with all my high school friends. They don't give a crap about Ryan Jackson, college quarterback; they're just my friends, and they don't treat me any differently than they did when I was sixteen. The only problem with Katie at the moment is that she likes to talk about feelings and all that crap. She's tried plenty of times over the summer to talk to me about Becca, but I refuse to. If I could wipe Becca from my memory, I would, and I especially don't want anyone else talking about it.

Katie signals to John, and he turns and waves at me too. She and John have done what Becca and I couldn't—they've lasted through college and are planning to move to San Diego together after they graduate. Katie steps toward me then stops when her eyes drop to my hand and see it laced through Kelly's. She looks at me with a question in her eyes, but I pretend I don't see it as I make my way over to her.

"Hey guys."

Katie's eyes flick to Kelly warily before she looks back at me. John's noticed our hands too and raises an eyebrow at me. "Hey man," John says before turning and smiling at Kelly. Katie doesn't say anything, and it takes John nudging her in the side before she plasters on a grin and smiles at us both. "Hey guys."

I roll my eyes at her effort. I knew this wouldn't be straightforward. "This is Kelly," I tell them, nodding in her direction.

"His girlfriend," Kelly tells them smugly.

Katie's head whips around to face me. "What?"

I shrug. "Yeah." I'm trying to act nonchalant, but it's unnerving having Katie just staring at me.

"Since when?" she demands.

I can feel Kelly stiffen behind me. "Since yesterday." There's an edge in her voice, and I know she's irritated by Katie's response. "We've been dating on and off since last October, and now we're official."

Katie's jaw falls open as she stares at Kelly. To be honest, I'm surprised Katie doesn't know; Kelly's plastered it all over social media, but then I guess if Katie's never met her before, she wouldn't be looking at her pages. I haven't changed my status yet, much to Kelly's annoyance. I guess what Kelly said about us dating since October isn't strictly a lie, but it's more that we've been sleeping together since last October. There definitely haven't been many dates, and we definitely weren't exclusive. It was just after Becca and I split up, and I took any willing girl to use as a distraction.

There's an awkward pause as Katie gapes at us. John nudges her in the arm. "Babe, you're being rude."

"Right." Katie snaps out of it and plasters a fake smile on her face. "Sorry. Congrats guys."

I roll my eyes.

"You want a drink, man?" John asks. I nod and ask for a beer, and then he turns to Kelly. "Can I get you anything?" She turns and follows him to the drinks station in the corner, leaving me alone with Katie.

"Seriously?" she demands. "A new girlfriend?"

"What?" I ask, looking around.

"She's not here," Katie snaps.

"Who?"

She narrows her eyes at me. "You know who." I don't respond to her, but I feel a certain disappointment that Becca's not here. It's the same disappointment I had when I first heard that she was away for the whole summer and wouldn't be in town. We'd always talked about traveling together, and I tried to tell myself it wasn't her I was missing, that I was just upset she was getting to travel somewhere I'd always wanted to go, but I knew deep down that was bullshit. As angry as I've been at Becca, as hurt and humiliated as she made me, some of that has started to die down, and now I think about other things too. I think about us, and I miss her—even if it's only myself that I admit it to.

"So." I swallow my pride. "Is she not coming or what?"

Katie narrows her eyes. "Who?"

I roll my eyes. She knows perfectly well that I mean Becca, but she's going to make me say it. "Becca." I sigh. "Come on, is she coming or not?"

"I don't know." Her eyes flash over to Kelly. "Is that why you brought her here? Trying to get one over on Becca?"

I glare back at her. That's a little too close for comfort. Kelly's here to show everyone I've moved on; I hadn't really thought about Becca seeing her. "Give me some credit, Katie."

"Ryan, I've spent the whole freaking summer with you, and you've not mentioned that girl's name once. Last week we were in a bar, and you went home with some waitress. Forgive me for thinking it's not serious."

"Shut up," I tell her. I don't need another lecture on my behavior. She's spent the whole summer trying to get me to admit the reason I'm sleeping around is because of Becca. *Well, no shit. It's pretty obvious.*

"I recognize her," Katie tells me. "She's always tagging you in pictures with her pressed all up against you, even back when you were with Becca." Her face turns into a sneer, and I already know she doesn't like Kelly.

"Hey guys."

I turn and see Jake approach us.

"Did you know he has a girlfriend now?" Katie demands.

Jake nods slowly. "Yeah, I saw it on Kelly's Facebook."

I don't look at him. He's tried calling me a couple of times since yesterday, and I knew it would be about this, so I haven't gotten back to him.

"When did you become official?"

I sigh in irritation. He's not going to let me get away with not answering. "Yesterday."

He snorts. "So this has nothing to do with those pictures Sam put up?"

"Don't know what you're talking about," I lie.

"Course you don't."

"What pictures?" Katie demands.

"Sam put up a bunch of pictures from their vacation trip. Becca's not in a lot of them, but there is one where she's next to some guy." I try to keep my face impassive; I don't want to admit that he's right. I've spent what feels like my whole summer checking her and Sam's social media, waiting for them to put some pictures up, but they didn't. Sam put up the odd one of the scenery, of gorgeous views that made me wish I was there with them like we'd always planned. She even posted a couple of her and the other girl who was with them. The only time she put one up of Becca was on her birthday—Becca's twenty-first birthday, the biggest birthday of her life, which I wasn't there to celebrate, just like she wasn't there for mine. My birthday fell on a game day. We played at home and my family came down for the game, and those friends from high school that were close enough to make the journey came too. We won the game, and then a huge group of us went to a bar downtown where we had food and I had my first legal drink with my dad. Then my family left and we all stayed out for hours, drinking and dancing before going back to my house and continuing the party there. It was awesome. I had a great time, but I couldn't shake the feeling that someone was missing, and I knew it was Becca. Becca should have been there, especially when my mom gave me a card from Becca's parents. There were two courtside seats to a Lakers game in there. My eyes flashed to her, and even though neither of us said it, we knew it had been Becca who told them this was the perfect present for me, and it just made me think of her even more. Her aunt's new boyfriend works in PR for the team, and I have a feeling that's how they got them. When I went to the game with Jake, we stopped by to say hi, but it all felt so weird. Everything feels weird without Becca.

I'd been thinking even more about Becca than usual during the week of her birthday. Her parents had been around at my house (I knew there had been a bit of tension between them when Becca and I first broke up, but they'd managed to sort that out), and when I walked in on her mom in the kitchen with mine, I tried to pretend everything was normal and not awkward as hell. I wanted to ask her how Becca was doing and what she was up to, but I didn't. I couldn't show any of them what I was thinking. When her birthday rolled around, I wanted to know what she was doing and how she was celebrating, and I waited and waited to see something on social media. Finally, when I woke up on the morning of her birthday, I saw the picture. Becca was sitting on the ground with her legs crossed in front of a massive bowl of pad thai. She had her hair pulled up in a messy ponytail and her sunglasses on top of her head. It was the first picture I'd seen of her in months, and I was shocked at how she looked. She was the skinniest I've ever seen her, and even though she was smiling at the camera, it didn't reach her eyes. It was a smile she'd put on for Sam, on demand, to please her. She's not happy in it. I can tell.

Looking at that picture is not what got me. When I was eventually able to rip my eyes away from it, it was Sam's caption that really hit me where it hurt: *Happy Birthday to my best friend, the kindest, strongest, funniest person I know. She's my favorite person.* That's what got me, because whether I liked it or not, Becca was my favorite person too, even after all this time, and I couldn't help but think it was a dig at me over our breakup. I mean, how is Becca strong? She's weak. Why else would she cheat? Even if she wanted Mulligan, she should have had the guts to break up with me first—but that's the thing, she's not with Mulligan. I've asked Mason about it enough times, but he said he never speaks about her, and as far as he knows, they haven't seen each other in months. And that just blows my mind, because it means she threw it all away for nothing.

"Is that what this is about?" Katie demands, waving her hand in Kelly's direction and pulling me back to the present.

"Is that why you've suddenly got a new girlfriend?"

"It's not that sudden," I tell her.

She throws her hands up in the air and stalks over to Jessica as I sigh with irritation. I turn back to Jake, who's watching me closely. "I knew that would cut you up, man."

"Don't know what you're talking about."

He rolls his eyes. "Sure you don't." I know I'm being ridiculous. It's just a picture of a group of people. Becca's not even looking at the guy, she's looking somewhere in the distance, and they're not touching or anything, but he's smiling over at her. It genuinely made my stomach flip, thinking she was out there, partying with a group of people I know nothing about.

"Hey Sam." I look up when I hear Sam's name called and turn to see her walking into the kitchen, heading to the corner where some of her old crowd from high school stand. My gaze immediately sweeps behind her, seeing if Becca's there, but it's her boyfriend, Chris, who follows her in. He looks in my direction and nods my way, but he doesn't make a move to come over. I frown. Chris is a good friend of mine these days, and I don't know why he'd ignore me.

Jake's gaze must follow my own. "Sam!" he calls, smiling over at her.

Her head turns to face us, and her eyes flick from Jake to me and then back again. The expression on her face doesn't change, and she turns away, dismissing us.

"What the hell?" Jake mutters. I turn to face him, and then turn back to Sam, but she's already over with her friends, greeting them and hugging them. She has no problems smiling at them. "Maybe she didn't see us?" Jake asks. Of course she saw us; she saw us clear as day but chose to ignore us, and I'd bet money on it having something to do with Becca. I watch as Katie approaches her with Jessica in tow. After a quick hug, Katie leans into her, clearly asking her something. Judging by the quick glance she sends my way, I'm guessing it has something to do with Becca. Katie nods her head sharply and then leaves the kitchen, with Jessica right behind her.

"I'll go find out what's wrong," Jake says, eyeing Sam.

We've all spent a lot of time together over the last couple of years, and we've both known Sam since middle school. The last thing I want is to lose her friendship just because Becca and I are no longer together. I watch as he moves over to Sam's group. Her friend Erica looks up as he approaches, smiling in welcome, but when Sam sees he's approached, her eyes quickly flicker to me, and I can see the flash of anger in them before she turns it back on Jake. She dismisses herself from the group before he has a chance to say anything to her and walks away without giving him a second glance. Chris looks confused, but sends Jake a quick, apologetic look before following after his girlfriend.

Jake turns back to me, shrugging his shoulders in confusion, and I put my red cup to my mouth and chug the remainder of my beer. It's going to be a long night.

# CHAPTER 22

**M**Y MOM'S WORRIED ABOUT ME; I CAN TELL. I see her watching me all the time, so much so that I want to just stay in my room. I want to crawl into a ball and never leave my bed. It's funny to think that all I wanted for so long was to be close to Ryan, and now, when I know he's only four doors down, I can't stand the thought of seeing him. I know that's crazy, but at least if I don't see him, it doesn't make it real; I can still live in hope. He's got a girlfriend now; I saw it on social media, probably within hours of it happening, and it's not just any girl. It's Kelly Taylor, the one girl I couldn't stand, and now he's with her. A part of me thinks maybe there was something there before, before we broke up when they were back at Cal State together. I think back on the words Ryan shouted at me when we broke up—that he fucked his way around Cal State—but I know deep down it's not true. I know Ryan was mine, only mine, which means that since we've broken up, he's chosen Kelly. Despite the desperation and heartache that hit me when I saw the picture she put up with him, declaring him her gorgeous boyfriend, I was also disappointed, really disappointed. Out of all the girls out there, he picked her.

I roll onto my side and pull out my phone, again looking at the picture of the two of them. I can't help it. I can't stop looking at them. As much as I hate it, they do look good together. There's no denying how good-looking Kelly is, and with her standing next to him, his arm wrapped around her, they look like they're ready to take on the world. They're devastatingly attractive. Kelly's the sort of girl he should have been with all along, someone happy to be on his arm, willing to move where he is, willing to put him first—not someone like me, someone who was too pigheaded to even see what was important when she had the chance.

My phone beeps with a message.

**Sam: Sure you won't come to the party?**

I drop the phone and turn and face the ceiling. We've only been back from our trip for three days, and it still feels weird not spending all my time with Sam. She's been amazing all summer. She made sure she was by my side every step of the way, and just seemed to know when I was feeling uncomfortable. We barely spoke about Ryan, to be honest; she just seemed to know that I needed to chill on this trip, to not have to think about things. Although I could tell she was worried about me, we had a great time. The trip was exactly what I needed. Still, I can't go to Jess's party. Sam wants me to go, and Jess and Katie have both texted me about it, but I can't face it. I thought I could for about a minute today, but then I overheard my mom in the kitchen with Mrs. Jackson, who was telling her that Ryan had brought Kelly home. I'd been in my room when they first came in, and my mom came upstairs and asked me to come down and see Kathy, said she's been asking about me and would love to see me. I just shook my head and told her I couldn't. I couldn't face Kathy Jackson, knowing she thinks so little of me. I don't care that my mom insists that their relationship with the Jacksons is fine now and that her and my dad spent time at their house over the summer, and even saw Ryan a couple of times. I don't care what she says because I'm way too ashamed to see Kathy Jackson. Then I felt bad and figured it wouldn't kill me to pop into the kitchen for a minute, but that's when I overheard Kathy talking about Kelly visiting, and I just turned and ran straight back upstairs.

I just want the new semester to start now. I want to get out of California and go back to Southern U where I can pretend that the guy I'm in love with hasn't moved on with his life and left me way behind.

◆

"You're like two hours late for my party," Jessica Murphy says, smirking at me.

My mouth falls open. The last person I expected to find on my doorstep at 10:30 p.m. was Jessica Murphy. Back in high school, she had a big thing for Ryan, and she definitely wasn't my biggest fan when we first got together. True, we've socialized over breaks from college over the last few years because she and Ryan have all the same friends, and we can most certainly hold a civil conversation these days, but still, *what is she doing at my house?* My gaze drifts to her right, and

Katie Thompson is there, grinning at me.

"Hello? Earth to Becca? My party?"

"Oh, right." I shake my head, snapping out of my daze. "I'm not going."

"That's what Sam told us," Katie jumps in. "So we came to get you." *Yeah, she's just as bossy as ever.*

I stare at her in disbelief and shake my head. "It's really sweet of you to come by, but I'm just gonna stay in."

Katie sighs. "Look Becca, please come." Her gaze drops to my frame, and I shift uncomfortably. I know I've lost a lot of weight since the last time she saw me. I've put some back on over the summer, but I'm still looking pretty skeletal. The way she looks at me with such concern is making me feel uncomfortable. "No one has seen you in months," she continues. "You were away the whole summer, and tons of your friends are at Jess's house. You need to come with us."

I shake my head. I have absolutely no intention of going there. I can't stand the thought of being judged. "I can't."

"Why? Because you and Ryan broke up?" Jess asks. It hurts to hear her say it, even after all this time. As far as she and everyone else was concerned, Ryan and I were locked down, and nothing was going to change that—but it's all different now. I hate the thought of them knowing why we broke up, or at least why they think we broke up. I hate that they think I betrayed him. That's another reason I don't want to go to the party—I don't want to face what they all think of me. It's easier to just pretend it isn't happening.

"I'm pretty sure everyone hates me now," I say quietly.

Katie sighs. "That's not true. People make mistakes. You fucked up. Big time. Come on, Becca. We all know what happened, but you can't lock yourself away forever."

"He won't want me there."

"Yeah? Then why does he keep staring at the door the whole time? Like he's waiting for someone to arrive?" Jessica asks.

My heart skips a beat; I can't help it. That tiny bit of information is like a gift to me, telling me that he still cares, even if only a little, but then I realize they're probably just saying that to get me to the party.

"I can't." No matter what they say, I can't go to this party, not with Kelly there. It'll hurt too much. "I know his girlfriend's with him. I can't deal with that."

Jessica rolls her eyes. "She doesn't have a thing on you, Becca. He's just being an idiot. It doesn't mean anything."

I smile at her loyalty. "He's moved on. It's fine. I just can't see it, not yet."

"You're coming with us," Jessica states.

I shake my head again. "I can't handle Kelly. I really, really can't deal with that right now."

Katie grins at me. "Yeah, she's there, which is exactly why you should come."

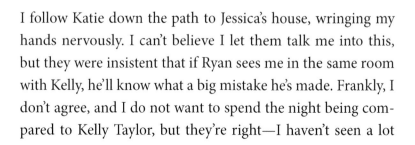

I follow Katie down the path to Jessica's house, wringing my hands nervously. I can't believe I let them talk me into this, but they were insistent that if Ryan sees me in the same room with Kelly, he'll know what a big mistake he's made. Frankly, I don't agree, and I do not want to spend the night being compared to Kelly Taylor, but they're right—I haven't seen a lot

213

of my old friends in a long time, and I can't lock myself away forever. Maybe I'll even get to have a chat with Ryan; I'm not expecting miracles, but even the slightest hint that he doesn't hate me as much as he did last year would be welcome right now. Besides, it was pretty clear that Jess and Katie weren't going to give up, so I gave in and came with them. Honestly, I'm lucky they let me change out of my pajamas. They were all ready to pile me straight into the car.

Jess opens her front door and I follow them inside. The place is packed; it looks like everyone from our class in high school is here, plus some. It reminds me of the last time I was at a party, but I force that thought from my mind. That is not this. This is my hometown, and this party is full of kids I've known for years. My stomach turns when I spot a brunette I recognize from being in one of Ryan's pictures over last Christmas. I'm pretty sure she hooked up with him. She sees me looking and quickly turns away while I continue to follow Katie through the house. The music is blaring, alcohol is flowing, and there are bodies everywhere. I keep my eyes downcast, not wanting to see anyone else he's hooked up with, but I feel eyes on me. It's like being back in high school again, when Ryan was the most popular boy in school and anything that happened involving him became big news. We might be four years older, but apparently nothing's changed. The girls continue hustling through the crowd, not stopping to talk to anyone. They only stop when they reach the kitchen.

"We're back," Katie announces loudly to the room.

I look up, and the room falls silent. I look around, and my eyes gravitate to him with a pull I can't control. There he is. It's the first time I've seen him in person in nine long months.

Ryan's standing by the fridge, holding a beer and chatting to Jake and a couple of others. He looks better than ever, and my heart starts beating a mile a minute just at the sight of him. If I thought seeing pictures of him on Facebook and Instagram was torture, this is a whole different level, being in the same room as him but not being able to be with him. I swear the whole room looks from me to him, as if waiting for his reaction. Ryan's eyes stay locked on my face with his jaw clenched. After a minute, I see his gaze drop to my frame, and I swear for a second I see him grimace before he covers the emotion and looks back at my face, his own face now a mask. He doesn't look away though; he stares back at me like I'm the only person in the room, and it's only when Kelly Taylor appears from nowhere and wraps her arms around him that he looks away. The sight of her on him makes me feel physically sick. That, combined with the scrutiny I feel I'm under, makes me pretty certain I'm about to bolt.

"'Bout time, McKenzie!" Jake suddenly says, walking toward me and pulling me into a hug. The tension in the room breaks, almost as if Jake talking to me gives the rest of them permission to do so, and the chatter resumes.

Jake squeezes me tightly and is followed by Sam, who is smiling widely, clearly delighted that I've come. Katie's boyfriend John comes over to say hi, and so do a couple others I was nervous about seeing. None of them mention Ryan; they all act as though they're happy to see me and there isn't this massive elephant in the room. I'm relieved and force myself to smile at my old school friends, some of whom I haven't seen in almost a year, and some of the tension leaves my body. It's nowhere near as bad as I thought it would be.

It's only when I glance back toward the fridge that I realize Ryan's left the room.

"You okay?"

I turn to Sam and nod my head. I've not left her side since I got here almost an hour ago. I've nodded and smiled at all the appropriate times when talking to various people, and my heart genuinely leapt with joy when Mason and Jake both went out of their way to ask me how my summer had been. The conversation was stilted and awkward and lasted for a maximum of two minutes, but compared to my last conversations with both of them, it was a huge step forward. Jake asked me at least five times how I was and I could feel him staring at my appearance, like he didn't recognize me. I just forced a smile and told him I was fine. I don't think he bought it. Since then though, they've both disappeared from the kitchen, and I'm guessing they're holed up with Ryan somewhere.

I can't relax. I just can't, knowing he's here and I still can't talk to him. He hasn't come back into the kitchen since I got here, and it's making me more nervous than if he were on the other side of the room. My anxiety is at an all-time high imagining what he's saying about me, but then I'm probably giving myself way too much credit. He's moved on completely. He's probably just talking football.

Sam's just starting to tell me her plans for next semester—something I know she's doing so I don't have to say anything—when I freeze at Kelly Taylor's voice.

"He's so romantic. He cooked me a candlelit dinner, three courses made from scratch, just before he asked me to make us official."

My breath catches in my throat. Ryan doesn't like cooking. He actually can cook and is way better than me, but if he actually went to the effort of cooking for her, that means he likes her. He really likes her. With me, we'd usually just get takeout.

Jessica snorts, and I sneak a glance and see that Kelly's standing with her and Katie.

"What?" Kelly demands defensively.

"Ryan probably ordered it and then put it on plate and pretended it was his."

I can't help but smirk at this. That does sound more like him.

"So was it his idea or yours to make it official?" Katie asks. The question's rude, but I want to hear the answer.

Kelly bristles next to her. "His." Something in the way she says it makes me think she's lying.

Katie scoffs. "Why would you even want to be with him? He's clearly on the rebound."

"Excuse me?" Her voice is shrill and louder than before. I glance around and notice that I'm not the only person listening. Sam rests her hand on my arm, but when she tries to nudge me toward the door, I shake my head. I want to hear this. Kelly glances my way with her eyes narrowed. "He has moved on." She's speaking to me. Her words might be directed at Katie, but she wants me to hear them. She wants me to know he doesn't think of me at all anymore.

Katie laughs. They've decided they don't like her already;

I can just tell.

"We're already making plans for next year," Kelly tells them, her voice steeped in irritation. "Thinking about where we could be."

It's like someone's stabbed me through the heart.

"Wait, what?" Jessica asks.

I'm a glutton for punishment, so I can't help it. I glance over at her, and she's smug. She's really smug.

"Yeah, you know, waiting to see where he'll be drafted."

"You're telling me you're gonna move to wherever Ryan is when you graduate?" Katie asks in disbelief.

"Of course," she replies. "He'll need my support after he gets drafted."

"Oh, come on. You guys aren't even seriously dating," Jessica states.

"We are totally committed actually," Kelly replies testily.

"You're crazy if you think Ryan even feels a fraction for you of what he feels for Becca. He's been in love with her since they were kids."

"*Felt* for her. He's moved on," she replies haughtily.

"Yeah, to numerous different people. From what I've seen, you're not the only one he's been hooking up with," Katie scoffs.

Kelly's eyes flare, and she straightens up, turning to look Katie straight in the eye. "Your opinion on my relationship isn't welcome, and if you want Ryan to keep getting you and your boyfriend tickets to his games, I'd suggest you quit while you're ahead."

Katie's mouth drops open at this threat, and a hush falls across the kitchen.

"Who the hell do you think you are?" Jessica demands, stepping forward. "You're just some girl he's passing the time with. We've known Ryan since we were kids."

Kelly flips her hair over her shoulder. "You're his past. I'm his future. You might want to remember that." With that, she turns and saunters out of the room.

I glance over at Jessica and Katie, who look like they're ready to march after Kelly and rip her hair out. I then turn to Sam, who is scowling. She looks over at me. "What a bitch."

I shrug. I've always thought that about Kelly, but I'm biased. How stupid can she be though, alienating two of his best friends the first time she meets them? Then I remember what she said about being with him next year, after the draft, and it's all I can do not to burst into tears. Sam nods toward the doors that lead to Jess's backyard, and I focus on putting one foot in front of the other as I follow Sam out of the kitchen to get some fresh air.

<hr />

"Becca!"

I stop and turn to see Katie standing in a room off to the right, and Jessica's next to her. Sam halts in front of me. We've been outside with Chris, not really doing anything, just sitting and watching the party from afar while I try to fight the urge to run straight home. I can't believe Ryan's so close to me after all this time, but it's like we're strangers. Scratch that— we're worse than strangers, because you acknowledge strangers, and he won't even do that. Then when Chris said he was going to head out, Sam told me she'd drive me home but just wanted to use the bathroom first.

Katie appears in front of me. Her face is slightly flushed, and my guess is she's been knocking back the drinks since I last saw her. "We thought you'd gone." I shake my head and she grips my hand. "Come in here."

Sam's eyes find mine, and she has a question in them. She wants to know if I'll be okay without her for the few minutes it'll take her to use the bathroom. This is what she does for me now. She stays by my side so she can protect me from things I never thought I'd need protecting from. She's my security blanket these days, and although I need to stop relying on her, I can't help but be grateful. I nod my head and force a smile at her, trying to reassure her as I let Katie pull me into the room.

My stomach instantly drops through the floor as I look around the small TV room. Ryan's in here. He's in the far corner, his eyes trained on my face. He has his friends around him: Jake, Mason, John, and a few others. He's swapped the red cup he was holding earlier for a bottle of liquor, and it looks like he's drinking straight from the bottle. My stomach twists. Ryan's always had the odd beer, but he's never gone hard. It reminds me of when my mom told me Ryan's dad blamed me for Ryan's behavior. It looks like he's taken to drinking a lot more since we broke up.

"You okay?" Jessica asks me, and I tear my eyes away from Ryan.

"I'm fine," I tell her. "It's really good to see you guys." It is. I hadn't realized how much I miss them. I might have avoided them throughout high school, but they're good friends. They're fun and they're loyal, and I regret not getting back to them when they've called me.

Katie suddenly pulls me into a fierce hug. "It is so good to see you, Becca. I promise things will get better."

I don't have to ask what she means by that. Judging from all the different looks and comments I've heard tonight, I know my appearance has caused a stir. I know I look bad. I'm the skinniest I've ever been, and it's definitely not in an attractive way. When I look in the mirror, even I can see how sad I am. Even with my summer tan, my skin has a gray tinge, and knowing they're all thinking it is making me feel more self-conscious than ever.

"Becca?" I turn at the sound and see Luke Masters, one of Ryan's friends from high school, behind me. He grins at me. "How are you?"

I smile back at him as he steps in and gives me a quick hug.

"I'm really good," I lie. "How are you?"

He doesn't skip a beat, doesn't grimace at my appearance or glance over at Ryan, doesn't nod sympathetically or look at me in pity. Instead, he launches into telling me about his summer and how he met a girl who goes to Southern U. If all goes well, he may be visiting her there next semester. He chats and jokes, and I'm reminded of how much I like him. He and I were in a lot of the same classes in high school, and we always got along really well. We didn't talk much after the first couple months he transferred here, but as soon as Ryan and I got together, we got our friendship back on track. I'm so engrossed in listening to him and not feeling like a complete freak that I almost don't notice Kelly strut into the room and sidle up next to Ryan—almost, but not quite.

Luke continues, and I stay focused on him. I force myself not to look Ryan's way, and when he cracks a joke, I actually laugh at it. My laugh is louder than it's been all night.

"So what?" Ryan's voice rings out from across the room. He's drunk. Just by the sound of his voice, I can tell. "You after my sloppy seconds now, Masters?"

I freeze at his words, and my eyes find Ryan's. He's in the same spot, glaring over at us. Jake scowls at his words and shoves him slightly in the arm, but Ryan doesn't look his way.

"Dude," Luke admonishes him. "We're just talking, man."

Ryan steps forward, walking away from Kelly, who has her arm around his waist. "You might get lucky, man."

"Ryan!" Katie's voice is a warning from behind me, but he doesn't turn to look at her.

"What?" Ryan continues, not looking away from Luke and me. His face is flushed, and he's swaying ever so slightly. "We're at a party, aren't we?" I suck in a breath, and tears prick my eyes. I can't believe the way he's speaking to me. Ryan steps even closer to me, only inches away now; it's the closest he's been to me in months, but he's never felt so far away. He dismisses Luke from his gaze and now is focused solely on me. "That's your specialty these days, isn't it, Becca? Fucking guys at parties?"

All the air leaves my lungs as a hush falls over the room.

"You are so out of line, Ryan!" Katie hisses angrily from where she's stepped up next to me. Ryan goes to say something else, but Luke steps in front of me, blocking Ryan's view of me.

"You're drunk, man. You should go home."

Ryan scowls back at him. "Why? So you can make your

move? Me being here didn't bother you a minute ago."

"Ryan." My voice is quiet. "We were just talking."

Ryan looks at me for a second, his eyes locking with mine before he turns back to Luke. "You're in for a treat, man. She's pretty good." His words stab me like a knife. Nobody makes a noise. "That's what Mulligan said, isn't it, Becca?" His gaze sweeps back to me. "That you were real good?"

The mention of Mulligan's name from his lips renders me paralyzed, and I want the ground to open up and swallow me whole. Luke pushes him away from me, and Jake appears next to Ryan. "Come on, Ryan. Let's go."

Ryan shrugs Jake off and turns back to me. "You were good, but not that good, Becca." I can't believe he's doing this. I can't believe he's talking about what I'm like in bed in front of everyone. I never thought he'd do this to me. I never thought he'd stoop so low. He wraps his arm around Kelly—I hadn't even noticed her appear at his side. "I've moved on to better."

I want to die. I want to die watching Kelly smirk over at me in a room full of my friends who have just watched Ryan degrade me completely. It's not just Ryan, my ex-boyfriend. It's Ryan, the boy I've known ever since I was born. The boy I played in the sand pits with. The boy who showed me how to ride a bike. The boy who showed me how to kick a soccer ball. That Ryan.

I start to tremble as I hear voices around me. I see Jessica and Katie with their mouths open, saying something to Ryan, and Luke stepping up to him, talking in his ear, but I don't hear any of it. I don't hear any of it because all I can see is his face and the complete loathing in his expression. It's only when Kelly steps even closer into him, wrapping her arms possessively around him, that I snap out of it.

"Come on, baby," she tells him. "Let's leave this whore to it."

There's stunned silence at her words; even Ryan seems to freeze in surprise. Complete shock surrounds me, and I start to tremble. Kelly Taylor just called me a whore, in front of all my friends. I wait for Ryan to defend me. Even after everything he's just said, I wait for him to tell her not to call me that…but he doesn't. He doesn't say a word.

"What did you just say?" Sam's voice is low behind me, and I turn to see her in the doorway, taking in the scene in front of her, her eyes wide and her fists clenched.

Kelly glances at her once and then dismisses her.

"What did you just call *my* best friend?" Sam's repeats, moving to stand next to me. Her voice is like ice.

"Sam," I say quietly. "Don't. It's fine."

"It is not fine, Becca." She turns back to Kelly and takes a step toward her, blocking Kelly's view of me. "What the hell did you just call my best friend?" Sam says again, her voice louder this time.

Kelly doesn't respond, just crosses her arms and levels Sam with a steady stare. She won't take it back, I know she won't. She doesn't care that this is my hometown and these are my high school friends. She has Ryan now, and she wants me to know how little she thinks of me.

Sam's head whips around to Ryan. "Really Ryan? You're gonna stand there and let her call Becca a whore?" Ryan doesn't answer her, and he doesn't look at me either. "Are you fucking kidding me?"

When he again doesn't answer, she shakes her head in disgust. "You know she's telling people she's going with you to the NFL?" she tells him. "That you guys are serious? She's gonna get herself pregnant and then you'll be stuck with her, just because you're too pigheaded to talk to the girl everyone in this room knows you're still in love with." There's silence around us. Complete and utter silence.

"Stop it, Sam." I try to sound confident, but my voice is thin. Sam doesn't even hear me. She's in full-on protective mode as Ryan's face grows redder and redder. He still doesn't look at me.

Sam throws her hand out in my direction, stepping aside so she's no longer blocking me. "Well, take a look at the girl you've been in love with since you were a kid, Ryan," Sam tells him, her voice loud and clear. "The girl you've known your whole life. The girl you're so desperate to hurt. Because she is hurting, Ryan. Fucking look at her." Sam's getting closer to him and practically snarling in his face. "She's hurting so fucking bad, and all you can do is attack her!"

"Stay out of it, Sam."

"I will not stay out of it, not when you're letting that bitch speak to Becca like that."

"What did you call me?" Kelly demands, stepping up toward Sam.

"I called you a bitch," Sam hurls straight back at her. "You're not even worthy of saying my best friend's name. You speak to her like that again, and I swear I'll make sure you regret it."

A shocked murmur ripples around the room at Sam's threat. This is not Sam. This is not what she does. Jessica is

225

staring at her with her jaw open, and Katie's eyes are wide. Jake's blinking rapidly, like he can't believe what he's hearing, and I don't dare look at Ryan. I don't want to see him take Kelly's side.

Kelly's face has turned bright red from anger. She turns to Ryan in fury. "Are you going to let her speak to me like that?" she demands.

Ryan's eyes flit back between Kelly and Sam, and I can see his own jaw is tense. He doesn't like this. He doesn't like that Sam is calling him out in front of everyone. He turns to Kelly. "Go wait for me in the kitchen. I'll be right there."

Kelly's eyes flash with anger, but she doesn't argue with him. She takes one last look at me, looks me up and down with a sneer on her face, making it perfectly clear to everyone in the room what she thinks of me, but she doesn't say another word. She turns and leaves.

"You owe Becca an apology," Sam tells Ryan.

Ryan scoffs in disbelief. "I owe Becca an apology? I owe Becca fuck all." I flinch at his harsh words, and I swear my whole body starts shaking. I can't stand that everyone's watching this. Everyone's witnessing this scene.

"You make me sick, you know that, Ryan? I don't know how you can claim to be so in love with her for years and then just drop her the second things get tough."

Ryan looks completely bewildered. To him, he hasn't done anything wrong. To him, he doesn't understand why Sam is being like this. To him, I'm the one in the wrong. I'm the one that cheated. He doesn't think she has any right at all to be angry at him.

"I get it though—you're *Ryan Jackson*." Sam's voice takes

on a mocking tone I know he'll hate. "You're the most popular guy at MacAllister High, that's right isn't it? And then you go to college and you're a freaking superstar there, am I right? They act like you're a fucking god, and it's *all hail Ryan freaking Jackson*. And that's why you've walked away from her, because you can't handle that people might not think you're Ryan Jackson, superstar jock and all-around popular guy."

"Sam." Ryan steps toward her, and his voice has a warning in it. "You need to—"

"I don't need to do anything," she hisses back at him. "Do you think this is bad?" Sam asks, waving her hand in my direction but not taking her eyes off Ryan. "Do you think she looks bad now?" she demands. Ryan doesn't answer, so she whirls on Jake. "What about you, Jake? You're supposedly one of her best friends since elementary school, but the second she needs you, you drop her too."

Jake's mouth falls open in disbelief. "What—"

"She's got a tan now," Sam says, cutting Jake off and waving back at me. "She's got a tan now, so it covers up the bags under her eyes and how pale she was at the start of summer, how sick she looked because she barely left her apartment and hadn't seen sunlight in months." Sam shakes her head at them. "And do you think she's skinny now?" Sam takes a step closer to Ryan. "Do you think she's skinny, Ryan? She's put on weight. She's put on weight because I stood over her every day while we were away and made sure she ate a meal. I made sure she ate, because when I saw her for the first time in months at the airport, she looked so fucking skeletal I wanted to start crying. Did you know that, Ryan? I took one look at my best friend and wanted to burst into tears." There's hushed silence in the room, and my heart is beating so fast, I'm scared it's going to burst. "Did you know that while you were fucking every girl that smiled your way and putting it on social media so she knew just how little she meant to you, did you know the girl you've known your entire life was falling apart from the stress of it all?"

"SHE CHEATED ON ME!" Ryan explodes. "SHE FUCKING CHEATED ON ME!" He hisses in a breath. "She fucked Robbie Mulligan, and I woke up to the pictures that proved it."

Hearing him say the words is like a punch in the face. Ryan finally glances at me, and I can see the anger in his eyes. He's still as angry as he was the last time I saw him; it might as well have been yesterday, but there's something else there too. It's hurt.

"Don't even mention that bastard's name," Sam spits back at him. She takes a step toward him, and they're leaning into each other, really going at each other now.

"I had a whole fucking stadium tell me how good she was," Ryan practically snarls, spit flying from his mouth. There's no doubt about how furious he is, and I feel like I'm going to throw up. He finally looks at me. "The whole stadium told me how good you were, Becca. The whole stadium told me how good my girl was." *My girl*—that's what he said. He called me his girl, and I cling to it. I go to speak, but the look he gives me stops me dead. I think back to that football game and what I saw on TV. How Ryan destroyed Robbie that night. How he outplayed him at every chance, and how his team made Robbie pay. But I forgot about the humiliation Ryan must have felt, in front of his teammates, in front of his family.

"I'm sorry." I whisper the words, so quietly I think I'm the only one who hears them.

"Do you know how that feels?" he demands. "Do you have any idea how that fucking feels, Becca?"

"I'm sorry," I try again, my voice paper thin.

He steps toward me, his eyes flashing. "After everything, Becca, after everything we went through, you threw it all away to fuck that bastard."

"Don't speak to her like that," Sam demands.

"Shut up, Sam."

"I will never forgive you, you know," she states fiercely. "I will never forgive you for how you've treated her."

"What the hell are you talking about?" Ryan demands in frustration. "She did this. She fucked Mulligan. She caused all of this."

"You don't know anything!" Sam snaps. "You don't have a clue what happ—"

"Stop! Sam, please stop!" I finally find my voice, and Sam instantly turns to me. Her face loses all the anger the minute she looks at me.

"Oh, Becca. I'm sorry."

She nearly spilled. She nearly told him everything, and I can't have that. I've buried it. I've buried what happened, and now I just want to move on, to forget it ever happened. That's all I want.

"It's fine, but I want to go home now. Will you drive me?"

Sam nods and takes a step toward me.

"Wait, what doesn't he know?" I glance over at Jake, who's staring back at me. I don't answer, so he turns to Sam. "You were just about to say he doesn't know what happened—what doesn't he know?"

"Nothing," I tell him quietly. I glance toward Ryan, but he's looking down at the ground. His jaw is tense, and you can see the anger radiating off him. "You all know what happened. I slept with Robbie Mulligan." I take a deep breath. "I'm sorry. I shouldn't have come."

Sam gently takes my arm and turns me around to walk out of the room. I stop just before I leave and force a smile. I want to tell Ryan that he looks good, that I hope he's happy and that his life is working out just the way he planned, but when he finally looks my way, I can't. He looks at me with so much hate and so much anger that I can't open my mouth to speak, and I can barely look him in the eye. I turn around and walk away.

# CHAPTER 23

*Becca*

THE DRIVE BACK TO MY HOUSE FROM JESSICA'S only takes ten minutes, but it feels like ten hours. Tension is radiating off Sam in waves, and she's gripping the steering wheel so tightly, I swear her hands will ache tomorrow. She pulls up outside my house and cuts the engine. She doesn't make a move to go, she just stares ahead. I sit beside her, not saying a word, just thinking again and again about what just happened at Jessica's house and the way Ryan spoke to me.

"Thanks for the ride," I tell her. She nods. "Do you want to come in for ice cream or something?"

She surprises me by stiffly nodding her head and opening her car door. I open my own door and lead the way into my house and through to the kitchen. Sam drops her stuff on the counter and takes a seat at one of the stools. I head over to the freezer, but before I get there, I hear a sniffle and look back in horror to see tears sliding down Sam's face. I reach out to comfort her, but she shifts away from me, shaking her head, wiping at her face furiously.

"Sam?"

"I'm sorry," she whispers. "I'm sorry."

"It's okay."

She starts to shake her head. "I can't do this anymore, Becca. I can't do this."

My eyes widen in horror. "What do you mean?"

She turns to look at me helplessly, and I've never seen her look so sad in my life. "I hate this," she whispers. "I hate seeing you like this. It is tearing me apart to see you like this."

"I'm fine," I insist.

She shakes her head. "You're not fine, Becca. You're falling apart in front of my eyes, and there isn't a damn thing I can do about it."

"Sam—"

"No, Becca. I know you're not going to counseling, and if you're about to lie and tell me you are, then I'll just say, it's not working—because it's not, Becca. Whatever you've been doing since that bastard raped you has not been working."

I close my eyes and sit down on the stool beside her. "I'm okay."

"No, Becca." Her voice is so desperate that I open my eyes and turn to face her. "You're not okay, and of course you're not. Not after everything you've been through. Not after what's happened to you."

"Sam—"

"You act like you did it," she tells me, turning her head so she's facing away from me, looking out the window into

232

my backyard. "You act like Ryan's right and you betrayed him. You're letting him talk to you like that, like you're nothing, but you didn't do anything wrong, Becca. You didn't do anything wrong."

I take a deep breath. "It's easier this way."

She shakes her head, fresh tears falling down her face. "I don't understand why you're doing this, letting Ryan treat you this way, letting Robbie Mulligan get away with it."

"I am not letting him get away with it!"

"But you are, Becca. I don't get it. I really don't get it."

"Sam—"

"I'm trying to be supportive of your decision, I promise I am, but I just don't get it. You're stronger than this. You're so much stronger than this, and you're letting him get away with it. You're letting him tear you apart."

I bite down on my lip, hard. I wish I hadn't told her. I wish she didn't know the truth, because now she's judging me. She thinks I'm pathetic and weak.

"I'm sorry," I whisper. My voice is weak. I'm so emotionally drained from tonight—from the whole year, to be honest. "If you don't want to be my friend anymore, I understand."

She looks horrified at my words, and more tears slide down her face. "Becca, no. That's not what I mean at all. I love you. You're my best friend, but I can't just watch you like this anymore. I can't just stand by and let you fall apart like this. I need to help you, and I don't know how."

"I'm fine."

"Explain it to me," she says eagerly, shifting closer to me. "Explain to me why you won't tell anyone, why you won't get help, why you let Ryan speak to you the way he did tonight."

"Because…"

"Because what?"

"Because if I act like I cheated on him, if I act like I made that choice, then I can breathe, Sam. I can get through it knowing I made the choice, knowing my choice wasn't taken away from me." I close my eyes. "If I let everyone continue thinking what they think right now, then it's like it's not real. It's like it didn't really happen. It's like Robbie didn't take everything away from me."

Fresh tears fall down Sam's face.

"Becca—"

"And nobody would believe me," I cut her off. I honestly believe that. Even if I did report it, Robbie would just deny it and I'd be the one called a liar.

"They would, Becca. I promise you they would."

I snort. "They wouldn't, Sam." That's the painful truth. No one would believe me over Robbie Mulligan, the star quarterback of the Southern U Kings, the son of old-school money and the nephew of a senator. I wouldn't have a chance in hell of anyone believing me.

"Becca—"

"No, Sam. I can't. I can't tell anyone."

"Please, Becca." Her voice is a whisper.

"Please leave it, Sam. This is the only way I can do this, Sam. It's the only way I get through the days."

Her head drops against her chest, and she keeps it there for a few minutes. When she looks back up at me, the light has gone from her eyes, and I know she's not going to push me on it again. "Please just go see someone," she tells me. "Or just tell your mom. She can help."

I shake my head violently. There's no way I'm ever going to tell my mom. Not a chance.

She closes her eyes at my answer, and her shoulders slump in defeat. We sit there silently for a few minutes, neither of us speaking, neither of us breaking the silence that feels so fragile.

Sam lets out a long sigh and offers me a weary smile. "Ryan was a real asshole tonight, huh?" She missed the way he spoke to me when she was in the bathroom, but when we left, Katie and Jessica followed me outside to make sure I was okay, and they filled Sam in. Sam was ready to march back in and go again with Ryan, but I convinced her to take me home. I'd had enough drama for one night and couldn't handle the thought of them arguing again.

I nod, but as thoughts of Ryan come crashing into my head, my lips start to tremble. Sam's eyes widen in alarm, and before I know it, she's pulled me off my stool and has wrapped her arms around me in a tight hug, whispering again and again that it's all going to be okay.

"I never thought he'd be like this," I manage to whimper through my tears. "I never thought he'd leave me. I never thought he could be this cruel."

Sam smooths down my hair and tries her hardest to soothe me, but with tonight's events suddenly fresh in my head, with the memories of him talking about me like I was nothing, talking about what I was like in bed and telling Luke he could get lucky with me, I'm suddenly inconsolable.

"Becca?" I startle at my mom's voice in the doorway, and I turn to face her. She's wearing her navy dressing gown over her nightdress, and her eyes are fixed on my face.

I turn my back to her quickly, wiping my face furiously. I can't let her see me like this; she's already worried enough. "Becca, what's going on?"

"Nothing," I tell her, trying to get my breathing back under control. "I'm fine," I tell her, "just being stupid."

I turn to face her, and she's staring at me like she's heartbroken. "Becca, please tell me what's happened."

I shake my head, and I feel Sam's gaze on me. I turn to her, and I know she wants me to tell my mom. I know she wants me to talk to her, to talk to anyone. I can see her eyes pleading with me, but I can't. I can't tell my mom. I can't tell anyone.

She must see that I won't tell her, because her face becomes resigned. "I'm gonna go," Sam tells me. She reaches out and gives me a tight hug before turning and walking away.

I still don't turn to my mom as I scrub the tears from my face and then rake my hands through my hair, trying to sort myself out. I turn back to her and force a smile onto my face.

She takes a step toward me. "You know I love your father, don't you?" I frown slightly, confused. "You know I've been in love with him for thirty years?"

I nod, unsure where she's going with this. My parents are crazy in love, always have been. She takes another step forward, slowly, cautiously, like she's scared she'll spook me.

"Well, if you were under attack, Becca, if you were in danger, I would use your father as a human shield to protect you. Do you understand that?"

Tears start to slip down my face again as she reaches out and cups my face in her hands. "I love you, Becca, more than anything else in this world. No one else even comes close." I try to choke back a sob, but it's not successful. Tears start to form in her eyes as she looks into mine. The same green eyes I inherited from her look so sad and desperate. "I would do anything for you. Do you know that? Anything. Your father would too, but you need to let us help you. You need to let me know whatever it is that's ripping you apart."

The tears are running freely down my face now.

"I can't stand to see you like this, Becca. It is breaking my heart to see my baby girl so broken. You just need to tell me what's going on. It can't just be Ryan. It can't be. I promise we can make it better. I promise we can fix it."

I see despair cross her eyes, and I realize I'm shaking my head, telling her I won't tell her. The first of her tears drop down her face before she takes a deep breath. "When you're ready, Becca, whenever you're ready to tell me, I'll be here."

She gives me one last sad smile and then turns and walks away.

"Mom." My voice shakes, and she turns back to me, her eyes hopeful. I let out a sigh. "Do you think you could give me a hug?"

She's by my side in a second and wraps me up in her arms, hugging me so tightly, I have no doubt that she's here for me, that she loves me and she cares, and it feels wonderful. It's the safest I've felt in months, and I didn't even know I needed it. She moves one of her hands to my head, gently stroking my hair back, and I think back to Sam's words and my mom's words. I know I have to do something. I have to find a way to move on from this and get my life back.

# CHAPTER 24

*Becca*

I STEP BACK THROUGH MY FRONT DOOR, AND I HEAVE a sigh of relief. It's been a long day, but it's done. I woke up this morning, and all I could think about was the look on my mom's face last night in the kitchen. Then my dad came in to say goodbye to me before going to work, something he would never usually do. He kind of hovered in the doorway, not really saying anything while I stared back at him. Then finally he blurted out that he loved me and walked away. I knew then that I was right last night. I had to find a way to move on.

I got up right away and made myself eat breakfast. I felt like stopping after the first few bites, already feeling full, but I made myself eat every bite of the granola and yogurt and then I even fried some bacon and ate most of that too. I need to start eating regularly again. It's not that I've cut down on food on purpose, but I just stopped caring about everything and completely lost my appetite. That's going to change now.

Then I pulled out my iPad and looked up those rape coun-seling groups I first found all those months ago. I sent one that's located a reasonable distance from Southern U an email, asking them for details about dropping in for support. I didn't have to wait long for a response. They emailed me back within a couple of hours, telling me their drop-in times and reassuring me that everything was confidential. I got the email when I was at the hairdresser. I decided I needed a physical change and got five inches chopped off my hair, which had gotten way too long over the summer, falling halfway down my back. It now sits just above my shoulders, the shortest it's ever been, and I also got a few caramel highlights through it to brighten it up.

Then I drove by Sam's house and showed her the email from the counseling center. Complete relief covered her face, and then she wrapped me up in the tightest hug and told me she was proud of me. It felt good. It felt really, really good to actually be taking a step in the right direction, and if it helps me start to make a change, start to move forward, then it can only be a good thing. I can't keep living like I have since the attack. I have to stop letting it consume me. I have to move on.

I walk into the kitchen, carrying my bags from the grocery store, and I see my parents at the counter drinking coffee. They both turn to face me when I walk in.

"Your hair," my mom blurts out. "Your hair looks really pretty, Becca."

"Thanks Mom." I take a deep breath. "It's time for a change."

She nods, looking at me cautiously. I set my bags down on the counter next to her and start pulling out the groceries I bought at the store. I can feel their eyes on me, but they don't say anything. Then I go over to the sink and wash my hands, drying them on a towel.

I turn back to them, and they're both just watching me cautiously. "I thought I'd make dinner," I tell them. "Well, at least attempt it."

"Really?" my dad asks.

I nod. "Yeah. I thought you could invite Aunt Ruth and Jay over if you wanted to?"

My mom raises her eyebrows. She's been trying to get me to do something with Jay and Aunt Ruth for the last few days, but I haven't wanted to, haven't felt up to it. "Yeah, of course, sweetie—if you're sure?"

I nod. The last time my aunt saw me, she tried to find out what was going on with me, but I just shut her out. I need to start showing all of them that I'm okay. I need to show myself. "And, maybe if Kathy Jackson comes over for coffee tomorrow, I could come and say hi?" My voice falters. "I mean, just for a bit," I tell my mom. I know this is what will mean the most to her, but it's also what's going to be hardest for me.

My mom's brow creases. "Becca, you don't—"

"Mom," I cut her off. I need to do this. I need to know that I'm trying to make a change, even if just for myself. "I'm trying, okay? I'm really trying here."

She nods immediately, and I'm sure I see tears well in her eyes before she rapidly blinks them away.

I pull out a chopping board and pick up the tomatoes I bought at the store, wondering how I'm going to manage to cook Bolognese when I usually burn toast. I feel slightly better, slightly better than I have in months.

# CHAPTER 25

## *Ryan*

PRACTICE IS OVER FOR THE DAY, AND MY BODY IS aching. I stood in the shower until the water ran cold, but even now, as I walk back into the locker room to get changed, Marty, Jason, Dean, and Evan are still in there. They're fully dressed, but have obviously decided to wait for me. My stomach growls with hunger, and Jason smirks as he hears it.

I walk over to my locker, throw it open, and grab my clothes, dressing quickly.

"You okay, man?"

I glance over at Marty. "I'm fine."

He narrows his eyes but doesn't push it any further. I've been on fire in practice, and we all know it. This is my best year yet—but off the field? Where thoughts are able to creep into my head? That's a different story. I've not been with it, and I know it.

"What's going on with you?" Jason asks. "You've been weird since you got here, and why were you late?"

I ignore him, putting on my watch. I'm not about to tell them I delayed coming here because I wanted to see my ex-girlfriend and rub it in her face that I've got a new girlfriend, and I'm especially not going to tell them I'm appalled at the way I spoke to her, that the look in her eyes when I let Kelly call her a whore has haunted me ever since—and don't even get me started on how she looks. I was physically shocked when she walked in. She's not the girl I remember, the girl I've always known. The girl from the party was a shadow of her former self.

"Did you see Becca?"

"What?" My eyes find Marty, who's looking at me in concern. "Why would you even say that?"

He shrugs. "Because she's the only one that can affect you like this."

I scowl at him. "Did Jake open his big mouth?"

"Doesn't take a genius to figure out you saw her."

"Well, so what if I saw her? She lives down the street from me. It was bound to happen eventually."

"How was she?" Marty asks, and I wonder what else Jake told him.

"I don't want to talk about it."

"Good. Forget her, man. She's not worth it. Think about what she put you through," Jason tells me.

"Like I could fucking forget," I mutter sarcastically. There isn't a day that passes where I don't think of her with Mulligan at least once.

Evan nods. "He's right, man."

"Why are we even talking about Becca?"

"Because she's the only one who can get in your head."

"Have I been off in practice?" I demand.

He shakes his head. "No, you're better than ever, but..."

"But what?"

He sighs. "It's senior year, man. We need to get to the playoffs. I just don't want her distracting you. I don't want you hurting again, man."

"Yeah, don't let her back in your head, dude."

I roll my eyes at Jason. It's too late for that. Becca's always been in my head, for as long as I can remember. "I don't even know why we're having this discussion. I'm with Kelly now."

Marty doesn't hide his sneer quick enough. He's not a fan of Kelly, just like Jake. To be honest, I don't quite know how we've ended up in a relationship. My breakup with Becca made me never want to get in another relationship again, but I couldn't be bothered to keep arguing with Kelly.

"Where did you see her?" Marty asks.

They're not letting me off; they know she's been on my mind and they want to know why. "A party."

"What happened?"

I sigh and look past Marty's head, concentrating on the crack in the wall behind him. "She looked like shit, like she hadn't eaten in months and was so tired. She looked really, really tired."

"Did you speak to her?"

I snort. In a way, I did—I talked about her, and then shouted at her. "She was talking to a friend we went to high school with and I told him he might get lucky because she fucks guys at parties now."

Marty's eyes widen and he glances over at Dean, who shifts uncomfortably. "Then I told him that she was good but I had better now." I close my eyes at the memory of her face at that. "And then Kelly called her a whore and I didn't say anything. I let her say it."

There's silence at my words. There's not much they can say to that.

"What did Becca do?"

I shake my head and sit down on the bench, running my hand over my face in irritation. "She didn't do anything. She just took it." I sigh loudly. "I was a fucking asshole."

No one argues with me, not even Jason, and he's been the most vocal when it comes to trashing Becca.

I slam my fist down onto the bench next to me. "I don't fucking get it," I tell them through gritted teeth, all my frustration from the last couple days spilling out. "She did this, she's the one who cheated on me, and I'm the one everyone was pissed at. I know I was a dick, but still…" I trail off. How am I the bad guy in this situation? And why do I feel so guilty? I'm not the one who's done anything wrong.

There's silence for a couple minutes before Dean clears his throat. "There's a bar about twenty minutes away that my brother reckons does the best chicken wings in the state," Dean tells me, changing the subject. "You wanna check it out?"

I shrug my shoulders as I pull out my phone. A distraction would be good right now. I need to not think about her.

**Jake: Her flight's tomorrow. That's when she's going back.**

I swallow as I read his words. After Sam and Becca left

244

the party last weekend, it was pretty much over. Katie and Jess were furious with me, and Luke walked away in disgust. Jake and I just stood there, trying to figure out what had just happened, trying to see how we were the bad guys in this. I mean, I know I behaved badly, but I wasn't the one that started this. I could see it in Jake's eyes that Sam's words had gotten to him. Just one glance at Becca showed how messed up she was, and I don't know why. It can't just be because we broke up. There has to be something else. The spark I always loved about her was completely extinguished. I type out a quick response.

**Me: Did you see her?**

**Jake: Yeah. She seemed a bit better than she was at the party, but still. I don't know what's going on with her but there's something not right.**

I glance away from my phone for a second, telling myself not to do it, telling myself she's brought everything on herself and doesn't deserve my sympathy. I tell myself I don't owe her anything—but then her face flashes in my mind, and I make a decision. I shove my stuff into my gym bag and sling it over my shoulders.

"Cover for me," I tell the guys over my shoulder, already on the way to the door. "I'll be back before practice tomorrow."

"Where you going?" Evan calls after me.

"Home."

# CHAPTER 26

*Becca*

THE DOORBELL RINGS, AND I PUT DOWN THE BOX of Chinese food I'm forcing down. I went a little overboard when ordering dinner, and though I've eaten way more in the last couple days than I have in months, there's still no way I can get through the mountain of food I've ordered. I wipe my mouth and hurry to the door, skidding on the wooden floors as I reach the doorknob and throw it open.

Ryan stands in front of me, and I freeze. My mouth is open, but nothing comes out.

"Hey," he says, awkwardly shifting on his feet. His eyes dart to my face and then look away again.

"Hey." I finally manage to breathe. *What is he doing here? Why would he be here?*

Neither of us says anything for at least a minute as we just stand there, watching each other.

Finally Ryan clears his throat. "Um, can I come in?"

I nod my head immediately, stepping back and letting him through the door. My heart's started hammering in my chest, and when he brushes past me and makes contact just for the briefest of seconds, I feel like I'm going to pass out. I need to calm down. *This doesn't mean anything.*

He starts to make his way down the hallway but then pauses as though he's unsure what to do. My heart aches at this. There was a time when my house was like his, and he'd move freely around without a second thought. Seeing him stand in the hallway, unsure about where to go, hurts more than I thought it would. I nod my head toward the kitchen and walk past him, leading the way. I hover by the stool I was eating at while he stands in the doorway, glancing around. He's bigger than I remember, taller somehow. Maybe it's because I don't ever let myself stand close enough to any guys anymore to notice the difference, but he feels so much bigger than me, he looks even more ripped than he used to be, and it makes me wonder exactly how hard he's been working out over the summer. The white t-shirt he wears clings to his abs and shows off his tan. The sweatpants he's thrown on sit low on his hips and the muscles in his arms are tense as he clutches the baseball cap he's had since high school. His hair is all messed up, the way it gets when he's been thinking about something and has been raking his hands through it.

"Are your parents in?" he eventually asks.

I shake my head. "My mom has a work dinner and my dad went with her."

He nods. "You've changed your hair from the other night."

My hand flies to my hair automatically, feeling

self-conscious. "Yeah." I pause. "I figured it was time for a change."

He nods and glances away. He's still kind of hovering in the doorway, and it's so uncomfortable, it's painful. "Do you want to sit down?" I eventually ask.

He glances back at me and offers me a wry smile before walking over and sitting on the stool across from me at the counter. His eyes briefly meet mine, and it takes my breath away. He's always had the most beautiful eyes. Back when I was dumb and naive and thought nothing could ever break us up, I remember telling him I hoped our kids had his eye color. He just laughed and told me he hoped if we had a girl, she'd look nothing like me, or he was going to lock her up for thirty years.

He still doesn't say anything, and I'm so scared he's just going to leave again that I blurt out, "I thought you'd gone to training camp." There's no point in pretending I don't know that's where he is, pretending I didn't listen intently when Katie called and dropped that into conversation.

He nods. "I did. Been up there all week."

"Oh." I frown. "Is it close by?" He'll have practice tomorrow too, so it must be close by, or else why would he be here?

He shakes his head. "No, it's a three-hour drive."

*Oh.*

Ryan smirks. "I'll have to head straight back after this."

*This.* My heart skips a beat. *What is this?*

"Jake came to see you?" he asks.

I nod. I was almost as surprised to see Jake at my door as I am to see Ryan now. He had a pizza in his hand and we ate a couple slices together. We didn't really say much but when he was leaving, he went all quiet and told me he was sorry he hasn't been around and that he hoped everything was okay with me. Then he crushed me into a hug before telling me he'd speak to me soon. "Yeah, at lunchtime."

Before he can say anything more, his stomach growls loudly. My eyes flash to his. "Are you hungry?"

He shakes his head. "I'm fine."

I hesitate for a second before I point at the Chinese food. "There's a ton of Chinese food left. I went a bit crazy when ordering." He glances over at the food but shakes his head. He doesn't want to take anything from me, I can tell. I sigh and try again. "It will only get thrown away if you don't eat it."

His eyes flit back to the food. "You ordered all that just for yourself?"

I nod. "Yeah." I pause. "I know I need to put on some weight, so I've been trying to eat more."

His eyes are back on my face in a second, only this time it's like they're searching for something, but I don't know what. "Have you been ill?" he asks. "Is that why you're so skinny?"

I don't know how to answer that, but I find myself nodding my head. "Yeah." It's the only way of saying it. "But I'm getting better now."

His eyes stay fixed on my face, "You sure you're okay, Becs?"

My heart slams in my throat at that old nickname. It's what he used to call me when we were little kids. He's the only one that calls me that. The only one that's ever called me that. It's not often he uses it, but when he does it has always made me feel closer to him. His eyes search mine and there's so much I want to tell him, so much I want to say, but I can't. Instead I make myself stand up and bring the takeout over to him. "You should eat. If you've been playing all day, you'll be starving."

"Bec—"

"It doesn't mean anything, Ryan, I know that, but you should eat. There's spicy chicken there too." That's his favorite. It's a habit I've gotten into since we first started dating—ordering that every time because I know it's his favorite. It's a habit I haven't wanted to break.

He nods and cautiously takes the fork I hold out to him then digs in. I sit back on my stool and watch as Ryan demolishes the food; it's all gone within minutes. When he's finished, he puts down his fork, leans back, takes a deep breath, and offers me a wary smile. "You're probably wondering why I'm here."

I shrug. Of course I am, but I don't care. He's here, and he's talking to me and not shouting at me, and right now, that's all I care about.

"I heard you were flying out tomorrow."

I nod, my heart pounding. *He's heard about me? He cares enough to have people tell him stuff about me?*

He sighs. "I owe you an apology."

That, I wasn't expecting. "No, Ryan, it's fine."

He shakes his head. "No, I do. The way I spoke to you the other night was unforgivable. I've been feeling guilty about it ever since. I was drunk and…I dunno…" He trails off. "It was the first time I'd seen you in so long, and I was just being an idiot." He pauses. "I know there's nothing going on between you and Luke, and even if there were, it's none of my business." That hurts. The thought that I could be getting with one of his friends and he wouldn't care, hurts. "I should never have said that stuff about you being good. That was rude and disrespectful, and I'm sorry."

"It's okay," I manage to whisper.

"I swear I don't talk about you like that. That was a one-time thing. I'd never talk about what we were like when we were alone together." He actually blushes slightly. "When we were in bed together. That's personal stuff, just between us."

I nod, my whole body on edge. It warms my heart that that stuff will always be between us, that nothing can take it away from us, no matter what has happened. That's something we'll always have.

"And Kelly." Any warmth I was feeling leaves my body at the mention of her name. "She should not have called you a whore, and I shouldn't have let her. I'm really, really sorry, Becca." He sighs. "I think she was just nervous and drunk and was trying to prove something."

I nod, but I'm not going to say it's okay. It's not okay that his girlfriend thought she could call me a whore in front of all my friends.

He stares at me for a moment, his blue eyes piercing mine, and I've never wanted to go to someone so badly in my life. I'm so desperate to be in his arms, to be absorbed by him so I can forget everything that's happened in the last nine months and be back with the only man I feel I'll ever love.

"You're not with Mulligan?" he asks suddenly.

I shake my head violently. "No. Absolutely not. I haven't spoken to him in months," I tell him.

He nods. "That's what Mason said." *He's asked Mason*

251

*about me? What does that mean?* "Are you seeing anyone else?"

"No. There's no one else," I reply.

He nods, glancing around again. Seconds pass, and still he doesn't say anything, but he doesn't make a move to leave.

"So, you and Kelly then?" I ask. I know I have no right to question him, but it hurts that he picked her, that he picked her so soon after me.

He shrugs. "It just kinda happened. I'm sorry." He pauses. "I'm sorry about that day you saw us together. I wasn't thinking properly at the time."

I nod. I wasn't thinking properly at the time either. All I could think about was what I'd lost. At least now I don't think about it every minute of the day—only every hour. I want to move past the subject of Kelly Taylor and me finding them in bed together. "It looks like you've done really well with the team."

"You've been following my games?" He sounds surprised.

"Of course, Ryan. Everyone says you'll definitely get drafted."

He shrugs modestly. "We'll see."

"Kelly's going to move with you wherever you go, huh?" He doesn't reply, and I can't seem to stop. "You must be pretty serious," I continue, torturing myself.

"Yeah, well, some people actually want to be with me, will actually put me first," he says bitterly.

It's like a punch to the face, hearing that he thinks I don't care.

"I take it all back, Ryan," I tell him. "About living on the East Coast and having my own life away from you." My voice cracks, and tears spring to my eyes. "It doesn't mean anything without you. Nothing matters without you." He's gazing at me so intently, like he's trying to read me, trying to see if what I'm saying is true. "I miss you so much, Ryan. I'd do anything if you'd just give us another chance."

"Do you know how much I loved you, Becca? Do you have any idea?" he yells, all his composure gone.

I blink and try to stop my mouth from shaking. *Loved.* He said loved, as in past tense.

"Fuck!" he continues, like he's annoyed he's revealed his true feelings. "I loved you since I was a kid, Becca. Since I was a little kid! I have been crazy about you for as long as I can remember. I'd have done anything for you Becca, anything!" He pauses and looks me in the eye. "Why'd you have to do it? You ruined everything."

I shrug my shoulders helplessly. I hate seeing the pain in his eyes and knowing I caused it. We sit there in silence for a few minutes. I don't know how to make this better. I don't know what to do.

"I want you to know how much I loved you too, Ryan," I tell him, my voice shaking. I want him to know this. I need him to know this. "I know you sometimes thought it was more you than me. You thought I didn't care, but I did. I swear to you, Ryan. I loved you so, so much."

He smiles wistfully. "And yet you were the one who went looking elsewhere."

*No! No, I didn't go looking anywhere. All I wanted, all I've ever wanted is to be with you.* But I can't say that. I can't change what started almost a year ago.

"I'm so sorry, Ryan. I love you. I love you so much.

Please, let's try again."

He shakes his head sadly at me. "I can't, Becca. Every time I think I can get over it, I picture you with him, and I can't get it out of my head. It's all I thought about for weeks."

"Ryan—"

"No Becca," he interrupts me. "I can't go through that again. I nearly fucking lost everything after I found out about you. I was a total mess. All I did was drink and drink, trying to forget, but I couldn't. Nothing helped me forget, and I nearly got kicked off the team over it."

"What?" I whisper. I didn't know that.

He sighs and looks at me. "I stopped caring when we broke up. I just wanted to forget about you and him, so I just drank and drank. Eventually Coach told me that if I didn't start showing up to training, they'd put the backup in instead of me. I nearly lost the starting spot."

My eyes are wide. "I'm so sorry. I didn't know."

He shrugs. "I told everyone not to tell you. I didn't want you to know anything about me."

Tears prick my eyes. He actually went out of his way to tell people not to talk to me about him. He was that desperate for me to know nothing about him.

His eyes find mine and he shrugs helplessly. "I can't go through that again. I can't risk it. I just can't."

I nod, looking away, and tears start to stream down my face. It really is over. It doesn't matter how I feel about him or how he used to feel or still does feel about me. He's not going to give me another chance, and I have to accept that.

I hear his stool scrape back, and I look up to see he's standing. His eyes are already on me, and he's frowning, like it hurts him to see me upset. He steps toward me, which is all the invitation I need. I fall onto him, wrapping my arms around him, burrowing my head in his chest and squeezing like I'll never let him go. He lets me cry. He doesn't move away, and eventually he cautiously wraps his arms loosely around me, but it's not like before. It's not the hugs from before, when he pulled me into him and made me feel like I was everything to him and he'd never let me go. After I've pulled myself together, I step back and look up at him.

"I'm sorry, I shouldn't have done that," I tell him, wiping my tears away with the back of my hand.

"I should go," he says.

I nod and watch him walk toward the door. He hovers in the doorway for just a minute, looking back at me.

"I love you," I tell him. I do; I don't think I'll ever stop loving him.

He shakes his head sadly, looking genuinely pained. "It's not enough though, Becca," he tells me. "It's just not enough."

# CHAPTER 27

*Becca*

I'M IN THE STUDENT CAFETERIA IN THE MAIN humanities building on campus, staring down at my plate of food. Tina was supposed to meet me here twenty minutes ago. I was very against meeting her here, but she insisted that I needed to stop being a hermit this year and that whatever drama went down last year was totally forgotten about now. When I saw her for the first time at the start of this year, she couldn't hide her excitement at my new hair. When she asked me to go for dinner with some of her friends during the first week and I actually said yes, I thought she was going to pass out, and she hasn't stopped pushing for me to do things ever since. I'm taking it slow, but I'm starting to try to get my life back.

When she first asked me to meet her on campus for lunch, my initial response was an immediate no. But, she can be incredibly persuasive, which is why I'm now sitting at an empty table, waiting for her to show up. A message flashes on my phone telling me she's been held up in study group and will be at least another twenty minutes. I sigh in annoyance and glance around. No one is looking at me, and I realize Tina was right; my paranoia about everyone gossiping was just that, paranoia. No one gives a crap; they all have their own shit to deal with.

A wave of noise hits the room. I look up and freeze when I see a group from the football team walking in. Robbie Mulligan is at the front, laughing and joking, and they're heading my way. This is the first time I've seen him since I went to his house to get him to drop the charges, and to my horror, tears spring to my eyes. I quickly blink them away. In a panic, I look around and realize they're heading to the empty tables just across from me. I thought I had this under control. I thought I could handle this. I've been trying so hard to sort myself out, but I didn't think about actually seeing him. I'm tempted to get up and run, but I force myself to stay. He does not have this power over me. I have just as much right to be here as he does, and I will not run away. Still, my heart starts beating faster in my chest, and I stare down at my plate. I may not be willing to run away, but I'm definitely hoping they won't notice me before I get a chance to get out of here inconspicuously.

Suddenly the noise dims, and I just know they've stopped in front of me. I can feel the stares. I glance up, and Robbie's standing there, staring down at me like he's surprised to see me. His eyes flicker over my appearance before coming back to my face. I swallow hard, refusing to look away first.

"Hey McKenzie," he says, looking around him at his

friends. He's nervous, I can tell. He doesn't want to ignore me in front of them, because to them, I'm someone he slept with, I'm the way he managed to fuck with Ryan Jackson—but he doesn't know where I stand with him now. He doesn't know if I'm still the same as I was last year or if I've changed my mind. A few of the guys he's with, ones whose names I don't know, have continued to the table, but a few are standing behind him. They're all looking at us, and I feel like my area of the cafeteria has suddenly gotten very quiet.

"You look good, McKenzie," Robbie tells me. His voice sounds loud, but he doesn't sound as cocky as usual. His hand is clenching nervously around the gym bag he's holding, and that gives me a bit of strength. If he honestly believed he'd done nothing wrong, he wouldn't be nervous. He'd be making suggestive comments and insulting Ryan like he used to. He wouldn't be uncomfortable. He clears his throat, his head turning briefly to look at the dude next to him. He forces a cocky grin onto his face. "We should go out sometime."

I force myself to look into his eyes—the dark, cold, unfeeling eyes I pleaded with in that bedroom. "Get away from me," I say calmly, my voice loud and clear, my outward appearance not reflecting the pounding in my chest. "And stay away from me." His jaw sets, and I see anger flash in his eyes. The arrogant fucker probably sees this as me publicly rejecting him rather than me being desperate for my rapist to get the hell away from me. He turns abruptly and joins his teammates, who are smirking at him, clearly enjoying his embarrassment. I pick my bag up off the ground, getting ready to leave, when a tray is set down across from me. I look up and see Mason there. He looks over at the table of his teammates, who are watching him curiously, and he shrugs and sits down across from me. Bernie is with him too, and he walks around the table and puts his tray down next to me, giving me a lazy smile as he sits down. A couple of their teammates who I'm pretty certain are also defensive players join them at the table.

I'm so surprised, I don't know what to do. Last I knew, Mason couldn't stand me. I look around in astonishment, and I'm suddenly so nervous being this close to Mason, worried I'll somehow mess up this opportunity, that when I go to grab my drink, I knock it over. Mason smirks and hands me a couple napkins.

"He's right, you know," Mason starts conversationally. "You look way better than you did when I saw you at that party at the end of summer." Jessica's party, where he awkwardly made small talk before disappearing and then watched along with everyone else while Ryan and Kelly went off on me.

I glance down at my body and realize he's right. The meals that initially were forced down my throat are now welcomed, and I know I've filled out. I'm still not quite the size I was before Ryan and I broke up, but compared to where I was a month ago, it's a huge difference. I look healthier too. My tan from the summer is lingering, and the bags under my eyes have started to fade. I am looking better.

"Thanks," I tell him.

He sighs and glances at his teammates. They take the hint and start talking about some party they went to the night before. He glances back at me.

"I'm sorry," he tells me.

My heart thuds in my chest. "What for?"

He sighs. "I'm sorry for the way I was last year, after you

and Ryan broke up."

*Oh.* I shake my head. "Mason, it's fine. You didn't do anything."

"No, Becca. I wasn't there. We're friends, and I should have been there for you. I know how hard it was for you, and I just acted like it was your fault and you deserved everything you got."

My mouth falls open. He's being brutally honest, and I wasn't expecting it.

"Look, Becca. I was pretty pissed about what you did to Ryan, and you know I can't stand Mulligan." He glances behind him, sending Mulligan a dirty look. A shiver runs down my spine when I realize Mulligan's watching us. His eyes flash to mine, and I know he hates having some of his teammates sitting over here, choosing to sit away from him. I quickly turn my attention back to Mason.

"Mason—"

"I'm sorry, Becca. Ultimately, your breakup was none of my business, and it was pretty obvious you really needed a friend last year, and I should have been there."

"Too fucking right," Bernie chimes in next to me, and I notice for the first time that he's been listening and not joining in the conversation with his teammates. I glance at him, but he's too busy glaring at Mason to notice.

Mason rolls his eyes at Bernie before looking back at me. "He told me he saw you," he says, nodding toward Bernie. "And that you weren't doing good. I didn't get it until I saw you at Jessica's."

"It's fine, Mason."

"I really am sorry."

I smile. "It's honestly okay."

He grins back at me, and I feel hope building inside me—just a little bit, but still. I know things will never be how they were before, and I know Ryan will never give us another chance, but Mason apologizing makes me realize that maybe I can get some of it back. Maybe I haven't lost everything.

I push my plate toward him. "You want a fry?" I ask. He grins back, reaches over, and grabs five, just like he always would have done before.

A burst of laughter erupts from behind Mason, and I know without even looking that they're talking about me. Mason glances around, annoyed, and tells them to shut up. He turns back to me, but not before I overhear the words "sloppy seconds". It's the second time I've heard that phrase in the last month, but it doesn't hurt nearly as much coming from Mulligan as it did from Ryan.

"Ignore them," he tells me.

"Look Mason, you don't have to sit with me. You can go sit with them."

"Shut up," he says. "I can't stand Mulligan. He's a total asshole, and I only put up with him for the team. Ryan's my boy. I'm Team Ryan."

I look at him and want to tell him there's no need to take teams like it's a competition. There'll never be anyone but Ryan for me, but of course I don't say that.

"How is Ryan?" I ask. "Have you spoken to him since he went back to Cal State?"

Mason shifts uncomfortably. It's pretty obvious he doesn't want to talk about Ryan to me. Eventually, after a pause, he nods. "Yeah, just briefly. He seems pretty good. Just focusing on football, you know?"

I nod.

"Is he still with Kelly?"

It's out of my mouth before I can stop it. I don't even know why I ask. I'm still looking at Ryan's social media pages daily, and she's constantly putting up pictures of both of them together. I know they're still together.

Mason glances at Bernie before looking back at me. "Yeah, they're still together."

There's another burst of laughter from behind, and I turn and see Liam stand up and head over to our table. He stands behind the chair next to Mason and looks at me.

"Do you mind if I sit here, Becca?" he asks.

I shake my head, surprised he's left that table for this. I'm also touched that he actually asked my permission before sitting down. "No, no. Sit." He plops into the chair.

"Mulligan's a prick," he announces to no one in particular.

"Preaching to the choir," Mason responds, smirking at me. I surprise myself by smirking back, something the old me would have done.

"How are you, Becca?" Liam asks, surprising me further. I look for something mocking in his eyes, but all I see is concern, like he genuinely wants to know how I am.

"I'm good," I tell him. "Thanks," I say after a pause.

He smiles, and I find myself smiling back. This kid is really sweet.

"So," Bernie says loudly, drawing my attention to him. "We're having a party at our place tonight. You should come," he tells me.

I immediately shake my head. I may be trying to force

myself to not be a hermit, but there's no way I'm going to a football party. I'd rather die first.

"No, I can't."

"Come on, we'll look after you, give you the VIP treatment."

I roll my eyes as Mason frowns over in Bernie's direction. "I really can't." I smile at him. "Thanks for the offer though." He winks back at me, and I remember how nice he was to me that day last year when he bought me lunch. He really is a great guy.

I reach down and pick up my bag; I have class, and Tina will just have to see me at home.

"I've got to go. It was really good to see you." I look directly at Mason. "See you around?"

He nods and grins at me, and I walk out of the cafeteria, not feeling quite as alone as I have been.

# CHAPTER 28

*Becca*

COUNSELING IS BETTER THAN I EVER DREAMED IT would be. I could kick myself for not going earlier, but in truth, I don't think I was ready. The first day I walked in, I wanted to bolt right away. I was so nervous that my whole body was shaking, and I had no idea what to expect. I was terrified that somebody I knew would see me, and that I had no right to be there. Those feelings vanished almost immediately when a young woman, probably in her early thirties, greeted me warmly and asked how I took my coffee. She made me feel at ease immediately. She didn't look at me like I was this strange specimen that needed to be treated with kid gloves; she simply walked me into a side room, poured me a coffee, and told me to take a seat. Then we talked, but not about me. We didn't talk about me at all. Instead she focused on the weather, told me about a wedding she'd been to that weekend, and about her daughter, who was just starting kindergarten. She was one of those people who can just put you at ease without doing anything at all; she made me feel relaxed and calm, and not like the completely useless, worthless fool I've felt like since Robbie broke my life.

Before I knew it, an hour had passed, and she told me she had another appointment, so we would have to leave it there. Then she explained that her name was Lucy, and she was the psychiatrist there who runs the counseling group. She informed me that they offer private one-on-one sessions once a week and also hold a weekly support group; Lucy recommended I attend both. She said it was helpful to know I'm not alone, and that it's good to see how other people deal with sexual assault. She gave me the group schedule, told me everything was completely confidential, and said she hoped she'd see me back there next week.

She did.

I haven't shared my story with the group yet. I'm not even sure I will, to be honest. I mean, I'd change the names and the details—I wouldn't want anyone to be able to link it back to me—but still, it's a big leap of faith to share my story, and nobody pushes me. Nobody makes me feel bad that I keep quiet or look at the ground when Lucy asks if anyone else wants to share. It's good to know that there are other people out there who have been through this. Other people who have moved past this and aren't letting it consume their every waking moment. Other people who are now using their experiences to help others. It's fascinating to listen to everyone else's stories, and sometimes it's just plain heartbreaking.

One poor girl is only seventeen, from one of the bad neighborhoods on the outskirts of town. She wears a nose ring and her clothes are cheap, and I knew just by looking at her that her life has been harder than mine has ever been. And I was ashamed, ashamed that I've wallowed in my own misery for the better part of a year and haven't been looking at how lucky I am in many ways. This poor girl was raped by one of her parents' friends. She told her mom, who just insisted she was lying. He still visits her house once a week, and her mom makes sure she sits at the table with them for dinner. It was the way she told her story that affected me the most. The way it was so matter-of-fact. She wasn't looking for sympathy or expecting anything from us in return. She was just telling us about her life while I sat there and listened in horror.

Watching Lucy with her was amazing. The way Lucy is with everyone is amazing, and so inspiring. She's at ease with everyone and just seems to know how to make people feel safe and comforted. She always knows what questions to ask and when to stop pushing. She has this innate sense of calm that she seems to pass on to everyone in her presence. She told me she's been doing this for five years, and she does it because she feels like she makes a difference. She definitely does. It must be amazing to know you can really make a difference in someone's life. I'm in complete awe of her.

I've been going for five weeks, and I'm starting to realize this isn't something I did. It isn't something I chose. This is something that was done to me, and I need to stop blaming myself for it. I get it, I really do, but it's easier said than done.

I just got home from today's session after spending the day in the library. I'm determined to do well in my studies this year. This is my last year in college, and I don't want the previous three years to amount to nothing. I want to do well, and I'm prepared to put in the hard work to get there. To be fair, it's not like I have much else to do. I might be way more sociable than I was for most of last year, but I'm still pretty reluctant to do anything that I think might put me in danger. It's pathetic, but I now consider people I don't know to be dangerous. I know that will change. After talking to Lucy, I know this is normal, and I know that as time goes on, I'll get more comfortable in unfamiliar surroundings and with unfamiliar people, but right now, I can't push myself to get there.

Tina wanted me to go out with her tonight. I could see the hope in her face when she asked me, but I declined. I've stopped drinking completely. I had a couple beers when I was away for the summer with Sam, but that's only because she wouldn't drink when I did, and I knew she wouldn't leave my side, because she knew the truth. If I went out with Tina, she'd assume we'd be knocking back the shots like we used to, and I don't want to have that discussion with her. It's not that she'd mind me not drinking, but I just don't want to put myself in that environment. It's the last place I would want to be.

I pull out my phone and order a pizza from my favorite local place, then go sit on the sofa and put on Netflix. I surf through the options until I find a film I want to watch, settling on a British romantic comedy I've never heard of before, and I'm about twenty minutes in when my pizza arrives. I settle back down, taking a bite of pepperoni, and feel as close to content as I've felt in a long time. I don't give a damn that it's a Saturday night and I'm spending it on my own. I finally feel like I'm moving forward and am starting to get a grip on things.

I'm fully asleep on the sofa when my phone starts ringing

next to me. I blink awake, groggy about where I am, then realize I dozed off in front of the TV. I squint at the clock on the wall and see it's after midnight. Yawning, I grab my phone, sitting up in surprise when I see it's Maddy.

"Hello?"

"Becca?" The noise in the background is so loud I can barely hear her. "Becca, is that you?" I roll my eyes. *Who else would be answering my phone?* Clearly she's had a few drinks tonight.

"Hey, I'm here," I tell her.

"Oh, thank God," she says dramatically. "I didn't know what to do."

I sit up straighter in my seat. "What's wrong? What's happened?"

"Oh, it's nothing too bad. It's just, well, Tina's here, and she's completely wasted, as in, she's thrown up and can barely keep her eyes open."

"Fuck, how did she get so bad?"

"Oh, you know, shots."

I shake my head. Tina is a shots fan. Every time she wakes up with a horrendous hangover, she swears she's not going to do it again. Then she does.

"Is she okay?" I say, standing up and looking around for my jacket.

"Not really. She's upset and was crying and stuff."

"What?" That's unlike Tina; she's not an emotional drunk.

"Can you come get her?"

"Yeah." I'm already pulling my boots on. "Where are you guys?" There's a pause on the other end of the line, and I think she must have lost reception. "Hello? Maddy?"

"Yeah, I'm here."

"So where are you?"

She sighs. "Well, that's the thing. We're at Carrington's."

# CHAPTER 29

*Becca*

I PULL INTO THE PARKING LOT OUTSIDE CARRINGTON'S and reach for my phone to check the time; it's nearly one in the morning. Then I look up and take in the scene in front of me.

Carrington's sits between a restaurant and a clothing shop on the main road that runs through Addington, the town where Southern U in based. To be honest, I've never seen what the fuss is about when it comes to Carrington's. It's a bit of a dive bar. I've only been three times—twice with Tina when we were freshmen and she was desperate to make sure we weren't missing out on anything, and then last year for Mason's birthday. The whole place stinks of fried food, and huge TV screens cover every wall, showing every sport imaginable. The beer is cheap, and the fact that it's a favorite hangout of the football team means it's never lacking college kids. Looking at it now, my fingers clench anxiously. I know the football team will be in there, the whole football team, and that means Robbie Mulligan is in there.

There looks to be at least thirty people in line outside the bar, and most of them are girls—girls who are dressed to impress with high heels, tight dresses, and big hair. The whole scene makes me want to throw up. I do not want to be here.

I get out of my car and slam the door behind me before quickly locking it and crossing the road. I walk straight past the line and approach the bouncer. The guy, who in truth isn't that much taller than me, obviously thinks he wields major power because he picks who can and cannot enter. He looks me up and down. I'm wearing black skinny jeans with a loose-fitting white t-shirt and a khaki jacket. I've got flat black boots on my feet, my hair is pulled back into a messy high ponytail, and there's not a scrap of makeup on my face. I'm definitely not the usual for this type of night.

"Hi," I say to the bouncer quietly. "I think Bernie Matthews put my name on a list," I tell him, referring to the text that Maddy sent me. I guess they knew what it would be like in here, and the football team holds major sway. They know the reason half the people are here tonight is because the football team is here, and Bernie Matthews holds more sway than most. If he tells them to let me in, they'll let me in, no questions.

"Name?"

"Becca McKenzie," I reply, trying to ignore the nerves that are building in my stomach. "Can I go in?"

He moves aside obligingly and I step past him, ignoring the bitchy comments I hear from the line behind me.

I take my first step inside the bar, and it's like walking

into a sauna. A wave of noise assaults my ears; the place is crammed, completely and utterly packed. It's filled wall to wall with half-naked girls, the whole football team, and probably anyone and everyone they've ever been associated with.

It's so crowded, it immediately makes me anxious—well, more anxious. I've never been a fan of big crowds in tight spaces. I've gotten better—I kind of had to get used to it in college—but looking around now, I know this is the last place I want to be.

I glance around, wondering how on earth I'm going to find Tina in this crowd. Even on my tiptoes, I can't see past the mass of tall football players. Then my gaze lands on Bernie. He's standing just to the side of the door with two girls who seem to be hanging off his every word. Seriously, they're staring at him like he's food and they haven't eaten in weeks. They're flipping their hair and fluttering their eyelashes, and it's all a bit nauseating.

He must feel my gaze because he looks up, and a wide smile crosses his face. He instantly steps away from the girls and moves toward me. "Hey. I said I'd wait for you so you'd know where we are."

I smile gratefully. At least now I don't have to wander around aimlessly trying to find them. I could try calling Maddy, but I doubt she'd hear me over the noise in here.

The two girls beside him shoot me dirty looks, and I swear I hear one of them mutter "slut" under her breath. My head snaps around to face them, but they've already walked away.

Bernie rolls his eyes. "Ignore them," he says, dipping his head next to my ear so I can hear him. "They're just jealous that you've arrived having made no effort and still look a million times better than them."

I roll me eyes. "Always so smooth, Matthews." He grins back at me, the full Bernie Matthews charm shining brightly. I know he's trying to make me feel better, but there's still the niggling doubt in my mind that they know who I am, that they saw the game last year, the one where my private life was splashed all over the TV.

Bernie jerks his head to the far corner of the bar, near the entrance that leads to the bathrooms at the back. "Come on. She's over there."

His right hand reaches out to touch the small of my back, and I breathe heavily through my nose, forcing myself not to flinch as he nudges me in the right direction. *This is Bernie, for Christ's sake.* We don't get very far. I try to dodge and duck my way through the mass of people, but it's so crazy busy that there's nowhere to go. My polite "excuse me's" are being ignored, and I'm getting more and more irritated by the drunk students surrounding me. I can almost feel Bernie's laughter from behind me, and sure enough, when I turn to face him, he's smirking down at me in amusement. He rolls his eyes and lets out a quick laugh before he grabs my shoulders and turns us so that it's him in front of me. He reaches back, grips my hand, and starts walking. Miraculously, the sea of people parts for him, and he pulls me along behind him. *I guess a six-foot-four wall of muscle is more effective than me.*

I see a couple people sending us curious glances, but I keep my eyes fixed ahead and ignore them. I'm so over football groupies and their pathetic need to be near a football player. I had enough of that bullshit when I was with Ryan, and I don't need it now when I'm just talking to a friend.

Finally Bernie gives my hand one last tug, and we break into some space where we can actually move around a bit. He lifts our hands that are still attached. "Is this okay?"

I snort and pull my hand back. "I would have let you carry me if it meant getting through that crowd quicker."

He grins in response and takes a step toward me, a playful look in his eyes. My eyes widen, and I change the subject before he even thinks about picking me up. "Why's it so busy?"

Bernie stares back at me like I just said the dumbest thing in the world. "Seriously?" I shrug. *How would I know why it's so busy?* "We won tonight, beat the Blue Tide. We destroyed them."

*Oh.* I really couldn't care less who they beat. Suddenly, chanting breaks out behind me. I register what they're chanting, and my throat tightens. Mulligan—they're chanting his name. When I look over, he's surrounded by his offense and has everyone around him cheering for him. It's the first time I've seen him in weeks, and just the sight of him makes me want to run screaming out of this place. I turn away quickly, knowing he's too occupied to notice me. *I'm here for Tina. I need to find Tina.*

Bernie's watching me though, and I know he noticed my gaze. "He had a good night," he tells me. "Hasn't fucking shut up about it since." I know he added the last part to make me feel better, and I plaster a small smile on my face because I know it's what he expects, even if smiling is the last thing I want to do.

My eyes turn to the corner, searching for my friend. I just

want to get out of here. Bernie turns and walks toward a corner, and I finally see Mason and Maddy standing with their backs to me, looking down at someone. I make my way over, and when Mason sees me, relief crosses his face. He steps aside, and I see Tina.

She's not looking good.

She's slumped over with her chin on her chest. Her dark blonde hair looks sweaty and tangled as it hangs over her face, and it looks like she's spilled various drinks down her cream-colored dress. Bits of vomit are splashed across the hem of it, too, and I try not to wince as I step closer. I can only imagine how bad she's going to feel tomorrow.

I crouch down in front of her so I'm level with her, ignoring the stench of vomit that's coming off her.

"Hey T," I say softly.

Somehow she hears me over the blare of the music, and she lifts her head. "You came," she whispers.

I chuckle softly. "Of course I came."

"But you came here."

My chest tightens, but I push past it. "Come on, T. I'd do anything for you, you know that."

"I'm sorry," she whispers as tears pool in her eyes and start dripping down her face.

"Hey," I say, alarmed. "Hey, it's okay, T. We all get drunk sometimes."

"But I made you come here," she says with a loud sob, and then I get it—she's brought me to the hub of Southern U football, to Robbie's domain.

I shake my head, refusing to think about it. "It's fine."

She shakes her head violently, and I feel Mason shift

275

beside me. I'm suddenly incredibly aware that he, Bernie, and Maddy can probably all hear this conversation. "No. I shouldn't have come. I know you would never want to come here, and then I drank too much, and you had to come get me." She lets out another sob, and I'm worried she's going to start crying hysterically any minute. She sits up straighter. "I haven't spoken to him, I swear Becca. I haven't even looked at him." I let a ghost of a smile play on my lips. That's her way of being loyal to me. She's never had a problem being around Robbie before, and even though, as far as she's concerned, we slept together, she knows I hate him with a passion now, and that's enough for her to ignore him.

"T, it's fine," I reassure her.

More tears fall down her face, and she looks like her world's ending. "I don't want you to be sad anymore, Becca. You're so sad, Becca, all the time."

"Shush," I tell her, trying to calm her down. The alcohol is not helping. "I'm fine."

"No," she says fiercely, wiping away her tears and sitting up even straighter. "You've been so sad ever since you and Ryan split up."

I shake my head. "Stop," I tell her. I do not want to get into this now, not in front of Mason, but she's suddenly full of life.

"I hear you crying in your room sometimes. You think I can't hear you, but I can. You act like everything's fine, but it's not. You're a good person, Becca. You don't deserve to feel like this." My face burns, even though it's only Tina that can see me. I didn't know she could hear me cry. Tina's eyes suddenly flash to Mason in anger. "You need to tell your friend to forgive her. You need to tell him she's always sad now, and it's his fault."

"Tina," I hiss, panicked. I can't believe she's saying all this. She's probably wanted to say it for a long time, and now that she's drunk, she has the nerve.

She turns back to me, and the fight leaves her eyes. Her body slumps back in her seat. "I don't get it, Becca," she tells me. "You hate Robbie, you always have. I don't know why you did it." She rushes on before I can come up with an answer. "It's my fault. If I hadn't left you to go dance with that guy at the party, it never would have happened." I'm shaking my head before I know what I'm doing. This is not her fault; none of this is anyone's fault but Robbie's. I know that now. I can't believe she thinks she's partly responsible for this. "And you had those bruises, Becca."

I stand abruptly at this. "She's drunk," I say, knowing Mason, Bernie, and Maddy heard that. I keep my eyes fixed on Tina, who is back to quietly crying in the booth. "She's just drunk." I can feel three sets of eyes on me, and I feel more exposed than I have in months. I have buried it. I've buried everything, and with a few drunken words, Tina's managed to rip me wide open. "I'll go get her some water."

Mason steps in my way. "What bruises?" he asks. His face is unreadable.

I force myself to roll my eyes and plaster a smirk on my face. "She's drunk, Mase. Everyone talks shit when they're drunk. There were no bruises."

I don't stop to see if he believes me. I step around him and head toward the bar. I walk quickly over there, grateful that it's slightly less crowded. I turn back and see that Mason and Bernie are still watching me; Maddy's more concerned with dealing with Tina. Bernie says something to Mason, and he looks away. Then they both return their focus to Tina. I pray she's back in her drunken stupor and they don't drill her with questions about me. I know Mason doesn't get it; he's never gotten why I hooked up with Robbie, but I'm not prepared to have that conversation with him, not when things are finally getting back to normal between us.

I reach the bar, but that too is packed. It's at least four people deep, and I know it'll take me forever to get served the usual way. I stare at it hopelessly before moving over to where the glasses are being collected. Luckily there's a guy loading the dishwasher there, and he agrees to get me a glass of water when I point out the state my friend is in. I'm just reaching for the outstretched glass when I feel someone step into my space. I look back and see Jones, the guy from the football team who lives with Robbie. He has a sneer on his face, and my heart drops to my stomach. I instantly step away from him.

"Becca McKenzie." He leers down at me. His breath stinks of alcohol. He smells like he's swallowed a brewery, and fear pours into my veins. *Stop it,* I tell myself. *Stop being so scared and pathetic. This is not you. He can't do anything to you. He's just drunk. That's all it is. He's just drunk.* I make to move past him, but he steps in my way. "Fancy seeing you here." He steps forward, and I move back, pressing my back against the area of the bar that holds the empty glasses. I glance quickly behind me, but the guy from earlier is gone. One glance to the side tells me all the bar staff are busy serving the massive crowd to the right. Everyone's drunk and laughing and joking. No one's looking my way. There's no one to help me.

He moves in even closer. "I hear you like football players," he tells me cockily. His breath is way too close to my face, and it smells vile. His eyes are glazed over, like he's taken something.

"Excuse me," I say, my voice barely above a whisper. I try to step to the right, but he just steps in closer to me. I freeze, trying to blink back tears. This is too familiar. This can't happen. I know it can't; I know it's not the same. I'm in a room full of people, but there's no one nearby, no one to help me, no one who cares. He reaches down, takes the water from my hand, and places it on the bar. Then he plants his hand on my waist before sliding it around to the small of my back and pulling me forward against him. My mind flashes back to that night and terror rips through my body, freezing me in place. *No, no, no.*

"I wanna see what all the fuss is about," he tells me gruffly, dropping his hand to my ass and hauling me up against his crotch. *Push him off!* my mind screams at me, but I can't move. I can't think past the terror that has taken over my body. Tears flood my eyes, and I look around desperately. To anyone who cared to look over, we'd just be a couple of college kids hooking up, but this isn't that night. This isn't an empty hall where there's no one around. This is the middle of the bar, and he won't be able to hurt me.

"Get off me," I hiss as my body finally manages to snap out of its freeze. I reach up to his chest and push him away from me, but he doesn't budge. He's too strong, just like they all are, and his grip on me is too firm.

"Aw, what's wrong?" he asks, his head dipping down, way

too close to my mouth. He gives my ass a painful squeeze. "You only go for quarterbacks?"

Suddenly, he's ripped away from me. "Get the fuck off her."

I feel like I can breathe again as I sag back against the bar. I take a couple deep breaths, relief flooding me.

"I was just messing, man," Jones defends himself. That's when I look up, and my blood turns cold. It's Robbie who's pulled him off me.

"Don't fucking go near her again, you hear me?" Robbie commands before giving Jones a hard push, which sends him staggering off into the crowd. Robbie watches him go as I try to back away from him. He turns back to me. "Are you okay?"

*No!* I want to scream. *No! I haven't been okay since the day you lost your fucking mind and raped me in a fucking bedroom to get one over on my boyfriend, just because he can throw a football better than you. No! My life is a mess. I can't sleep, I stopped eating, I am only just getting my life back together after you destroyed it, after you destroyed me!* "Go away," I tell him. My voice is quiet, but he hears it. "Get away from me."

His eyes flash in anger. *Anger! He's actually angry at me?* "I just fucking helped you out there."

Does he actually think I'm going to thank him? He's the reason Jones thought he could pull that bullshit. The Becca of before would have kneed him in the balls and punched his lights out for thinking he could do that. She wouldn't have frozen in fear. She would have fought back, wouldn't have been so scared and weak and pathetic. She wouldn't have to live with fear every day of her life because of what he did to her. *What he did to me!* "Go away," I repeat, my eyes trained on his face.

"You came here, Becca. You know this is a football place."

"You okay?"

I jump out of my skin and see Mason has joined me. *Where the hell was he a few minutes ago?* He's looking warily between me and Robbie. Robbie shoots me one last look of anger then turns and leaves. I release the breath I've been holding and watch him go, not caring what Mason thinks of it. I need to know where Robbie is so I know how far away from him I can stay. He walks over to a crowd from the team, hanging out in the opposite corner. The group breaks for him, the way it did for Bernie, and a few of them shoot me looks. I wonder how many of them saw Robbie pull Jones off me. What Robbie does gets noticed, and I realize that's probably what caught Mason's attention. Then I realize that for Robbie to know what was happening, he'd have to have been watching me. Robbie shakes his head at whatever his teammates say then turns and tugs a beautiful blonde who is hovering nearby over to his side, wrapping his arm around her waist. My stomach tightens at the sight of it. My eyes find hers, and she's already watching me, not unkindly—there's no scorn on her face, just curiosity. My eyes take her in, and she really is beautiful with clear dewy skin and soft blonde curls that fall around her face. I can't tell what color her eyes are, but I'd bet money on them being blue. She looks like an angel, a very, very young angel. Robbie must tighten his arm around her, because her attention is diverted, and she smiles adoringly up at him. I blink rapidly and turn to Mason, who is watching me watch them. I can't read the expression on his face. I would say he thinks I'm jealous, but he looks concerned, not annoyed. He rests a hand on my arm, and this time I can't hide my flinch at the contact.

His eyes widen. "Are you okay?" he asks again.

I sigh. "I'm fine. Can you just help me get Tina out to my car?"

---

It takes an age to get Tina outside. She'd fallen asleep by the time I got back to her, and she really didn't want to move, but the situation helps to get my heartrate under control and I'm able to push the panic of seeing Robbie away. We finally manage to load her into the car without any more tears, and her head rolls to the side against her shoulder. She's back asleep almost instantly. I chuckle softly and close the door behind her. I turn around and send Mason and Bernie a grateful smile before waving them off and walking around to the driver's side.

"Becca?" I look back up, and I'm surprised to find Bernie still there. Mason sends him a look, hesitates for a moment, glances back at me, and then heads back into the bar. "You sure you're gonna be okay getting her back into your apartment?"

*No idea. I guess I'll find out when I get home.* "I'll be fine. Thanks for your help though."

"You sure?"

I grin. "Yeah. I wouldn't want to drag you away from your adoring fans."

He smirks. "I think they can survive without me."

I roll my eyes and go to open the door handle. He still

hasn't moved. I glance back at him, waiting for him to turn and leave, but he just smiles at me and shoves his hands deep into his pockets, rocking back slightly on the heels of his feet. He doesn't make a move to go. "You don't want to head back inside? Looked like you were pretty popular in there."

He chuckles. "It gets pretty old. They want anyone with a jersey. It's the same for any football player across the country."

I swallow at his words, my mind flashing back to all those pictures of Ryan with various girls, and Bernie must see it on my face. "I'm sorry, I didn't mean…Ryan—"

I shake my head. "Bernie, it's fine. We're not together."

"Y'know, I always thought he'd wake up and realize he made the dumbest mistake breaking up with you."

I smile sadly, thinking back to that day in my kitchen when he told me he could never get over it. "I guess he doesn't agree."

"He's an idiot. He'll wake up one day and regret it. Girls like you don't come along very often."

"You're sweet, but he's moved on."

"Have you?"

My eyes shoot to his in surprise, and I frown slightly. This is unchartered territory for us. We've always gotten along, but he's always just been Mason's friend at college. The only time we've ever really spoken (except for that one time we had lunch together) has been when Mason was there, or just briefly in passing. We've never had anything more than a generic conversation.

"Um, well—"

"I'm sorry, I'm messing this up." He pauses, and I actually see his cheeks turn slightly pink. I didn't think it was possible for Bernie Matthews to blush. "What I'm trying to say is that you're awesome. You're smart and you're funny. You don't give a crap about football, which just makes me like you more." He pauses again and looks me straight in the eye. "I'm asking you if you'll let me take you out on a date."

My jaw falls open, I'm so surprised. That is the last thing I expected him to say.

"What?"

"A date, Becca. Let me take you out."

I shake my head before I even register I'm doing it. "You don't want to date me, Bernie."

He smirks at me. "Oh, don't I? Yeah, clever, sassy, beautiful women are a total turn-off for all men everywhere."

I just stand there, gaping at him.

"Did I mention that you're beautiful?"

I come crashing back to reality, and I actually flinch at the word, because I'm not—not anymore. I'm so far from beautiful, it's ridiculous. Maybe I was before, but that feels like a different lifetime now. All I feel these days is used and dirty, like I'm rotten, secondhand goods—someone who's not good enough for anyone. When I'm feeling my worst, when I'm allowing the memories to creep back in and I can't cover them with other thoughts, I still feel his hands on me, and when that happens, I can't breathe. I can't breathe again until I've gotten in the shower and scrubbed my body raw, scrubbed away the feel of him on me, but the feeling always comes back. Even now, even with the counseling and forcing myself out of my apartment, the feelings are still there. It's not that I never cared about my looks, I just never really focused on them. I knew Ryan thought I was beautiful; he used to tell me all the time. I knew when I got dressed up and made an effort, I could turn heads with the best of them, but that was before. I remember the last time I looked my best, the night of the short skirt, cropped top, and high heels. Tina told me how beautiful I looked, and then he did. Robbie did right before he turned my life upside down, and the word beautiful makes me want to throw up.

He laughs at my reaction, mistaking it for disbelief at the word and not disgust. "I promise I wasn't scamming on you when you were with Ryan. I always knew you were out of bounds, and I knew Ryan had you locked down, but I always liked you, and then when you and Ryan broke up and didn't seem to be getting back together, I figured I'd take my chance. What do you say?"

I stare back at him for a few seconds. He's smiling at me, but his shoulders are tense, which makes me think he's not as relaxed as he's trying to seem. "Bernie, I-I'm sorry. That was the last thing I was expecting you to say." I pause and look at him. He's a great guy, funny and kind, and he's gorgeous to look at. Dark blond hair that is just long enough for him to tie back in a short ponytail, warm brown eyes, and a body that half the girls all over campus dream about. I'm sure he has girls lining up to date him—they'd be crazy not to—but he's not what I want. He's not Ryan. "I'm sorry, Bernie. I'm just…" I pause and let out a sigh. "I know he's done with me, I get that, but I'm not over it yet. I don't want to date anyone. I just can't. I'm sorry."

His gaze drops to the ground, and I bite my lip, hoping I've not ruined whatever small friendship we had. Then he looks back up and offers me a small smile. "I kinda knew you'd say that," he tells me. "But it was worth a shot."

"Definitely worth a shot," I reply, relieved that he doesn't seem to be mad at me.

"Ryan's an idiot," he tells me.

I laugh. "Maybe you could try telling him that for me?"

He laughs at this. "You deserve better, Becca."

I grin and look away, unsure how I've gotten into a conversation about Ryan with Bernie Matthews, of all people. "I should go," I tell him, gesturing toward the car.

He nods and turns to head back into the bar. I open the car door, and I'm just about to slide in when I hear him call my name. I glance back up.

"I know you're not ready now, but just so you know, I'm gonna ask again." With that, he gives me a wink, turns, and saunters into the bar, leaving me looking after him.

# CHAPTER 30

*Becca*

"WHERE WERE YOU LAST NIGHT?"

I glance across at Tina. I had a session with Lucy, and I finally spoke about the whole thing, from start to finish. I didn't leave bits out like I have before, and it was the first time I've described the night in full. Even with Sam, I just gave her a brief overview, but I told Lucy all of it, every last detail, and I feel better for it— way, way better.

"I was in the library until late."

Her eyes narrow on my face. "I stopped in there on the way home but I didn't see you."

I don't miss a beat. "I popped out for a coffee at one point. It must have been then."

She looks at me for a second and then nods. "Must have been."

I look away across the student quad, trying to act

nonchalant. I know she's wondering where I've been disappearing to twice a week, and I'm going to have to start coming up with better excuses. There's no way she can ever find out the truth.

"I have news," I tell her.

"Oh, yeah?"

"I'm switching my major."

Her jaw falls open. "What? Again?"

I laugh at her expression. "Yes, again, but for good this time. I've decided to go to medical school, and now I just need to make sure I can get enough credits to get there. I'm going to pick up physical sciences and psychology for the rest of the year."

Her eyes bug out of her head. "Medical school?"

I smile. "Yeah. I want to be a psychiatrist."

"What? Since when?"

Since I met Lucy, since I saw the difference she's made in my life and the lives of everyone she works with. I've finally found something I am passionate about, something I can be good at. I know it'll be hard, but I know it'll be worth it, and I'm going to do it. I told my mom last night, and though she was shocked, she told me she'd support me in whatever decision I wanted to make. "I just really want to do it. I want to make a difference."

"Are you being serious?"

I laugh. "As a heart attack. I just need to make sure I study my ass off for the rest of the year so I can pass the entrance exams."

"You're being serious?"

"Yes, Tina. Becca McKenzie has finally figured out what

she wants to do with her life."

She stares at me openmouthed for another second then pulls me into a hug. "I think that's amazing, Becca. Really, really amazing."

I smile at her, returning her hug, but when I glance behind her, Robbie Mulligan walks into my line of sight, and I automatically freeze up. I can't tear my eyes away from him though. If he's in my vicinity, I need to know exactly where he is so I know to stay away. He's with the same blonde girl he was with at Carrington's, and he's holding her hand and smiling down at her possessively while she tells him something. My heart tightens at the sight of it. A redhead and a brunette trail behind them, calling out to the girl, and she turns and smiles at them. They must be her friends—I saw them at Carrington's too.

"Becca?" I force myself to face Tina. She has her eyes pinned on Robbie too.

"Who's that girl?" I don't care what she makes of the question. I've seen him with her twice now, and I want to know what she is to him.

Tina's eyes widen just slightly before she glances back at them. "I don't know. I can find out though?" It's a question.

My eyes find Robbie again, and I watch as he bends and places a gentle kiss on her forehead. I swallow hard. I hate seeing him with anyone. I know what he did to me was all about Ryan, but still, I hate seeing him with someone. "Yes." My voice is firm and hard. "Find out who she is."

The blonde girl wraps her arms around his waist, throwing her head back and laughing at something. Then she takes his hand and tugs him toward the business buildings, pulling them out of my eyesight. I let out a visible breath of relief when he's gone, but I still feel uneasy. Something is still niggling at me.

I turn back to Tina, and she's watching me, concern written all over her face. "What should I cook for dinner tonight?"

She snorts. She's not on board with me trying to cook. I burned rice the other day.

"I'll cook," she announces. "Come on." She pulls me out of the shelter of the arts building, where I met her after class. I reach down and zip my jacket, making a mental note to dig out my winter gear when I get home. It's definitely getting colder.

"So I have another date with Max tonight," Tina tells me. I glance over at her and she's grinning from ear to ear.

I smile back at her. "That's great." She met Max in her sociology class earlier this year, and they've been on at least five dates now, so I know she really likes him. I've met him a couple times, and he seems really nice.

"Do you have plans tonight?" she asks.

I shake my head distractedly. Mason has just walked into view, talking with a couple of guys. I haven't seen him at all recently, and my heart starts beating a little faster at the sight of him. He's my link to Ryan. He stops midstride and starts laughing at something one of his friends has said to him.

I wonder if I should go speak to him. We're friends again now, right? I hate that I'm second-guessing this; I wouldn't have thought twice about approaching him before.

"Becca?" My gaze snaps back to Tina, who is watching

me watch Mason. I turn to face her.

"What?" I ask. She lifts an eyebrow at me. "Sorry, what were you saying?"

She narrows her eyes in Mason's direction. "What are you doing tonight?" she asks, turning back to me with a mischievous glint in her eye.

"No plans. You're cooking for me, and then I'm staying in and studying."

"You should come with me."

I frown. "I'm not third-wheeling on your date, Tina."

"It doesn't have to be a third wheel," she tells me, looking at something over my shoulder and smirking. I cock an eyebrow at her. *What's she talking about?* "Remember Max's friend, Jacob? You met him when we saw them at the mall that time?"

I nod my head, recalling the tall blond-haired guy who made me feel like a total dwarf next to him.

"Well, he's asked about you a couple times and wants to take you on a date. We could double tonight."

I immediately shake my head. "No. No way," I tell her. "I'm not dating."

"He's really, really hot," she tells me, not giving in. I sigh, knowing she's going to push this. Tina is not good at accepting no, and she's decided I need to get back out there. "And he's so sweet!"

"I don't care."

"And smart. He's really, really smart."

"Tina—"

"Just come with us."

"No!"

"Becca!"

"There's absolutely no way in hell I'm going with you," I tell her.

"No way in hell you're going with her where?"

I jump at the sound to my left and turn to see Mason. Bernie's beside him. A smug smile crosses Tina's face, and I realize she must have seen him head our way. Apparently she's pleased. "I'm trying to get Becca to go on a date tonight," she tells him.

My eyes widen in horror, and I turn to Mason.

"I'm not going," I tell him quickly before turning and glaring at Tina.

"What? You've started dating again?" Bernie asks in surprise. Hurt crosses his face. "Who's the guy?"

I shake my head emphatically. "There is no guy." I turn to glare at Tina. "She knows I'm not dating."

Tina just grins back at me. "He's gorgeous," she tells Mason, who is looking at her with an amused smile playing on his lips. "Really sweet, and he's on the basketball team. Did you know that, Becca?"

I stare back blankly at her. She knows I don't know that; I met him for two minutes when we bumped into them once. "So if you want to stick with jocks, like your dating history suggests, he still counts, only a different flavor."

My jaw falls open. I can't believe she just said that. Bernie starts to chuckle next to me, and I send him a look too. She doesn't need any encouragement.

He holds his hand up to me. "Hey, you know I think you should start dating again, but you don't have to go to the basketball team. You know there's a willing football player right here who wants to take you out."

My stomach drops to the floor. He just said that in front of Mason and Tina.

"What?" Tina squeals next to me.

I've gone bright red, I just know it. I sneak a peek at Mason, who is watching me with interest.

"If anyone's taking her out, it's going to be me—right Becca?"

I flush an even deeper red.

"You asked her out?" Tina demands.

"You mean you didn't tell your friend?" Bernie teases me. "That cuts deep."

I roll my eyes, willing my flaming cheeks to cool down.

"This is perfect," Tina declares, clapping her hands together. "You guys would make a gorgeous couple."

"Stop," I tell her, shoving her with my shoulder.

Bernie starts laughing. "I agree, but we have to convince Becca first." He glances at his watch. "I've got to go," he tells us. "Tina, keep working on her." He looks at me and flashes me a disarming smile, which does nothing to stop my embarrassment. "Remember, when you're ready, I'm first in line." Then he turns and struts off like he owns the whole campus. His confidence is ridiculous.

"You did not tell me that!"

I turn to Tina, who is looking at me accusingly. "There's nothing to tell," I mutter, wishing Mason weren't witness to this conversation.

"What's the problem? Bernie's gorgeous. You'd have half the campus crazy with jealousy."

My stomach rolls at the thought. I can't stand having

people think about me at all. I just want to get through this year and forget that anyone has ever had an opinion on me and my private life.

"Tina—"

She whirls on Mason. "So, is he like, really into her or what?"

"Tina!" This time my voice is loud and sharp. It is not okay that she's saying this in front of him.

She just rolls her eyes. "But you and Bernie would be great together." I glare at her. She's really pissing me off now. She notices my look and just smirks. "Okay, so if you don't want Bernie, then date Max's friend."

"Arrgh! I'm not dating! I'm not interested in anyone."

"Well, people are interested in you," she tells me, sending me a wink.

"Please stop," I manage to snap after a brief pause. "Now."

Tina turns back to Mason. "She's mad I'm saying this in front of you because there's the possibility that it might get back to Ryan." She gives me a pointed look, which basically tells me she can see straight through my irritation. "However, I think it would do him some good to know Becca's got options, and he should get the massive stick out of his ass and forgive her already, because the poor girl can't do anything else to prove she's sorry."

Mason raises an eyebrow, and a low chuckle comes out of his mouth.

"I'm being serious," she continues, crossing her arms. "Ryan Jackson needs to get the fuck over himself and realize what he's missing, because she's not going to be hanging around forever."

My jaw drops open. Mason's gaze doesn't budge from Tina. She steps toward him, in full-on rant mode. "My girl is freaking beautiful. She's kind, she's clever, she's funny, and if he doesn't want her, there are plenty of others that do. Might do him some good to be reminded of that."

Then she turns to me and grins, gives me a wink, and starts walking away, calling over her shoulder that she needs to return a library book and will see me back at our apartment. I watch her walk away and feel slightly bewildered, but am also reminded of what a good friend she is.

I turn back to Mason, shrugging my shoulders at Tina's antics. "Sorry about that," I tell him. "She's just, y'know, being my friend." Mason smiles and nods. "I'm not going," I continue. "I'm not dating anyone. Please don't tell Ryan."

Mason doesn't say anything, just stares back at me, and it's making me nervous.

"I swear I didn't encourage Bernie," I continue. "He probably just feels sorry for me, and that's why he asked me out."

Mason snorts. "Bernie's liked you for a while. It's not because he feels sorry for you." I don't know what to say to that, and Mason smirks at me. "He knew you were off limits, and now you're not. He took his chance."

"I didn't say yes."

"I know."

"I'm not dating anyone. I'm not interested in anyone."

He looks at me for a long time, weighing something up. "I know. You don't want anyone except Ryan."

"Please don't tell him about any of this."

Mason grins at me. "I'm not gonna tell Ryan you're dating, Becca. Do I look like I want my ass handed to me?"

My eyebrows burrow in confusion. I have no idea what he's talking about.

Mason laughs at my blank expression. "You never did quite get how Ryan feels about you, did you?" he asks. I shrug in response. Ryan told me he was in love with me for years before we got together, but that's all in the past now. Mason narrows his eyes and crosses his arms. "Did you never wonder why no one ever asked you out in high school?"

My face burns red. "Mason! I did get asked out. I went out with Charlie!"

He starts to laugh at me. "I mean, anyone from our school?"

I let out an annoyed huff and rearrange my bag on my arm. This is kinda rude. I would never point out Mason's dateless state to him! I met Charlie through Sam's boyfriend who attended a different school. "I don't know, but thanks for pointing that out!"

He grins. "It was because of Ryan, you idiot. Everyone knew you were off limits, and everyone listened to Ryan, did what he said. I mean, we all had an idea he liked you, as far back as middle school, but when we got to high school, it just became more and more obvious, especially after he dealt with Fran Cunningham for you." I'm listening to him intently. Fran Cunningham was this horrible bully back in high school, and when I stood up to her, Ryan made sure she didn't come after me. "I swear he used to stare at you in the cafeteria when he thought no one was watching. It was funny, really. Then remember when Luke Masters transferred to school sophomore year?"

I nod my head. "Well, he had a thing for you. He

mentioned that he was going to ask you out at practice one day, and everyone just kind of went silent and looked at Ryan. We all knew he was into you, and Luke got the message and backed off. That's why Ryan was a dick at Jess's when he saw you talking to Luke. He knew he used to like you and jumped to conclusions."

"What? Are you being serious?"

Mason laughs. "Yeah. Everyone knew back then that Ryan was into you, so they stayed away."

I'm totally dumbfounded. "Ryan cock-blocked me throughout all of high school?"

"Yup!" Mason replies cheerfully. "Although it wasn't completely his fault. He never spoke about you or anything, we just knew, and you know what it was like at MacAllister. No one ever really went against Ryan." I can't believe this. I had no idea about any of this, but something tells me it's true. Ryan was ridiculously popular in high school; he pretty much ruled the place, and whatever he said stood.

"Remember that time," Mason continues conversationally, "when we all came over to you and asked you to tutor Ryan? We could tell you weren't impressed that we all surrounded you." He winks at me, and I grin back. It's no secret I spent all of high school avoiding Ryan, Mason, and their friends, but one afternoon, they all surrounded me, trying to talk me into tutoring Ryan. "Anyway, some kids started running past and banged into you, you went flying, and Ryan had to reach out to catch you before you fell, remember?"

I smile. Yeah, I remember that. They were all being weird, and then I fell and was really embarrassed that I looked like an idiot in front of them.

"Well, I swear the guy stopped breathing because he was actually touching you. You detached yourself from him, probably didn't even thank him, and then walked away, and we all just starting pissing ourselves at Ryan. It was so funny. He was bright red and everything. We all loved it, since he got every other girl in that school so easily."

I smile at Mason. There's no point in pretending I don't like hearing this stuff. It makes me feel closer to Ryan, hearing about our past, even if at the time I was completely oblivious to it. It's horrible that it's so different now.

"Thanks Mason, but it's different now. He doesn't feel like that anymore."

"I don't know. Remember when we were kids and I kissed you in spin the bottle?" I nod my head, remembering back to that day when we were twelve. Ironically, Mason was my first kiss. "Well, Ryan was so pissed at me that he didn't speak to me for a week. I swear it still pisses him off today. And then when we were in high school and Kevin Wilson groped you that time?" I nod, grimacing at the memory. "Well, Ryan threw him into the lockers so hard afterward, I swear I thought he'd have broken bones. Then he didn't speak to him again. And whenever he saw you with that idiot boyfriend of yours when we were seniors? Well, we all avoided him like the plague whenever that happened, because we knew he'd be in a shitty mood about seeing you with another guy." I force a smile, but really I want to cry. We have so much history, and yet he won't give us another chance. Mason must see my face, because he steps toward me and puts his hand on my shoulder. "My point is, the guy fucking adores you, Becca. Always has."

I smile sadly at Mason. "Not anymore, Mason. He doesn't want anything to do with me now."

Mason shrugs and smiles back at me. "You don't just switch that shit off, Becca. No matter how much you want to. You really hurt him, but…" His voice trails off, not finishing his sentence.

My eyes snap to his in earnest. *Does Mason think there's still a chance for Ryan and me? Does he think Ryan might one day take me back?* Surely, if anyone would know, it would be him, one of Ryan's best friends. The questions I've been trying to force out of my head after seeing him over the summer come to the forefront of my mind.

"Look, just give him time, okay? Let him figure it out on his own. I don't know for sure, but I know him, and I know deep down he loves you. So no, I wouldn't be going on any dates with anyone else, because I'm pretty sure Jackson's not done with you yet."

My heart soars, and I feel tears well in my eyes. Mason rolls his eyes at my response. "Geez McKenzie, don't start bawling on me. Come on, let's go get some pizza." He throws his eyes arm around my shoulder and leads me toward the student food hall. "I might even take a picture of us and put it on Instagram, just to mess with Jackson's head. You know he'd be checking that shit out," he says, grinning wickedly and giving me a wink.

I smile back at him. For the first time in what seems like years, I return his smile with a genuine smile of my own.

# CHAPTER 31

## Ryan

**"W**HERE'S JAY?"

I look up and sigh at the sight of Jake in the doorway. Jay had come to visit; we arranged it weeks ago, and I know he's been really excited. I had been too. I missed him. Ever since Becca and I broke up, I tried to make sure I saw him. I know he finds it hard to understand why we're not together. He used to ask me about her at first, but that's stopped recently, and I was looking forward to a full day of Jay's energy. That's what I need at the minute, and even though I hate to admit it, he reminds me of Becca, and I need that too. Ever since I saw her over the summer, it's been harder and harder for me not to think about her.

"He's not here."

"What? I thought you weren't dropping him off until later?"

"He wasn't feeling great, so we took him home." Jake's

eyes swing to my side at Kelly's words, and his eyes narrow before turning back to me. I can see right away he's pissed. I don't think he knew she was there before.

"You took her to meet Jay?" he demands, not even looking at Kelly.

"What's the problem?" I ask, but I know the problem. I hadn't invited Kelly, but she'd shown up when I was leaving and then invited herself along. I could tell Jay hated her being there. I think Kelly was really trying with him, or at least attempting to try with him. I think she knew how much he means to me, but Jay wasn't having any of it. His face fell when he saw her, and then he was sullen and moody all day. Plus, I'm pretty certain Kelly didn't want to be there either; she was just doing it because she thought I'd want that. Then Jay asked me to take him home early, and as disappointed as I was, I knew it was for the best. I didn't fail to catch the look on his mom's face when I dropped him off and Kelly insisted on walking to the door with me. His mom didn't say anything, but I knew she wasn't impressed.

"Seriously, Ryan? Are you fucking kidding me? Becca's cousin?"

"Hey." Kelly sits upright and places her hand on my knee. "It was important that I meet Jay. He and Ryan are close, and therefore it's important that I'm in his life too." Jeez, even I want to roll my eyes at her. "It doesn't matter if he's related to that girl." She wouldn't ever refer to Becca as my ex-girlfriend. "If he wants to continue to be in Ryan's life, then he needs to accept me."

I'm stunned into silence at her words. Does she actually think I'd discard Jay just because they didn't get along?

Jake lets out a humorless laugh and turns to face her straight on. "Don't ask Ryan to pick between you and Jay, Kelly," he tells her, his eyes flashing with anger. "Because you'll lose."

Jason, sitting across from us, lets out an awkward whistle. Kelly gasps in indignation and whirls to face me. "Are you going to let him talk to me like that?" she demands.

I look at Jake, and he crosses his arms. To be honest, this has been coming for a while. Jake doesn't like Kelly—can't stand her. He didn't like her before we got together, and his dislike has grown even more intense since we started dating. He thinks she's shady and hates that she was chasing me when I was with Becca. He also thinks I'm only with her because I know it'll hurt Becca. I didn't say anything when he said that, but I know he dislikes Kelly with a passion, and Kelly knows it too. She used to make a real effort with him, knowing he's my best friend, but I think she's given up now and is just generally bitchy to him. She won't push me to choose between them though; she knows I'll pick Jake. He's been my best friend forever, and the only person I'd ever pick over him would be Becca—that is, until I wiped her out of my life.

Jake is staring back at me, looking like he's ready for a fight. I have no idea what his problem is, but I could really do without this right now. "Babe, why don't you go up to bed? I'll be right up."

She looks pissed that I'm not jumping to her defense, but she doesn't say anything. She never really challenges me—not like Becca, who was never scared of putting me in my place. With Kelly, it's like she's scared I'll end it. The truth is, I'd actually like a bit of bite. I know she has it; I've seen her use it on other people, but never on me. She shoots Jake a dirty look, picks up her phone and her purse, leans over, and attacks my mouth. She kisses me like we're alone in the room and about to go at it, even resting her hand on my upper thigh and squeezing just below my dick. It's a promise of what's to come upstairs, and it should excite me. It should make me want to throw her over my shoulder and drag her upstairs, but the thought of it just makes me tired. Kelly is great in bed, but it just isn't right for me, not anymore. My heart isn't in it.

When she finally finishes mauling my face, she straightens up, shoots Jake another dirty look, and brushes past him out of the room. He looks back at her in disgust.

"Dude, you're getting lucky tonight," Jason chuckles.

"Yeah, real lucky," Jake says sarcastically. He steps toward me and crosses his arms. "Seriously, what the fuck were you thinking having her meet Jay?"

"Jay didn't care," I lie.

"Yeah? And what about Becca? How do you think she'd feel if she knew?"

"It has fuck all to do with Becca."

"Course it does. Everything you do has something to do with Becca, whether you'll admit it or not."

"Shut up."

He shakes his head. "For you, everything comes back to Becca."

"Why are you sticking up for her all of a sudden?" I've noticed recently that he is dropping her into conversation more, trying to act casual and asking how I felt about it. I always shut it down immediately, not wanting to talk about her, but I know his position on her has changed. He isn't mad at her anymore.

"Because Sam was right," he says quietly. "I was a shit friend when she clearly needed me, and I feel guilty as fuck about it."

"That's Becca's problem, not ours."

He stares at me. "I get it. I get why you're acting how you are, and I know she broke your heart, but I didn't have to cut her out."

"She didn't break my heart," I lie. Dean snorts from his seat to my right, and I turn to glare at him. "She didn't," I repeat. I glance around at them all, and I know not one of them believes me. They were all there in the months after it happened. It was pretty obvious how much she hurt me.

Jake lets out a long sigh. "People make mistakes, Ryan, and I think she's been punished enough. If you're done with her, then fine, but don't use Jay to try to hurt her even more."

"I wasn't using Jay."

"Yeah, right," he says sarcastically. "How would you like it if she took Amy out on a date with her and Mulligan?" he continues, referencing my niece, who does nothing but ask me about Becca whenever I see her.

"What the fuck?" I demand, sitting up straighter. "Is she with him now? What did you hear?" I realize too late how desperate I sound and how little I'm hiding my interest in her.

Jake just smirks back at me and shakes his head. "I didn't hear anything," he mutters before sitting across from me. "But good to know you don't care, Ryan."

I flip him the finger and take another swig of my beer. I want the conversation over.

Marty chooses that moment to walk in. He looks around

in confusion, sensing the tension, before flopping down next to Jake.

"What's up, man?" Jason asks.

"Ellie's pissed at me."

"Why?" I ask, eager to change the subject.

"I dunno, she said she loved me."

Jason bursts out laughing but quickly covers it with a coughing fit when Marty reaches over and smacks him on the head.

"What did you say?" I ask, genuinely curious. He's only been dating Ellie for a couple months, but I'm pretty sure he's into her.

He sighs dramatically. "I just said thanks." Jason bursts out laughing again, and this time I can't help joining in. Marty glares at us. "I didn't know what to do! I was so surprised. I don't know how I feel. I mean, I like her but..." He trails off before turning to me. "How do you know when you're in love?"

I actually snort with laughter. "I don't love Kelly." I don't, not even close—even Kelly knows that.

Marty rolls his eyes. "I wasn't talking about Kelly."

Becca. Of course he's talking about Becca. I look at him for a moment and then shake my head. "Do yourself a favor and forget it. It's not worth it."

Jake's eyes snap to me. "It's not worth it? So, what? You'd rather not have had the years you had with her because of how it ended? You'd rather it never happened?"

*No. I don't regret a second of it.* If anything I wish it had happened sooner. When Becca and I got together, she turned my life upside down in the best possible way. It felt like I became whole. We were a team from the minute we got to-gether. We were Becca and Ryan, and nothing could touch us—but then it did, and it hurt when it ended. It hurt more than I could ever possibly imagine, and I honestly don't think I could go through that again.

"Leave it," I bite out at Jake.

Marty glances between us but doesn't let it go. "But how do you know when you're in love?" he asks me. He can't ex-actly ask anyone else. Jason, Dean, and Jake have never been close to love. I think their longest relationships total six months combined—not that there's anything wrong with that, because they don't know what they're missing. But I do. I know every single day what I'm missing. "Seriously, Ryan, I need to know. What does it feel like?"

I still don't answer, and that's when Jake decides to pipe up again. I get the feeling he's been waiting to say this stuff for a long time. He's kept his mouth shut up until now, but clearly he's finally ready to tell me what he thinks. "I would say it's when you can't stop thinking about someone, when they're on your mind constantly, and no matter what you do, and no matter what they do, you can't stop wanting them, even when you don't want to. That sound about right, Ryan?"

"Shut up." I practically snarl the words at him. I don't care if every word he said is right; I don't want to hear it.

"Mason told me Bernie Matthews asked her out."

I feel like I've been punched in the face. "What?" I demand.

"Yeah, last week."

"What the fuck?" I'm not happy. Although I wouldn't exactly classify Bernie as a friend, I never thought he'd go behind my back after Becca. "Were they getting into it when I was with her?"

Jake rolls his eyes. "Get your head out of your ass, Ryan. No, of course they weren't, but Mason said he asked him a couple of weeks ago what was happening with you guys, if you were going to take her back."

"And what did he say?"

Jake shrugs, a smirk on his face. "He said you were done with her. That's right, isn't it? That's what you keep saying?"

I don't have an answer to that, and he knows it. It is what I've been saying all along, but he can see straight through me. He knows I'm not done with her—not even close—even if I'm not fully prepared to admit it to myself yet. The truth is that the anger and the hurt are starting to fade, and now I just miss her. I really, really miss her.

"So what, are they dating now?" I can't help but ask the question. I feel a bit sick at the response I might get. I know its rich considering I have Kelly waiting in my bed, but Bernie Matthews is different from Robbie Mulligan. Bernie is actually a good guy, funny and relaxed, and even I can appreciate that the dude's good-looking. If Becca gave him a chance, I'm sure it wouldn't take long for him to win her over.

Jake stares at me for a long minute and then finally shakes his head. The relief I feel is instant. "No. She said no. But he'll ask again, and one day she'll say yes. And if it's not him she says yes to, then it'll be someone else."

I don't respond. I don't want to think about the day when she'll say yes to someone else. At the moment it's enough for me to know she still wants me, still loves me. As soon as that stops, I don't know what I'll do.

Dean chuckles. "What?" I demand.

He rolls his eyes. "Oh, come on, Jackson. You can't expect her to stay single forever. Becca's hot, like hottest-chick-in-the-room hot. There's probably a line of people waiting to take her out."

"Yeah," Marty chimes in. "She's like, seriously beautiful, right? But there's something else about her too, like you notice her when she walks in the room." His eyes widen when he sees the look on my face. I don't need to know that my friends have been noticing Becca like that, and I certainly don't want to think of other people, people I don't know, thinking of her like that.

"Actually," Jake continues, dragging me out of my thoughts. He's got a steely look on his face, and I've got a feeling I won't like what I hear. "Becca's a fucking catch. I mean, she's funny, she's smart, and she's fucking hot. She's a solid nine." *A ten,* I want to say. *She is a solid ten. She is absolutely perfect.* "I mean, she's pretty much the whole package, looks and personality, and I know we already get along—"

My eyes snap to his when I realize where he is going with this. "Don't," I warn.

"And I've been thinking about getting a girlfriend for a while now—"

"Jake!"

"I mean, I've seen her in a bikini, and her body is fucking unreal—"

"Jake, I'm warning you."

"That ass and those tits—"

"I swear to fucking God, Jake," I say through gritted teeth. I feel like smoke is coming out of my ears right now.

"And she must be good in bed, right? She kept you satisfied for years, and Robbie—"

I fly out of my chair before he can even finish his sentence, and my fist connects with his jaw so hard my knuckles ache. Jason hauls me off him and pushes me away while Marty and Dean stare at us, openmouthed. Jake rubs his jaw, but he's laughing at me, his eyes mocking me from the sofa where he's still sitting. He shakes his head at me as I seethe in the corner. I know he doesn't mean it. I know there's only ever been friendship between them, but I can't help it. The thought of anyone talking about her like that makes me want to kill.

"In the bar last week, some guy was hitting on Kelly all night, and you didn't even glance her way. I mention Becca's ass, and you're ready to kill me." He pauses, wincing in pain. "Do yourself a favor and get your head out of your ass." He shakes his head one last time. "Fucking think about it, Ryan, because you're not just punishing her anymore. You're punishing yourself too." Then he stands and leaves the room without giving me a second glance.

I stare at the empty doorway for a full minute, taking in what he said and feeling my heart beating loudly in my chest. I let out a deep sigh and lean back against the wall. I glance at Marty, who is staring at me, eyes wide. Jake and I don't fight. Ever. "You don't love Ellie," I tell him. Because when you're in love, you know without a shadow of a doubt that you'd do anything for them and that life without them is empty. "You know when you're in love."

I break up with Kelly the next day.

# CHAPTER 32

*Becca*

'VE GOT THE FRIDGE DOOR OPEN, AND I'M SCANNING the shelves, looking at a bunch of ingredients I have no idea how to turn into a meal. If Tina were here, she'd be able to whip something up in minutes, and it would taste amazing. Me? I've realized my skills do not lie in cooking. I'm just wondering how I can turn a wedge of cheese and an onion into something edible when my phone starts ringing.

I reluctantly close the fridge door and turn to the counter. A glance at the phone tells me that it's an unknown number. Either it's someone trying to sell me something, or whoever is on the other side doesn't want me to see their number. I swipe my thumb and answer anyway.

"Hello?"

I wait for a response but don't hear anything. I pull the phone away from my ear to make sure I've answered and it's connected—it is.

"Hello?" I ask again. "Becca speaking."

There's another long pause at the other end, and I'm about to hang up when I hear a throat being cleared on the other end. "Hi." My whole body goes still. "It's me." I don't dare move a muscle. "It's Ryan." Of course it's Ryan. I'd know his voice anywhere. I've known his voice my whole life. I hear his voice in my dreams, but in truth, I didn't think he'd ever call me again. "You there?" he asks, and I realize it's been a minute since I've spoken.

"H-Hi," I manage to stammer out.

There's more silence, and fear suddenly grips onto me. *Why is he calling me? Something bad must have happened.*

"Has something happened?" I ask, my heart in my mouth. Maybe something's happened to his parents, but then surely my mom would have let me know. "Is something wrong?"

He must hear the panic in my voice. "No. No, nothing's wrong." He sighs loudly. "I don't even know why I'm calling you. I should probably—"

"No!" I interrupt. He can't go, not when he's finally ready to speak to me. "No, it's good to hear from you." I pause and take a shaky breath. I really don't want to mess this up. "How are you?"

"Yeah, I'm…" He trails off, like he doesn't want to tell me anything about himself, doesn't want to give me any of the information I'm so desperate to hear. "I, um…" He stops himself again. It's like he's warring with himself. He doesn't want to talk to me. I mean, a part of him does, and that's why he's called, but he doesn't *want* to want to talk to me. He wants to be done with me, and I honestly thought he was. I'm praying this call means he isn't.

He still doesn't say anything so I clear my throat. Maybe if I tell him some of my news, he'll then share some of his. "I finally decided what I want to do for a job."

"Oh yeah?" His response is instant, and I know he's grateful that I've started talking to take some of the pressure off him.

"I'm going to train to be a psychiatrist. I'm going to medical school."

"What?" His voice is full of surprise.

I laugh softly. "I know, right? Kinda random but it's what I want to do. I've been studying nonstop to make sure I get the grades to get into medical school."

"Medical school?"

"Yeah."

A long pause follows. "Where are you going to medical school?" His voice sounds strange. Distant.

"Hopefully here in Texas. I've applied and I should have everything they need to secure a place."

"So you're staying in Texas?"

"Well, that's the plan."

"For the next few years?"

"Yeah. I want to."

He doesn't say anything for what feels like forever. "Wow," he eventually says. His voice is quiet. "That's huge, Becca. Congrats."

"Thanks Ryan. That means a lot." I mean it. I wanted to tell him when I made the decision. I wanted him to know that I'd finally made a plan, but I couldn't. I didn't think he'd want to know, and I definitely didn't think he'd care—and I couldn't stand the thought of that. Now he knows and I'm glad.

Neither of us say anything for a couple of minutes.

"I signed with Bobby Douglas," he says eventually.

I actually gasp in surprise—this is massive. Bobby Douglas is one of the biggest, if not *the* biggest, sports agents in the country. He's notoriously selective when taking on new clients, and he only goes for those he thinks will genuinely be superstars of the game. I know last year he went to watch one of Ryan's games.

"That's amazing, Ryan. Congratulations."

"Thanks." He lets out another long sigh and then doesn't say anything for another minute. "He's been to a few more of my games this year, and I met him a bunch of times. Your dad introduced us."

"Oh." I didn't know that. My dad is a sports journalist and pretty big on the NFL scene. He's always been interested in college football, but has taken a special interest in it since Ryan started playing for California State. He's known Bobby Douglas for years—they went to college together—and although neither of them managed to go pro (my dad because he suffered a career-ending injury and Bobby Douglas because he wasn't quite good enough), they've both forged careers in the game.

"You didn't know?"

"No." I shouldn't be surprised really. My dad would do anything to help Ryan. I know he sees him as the son he never had, and I'm once again reminded of how our breakup has affected our families. "But that's great, Ryan."

"Yeah?"

"Yeah, of course it is. You deserve it. You deserve

everything that's coming, Ryan. You're unbeatable at the moment. Buckton couldn't get near you last week."

"You watched that?"

I feel like laughing out loud. "Of course I watched it, Ryan. What else would I do?"

He doesn't respond.

"I'm so proud of you," I tell him quietly. I know I'm pushing it now, making it more personal than he wants it to be, but it's true. I'm so, so proud of him and everything he's achieved, everything he is about to achieve.

"Your parents came to the game."

"I know," I tell him, thinking back to that phone call when my mom told me they were going to watch him and how alone I felt at her words, how I knew I should have been there too, watching the boy I'm in love with dominate his senior year of football. I clear my throat. "My mom told me. I know they're really proud of you too."

"Yeah," he says, his voice flat. The conversation stops again. Neither of us knows what to say.

"Kelly must be really proud of you too," I tell him, and I hate myself for bringing her name into this. It's like I'm a glutton for punishment. I hate the thought that she's there, cheering him on. For the first time, it crosses my mind that she may not have just met his parents, but his sister too, and then I want to throw up thinking that maybe even my parents saw her.

He doesn't reply for what feels like an hour, but in reality it's probably only around ten seconds. "I wouldn't know," he finally tells me. "We broke up two weeks ago." Hope slams into me and I'm left reeling, but I force my hopes down and try not to get ahead of myself, try not to read too much into this.

He clears his throat, and I'm brought back to the here and now. Before I can ask him any questions about Kelly, he speaks again. "I heard Robbie Mulligan signed with Sam Carlton."

"I wouldn't know," I say instantly, and I know I'm not hiding the edge in my voice, but I don't care. He just tells me he's broken up with Kelly, and he immediately jumps to Robbie fucking Mulligan. I don't want to know who Mulligan signed with. Sam Carlton is no Bobby Douglas. He's not quite on the same level, but he's still a pretty big deal as far as agents go. It makes me livid that once again everything's just fallen into place for that bastard, and I hate that Ryan's asking me about Mulligan again, like it wasn't enough when I told him last time that I didn't see him.

"So you're not—"

"No, Ryan," I cut him off. "I have nothing to do with him." My tone leaves no room for argument, and I swear I hear him breathe a sigh of relief.

"Do you know who Bernie Matthews signed with?"

I shake my head and then realize he can't see me. "No. Mason will know."

He pauses on the other side of the line. "So you haven't seen Matthews recently?"

*What?* "No. I bumped into him when he was with Mason on campus a few weeks ago, but that was for like two minutes, and I haven't seen him since."

"Right." That's when I figure it out—he knows Bernie asked me out. Mason must have told him.

"I'm not dating him, if that's what you're trying to ask me." I'm trying not to get my hopes up here, but the fact that he's asking about Bernie must mean he doesn't like the fact that I could start dating someone else. *Right?* Maybe I'm just clutching at straws. "I haven't dated anyone since you, Ry."

"That's not what I was asking," he insists immediately. "You can do what you want, date who you want. I don't care. We're not together anymore."

"Gee, thanks Ryan," I snap back sarcastically before I can even think. "I hadn't noticed that we're not together anymore. Thanks for pointing that out."

My eyes widen when I realize what I've said, and I immediately want to take it back. Just talking to him over the phone makes me feel more like my old self. I open my mouth to apologize when a soft chuckle drifts through the phone. It's like music to my ears.

"So you noticed, huh?" he asks me softly.

I sigh. Every minute of every day, I notice we're not together. Not a second goes by when I don't notice that he's not in my life anymore. "Yeah, I noticed," I whisper back.

I stand there, frozen still, waiting for him to say something else, waiting for him to tell me why he called, desperate to know if he's finally ready to talk. He clears his throat.

"Becca—" I hear a loud noise in the background. It sounds like a door has just been slammed, and male voices drift through the phone. He stops immediately. "I gotta go," he tells me. I try not to feel overwhelmingly disappointed, but I can't. It's not possible. "Look, this conversation doesn't change anything between us, right?" His voice has turned hard, like he's remembered himself. "Nothing has changed."

He pauses for a second. "Okay, bye." Then he hangs up on me without another word.

I stare at the phone in my hand.

Ryan's wrong. Everything has changed.

# CHAPTER 33

*Becca*

"**B**ECCA." I GLANCE TO THE RIGHT AS I WALK through campus, and Tina appears at my side. She grips my wrist and pulls me to a halt.

"What's wrong?" I ask, taking in her drawn face. Tina always has a smile on her face—always. "Are you okay?"

She nods and pulls me over so we're standing against the side of the library, out of the way. "I heard something."

"What?" I ask, glancing around and wondering why she being so secretive.

"Robbie Mulligan was arrested over the weekend for attempted rape." My whole world grinds to a halt as I stare into her worried brown eyes.

My mind reels, and my stomach starts churning. *This can't be right. He wouldn't. There's no way he would. He only did that to me because of Ryan. He wouldn't do it to someone else.*

"What?" I manage to whisper.

Tina's eyes flash over my face. "That blonde girl we saw him with? Her name's Grace. They've been dating, and this weekend, he tried to take it further. He tried to force her."

"How—" My brain can't process this information. "How do you know this?"

"It's all over campus. Everyone's been talking about it in classes."

"So he's in jail?"

Tina shakes her head. "No. He's been released on bail. He said she's lying."

I'm shaking my head before I even know what I'm doing, and Tina's eyes widen. She's not lying; I know it. "Is she okay?"

Tina shrugs. "I don't know. People were saying some pretty harsh things about her this morning."

"Like what?"

"That's she making it up. That she's a liar."

*She's not a liar. She's telling the truth. I know it.*

"I mean, I know he's a dick, but surely he wouldn't do that."

I straighten up and look around, my eyes flashing to the students filing past us. "I think Robbie Mulligan is capable of anything."

Tina's eyes widen, and she steps closer to me, gripping my arm. "Are you okay?"

I nod, but tears well in my eyes as I realize the magnitude of what she's told me. I could have stopped this. I could have told someone.

"Becca." Tina's staring at me in alarm, and I quickly wipe my eyes and look away.

"Guys!" We turn and see Maddy approaching. "Did you guys hear?"

Tina nods at her. "About Robbie? Yeah."

Maddy shakes her head. "People are saying some horrible things about Grace."

"Why?"

"Because he said she's lying."

"Why would she lie?" Tina asks. I don't say anything. I can't think. I can't think about this.

"I don't know. I mean, it's Robbie." She gives me an apologetic look. "It's not like he needs to force anyone. There are plenty of girls lining up for him."

"And that makes her a liar?" I ask sharply.

Maddy's eyes widen at the anger in my tone. "No, no, of course not. It's just, he's saying one thing and she's saying another. It's hard to know who to believe."

*Her.* Her without a shadow of a doubt. He did it—I know it with every fiber of my being.

"Has he been suspended from the team?" Tina asks.

Maddy shrugs. "I don't think so. They're standing by him."

Of course they are. He tries to rape somebody, and they believe him when he tells them he didn't do it.

"Poor girl," Tina says.

"Have you spoken to Mason?" Maddy asks me. "What is the team saying?"

I shake my head. "I only just heard about it." My voice is trembling, and they're both watching me suspiciously. I force myself to pull it together, rearranging my bag and standing up straighter.

"Are you okay?" Maddy asks with concern.

I nod and look away. *Oh Jesus. This can't be happening. I could have stopped this.*

"What did he do to her?" I ask.

"She said he tried to force her. Apparently she had a few bruises, but he said she's lying and she got the bruises from somewhere else."

Tina's eyes fly to mine at the mention of bruises, but I look away and refuse to look back. I need to figure out what to do, how to deal with this.

"It's horrible," Maddy says. "Apparently none of her friends have stuck by her. They're all groupies and don't want to go against him or the team."

I suck in a breath. I recall the redhead and mousy brunette, gazing up at Robbie like he's a fucking Greek god. I don't know how Maddy knows all this, but it sounds painfully true. *That poor, poor girl.*

"Becca?" I glance back at Maddy, and she's looking at me like she's been waiting for me to say something.

"Yeah?"

Her brow furrows. "Do you want to grab some lunch?"

I nod, even though I have no appetite. I follow behind them without a word as they lead me across the lawn and up the steps to the student cafeteria. My mind is reeling. I don't know what to think or what to say. When I spoke to Lucy about this, she asked me why I didn't go to the police. I told her about the deal I made about dropping the charges against Ryan, and then when she said he could be a danger to others, I just dismissed her concerns. I genuinely didn't think he'd ever do this to someone else. It was all about Ryan, that's all he cared about, and I was a way to hurt Ryan. That's what it was about. I didn't even think about him being dangerous to other women.

Suddenly Tina grips my hand, squeezing tightly, and I look up in surprise and see her and Maddy have stopped completely still just inside the doorway to the cafeteria. I gaze around in confusion, taking in the large room, which seems even fuller than usual today. Each table is completely full, and loud obnoxious laughter is ringing out from the back wall. When my eyes flick over to them, I see him. Robbie Mulligan is standing, arms crossed, holding court without a care in the world. He's throwing his head back and laughing with enthusiasm, entertaining the numerous people surrounding him. It's not just football players over there, although I recognize some of the offensive players. There are girls, too, lots and lots of girls. Then I see Grace's friends. They're with Robbie Mulligan, the guy she said tried to rape her. They're laughing at his jokes, flipping their hair and trying to get his attention.

I feel sick for Grace. I feel physically sick for her.

"Oh my God," I hear Tina whisper beside me. I turn my head to her and follow her gaze. Grace is here. Grace is here in the cafeteria.

I take in the scene in front of me, and I want to cry for her. She's all alone at a table that's big enough to seat eight people, and the cafeteria is crazy busy. There doesn't seem to be a spare seat in the room, and yet she's surrounded by empty chairs. People are filing past her, sending her curious looks, and I physically flinch as I see two guys wearing Kings shirts purposely walk right by her and barge into her chair, just slightly. They're sending her a message. They're telling her they don't believe her, that their quarterback wouldn't do that, that she's not welcome. She doesn't look at them though. She just stays focused on the tray in front of her, and when she reaches for her fork, I swear her hands are trembling.

I'm devastated for her. There's no other way of putting it. She has her hair pulled back, and she's wearing a simple black sweater and jeans. I can't see her face because her eyes are staring at the food in front of her. Loud laughter again rings out from the back of the cafeteria, and I swear she winces at the noise. I look back at Robbie's table, and sure enough, they're looking over at her. They're laughing at her, mocking her.

I stand there for another moment, watching across the hall as some new girl I've never seen before wraps her arms around Robbie, and I want nothing more than to scratch his eyes out. He's just destroyed another girl and is getting away with it. Then I look back at Grace, this young eighteen-year-old trying desperately to keep her emotions in check, eating her lunch despite the fact that her hands are shaking so badly. She knows she didn't do anything wrong and refuses to be made to leave. Someone else walks past her chair and knocks into her as they go. She flinches but doesn't get up. She doesn't leave.

Something inside me snaps.

"Mulligan," I scream his name across the cafeteria.

My feet propel me forward, and I march across to his table, my eyes glued to his face as his head snaps up to meet my stare. Tina and Maddy are a step behind me. They don't say anything, but I can feel their presence, and it gives me the confidence I need. Grace's friends might have dropped her like a stone, but mine won't do that. My friends are loyal and would do anything for me.

My eyes quickly scan his table, but Mason and Bernie aren't there. In fact, the only player I recognize except Robbie is that asshole, Jones, and I'm relieved. I'm so relieved they're not here mocking Grace too. His table's gone silent as I get closer, and I can see it. I can see the panic in his eyes before he quickly masks it and covers his face with an arrogant sneer.

"What's up, McKenzie?" he asks. "Finally ready for round two?"

"Fuck you," I snarl at him, my voice louder and stronger than it's been in almost a year. It's been a full year since he broke my life, and now he's tried to do it to someone else.

"You already did," he throws back. I hear sniggers from the watching crowd and realize it's not just his table that's gone silent. The whole room is so quiet, you could hear a pin drop, but I don't back down. I stare straight back at him, and his face pales slightly, like he's worried I'll spill his secret to everyone right here and now. I take a step closer to him, and he must see it, the determination in my face, because he breaks my stare first. "What do you want?" he eventually asks.

"I want you to call off your fucking dogs!" I say venomously.

Confusion crosses his face, and I point over at Grace, who is staring at me along with the rest of the cafeteria.

"I don't know what you're talking about," he tells me.

"Yes you do." I step forward, looking him dead in the eye. "You know exactly what I'm talking about."

"She's lying," he hisses the words at me, and I can see the hatred in his eyes. He hates me. He really, really hates me right now, but I don't care. He can't hate me even a fraction of the amount that I hate him. "She's lying," he insists again.

My mouth curls into a sneer and I shake my head. She's not lying. As I look into his eyes, we both know it. We both know the truth. We both know he tried to do to her what he did to me.

"Becca—"

I cut him off. "You need to tell all your fans and all your little groupies to leave that girl alone," I tell him, my eyes flashing around his table accusingly. A couple of them look away, ashamed, but a couple of them just sneer at me, waiting for Robbie to respond. They expect him to shut me down and for me to walk away humiliated, but I suddenly know with absolute certainty that that's not going to happen. It won't be me who backs down.

He doesn't respond, just briefly glances at Grace and then back at me, but I refuse to look away. At this stage, he has more to lose than me, and I refuse to let everyone bully this girl for being brave enough to do what I couldn't. Seconds pass as he looks back at me, trying to make up his mind, trying to see if I'm bluffing. Eventually he shrugs his shoulders and stands up. "Let's go," he says to his table. "They're not worth it."

There's a murmur around the room at his concession, and I know it will set people wondering—wondering why he's listened to me, why he's backed down in front of me. Everyone at his table shoots me curious glances, amazed that he's listened to me, amazed at the power I seem to have over him. They know who I am. They know I was Ryan Jackson's girlfriend and that Robbie slept with me, but now, they see that he's listening to me. He's doing what I want, but they don't know why. After a minute they get up and follow him out of the room without a word. I stand and watch them, and I watch him. I watch Robbie Mulligan skulk out of the room with his head down, and I feel stronger than I ever have. I can do this. I know I can do this.

I spin on my heel, walk over to Grace's empty table, and sit down beside her. Maddy and Tina follow me and sit down across from her. They send me worried glances, but I don't look at them. I know they want to know what's going on, why I did that, what it's all about—but I can't tell them yet. I'm trying really hard to get my breathing under control, and the realization of what I need to do is coursing through my body. Eventually Tina and Maddy get up and join the line. They come back with their lunches and a slice of pizza for me. None of us speak though. We just sit there silently, eating and ignoring the looks we're getting from the rest of the students.

Eventually everyone stops staring and goes back to their lunch. Soon the cafeteria empties out, and Tina and Maddy head off to their afternoon classes. Everyone leaves until it's just Grace and me. I glance over at her. "Do you want to talk about it?"

"No one believes me," she answers quietly. Her huge blue eyes are pools of complete sadness.

I take a deep breath and look her straight in the eye. "I do."

# CHAPTER 34

*Becca*

BITE MY LIP AS THE PHONE STARTS TO RING. TINA reaches out and grips my free hand tightly. Her face is pale, but her expression is fierce. I just told her what happened. When I got home from the police station after making my statement, she was waiting for me, and I knew I had to tell her. She burst into tears, told me she suspected something had happened, but that she never, ever envisioned something like this. I was terrified she wouldn't believe me, but the second I told her, I knew she did. I knew she believed me and would do anything to help me. Then she pulled herself together, hugged me tightly, and told me everything was going to be all right. Now she's sitting beside me as I make the single hardest phone call I've ever had to make.

"Hello?"

"Hey Mom."

"Becca, honey, how are you?"

"I'm okay." I pause. "Is Dad there? I have to tell you guys something."

"Yeah, he's here next to me."

"Can you put me on speakerphone? I want to tell you both at the same time." I know I'll only be able to say this once.

There's a pause on the other end. "Is everything okay, Becca?"

"Can you just do it, Mom? Please?"

There's another slight pause, and then my dad's voice comes on the line. "Hey Becca."

"Hey Dad."

"Is everything all right?"

I take a deep breath. I really don't want to have to do this, not like this, not when they're miles and miles away and won't be able to do anything, but I need to. I've made a statement, and Robbie's been taken in for questioning. There's no way it will stay under the radar, I know that. I know the shit-storm it's going to bring, know I just have to deal with it, but I need to be the one who tells my parents. They can't hear it from anyone but me.

"I have to tell you both something. I'm fine now—I promise I'm fine—but last October, I went to a frat party and I went to find a bathroom"—I close my eyes and take a deep breath—"and Robbie Mulligan, the Southern U quarterback, raped me in a bedroom."

I press my lips together, waiting for a response, my heartbeat going crazy in my chest. If they don't believe me, I can't go through with this. If they don't believe me, I'll drive down to the station right now and withdraw my statement, because

I don't think I can face this without them.

Tina squeezes my hand, and when I glance at her, she gives me an encouraging smile as she blinks back tears. There's painful silence on the other end of the line.

"Hello?" I manage to whisper.

That's when I hear it—a heart-wrenching sob comes down the line, and I know it's my mom. I wish I didn't have to do it like this, and it kills me that I'm not telling her face to face so she can see that I really am okay. It's not just one sob; more and more follow it, and it breaks my heart to hear my mom crying over the phone.

"I promise you I'm okay now. I really am fine." My voice is trembling.

"Becca." My dad sounds like I've just ripped his heart out. "My little girl." I hear him suck in a breath on the other side of the line, but he doesn't say anything else. My mom's cries become muffled, and I have a feeling that her head is buried in my dad's chest.

"You believe me, don't you?" I ask them, my voice shaky.

"Of course we believe you, Becca." My mom's voice is fierce, despite it cracking with emotion. "Of course we do, and we love you. We love you so, so much, Becca. I promise it's going to be fine. Everything is going to be fine."

The relief is instant. They know. I've told my parents, and they believe me. The worst thing that could have happened is them not believing me, and they did. Everything is going to be okay.

"We love you, Becca," my dad says. He sounds devastated, completely and utterly devastated.

"I love you too."

"We'll get on the next flight to you," he tells me.

"No, no, I promise I'm okay. I've reported it to the police, and they have my statement. I just have to wait and see what happens next."

"Becca, we're on the next flight."

I'm about to tell them no, but then I stop, because the truth is, I want them here. I want to see my mom and dad, and as much as it hurts that it's because of this, it'll be the first time in a year that I can be honest with them, and I think I need that too.

"Okay," I whisper.

"I love you, Becca," my mom states loudly. "We both love you so much, and I promise you that everything is going to be okay."

I nod my head, and for the first time in what feels like forever, I feel like they might be right. Everything will be okay.

# CHAPTER 35

*Ryan*

STRETCH OUT MY NECK AND GLANCE AROUND THE room. We played well today, really well. We destroyed St. Michael's, one of the best teams in the division. We completely dominated them, and we're all feeling pretty good. There's a huge celebration party going on at our house, but I'm holed away in a side room with Dean and Marty. We're pretty much hiding from the party. I'm not feeling it, and I know why.

Becca.

I can't stop thinking about her, not at all. It's been close to a year since we broke up, and I still can't get her out of my head. The girls I initially used as a distraction have stopped distracting me, and she's always on my mind. Constantly.

I can't get the news that she's staying in Texas for medical school out of my head. I don't know where I expected her to go after college, maybe New York, maybe back to California, but I didn't think she'd want to stay in Texas. And I definitely never expected her to go to medical school. I didn't know how to react when she told me that. This is huge news for her; a massive decision that she's actually committed to and it's just made me feel further away from her than ever. She's made this huge, life changing decision and it's so separate from me and has made me realize that maybe she's ready to move on with her life away from me. And that thought makes me feel sick. This is the sort of thing that I should have been the first to hear about, the sort of news that she should have asked my advice on and confided in me. Just like she was the first person I wanted to call when I signed with Bobby Douglas. I wanted to ask her why she'd decided on medical school and how she'd come to that decision, but of course I didn't. I didn't do anything. And now all I can think about is that she'll be in Texas for the next few years and I could get drafted anywhere in the country. I could realistically not see her in years and from the way I've acted over the last year, you'd think that would make me happy, but in all honesty I couldn't be further from happy at the news.

Jason wanders into the room. "What are you pussies doing in here?" he asks, dropping down onto the seat next to me and spreading his long legs out in front of him. He snags the bottle of Jack out of my hand and refills his own glass. "Dude, you wanna get out there," he tells me, slapping his hand on my knee. "There is this smoking blonde with the best legs I've ever seen asking about you." I smile and reach for the bottle, topping my own drink. "Although, if you hit that, you should do it privately, because Kelly's out there, and she'll rip the girl's hair out if she sees you," he adds, smirking at me.

I let out a groan. Kelly has been driving me crazy. She won't accept that we're over. It was never serious as far as I was concerned, but she seems to think we were destined to be together forever, and now she keeps showing up everywhere I am.

Marty starts laughing across from us. "Dude, Ryan doesn't care about that." I look over at him, raising an eyebrow, and he chuckles again. "Don't think we all didn't see that picture Mason put up of him and Becca. Don't tell me you haven't had that on your mind ever since."

"Shut up." The guys all know Mason from when he visited, and they all followed him on social media.

"She looked good, bro," Dean pipes up.

I sigh. "I know." She looked freaking beautiful in the picture. All she'd been doing was laughing at something Mason had said, but I couldn't help but wish it was me who had made her laugh, me who had made her look like that. It gave me an ache in my chest that I've been trying to ignore ever since.

"You think they're—"

"No!" I snap. "The little bitch put it up because he knew I'd see it." I know that's the truth. Mason wants me to get back with Becca. Jake thinks I should give it another go too. They've both told me enough times that I should forgive her, and Mason put that picture up so I'd see her and have her stuck in my head even more than usual. It worked. He put one of them up just after the start of the fall semester, and I must have spent hours staring at it. Then he put another one up a couple days ago, and she looked happy and healthy, way better than she did when I last saw her. I was relieved, relieved she was doing better, but scared that the change in her was due to someone else making her happy. The news that Bernie asked her out has also been messing with my head, and I've been dreading confirmation that she's started dating someone else. I know she's not dated anyone since me; I know she wanted to give it another go too, but I just don't know if I can get over it, no matter how much I want to. She broke my heart—actually, scrap that, she *destroyed* my heart.

"Dude, maybe you should talk to her. People make mistakes. She makes you happy," Marty says.

"Fuck that! Forget her," Jason says. He used to love Becca, but I know he thinks what she did is unforgivable.

"Shut up, man," Dean chimes in. "He's not happy without her, and we all know it."

I just sit back, ignoring them all. I'm grateful when Dean changes the subject and starts talking about the girl from his study group that he invited to the party. Jake walks into the room and closes the door behind him, blocking out the noise from the other room. I glance over at him, ready to offer him a drink, but I know instantly that something's wrong. He's tapping his right hand against his leg, which has always been his give, and his face looks pale and drawn.

"What's up?" I ask, sitting up straighter in my seat. Jake is one of the most chilled-out people I know. To shake him up like this, it must be something bad. He presses his lips together, glancing around the room, almost as though he's checking out who's present. My brow furrows; he's making me nervous. "What is it?"

"I just got off the phone with Mason. He's been trying to call you all day."

"My phone's broken. I'm getting a new one sent tomorrow."

He nods and takes a deep breath. "Robbie Mulligan's been arrested for attempted rape."

The room falls deadly silent, and I swear my heart stops beating.

"Wh-What?" I manage to stammer out. I stare at him while he stares back at me. All the horror, worry, and disgust I feel is reflected on his face. He starts to shake his head at me, and that's when the reality starts to creep into my head, the horrifying reality of what he's telling me.

"What happened?" Jason eventually asks.

Jake doesn't take his eyes off me. "Mason said it was a freshman he's been dating. Apparently he was trying to get her to sleep with him. She said no, and it turned nasty. He's been released on bail."

"Bastard," Dean mutters under his breath.

"He's denying it. It's her word against his."

None of us say anything as his words settle in. My mind races as I think about what this means, and horror and dread rip through my entire body when I think about him with Becca. My eyes find Jake. I know Jake well enough to know what he's thinking.

"No," I state firmly, shaking my head. "No. No. It's not what you think," I say to him. "No," I say again, desperation creeping into my voice. I'm being stupid. Mulligan's a bastard, a total bastard, but this is separate from Becca. He didn't do this to Becca, because as much as I hate that Becca betrayed me, the alternative is worse. It's so much worse.

He shakes his head sadly. "It didn't make sense, Ry. She never would have done that to you."

"No!" I snap back at him, unable to comprehend what

he's saying. "No, she would have said something!"

"What did she say, Ryan? When you first confronted her about it?" Jason says quietly, pulling my eyes away from Jake. I look around, and the boys are looking at me intently, waiting for my response. The party atmosphere is long gone from the room, and their faces are deadly serious.

I think back to that day when I woke up and first saw the pictures of her. I didn't think. All I felt was devastation, total devastation, and then I got mad, drove straight to the airport, and got on a flight. I burst into her room and screamed at her. I didn't let her speak; I just wanted her to feel as bad as I did, to feel as hurt as I did, but if I think about it, really think about it, she didn't look guilty when I burst into her room. She didn't look shameful. She looked broken. She looked utterly devastated, and all I did was scream at her. "She didn't say anything," I say after a pause. "I didn't give her a chance." My words come out flat. No one responds, and I realize I'm gripping the bottle of Jack so hard, my knuckles are white.

"She didn't tell me what happened either, Ry. All she ever said was that it just happened."

"No," I repeat, desperate for it not to be true, desperate for it not to be a possibility. "No, no, no. I swear to God, I'll kill him."

"Wait, don't jump to conclusions. Has Mason spoken to Becca?" Marty asks.

Jake shakes his head. "He can't get ahold of her. She's not at her apartment, and she's not answering her phone. I tried calling her too." He pauses, dragging his hands over his face, screwing his hands into fists and rubbing his eyes in despair.

"Say it!" I bite out, knowing he's holding back about something.

He sighs. "Mason said he heard she was talking to the girl who pressed charges. Becca stood up for her in front of everyone." He pauses again, and I know he's not finished.

"Jake, fucking spit it out."

"One of the guys thinks he did the same to Becca. That night, when they supposedly had sex? Apparently, when she got to the party, Robbie told them all he was gonna get her that night. He's been after her for years, wanting to get one over on you. Someone said they saw him follow her upstairs, and this one kid said he saw her just after they came out of the room." He pauses and closes his eyes. When he opens them, I see tears as he looks straight into my eyes. "He said she was shaking all over and looked a complete mess. Apparently he tried asking her if she was okay, but she just ran away. When Robbie said they had sex and she never said anything different, he just assumed that was what happened and left it."

I can't breathe. I officially cannot breathe. It feels like someone has reached into my body and ripped out my heart.

"Mulligan's been pulled in for questioning again. Someone else has filed charges against him. Mason doesn't know who but—"

"Fuck." My eyes find Marty at his words and his eyes are wide as he watches me. He's turned pale.

I shake my head. "No, it can't be Becca."

"It makes sense. That's what Sam would have been talking about at the party."

"Who's Sam?" Jason asks.

Jake turns to him. "Becca's best friend. Over summer, we

were all at a friend's party, and Kelly was saying something to Becca. Sam flipped. She's usually pretty chill and quiet, but she told Ryan to get Kelly away from Becca or she'd lose it. She's never like that. Then when Ryan tried to defend himself, she told him he didn't know anything, but Becca cut her off before she finished."

"You think Sam knows something?"

"Fuck, Ryan! I don't know. She got Mulligan to drop the charges against you. She had to have something over him to get him to do that."

I feel sick. Gut-wrenchingly sick. My entire body is shaking and my breathing is heavy.

"We need to call Sam."

Jake shakes his head. "I tried. She's not picking up either."

"Give me your phone," I demand of Jason.

He hands it over without a word, and I call the only person I can think of that might know something—my mom. I speak to her for a couple minutes before hanging up, dread filling every pore of my body.

"Her parents are on a flight over there now," I tell Jake. My voice sounds hollow, like it's not mine, and I really wish it wasn't. I really wish it wasn't me having this conversation. "Mom doesn't know what it's about, but she knows it was serious, and she said Becca's mom was distraught." The gravity of the situation hits me as I realize what this probably means.

There's complete silence in the room, complete and utter silence, and it's deafening to my ears. I shake my head. "She would have told me, right?" I turn to Jake. "She would have fucking told me, *right*?"

He shrugs and a few tears streak down his face which he

quickly swipes away. "I don't know, Ry, but it would explain everything. She never would have cheated on you and then she looked so sick over summer and Sam was so angry. She must have known."

"You think it's true? You think he raped Becca?" I glance around, my eyes wild.

No one replies.

"He fucking raped her, didn't he?"

Jake lets out a shaky breath and shrugs helplessly at me. The guys don't say anything. They're frozen. Complete horror covers their faces. *Holy fuck.* That bastard raped her. That bastard raped Becca.

My Becca.

"I need to go to her," I say, my voice actually shaking from the horror of it. I stand up and stride toward the door, but Jake steps in front of me, blocking my way. "Move," I demand, going to walk around him, but he pushes me back. "MOVE!" I shout again, getting in his face, but he pushes me back roughly again. I move forward, clenching my fists, prepared to do anything to get past him.

"You can't, Ryan, you need to wait."

"She needs me!"

I go at him again, and he struggles with me, pushing at my arms, not letting me through. Jason pulls me off him, and when I turn back to Jake, I see his fist coming out to meet my jaw.

I'm frozen in shock. Jake hit me. My best friend hit me. He drags his hands over his face and sighs in frustration, staring back at me. "No, Ryan! She fucking needed you a year ago when it happened," he says breathlessly. He groans, and I can see the despair in his eyes. "She fucking needed all of us, and we weren't there for her. We just fucking dropped her like she was nothing." His voice trembles, and I know how devastated he is; Becca was one of his best friends. "Now she needs to deal with this in her own way." My whole body starts trembling as the realization of our conversation hits me. "She let us all think she cheated so she could protect you. That's why he dropped the fucking charges, so she wouldn't tell."

I turn to the wall and start punching it again and again. I punch it until there's blood pouring down my hand. I punch it until I'm pretty certain I've broken at least one of my knuckles, and when that happens, I start kicking the wall again and again. Finally, after Dean and Marty pull me away and I collapse onto the sofa, I start to cry. I cry like a little girl, because the worst possible thing happened to the girl I love, the girl I thought I'd spend the rest of my life with, and when it happened, I abandoned her. And now, I can't do a damn thing about it.

# CHAPTER 36

*Becca*

I REACH FORWARD AND ACCEPT THE CUP OF COFFEE my dad has passed to me, not because I want it, but because I know that making it has made him feel useful, and if I don't drink it, he'll just need to find some other way to try to help me. He's already changed a bunch of lightbulbs and erected a few shelves, putting them together in the corner. It's stuff that didn't really need doing, but it keeps him busy and makes him feel better, so I let him do it. He watches me take a sip and then resumes the pacing he was doing before. I turn to my mom, and she offers me a tight smile and reaches out to rub my back. She's barely moved from my side since they arrived here; I swear she'd follow me to the bathroom if I'd let her. They don't know what to do, and I don't blame them. There's really nothing that they can do.

My mom's legal knowledge has been useful. After speaking to the policemen at the station, she's been able to find out that Robbie's been pulled in for questioning again, but she's warned me that he'll probably make bail again. She's told me it's going to be hard, and that it's really tough to get a conviction for rape, but when my belief faltered and I suggested that maybe I should drop it, her response was instant. She told me they will fight for as long as it takes and do whatever it takes to put Robbie Mulligan behind bars. She told me I couldn't risk him trying to do this again in the future, and said he deserves to pay for what he's done. She's right. He can't get away with this anymore, and I haven't backed down. I haven't withdrawn the charges, and I'm not going to. I'm going to see him in court, and I'm going to tell the jury exactly what happened.

Mason showed up at my apartment earlier; he had Bernie with him, and to my surprise, Liam was with them as well. Mason hugged me so tightly I thought I was going to get bruises, and then he sat down next to me and told me it was all going to be okay. He told me he believed me and is willing to tell anyone who asks him that he believes me. Bernie nodded his agreement, and I wanted to cry with relief. I know it won't be this easy with everyone, and I know a lot of Robbie's teammates will stand behind him and call me a liar, but it means a lot that it's not all of them. It means a lot that they're willing to stand by me and that I'm not alone.

Then Liam shocked me to the core by telling me he made a statement to the police about what he saw that night. I listened, astonished as he told me he thought something bad had happened when he saw me on the stairs. I swear he choked back tears as he relayed how guilty he felt that he hadn't gotten there sooner, that maybe he could have helped me. That's when I remembered bumping into him on the stairs. I've spent so long trying to block out that whole night and pretend it never happened, I'd forgotten I'd seen him. He had no doubts I was telling the truth, and he'd told the police that. He'd checked back on all the pictures from that night and had spotted a picture of Robbie with a scratch down his face. He reported it to the police and showed them pictures of him earlier in the night when he didn't have the scratch. Bernie said some of the guys had mentioned it the next morning when they saw him at a team meeting, but because Ryan showed up then and pulverized his face, the scratch had disappeared amongst all the other cuts and bruises and had been forgotten. Hopefully, they could use it as evidence against him. I glanced over at my mom at this, and she sat up straighter. I knew it wasn't proof, but this would help. It would show that I tried to fight him off. Coupled with Liam's testimony, it has to help. Maybe, along with Grace's story, we'll have a better chance than we thought.

My mom's already arranged a lawyer for me. One of her law school friends is a partner at one of the biggest firms in town, and Mom's stayed in touch with him over the years. In fact, Mom told me that Robbie's family contacted them, requesting that he defend Robbie, but he refused out of principle. Then he took on my case. I know it's only a small win, but the fact that Robbie's had to get his second choice attorney feels like a victory, and I'm taking it as one.

There's a knock on the door of the apartment, and Tina rises from her seat across from me and goes to answer it.

Tina turns back to the room and looks at me. She's not fully opened the door, so I can't see who's there.

"It's Ryan," she tells me quietly. "And Jake."

343

"No." My dad's response is instant, and he marches over to the door, opens it wider, and tells them both to get the hell away from me.

I turn to my mom in panic. She stands swiftly and pulls him away from the door, back toward the kitchen area. Tina glances at me questioningly, and I nod my head. She opens the door wider and steps aside. They both step in, Jake looking nervously toward my dad, and Ryan instantly finding my gaze. He looks like a shell of the Ryan I know. His eyes have black bags beneath them, his hair's disheveled, and his complexion's gray. Jake steps toward me quickly and grabs me in a fierce hug, wrapping his arms tightly around me. After a second, I return his hug, cautiously wrapping my own arms around him. His mouth finds my ear. "I am so, so, so fucking sorry, Becca," he whispers fiercely in my ear. "I promise I will make this up to you, and I promise you'll be okay."

I nod my head against his body, and I know I will be. For the first time in a long time, I feel like I will be okay.

He gives me one last tight squeeze before releasing me and stepping back. He gives me a tense smile and then moves away so it's just Ryan standing in front of me. I look at him as he stares back at me, and it hurts to see him like this. He looks like hell, like he hasn't slept in days. He looks completely and utterly broken, just like I did a year ago.

I turn to Tina and my parents and Jake, who are to the side, watching us. "Do you think you guys could give us a bit of space?"

"No." My dad's voice is hard, and he's staring daggers at Ryan. "I'm not leaving you alone with him."

"Dad," I admonish him quietly. "Come on, this is Ryan

we're talking about."

"Yeah," my dad says sharply. "And where was he a year ago when you needed him?"

"I know, sir." Ryan's voice cracks slightly at the words, but he doesn't look at my dad. He doesn't look away from me.

I turn to my parents, and my mom tugs on my dad's arm. When he dips down to speak to her, she whispers something in his ear. He frowns, but she keeps talking, and when he eventually looks back up, I know she's convinced him. "Thirty minutes," he tells Ryan, who eventually turns to face him. "I'll be back here in thirty minutes, and I swear to God, if you've upset her, I will strangle you with my own bare hands."

I roll my eyes at his words and watch as Tina grabs her things and then leads my parents out the door, with Jake following behind them.

"Ignore him," I tell Ryan. I suddenly feel nervous being in the same room as him, and I glance away. "He's just being protective. They're pretty upset."

"I deserve it."

I swallow hard. There's no point in pretending I don't know why he's here. "Who told you?"

He blinks. "Jake. Mason called him."

I nod and try to force a smile. Ryan's lips start to tremble. "I'm sorry," he whispers. "I am so, so sorry."

I don't know what to say. What can you say to the boy you're in love with when he's just realized you've been raped? When he's spent a year treating you like crap, and now realizes you didn't do anything wrong, realizes it's you who was the victim?

He rakes his hand over his face, and a heartbreaking sob

forces its way from his throat. He steps toward me, his clear blue eyes filled with pain, and he throws his hands up in despair. "Why didn't you tell me?"

I shrug my shoulders helplessly. "I tried." My voice is a whisper. "But you ran off. Then I tried calling you, and you blocked my number. I came to see you…"

He sucks in a breath like I've physically punched him and closes his eyes like he's in actual pain. When he reopens them, his eyes are full of tears.

"I hate myself," he tells me. "I will never, ever forgive myself."

I shake my head. "Ryan, don't. It wasn't you that did this to me."

"I swear to God I'm going to kill him," he tells me fiercely, blind rage taking over his features. "I'm going to fucking kill him."

"No, Ryan. It's with the police. We need to let them deal with it."

His hands clench into fists at his sides. "I need to do something, Becca."

I look at him, taking in the helplessness and desperation radiating off him, and I shrug my shoulders. "You could give me a hug," I whisper.

His eyes flash to mine, and within a second, he's in front of me, crushing my body into his, wrapping his arms around me so tightly. There's no doubt he's there and he cares. He hauls me against him and buries his head in my neck, telling me over and over again that it's going to be okay, that he loves me, and that he's sorry, and I hug him back, letting myself melt into him, just the way I've wanted to all along.

———————◆———————

"Remember the night we got together?" I ask. I'm curled up next to him on the sofa with my head on his shoulder. It feels like a dream being this close to him again. He's gripping my hand tightly, like he's scared I'll let go.

He nods, and a smile ghosts across his face. "I'll never forget it. It was the best night of my life."

I flash a genuine smile at his words, and lift my head to look at him. It was the best night of my life too. "Who'd have thought that four years later, this is where we'd be."

"I love you," he tells me, holding my gaze. "I never stopped. Even when I wanted to, I couldn't stop loving you."

I smile at his words. "I love you too, Ryan." And I do. I doubt there'll ever be a time when I don't love him.

He closes his eyes for a second, like it's painful for him to think it, and then he opens them again and leans forward, his forehead touching mine. "I know I don't deserve it. I know you won't be able to forgive me, but I promise I'll make it up to you. I'll spend the rest of my life making it up to you."

"Ryan—"

"I mean it, Becca. You will never understand how much I hate myself. I am so sorry."

I'm about to tell him it's okay, that it was Mulligan who did this and not him. That I understand that he was hurt, and that's the reason he behaved how he did—but the truth is, it's not okay.

"You know, Ryan, if I'd have gotten those pictures of you with another girl, I would have been pissed off too. I'd have been hurt and I'd have been furious, and I probably would have jumped to the exact same conclusion you did. And yeah, I would probably scream and shout at you too." I swallow hard because I need to say this. "But I wouldn't have not listened to you. I wouldn't have blocked your number. I wouldn't have refused to talk to you. I wouldn't have had sex with another guy that you can't stand just to hurt you, and I wouldn't have told you to go away and said I never wanted to speak to you again when you walked into the room and stood there in the doorway, completely broken after seeing me in bed with someone else. I wouldn't have splashed pictures of myself with different guys all over social media so you could see how much better I am without you." My voice has started trembling now, all the heartache and hurt of the last year overwhelming me. "And I wouldn't have taken my new boyfriend to a mutual friend's house and then not stopped him when he called you a whore." I take a deep breath and watch him as he tries to battle his emotions. He sits there and takes what I have to say, because he knows it's the truth, and he knows that what he did is unforgivable. "I wouldn't have done those things, Ryan. I would have thought that that wasn't you in the photos. I would have thought that maybe there was some explanation I was missing, or I would have at least asked how it had happened, because I'd know how much our relationship meant, how much I loved you and you loved me. I'd want to know why it happened, not just wipe you out of my life."

He's crying now. Big, fat tears are sliding down his face, and he doesn't attempt to wipe them away. "I'm so sorry, Becca." His words are barely above a whisper.

"It's not okay, Ryan."

He nods. "I know."

"You get that we can't be together again, don't you? That we can never be together again."

A loud sob echoes from his throat, and I realize for the first time that I'm crying too. Because it's the truth. We can't ever be together again. This horrible, horrible thing has happened to me, and it can never be unchanged. The events of the last year can never be taken back. I'll never be able to wipe away the memories, and Ryan and I will never be together again.

"I love you," he whispers.

"It's not enough, Ryan. It's just not enough," I say quietly, repeating the words he told me over the summer.

He starts shaking next to me, his sobs becoming hysterical, although he barely makes a noise. I reach out and pull him into me, wrapping my arms around him and hugging him tightly. "Sssh," I tell him, trying to soothe him. I squeeze him tightly and try to make him feel better, just as he should have done for me a year ago.

# CHAPTER 37

## Ryan

I SEE HER BEFORE SHE SEES ME. SHE'S WALKING PAST the library, and she's got her head down, powering forward. She glances up briefly to make sure no one's in her way, but then her eyes hit the ground again. I see Tina walking toward her, coming from the opposite direction. Tina shouts out to her, but Becca makes no motion to show she's heard her. Tina joins her and reaches out a hand to grab her attention. Becca immediately flinches, and panic crosses her face before she realizes who it is. It makes my heart ache that this is her world now, that when anyone nudges her or touches her unexpectedly, she thinks it could lead to an attack. I turn to my right to look at Mason, and his jaw is tense. I know he saw it too, and he turns to me and offers me a sad smile. Tina says something to Becca, and I see her relax now that she's in the presence of her friend. Tina's talking to her intensely about something and flashes a grin. Becca throws her head back and laughs at whatever she's said. I'm not prepared for the feeling it gives me to see her laugh. I've not seen her laugh in over a year, not once, and I've missed it. I've missed it more than I'd realized.

Tina links her arm through Becca's and keeps talking in Becca's ear. Becca's whole demeanor has changed now that she's with her friend. She's relaxed so much, compared to even a minute ago, and I'm reminded how much I like Tina. She's been there for Becca so much over the last year, back when it should have been me, and I make a mental note to do something for her to show her how much I appreciate all she's done.

They're getting closer to us now, to where we're leaning against the wall of the business building on the Southern U campus. It's on the way back to their apartment, and I knew she'd come this way. That's why we're waiting here.

Becca glances my way, and her gaze continues past me before snapping back to me in shock. She freezes in place. Tina carries on walking, but is pulled back because Becca's stopped dead. It's pretty comical. Tina turns and questions her, and then follows her gaze. I wave casually over at her as Mason chuckles next to me. She looks absolutely dumbfounded to see me. It takes a minute for her to snap out of her trance, and she slowly makes her way over to me, her eyes flicking between Mason and me suspiciously.

"Hi," I tell her, unable to hide my smile at her shocked expression.

"Hey," she responds, biting on her lip and furrowing her eyebrows. "What—what are you doing here?"

I grin and shrug my shoulders nonchalantly. "Just getting

used to my new neighborhood."

Her eyes widen. "What?"

"I just moved my stuff."

"What are you talking about?" she demands. She looks at Mason. "What is he talking about?"

Mason grins. "I've got a new roommate."

"You've got what?" She looks completely confused.

I smile at her. "I've always liked Southern U. You know that."

She looks between Mason and me again, then to Tina, who just shrugs back at her and then back to us again. I'm guessing our smiling faces must piss her off, because her mouth sets into a straight line and she turns a steely gaze on me, her beautiful green eyes flashing irritably. "Ryan David Jackson, you better tell me what's going on right now!"

Mason clears his throat. "T," he says, cocking his head to the left. "Let's give them a minute."

Tina sends Becca a questioning look, and Becca nods her head in agreement. She watches as Mason and Tina walk away to give us some space. Then she turns back to me and raises an eyebrow.

"I moved here," I tell her.

"You moved here?"

"Yes."

"To Southern U?"

"Yes."

"From Cal State?"

"Yes."

Her jaw falls open, and I can see her brain working over the information I've just thrown at her. "Are you crazy? Ryan,

352

you can't do that."

I laugh. "I can, and I did."

"What? I don't get it."

I laugh. "Becca, I moved here."

"But you go to Cal State."

"So?"

"You have a scholarship."

"I don't care about that."

"So you left the team?"

I shake my head. "There are only three games left in the season. I'll fly back for them."

"Your coach was okay with that?"

"He doesn't have a choice." And he doesn't. Coach was pissed when I told him I was moving here, to say the least. He was fucking furious with me, but I told him I was going and wouldn't change my mind. He tried everything he could to make me stay, told me I'd have to pay back my scholarship if I didn't honor it, told me everyone in the industry would think badly of me and I wouldn't have a future in it. He told me I was throwing away my future over this. I told him he had a perfectly good backup, and he could use him for the rest of the season. I left his office, and he immediately followed me out into the locker room and barked at Evan that he needed a meeting with him. Evan sent me a sympathetic look and then followed him back into his office. I'd already told Evan what I planned on doing, and even though I knew he was disappointed, I knew he supported me. I'd showered and was ready to leave when Coach appeared again, asking for another word with me. This time he was calmer and told me he respected my decision. Evan must have told him why I made it, and

353

he asked me to consider if I would finish the season as their quarterback. He told me he'd clear it with the college as long as I agreed to fly back two days before the games for practice and made sure I was training when I was away. If I'm honest, relief flooded me at the solution he'd come up with. I didn't want to let the team down, and I didn't want to finish my college career this way, not when we were going for the championship, but if it was a choice between that and Becca, I was going to pick Becca every time.

"But what about your classes?"

"I'm working on that. I'm hoping they'll let me just pick up the notes from the lectures online, and then I can fly back again for finals."

"But what if they don't?"

"Can you believe they have classes here, Becca?" I tease her.

She rolls her eyes. "You can't transfer to Southern U. You're not exactly popular around here."

I shrug. Southern U is a huge football school, and I know I'll probably take some abuse if anyone recognizes me, but I don't care. If they don't let me finish my degree at Cal State from over here, I'll just show up for my exams. I can handle anything for a couple months, and this is where I need to be right now. I'm worried somebody might say something to Becca with the court case coming up. If anyone even dreams of saying anything about Robbie Mulligan to her, I want to be there. Mason says it's pretty mixed. There are still some die-hard Mulligan fans out there who think she led him on and he's the victim in this, but there are more that believe her, more that can see the truth. I think it helps that

Bernie, Mason, and some of the other players have publicly sided with her. By all accounts, their whole team is in complete disarray, and the administration has had to relent to the mounting pressure and suspend Robbie from the team. I'm hoping it's made Becca's life a bit easier, and I know she's always surrounded by people looking out for her. If it's not Tina or Maddy, then its Mason or Bernie, and even that kid Liam who made a statement. "I'll make it work."

"When did you decide this?"

"Over Thanksgiving." I can't believe it took me that long, to be honest. The day after Thanksgiving, the old crowd came over to my house—Jake, Mason, John, Katie, Jessica, and a few others. The plan had been to go to a couple of bars—but I wasn't in the mood to party. Really, neither were they. Even though nobody was saying it, I knew Becca was on everybody's mind. She'd gone with her parents to Hawaii for the break; they wanted her to have some space. I'd wanted to join them but she told me she needed to spend some time with her parents. We ended up sitting around at my house with a couple of beers and some music playing in the background. Marty and Jason showed up too, since they were fairly local. I sent Sam a message, inviting her over, but she didn't reply. It hurt knowing I'd probably ruined my friendship with her. She wasn't as quick to forgive my behavior as Becca was.

Mason was talking about one of his roommates that had dropped out, and I suddenly realized he had a spare room. It was like a lightbulb went off in my head. I invited myself to move in with him and was working out when I should fly over there by the end of the night. I expected Marty and Jase to be pissed with me for just up and leaving; they were some of the best friends I'd ever had, and I loved being their room-mates and teammates, but they never once said anything against it, even though this was before Coach made his of-fer. It was Marty who trolled online to find me the cheapest flight to get here. Jake was all for it too, and I knew I'd miss him the most. I've seen Jake practically every day ever since I can remember, throughout school, over summers, holidays, and college, but we both knew this was the right thing to do. Becca comes first.

"So you're living with Mason?" she asks, her head turn-ing to face him.

"Yeah, and Bernie and those other guys." To be hon-est, I thought it might be a bit weird seeing Bernie, know-ing he's into Becca, but we only mentioned it once. He apol-ogized for stepping on my toes, but I just shrugged it off and told him he'd be crazy to not be interested in Becca. I get the idea Becca's not interested in dating anyone right now, but if it comes to it, I'll just have to deal with it when it happens (whether it's Bernie or not). I just want her to be happy, and if that means she has to date someone else, then so be it.

"Seriously? You swear you've really moved here?"

I start to laugh. "Yes, Becca. I've really moved here."

"Why would you do this, Ryan?"

I'm honest with her. "Because I want to be closer to you."

Her face softens, but she's shaking her head. "This won't change anything, Ryan. I meant what I said. We can't be together."

The words hurt just as much as they did when she said them the first time, but I nod my head. "I know. This isn't about us being together. I just want to be here for you. I've got a lot to make up for, Becca. I can't do that from California."

"Ryan—"

"I don't expect anything, Becca. I just want to be your friend. I know you can't forgive me—"

This time it's her that cuts me off. "Ryan, I do forgive you."

"So—"

"What do your parents think about this?" she asks suddenly.

I shrug. "They're supportive. They know I have to be here." I was surprised, actually, by how supportive they were. My dad made no secret of the way he felt about Becca after we broke up. He blamed her for my behavior, and I know it caused tension between my parents and hers. When he found out the truth about what happened, he turned pale, and I knew he was ashamed of himself. Regardless of that though, he's really into my football career, not in a pushy, forceful way, but I know he's really proud of me and is my biggest supporter. When I told them I was moving, I expected some resistance, but my mom just smiled and told me she was proud of me. My dad shook my hand and told me I was doing the right thing. I wasn't sure they fully understood, and I reiterated that it could mean the end of my football career, but my dad just told me that if it was a choice between football and Becca, I should pick Becca every time. I loved them even more in that moment. My sister, Lisa, is totally on board too. She called me when she heard and told me how proud she was of me. She gave me a full-on lecture about how I couldn't put any pressure on Becca and couldn't expect things to go back to how they were, and she mentioned again and again (as if I didn't know) that I had a lot of making up to do. But, she also told me I was doing the right thing and promised to come visit with her husband and kids, and then she told me she loved me.

"Really?"

I smile. "Really. They're looking forward to visiting."

"So you'll be here until you enter the draft?" she asks uncertainly. I can tell it's starting to dawn on her that I won't change my mind, and she's calculating how long I'll be around for her.

"I'm not entering the draft."

She actually gasps in shock, and her eyes go wide. I force myself not to laugh at her.

"Ryan! What the hell?"

"Relax, Becca. It's not that big a deal."

"It is a big deal!" I chuckle at her words and glance behind her to see Mason and Tina watching us with interest. I'm guessing Mase has filled Tina in on what my plans are. I look back to Becca, and she rolls her eyes at my laughter.

"Ryan, this is your future!"

*No*, I want to say. I want to say that she's my future, that nothing else matters to me, nothing but her, but I know she can't hear that right now. I know it's not fair for me to say that to her. I don't know if I'll ever be in a position to ever say that to her again. "Becca, you don't need to worry about it."

"But you're a football player. My dad said you're predicted to be a first round pick."

"None of that is important, Becca."

"Not important?" Her voice is getting shrill, and I can tell this is making her anxious. I need to calm her down. "This is your life, Ryan."

I rest my arms on her shoulders and look in her eyes. "Becca, it's fine. It's only throwing a ball around a field, remember?" I wink at her, and I see her relax just slightly. I know that's all Becca thinks football is. I know the only reason she's ever shown any interest in it is because of me.

"Ryan, I can't be responsible for you not going pro. It's what you've worked toward for years."

"I know." It's true, I have. "But if it's meant to be, it'll still happen. I've spoken to Bobby Douglas, and he's going to speak to some of the local teams to see if I can do some training with them over the summer."

"Local teams? There's only one local team, Ryan!"

She's right; there's only one professional team in the area, but they're pretty good, and if I could get in with them, I'd be more than happy. "So, I'll have to get in with them."

She looks horrified. "But isn't the point of going into the draft so that you'll make a ton of money?"

"I don't care about the money, Becca." I really don't. I'm lucky to never have had to worry about it, and as an NFL player, I'd have more money than I've ever dreamed about, but if that doesn't work out for me, I'll find another way to enjoy football, even if it's just coaching peewee. I honestly, hand on heart, don't care.

"But what if it doesn't work out, Ryan? What if you don't get to train with a team and they don't want you?"

"Becca, in a few months, I'll have my business degree. Seriously? Your lack of faith in me is pretty embarrassing. Football doesn't define me. I'll find something else I want to do. I'm twenty-one, I can do anything I want."

She's not convinced. She stares at me for a few beats then looks away. After another minute of her processing everything I've just told her, she turns back to me. "I can't be the reason you don't achieve your dreams, Ryan," she tells me quietly.

She's my dream, always has been. I still can't believe she'd doubt that, but then I guess that's my fault. I've always told her how much I love her, how long I've loved her, and then as soon as I thought she betrayed me, I bailed on her and let her down in every way possible. I'm going to make it up to her if it's the last thing I do. "Becca, dreams change. I'm doing this, and I won't regret it. I promise you."

She bites her lip. "And you know we can only be friends, right?"

I nod. As much as it hurts, I know that's all she can give me right now. Maybe that's all she'll ever be able to give me. "I know, and I need to be here for that to happen. It won't work if I'm in California and you're here. Texting and phone calls aren't the same. We need to be in the same place."

"I'm not moving, Ryan. After I get my undergrad, I want to go to medical school here too."

"I know, and the day you graduate, I'm gonna be there, and I'm gonna be so proud of you."

"You don't have to do this."

"I want to, and I don't expect anything. I'm just hoping that every once in a while, you'll let me walk you to class or take you to dinner, just as friends."

"You're really moving here?" she asks again, like she can't believe it.

I nod my head. "I'm already here. There's just going to be

a month of flying back and forth for games, then I'll access my lectures online and hopefully be able to fly back for finals and my graduation. This is my home from now on."

Her eyes fill with tears, and she starts blinking her eyes rapidly, trying to brush them away. "You're really doing this for me?"

I smile at her. "I'm really doing this for you." I pause. "And the pizza. I hear they have really good pizza here."

She starts to laugh and playfully hits me across the stomach. It feels so good to hear her laugh. I've done the right thing; I know it with every inch of my being. Then she surprises me by stepping forward, wrapping her arms around me, and burying her head into my chest. My heart literally skips a beat at being this close to her again, and I wrap my arms around her and hug her tightly. I suddenly feel this strange sense of calm, and it's the most right I've felt since I found out what Mulligan did to her. I think about it all the time, about what he put her through, and how I've let her down. I spend most of my days thinking about how I can punish him, how I can make him suffer as much as he's made her suffer, and it's getting to the point of obsession. But, when she's in my arms, nothing else matters. It's just the two of us in the world, and everything just feels right.

She pulls away too soon. "You know you're crazy right?"

I shrug. "Actually, I think it's the best decision I've ever made." She rewards me with a blinding smile. I turn her so she's facing Tina and Mason, who are trying to pretend they're not watching us, and gently nudge her in their direction.

Becca playfully shoves Mason away when she gets close to him. "Did you know about this?" she demands.

He throws his arm around her and hugs her into his side. "Pretty awesome, huh?"

She looks over at me, her eyes shining. "Yeah, pretty awesome."

"So," Mason says, clapping his hands together to get everyone's attention. "I was thinking we should go for some drinks tonight." He glances at Becca. "Just something low-key, I promise, just a quiet bar. I'll invite some guys you already know, Bernie and a few others, so we can give Ryan a bit of a welcome and introduce him to some people. Tina said you're free, and you should invite Maddy and whoever else you want."

She bites her lip, unsure. "I don't drink in public anymore," she says quietly.

My heart slams into my throat at that admission. The fact that she doesn't feel safe enough to have a drink in a bar breaks my heart, but I don't miss a beat. "Okay, so I won't either."

She rolls her eyes. "Ryan, you can't not drink at your own welcome drinks."

"Yes I can," I tell her firmly. "I'll be there, Mase will be, Tina too. Nothing will happen to you, I promise. Come on, tell me you'll come."

She pauses, considering the situation, and after a minute, she nods. "Okay. I'll be there." She turns to Mason. "What time?"

"Eight? I thought we could go to Salloway's, near the river. It's usually pretty chill."

"Sounds good." She links her arm back through Tina's. "See you guys later," she tells us before turning Tina and heading home. I watch as she leaves, and I know without a shadow of a doubt that I've done the right thing.

For me, Becca is the right thing.

# EPILOGUE:
# FOUR YEARS LATER

*Becca*

"TO RYAN!" JAKE MAKES THE TOAST, AND WE ALL clink our glasses together while Ryan squirms with embarrassment. I smile over at him, and he grins back. Tonight Ryan started in his first NFL game, and he was unbelievable. He got his chance when their starting quarterback got injured a couple days ago, and he got the call saying he'd be starting. He didn't disappoint. He got a bunch of us tickets for the game; Jake flew in, along with his parents and mine. Even Evan Princely flew in from Miami, where he got drafted, and his old roommates from Cal State, who no longer play football, came too. I honestly thought I might burst with pride at one point. It's amazing to see someone's dreams come true.

We're in a downtown bar, where the team after-party is being held. We all went for dinner after the game, and when our parents decided to head back to the hotel, we decided to stay out and celebrate. Even his sister is with us. I lean over Mason, who is sitting between us, and hand Ryan my phone, indicating that he should read the message. It's from Sam, telling me to tell him congratulations and that she's really happy for him. I know it'll mean a lot to him. Their relationship has been pretty strained over the last few years; Sam never really forgave him for the way he was with me when we broke up, but they've seen each other a lot more recently, and I think the fact that I've forgiven him has helped Sam finally stop blaming him. I know he's always thought a lot of Sam and hates that she stopped caring for him.

Chatter resumes around the table, and as I look around, I realize I'm actually comfortable here. Usually in a bar like this, where the drinks are flowing and there are way more football players than should be allowed in one room, I'd be on edge and nervous, thinking about what could happen. Tonight, I'm not. I'm actually just enjoying the moment. I've come a long way in the last four years. I've even plucked up the courage to wear a dress. I've also styled my hair, and I'm wearing more makeup than I have in a long time.

"Are you okay, Becca?"

I glance over at Abbey, Jake's girlfriend, and she's smiling sweetly at me. I watch as he laces his fingers through hers, and I grin. Jake is seriously loved up, and it's so cute to watch. They met almost a year ago, and he went from being a complete player to a one-woman man within the space of a week. He catches my gaze on his fingers and rolls his eyes at me, but he doesn't loosen his grip on her. He's completely and utterly smitten.

"I'm great," I tell her.

"How's medical school going?"

I grin. It's tough and I have to work my ass off to keep on top of everything, but it's worth it. It's where I'm supposed to be and I can't wait until I actually get to meet patients and help them. "It's awesome."

She smiles back at me. "What time is Mike getting here?"

Mike is the guy I've been dating for the last four months. We met through mutual friends. He couldn't make the game today, but is supposed to be coming for drinks. "Soon, I think."

"You guys seem pretty happy."

I smile. "Yeah, he's great. He's meeting my parents tomorrow."

The table falls silent at this, and I realize I maybe shouldn't have shared this in front of Ryan.

"Anyone want a drink?" Ryan stands abruptly and quickly walks away toward the bar before anyone can give him an answer.

I bite my lip as I watch him go. I try not to talk about guys in front of Ryan, just like he never talks about girls in front of me, but I didn't think before answering Abbey's question. Ryan's met Mike a couple times, and he even told me to invite him tonight. I glance over at Jake. "Is he okay?"

Jake shrugs. "I'll check." He stands and goes to follow him to the bar. Mason trails behind him. Most of the other guys are already over there.

"I'm so sorry, should I not have said anything?" Abbey looks at me in panic, but I shake my head.

"It's fine." My gaze finds Lisa, who is watching her brother with a strange look on her face. She turns to me and offers me a sad smile. "Should I leave?" I ask.

She shakes her head violently. "No. Trust me, out of everyone here tonight, he'd only be upset if you left."

I sigh as I watch Ryan at the bar. He's listening intently to whatever it is Jake's saying to him. Things were complicated between Ryan and me for so long, and I thought we were finally in a good place. The last thing I wanted to do was upset him on his big night.

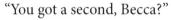

"You got a second, Becca?"

I look up to see Jake standing over me. I nod my head and move over so he has room to pull his chair next to me. Lisa and the rest of the group discreetly get up to go to the bar or the bathroom.

"Is he okay?" I ask.

"Yeah."

I swallow. "Is he upset about Mike?"

Jake glances over at Ryan, who is standing by the bar, looking lost in his own thoughts while people chat around him. "I think he was just surprised that Mike was meeting your parents. It's a pretty big step."

"It's not like that. He just knows they're in town and that I'm meeting them tomorrow. He has the day off, so he said he'd come along."

"Are you guys just dating or are you officially his girlfriend now?" I don't know how to answer that question. We haven't really had the conversation, but it's definitely moving in that direction. Jake sighs and takes another look at Ryan. "It's just hard for him, that's all."

"Yeah." I get it; it would be hard for me too. I just haven't met any of the girls Ryan's dated over the last few years. He's kept them away from me.

"You know, you look really great tonight, Becca."

"Thanks."

"I mean it. It's been a long time since I've seen you dress up."

I look down at the black dress I'm wearing that stops at mid-thigh. I saw it in the window of a shop in the city a couple weeks ago. It's sleeveless and high in the neck, short and formfitting. I haven't worn anything revealing since the night Robbie raped me, have never felt comfortable enough to do it, but this dress kept playing in my mind, and I went back and bought it. When Tina said she wanted to go home and change after the game before coming here, I knew now would be a good opportunity to wear it. When she saw what I was wearing and asked me if I wanted her to do my makeup for me, I didn't say no. I wanted to look good tonight.

"I'm wearing it because of Ryan," I tell him with a sigh. He raises an eyebrow. "Not because of that, not because I want him to like how I look." That's not strictly true; of course I want Ryan to think I look good, but it's more than that. "I know he's here, and because of that, nothing will happen to me." It's true; Ryan's here, so I know I'll be safe. I know nothing will happen to me with him looking out for me.

Jake's face falls. "Nothing like that is ever going to happen to you again, Becca."

Deep down I know that, but I feel like you can never be

too careful. I hate that this is what I'm like now. I was always so spontaneous and do-what-you-want; sometimes it feels like I'm scared of my own shadow. At the same time, I'm so much better than I was, and that's largely due to Ryan. I know nothing bad will happen to me whenever he's around. He watches me and makes sure I'm comfortable. I'm safe when Ryan's around.

As if to prove my point, Ryan comes over at that moment and places a glass of wine in front of me. My gaze immediately falls to his other hand, and I see the bottle of water he's clutching. "No. Honestly, this is your night," I tell him, pushing the glass away. He shakes his head, and when I reach for my wallet to try to give him some cash, he rolls his eyes and waves me off before walking back to the bar and joining Dean and Evan. He never accepts any money from me, and it drives me crazy. I know he earns more in a year than I'll probably earn in twenty, and that amount is only going to grow, but I don't want him to think I expect it of him.

"He's still doing that?" Jake asks, nodding toward the water bottle.

I nod. He does it every time we're out. He knows I like to have a drink, but I won't drink in a crowd, and especially not with people I don't know, and therefore a bar is definitely off limits. That's why he stays sober and lets me drink. The only time he ever drinks when I'm there is when we're in a small group at someone's house and he knows I'm comfortable and can relax. Jake's done it for me too, and so has Mason, but only when Ryan's not there. If Ryan's there, he sees it as his job. I did feel bad for a while, but now I think he enjoys it.

I glance at the bar and see a brunette has approached

him. She's smiling shyly at him, and she looks beautiful, even from all the way over here. My heart tightens at the sight of it, but I push the feelings away. It's hardly fair when I'm waiting for Mike to arrive.

"Why aren't you together?" Jake asks suddenly, and my gaze snaps back to him. He knows why we're not together. "I get it, Becca. Trust me. I can't even begin to imagine the hell you went through that year and the way Ryan dropped you"—he shakes his head at the memory—"the way I was with you. The only person who feels worse than I do about it is him. But, you should know, he never stopped thinking about you that whole time, not once. And the day he found out the truth? I've never seen a man so broken in my life."

I swallow hard. We barely talk about that time. I don't like to think about it.

"It was a long time ago now."

"I know. I just, I don't get it. I've never seen either of you as happy as you were when you were together. You two are meant to be together."

"Jake—"

"Doesn't that bother you?" Jake asks, nodding toward the bar and the girl who's talking to him. She steps closer to him on the pretense that she can't hear him, and it actually makes my jaw clench in anger. He smiles back at her, but it's not his usual cocky grin. He reaches for his water and takes a pur-poseful step away from her.

"Of course it does, Jake, but I want him to be happy."

Jake sighs. "Don't you get it, Becca? He's never going to be happy with anyone but you."

My eyes snap to his in surprise. *No.* Ryan doesn't feel like that about me anymore. It's been almost five years since we were a couple. He cares about me, I know that, and he loves me, just like I love him. It would be impossible with our history not to have feelings for each other, but we've both moved on. We both knew we couldn't go back, and we're friends now, friends that care very deeply about each other, but that's where it ends. I shake my head, and Jake leans forward so he's closer to me. "Look, Becca, you know that I love you, don't you?" I nod my head. Jake's been my friend since we were little kids, ever since he transferred to my school, all through elementary, middle, and high school, and all of college (except for after he thought I cheated on Ryan). He still calls me at least once a week to see what's going on, even from all the way over in California. "You're one of my best friends, Becca, and so is he. That's why I'm telling you this. I hate seeing you both like this when I know how good you are together."

"I know he loves me, Jake, but not like that, not anymore."

Jake smiles kindly at me. "You've managed to convince yourself of that because you haven't been with anyone else since him, and neither has he, not properly, not since he moved here."

"What are you talking about?"

"It's easy for you both to act like you're just friends when there's no one else in the picture. Now that Mike's around, it's threatened that, and he's upset."

I swallow hard. I knew he wouldn't be happy about it, but I didn't expect him to be upset. "But he's dated other girls too."

"Has he? Or has he just taken the occasional girl for dinner every now and again but not cared about any of them because the only girl he's ever given a crap about is you?"

"Jake!" This is all coming from nowhere. Ryan and I are friends now, best friends. It took a while, but we've made our relationship work, and we both know why we can't be together again. "He doesn't feel that way about me anymore."

Jake shakes his head. "He is so in love with you, Becca. He always has been. You need to forgive him, and then you can both move forward."

I'm surprised. "I have forgiven him."

"You really think so?"

I pause. I have forgiven Ryan. I've chosen not to let Robbie Mulligan dictate my life, and that means forgiving Ryan, Jake, and everyone who didn't treat me well throughout that horrible year. "I don't blame him for anything," I tell Jake after a minute.

"Then do something about it. Give you and Ryan another chance. Mulligan wanted to break you up—don't let him win."

My jaw tightens just at the mention of Robbie's name. He hasn't won. He was found guilty of rape and attempted rape. That week in court was the worst of my life. Sitting there and having the prosecution rip apart my character and try to paint Robbie as the victim was horrendous, but I didn't back down and I didn't crack. I stood my ground and I told the truth. To be honest, I didn't think the jury would believe me. I thought they'd be taken in by Robbie's smooth manners and stellar appearance, and when I was on the stand and my lawyer was making me go through every horrid detail for the benefit of the jury, I made the mistake at glancing at my parents. My mom forced a smile on her face when she saw me looking and nodded in encouragement, but it was my dad that got me. He was sitting there, looking straight ahead with tears dripping down his face as he tried to control his emotions at hearing me describe what happened. That's the only time I seriously considered getting up from the stand and not continuing. I hated seeing that look on my dad's face; it was the worst point for me. Ryan was there too, had been the whole time I was at court, but I couldn't look at him when I was talking about the rape. He could barely contain his fury when Robbie's name was mentioned, let alone when I described what he did to me. It was Robbie's arrogance that was ultimately his undoing. Turns out no one took the pictures of us outside that bedroom that night, which was a relief—I was glad to know no one stood by and let that happen to me. After having one of his friends take the picture of us on the dance floor, Robbie must have planted his phone somewhere and recorded the whole thing as a video and then took still images from it to send to Ryan. He was too dumb to get rid of the video, and the police found it when he was arrested. When the video was shown in court, it was pretty obvious what happened next. I made sure I didn't look at my parents when it was playing; I knew I wouldn't be able to handle that.

The relief I felt when he was found guilty was overwhelming. I wish I could tell you he spent years behind bars, but he didn't. He got sentenced to two years in prison and is already out. As far as I know he's working for his dad's firm now, spending his trust fund, and telling people he's the victim of my lies and saying he didn't do anything wrong.

I turn back to Jake. "I'm not letting him win. I'm with Mike now. Ryan's moved on too. I honestly don't think he feels that way about me anymore."

Jake shakes his head. "Ryan's dated a couple of girls, but he hasn't been interested in any of them. And to be honest, once they see how much he cares about you, they move on. They know they can't compete with that."

"What?" I knew Ryan had dated a bit, but we never talked about it in front of each other. The only reason he met Mike was because we bumped into him in a coffee shop. "They've broken up with him because of me?"

Jake smiles. "It never got to the stage where they could break up with him. He never let it get that far, and you and I both know that's due to his choice and not theirs. Even if he did give it a shot, it wouldn't last. No girl wants to be with someone who's crazy about someone else."

"Do you think I should back off? Give him some space?" I hate the thought that my presence is ruining his dating life, but I'm selfish. I have him back in my life, and I don't want to give him up.

"No." He sighs. "I'm gonna be honest with you, okay?" I nod my head. "I get it. What happened to you was terrible. Jesus, even thinking about it now makes me so mad, and so ashamed about the way I was with you, so I can only begin to imagine how guilty Ryan feels. But, I can promise you that boy has been in love with you since he was a little kid, and nothing has ever changed that, not even when he thought you'd slept with Robbie Mulligan. He gave up the draft for you, moved across the country for you, didn't care if he never got a chance with a team for you, and he was happy to do it. He didn't even give it a second thought, and that's the way it's supposed to be, because to him, you're all that matters." He pauses, looking into my eyes. "Do you get that, Becca? You're all he cares about. Nothing and nobody comes above you, not for him. I've seen you guys together, and I've seen you apart, and I can honestly say I have never seen either of you happier than when you were a couple."

"You think he's still in love with me?"

"I know he is, and I think you're in love with him too, Becca."

He reaches out and grips my hand. "Try to imagine your life without him, Becca. You don't have to right now because he's always there, but if you're moving on, then imagine if he did the same. He'll wait forever for you, but if you saw him with another woman, eventually settling down and starting a family with someone else, do you honestly think you could handle that?"

The simple answer is no. I can handle him dating other people occasionally because it's never in my face, and I know if I need him, he'll be there for me in a second—but the thought of him moving on and setting up a life away from me? No. I can't even begin to imagine my life without him.

"If you can honestly tell me that when you picture your life thirty years from now, Ryan's not in it, then I promise I'll never mention it again, but I bet you can't. You two are supposed to be together, Becca. You just have to move on and really forgive him." He smiles at me, squeezes my hand, and bends down to kiss my cheek before standing and leaving me alone with my thoughts.

My eyes find Ryan across the bar, and he's laughing at something Dean said to him. The girl he was talking to is long gone. It's like he feels my gaze, because he turns to face me and smiles.

Ryan really has been amazing over the last few years. It was strange how quickly I got used to him being at Southern U. After a couple weeks, it was like he'd always been there. The day after he moved, he showed up at my door with a coffee in hand and walked me to class. Then he was there waiting for me when it ended. I told him he didn't have to do that, but he just kept showing up every day. It was weird how quickly we fell back into our old routine. He was as easy to be around as ever, and he instinctively knew when I needed to be made to laugh and when I needed to be left to my own thoughts.

After a few weeks of this, I started to feel guilty. Ryan had given up Cal State and all his friends for me, someone who wasn't even his girlfriend anymore. I knew this should have been his time, basking in the glory of his college football career and celebrating the end of college with all his friends in California, but whenever I mentioned this to him, he just told me there was nowhere else he'd rather be.

Ryan's never had any problems making friends, but when he came to Southern U, he turned down most of the parties he got invited to. He joked that he couldn't show his face because he was the enemy, but I know it was because he knew I wouldn't go and he was happy to stay in and watch a movie with me. The only time he ever seemed interested in going to a bar or a club was on the rare occasion when I'd go. Then he'd be right there next to me, making sure I was okay.

He never once complained about anything, not even when I walked out of class one day and saw a bunch of idiots wearing Kings t-shirts surrounding him. I watched for a second as he ignored them, as they tried to taunt and antagonize him. It was only when they referred to his "slut" that I realized they were talking about me. Ryan flattened the guy within seconds and looked ready to take on the rest of them when he spotted me. He broke away immediately, grabbed my hand, and pulled me away. Then when we'd put enough distance between us, he pulled my trembling body into his arms, wiped away my tears, and told me again and again that they were assholes who didn't matter and that anyone who thought they could pull that shit could answer to him. That's when I realized that maybe his move here hadn't been as easy as I'd thought it had been.

I think the guiltiest I felt was on the day of the draft. A bunch of us sat around at Mason's house watching it on TV. Bernie had decided to stay home, and his family and a bunch of his high school friends were there. There were camera crews there to watch his reaction, and he was predicted to go high. I'd felt anxious all day, knowing this was the night Ryan had been working toward all his life, but instead he'd have to sit there and watch his friend achieve his dream. I know it must have been tough for him, know he must have wondered what if, and when the commentators on screen actually commented on the top pick being a quarterback from Florida now that Ryan Jackson was out of the running, I'd felt sick for him. But, he didn't seem to care at all. He laughed and joked with everyone, wished Bernie the best of luck and cheered along with the rest of us when he went as the tenth pick of the first round. I kept apologizing to Ryan, telling him he should have entered, but he just rolled his eyes and told me to shut up. He told me there wasn't enough money in the world to get him to move away from me, and the truth is, I believed him. I knew to him, I was more important than his career, and even though we were just friends now, that meant more to me than I could ever explain. Luckily the Devils asked him to train with them within a month, but I honestly think, even if they hadn't, he'd still make the same decision again.

He's even the reason I started dating again. When Tina asked me to double date with her a couple months after the court case, I was ready with my standard rebuttal, but it was Ryan who convinced me to go. He was the one who told me I deserved some fun and that I could end up having an amazing time with a fantastic guy. He also told me he'd have his phone on him at all times and if I didn't feel comfortable, he'd come get me in a second. It felt so weird having that conversation with him, and even though he covered it well, I knew it was difficult for him to encourage me to date other guys. He did it though, because that was what was best for me.

I really don't know much about Ryan's dating history in the last couple of years. I know that when we're out together, he garners plenty of female attention, but he never looks at them twice. I know he's been on the occasional date, mainly football events where I've seen pictures of him with his date on gossip sites afterward, but we never discuss them. We never have to because they never seem to stick around.

As I watch him from across the bar, I can now see it for what it is. He never wanted any of them. He only wanted me, and he's spent the last four years trying to prove to me how much he loves me and how sorry he is. I thought I had forgiven him, I really did, but now, after speaking to Jake, I realize just how much he's done for me and just how much I love him.

I wave my hand at him, and he starts to walk over, but he

stops suddenly, a frown covering his face, which he quickly masks. My brow creases in confusion before a shadow crosses the table and I see that Mike has arrived.

"Hey." He grins down at me, dropping a quick kiss on my lips before he sits down next to me. "I'm about to start fangirling all over this place."

I chuckle. Turns out Mike is a die-hard Devils fan. I had no idea until a couple weeks into our relationship when we were at a coffee shop, ordering our drinks at the counter, and he suddenly gripped my hand tightly and whispered in my ear, "Oh my God, don't look now, but there's a Devils player in the corner, looking over here."

"What?" I looked up at him in confusion and then turned to look around the coffee shop.

"Stop," he hissed in my ear as the barista put his drink down on the counter. "Be cool."

"Who is it?"

"You know football?"

I shrugged. "A bit."

"Ryan Jackson." My heart sank. I hadn't told Ryan I'd started dating Mike. "He was the best college quarterback in the country a few years ago, but he didn't enter the draft. The Devils signed him, and I swear as soon as Miller has an off game, Jackson will get his chance and not look back. The guy's ridiculous."

"I didn't know you liked football."

He just grinned back at me and dropped an arm around me, and I resisted the urge to shrug it off. I would hate it if I saw Ryan with his arm wrapped around another girl. "Diehard, baby."

I laughed at the expression on his face and picked up my cappuccino before turning around. I spotted him right away. He was at a corner table with Mason across from him, and they were both looking at me. Mason smiled when he saw me, but Ryan had an impassive look on his face. I suddenly felt really uncomfortable, but I forced a smile anyway and waved over at them.

I looked back at Mike, who was looking at me in surprise. "Come on," I told him, walking over to their table.

"Hey Becca," Mason greeted me, standing up to give me a hug. Then he turned to Mike and held his hand out to introduce himself.

Ryan was just kind of staring at us in surprise, but then Mason cleared his throat, and that suddenly spurred him into action. He stood to shake Mike's hand and introduce himself.

Mike seemed a little star-struck. "I know who you are, man. I'm a huge fan."

I forced a laugh. "This is Mike," I told them. I turned to him. "I went to school with these guys."

Mike's eyes widened with surprise, and I almost laughed for real. It was so weird seeing people get star-struck around Ryan. "Mason actually went to school here too, and Ryan and I grew up together. Our parents are neighbors."

Mike's eyes widened even more, and I thought I could actually see him immediately calculating how I might be able to get him tickets to the games.

"Yeah, neighbors," Ryan echoed behind me.

I turned to him, and I could see the hurt on his face. I suddenly felt even more guilty. "Neighbors and friends," I told Mike. "Ryan is my very good friend."

"No way!" Mike grinned like a fat kid in a candy store. "My girl grew up with Ryan Jackson? That's crazy."

I flinched at the way he said "my girl" in front of Ryan, and I glanced sideways to see Ryan staring at me. I knew he was wondering why I hadn't told him about Mike. We'd seen each other a couple days before for dinner, but we never talked about our dates, and even though Mike was the guy I'd dated the longest since Ryan, I still couldn't bring myself to tell him.

"How long have you guys been dating?" Ryan asked, directing his question at Mike.

Mike looked over at me and stepped closer to me, dropping his arm around my shoulder. I tried not to tense. "Nearly three months?"

I nodded my head, unable to look at Ryan. I felt so guilty. I glanced over at Mason, who raised his eyebrows at me. He was not impressed with me, I could tell. I rolled my eyes back at him, but I knew it was me who was in the wrong. It didn't matter that I was dating Mike, but I should have told Ryan.

"You should come to a game sometime," Ryan said, and I turned my attention back to him. He smiled at Mike, and when he saw me looking, he grinned at me too, only it didn't quite reach his eyes. "Tell me which games you want to see, and I'll give Becca the tickets."

"That'd be awesome, man." Mike looked like he was about to explode with excitement.

"We better go," I told Mike. I turned to Ryan and Mason. "I'll see you guys later." I walked off without another word, and Mike followed. When he reached down and took my hand, it suddenly felt like the most unnatural thing in the world.

"You okay?" Mike asks, pulling me out of my daydream.

"Yeah, I'm good."

"How was the game?" Ironically, he couldn't even come to the game with us tonight. He's a doctor at the local hospital, and he got called in at the last minute.

"Good. Ryan was awesome."

"Told ya. I was watching it in between patients and caught a bit of it. He's gonna be a superstar, that guy. No doubt about it."

I smile, and my eyes go back to Ryan, standing at the bar. He's facing me, and even though it looks like he's in deep conversation with Evan, Mason, and now Jake, I can tell he's not really listening. He keeps shooting glances over here at us.

"Yeah. He deserves it, y'know? He's worked so hard."

"You must be really happy for him, what with you guys going so far back."

For some reason, tears flood my eyes, but I quickly blink them away and force a smile in Ryan's direction. Happy for him is an understatement; it's not possible for me to be any happier. "I'm so proud of him. This is everything he's ever wanted."

Mike eyes me for a minute, taking in the emotion I'm sure is written all over my face. Then he looks over at Ryan, who quickly looks away. He nods like he's had something clarified and then straightens in his chair, removing his arm from the back of mine.

"I'm surprised he's not surrounded by girls right now. A guy like him won't be short of offers any time soon."

I shift uncomfortably in my seat. Ryan's never been short of offers, ever, and Mike's right—he'll get even more now. I hate the thought of it.

"Becca, look at me," he says gently. I turn to him and see the small smile playing on his lips.

"You know I'm a huge football fan, right?"

I nod my head, unsure where he's going with this.

"Well, I followed Ryan's career when he was back in college. I swear he was going to be a first round pick, maybe even first pick. He was the best quarterback at Cal State in over twenty years, and they've had some pretty good ones." I nod my head; I know all about how good Ryan is. Even before we were together, back when I thought I hated him in high school and did everything to avoid him, I'd hear he was pretty special. My dad has told me countless times over the years that Ryan is the real deal when it comes to football. "Well, everyone was pretty shocked when he bypassed the draft and moved across country without a team to go to. By all accounts, he didn't care if he never went pro, he just wanted to make sure he was living in a certain city. Of course, his talent couldn't be ignored, and he got snapped up by the Devils after training with them for a couple weeks. I mean, that cost him easily a couple million. He would have gotten a huge deal if he'd gone into the draft, but he didn't care. When he was asked about it in interviews, he said there were way more important things than football and money." Tears start to prick my eyes, and I bite down on my lip. I remember that interview. "The rumor is he did it for a girl. His ex-girlfriend had been assaulted by that shithead, Robbie Mulligan, and he wanted to be closer to her, no matter what it took. He didn't care about his career or what anyone else thought. He was moving to be near the girl he loved, and that was that." Tears start to run down my face. "I remember at the time thinking, what a guy, what a sacrifice—he must really love her. Then I met you, and I realized it was actually a no-brainer." My eyes find his, and he smiles kindly down at me, his gaze locked on mine. "You're that girl, aren't you? The girl he moved here for, the girl he was willing to give everything up for?"

I nod my head, because it's true. I never really allow myself to think about it, about everything he could have lost because of me, but it is true, and I know he would do it all again tomorrow. "How did you know?"

He sighs, but not unkindly. "I see the way he looks at you, the way he watches you. I probably would have noticed it in the coffee shop that first day I met him, but I was so starstruck. Then I remembered how he came to be here, and it all started to make sense."

"I should have told you."

He shakes his head. "You have nothing to apologize for." He pauses. "I don't understand why you're not together."

"It's complicated."

He nods. "I'll bet. You were the girl from the Mulligan court case?"

"I was one of them," I whisper.

He inhales sharply, and his eyes flash with anger. "That fucking bastard."

I don't argue with him. Mulligan is a bastard, but I'm done letting him rule my life and affect my choices. Mulligan has nothing to do with me, and if I can help it, I refuse to even think about him.

"It kinda makes sense now," he mutters quietly.

I don't say anything as I see things become clearer to

him. We haven't slept together, even after nearly four months; I haven't slept with anyone since the rape. I had every intention of sleeping with Mike once I realized I wasn't just a one-night stand for him, realized he wanted a real relationship. I fully intended to, even daydreamed about it when I should have been studying, but when it came down to it, when I was in the situation, I just couldn't. He never pushed me, never made me feel guilty or acted annoyed with me; he just accepted it and let me take the lead on things. He really is a fantastic guy.

"Ryan's a really good guy, Becca."

"So are you."

He grins. "I am, aren't I?" I laugh. "And you, Becca McKenzie, are a very special lady. I can see why he's head over heels in love with you. I think you probably love him too, deep down, am I right?"

"I'm so sorry, Mike. I didn't mean to lead you on."

He shakes his head. "You didn't. It's been great hanging out with you, Becca." He looks me in the eye. "I mean that with all my heart, but it's not me you should be with." He pulls me into a hug, kisses me on the forehead, and gets up and leaves the bar without another word.

Half an hour later, I've pulled myself together. After Mike left, I got up and went to the bathroom to sort out my appearance, and then I joined Tina and Abbey, pretending to listen to what they were talking about. I've seen Jake glance over at me a couple times and smile at me reassuringly. His eyes seem to be talking to me, telling me I know what to do. I get the impression he was watching the scene with Mike and has an idea what happened.

Ryan's been surrounded by people for the last half hour. It's not just his friends, but Lisa and her husband, his new teammates, and the couple of girls who are trying their luck. When he finally steps away from them and goes to the bar with just Evan by his side, I stand up on shaky legs, smooth down my dress, and take a deep breath. I walk over to him, feeling more nervous than I ever have in my life.

He looks up as I approach. Evan grins at me and slaps Ryan on the back. "You must be so proud of your boy!" he exclaims, grinning from ear to ear.

Ryan shakes his head. "I'm not her—"

"So proud," I say, cutting off his words. "I've never been prouder. He deserves it all."

Ryan's eyes flash to me, and I smile at him. I mean every word.

Evan grins, looks between us both, and then turns and walks away, leaving us alone. Ryan takes a step closer to me and reaches his hand out like he's going to rest it on my hip-bone, but he stops himself and lets it fall to his side. I guess old habits die hard, even now. I look back up at him and take in his fitted jeans, tight t-shirt, and ruffled hair. My stomach flips. Even after all these years, he's still the best-looking guy I know. No one else even comes close; he's just so handsome. I swear every single year he gets better looking, and for the first time in four years, I'm allowing myself to think this instead of pushing my feelings aside.

"You don't look very happy, Ry." And he doesn't. This is

the moment he's been waiting his whole life for. He played the game of his career, and even though he's smiling and laughing at all the appropriate moments, I can tell he's not really into it. He shrugs. "You should be on top of the world," I tell him. "Everything you've ever wanted has come true."

He tilts his head to the side and offers me a small smile. "We both know it's not everything I've ever wanted."

My heart skips a beat, and I stare back at him for a minute, unsure what to say next. I'm pretty sure he's telling me I'm all he's ever wanted, just like he's the only person I've wanted since I was seventeen years old, but suddenly I'm tongue tied and don't know what to say.

"You know you look beautiful tonight, right?"

I smile at him. I think I already knew he thought that. When Tina and I walked in, he was talking with his friends with his back to us. When we joined them, he turned around, and I swear I saw him swallow before he flashed me his normal smile and told me I cleaned up well.

Out of the corner of my eye, I see the brunette he was talking to earlier watching us with interest. She's not glaring or anything, but it looks like she's trying to work out if he's taken or not. I suddenly decide, right then and there, that he is.

"That girl you were talking with is really pretty."

He raises his eyebrows and follows my gaze. I know a few years ago he would have loved to hear me say that. He loved when I noticed that someone else was interested in him, but now he doesn't know how to take me. Eventually he winks at me. "She's no Becca McKenzie."

"She keeps looking over here."

"She's probably just a jersey chaser."

"Maybe, maybe not. You won't know if you don't give her a chance." It comes out before I even know what I'm saying, and I feel like punching myself in the mouth. I don't know why I said that or what I'm trying to get out of it.

His brows furrow in confusion. "You really want me to go over there and talk to her?"

*No.* I suddenly realize, even though I'm the one that's started this ridiculous line of conversation, I desperately don't want him to go over there. It's like I'm trying to test him or something, and all of a sudden, I know with absolute certainty that's the last thing in the world I want him to do. I don't want him to talk to any other girls—ever. I just want him to be mine.

"No," I whisper.

His eyes bore into me. "Good."

I open my mouth to say something else, but no words come out as he waits for me. I glance around the bar, trying to muster up the courage to say what I really want to, and I am so, *so* nervous. I feel like I could throw up.

He clears his throat, and when I look back at him, he's pointing toward my empty hand. "You need another drink?"

I nod my head, hoping some liquid courage might do the trick and get me to say what I've always known but have been hiding for the last few years.

A minute later, he's facing me again and passes me a glass of wine. I put it to my mouth and chug half of it down. His eyes widen in surprise, but he doesn't comment. He's still clutching his water bottle. Suddenly I feel really exposed, standing at the bar in a crowd full of people who all want to know what Ryan's doing.

I glance around quickly and see a dark empty corner. "Can we talk over there?" I ask, nodding toward the space.

He looks over at the corner and doesn't question it. He follows me as I walk over there then I turn around, ready to lay my heart on the line, but he jumps in first.

"Where's Mike? I saw him come in."

"He left."

"Why? He just got here." I get the idea he knows exactly when Mike left, and I'm pretty sure he didn't miss the intense-looking conversation we were having.

"We broke up."

"What?" His mouth falls open in surprise. "But you really liked him. What did he do?"

"Nothing."

"Did he hurt you?" His face sets into hard lines. "I swear to God, if he did anything to upset you, I'll kill him."

"He didn't do anything, Ryan." I take a deep breath, close my eyes to summon all my courage, and then open them and look straight into Ryan's gaze. "He's just not the one."

He stills completely, and we stare at each other for several breaths. My heart starts beating faster in my chest, and he seems frozen in place.

"Do you love me, Ryan?"

He blinks at me for a minute before stepping in closer to me. He doesn't say anything for what feels like the longest time. "More than anything else in the world," he finally says. I can hear the truth in his words.

"I love you too," I tell him. His entire face softens. I haven't said that since the night he came to see me after he found out the truth about Robbie. He told me he loved me that night too. Then he told me a year after when Robbie was found guilty, but I didn't say it back. The only other time he's told me in the last couple years was when he was hanging out at my place, having a couple beers and eating pizza. I burst out laughing at something on the TV, and when I turned to him, he was watching me, and he came out with it. I didn't say it back. He left pretty soon after that, and neither of us mentioned it again. I take another deep breath. "I know you love me, but are you in love with me?"

He steps ever so slightly closer to me, and my heart starts beating even faster in my chest. His beautiful blue eyes don't leave mine.

"I have been in love with you, Rebecca Louise McKenzie, ever since I was a little kid, for as long as I can remember."

My eyes bore into his, and even if I didn't hear the truth in his words, I can see the emotion in his eyes. I know he means every word.

Suddenly he looks down, like he's remembered himself. "I'm sorry, I shouldn't have said that. I wasn't thinking, I know you can't forgi—"

I step forward into his body, reach up onto my tiptoes, and press my mouth against his, cutting off his words. He reacts almost immediately, reaching up to cradle the back of my head with one hand and gently resting the other hand on my hip. It starts off cautious and gentle, our mouths gently brushing over each other, testing each other out and not pushing the boundaries, but the old passion soon takes over, and he wraps his arms around my waist and pulls my body against his. I don't give a damn when I hear hoots break out from the people in the bar watching us, and I don't give a shit that all our friends and family are probably watching us make out like teenagers in front of a bar full of people and half of his football team. I don't care at all, because this feels like the most right thing I've done in years. It feels like I've come home.

After another couple of minutes, we break apart, breathless. He leans his forehead against mine and looks into my eyes. "Becca." His voice is choked with emotion.

I smile at him and take his right hand in my left, just the way we always used to.

"No more wasting time, okay? I want to be with you, Ryan."

He closes his eyes, and when he opens them, his whole face is shining. "I love you so fucking much, Becca."

"Good, because you're stuck with me."

His chin dips again, and his lips find mine. It's even more heated this time as he backs me up against the wall, and the cheers are getting even louder. It reminds me of high school, when he kissed me in the cafeteria in front of everyone, and the memory makes me smile against his lips. I pull away and look behind him. It's Jake who's leading the applause; he's standing, facing us, his face positively glowing with happiness. Lisa stands next to him, wiping away a tear, and Tina is practically jumping up and down with excitement next to them while Mason and the rest of our group are laughing and smiling from behind them. It warms my heart that they're all so happy for us.

I look up at Ryan, and he's already looking down at me. He looks the happiest I've seen him in years, and my heart swells to know I'm the one who caused it. I beam back at him, and I know my face probably mirrors his own.

"Come on," I tell him, tugging on his hand. "Let's go. Let's go back to your place." I want more than anything to be alone with him, and I realize in surprise that I want to be in his bed again, something I haven't wanted in years.

He swallows hard. I see his eyes flare, and I know he wants me too, but something stops him. He still looks cautious. "Are you sure?"

I nod. "I've never been more sure about anything in my life."

And that's the truth—nothing has ever felt so right to me.

---

I married him six weeks later. There was no fuss and no planning. We sent a message out to our family and closest friends a week before, and those who could make it did. I wore a dress I bought with my mom from a boutique downtown the day before. I carried a bunch of flowers Sam picked up for me that morning, and my dad walked me up the steps to City Hall because we didn't have an aisle. There weren't many people allowed in the hall when we did it, just our parents, Lisa, Sam, and Jake. I wasn't nervous when I walked toward him. When I first caught sight of him standing there in his tux, smiling at me with so much love, I knew I'd made the right decision. I knew this was the best decision I would ever make.

Afterward, we went to a nice restaurant downtown, and my dad insisted on making a speech. Then, when Ryan stood up and told me he loved me more than I could ever possibly imagine, I knew he was telling the truth, because that's exactly how I feel about him.

The next day, Ryan got up and went to practice, and I went to a lecture.

And I've never been happier.

The End

# AUTHOR'S NOTE

Becca's story is a fictional story set in fictional places with fictional characters, but unfortunately it is the reality for some people—for far too many people—and I'm not just talking about a pretty girl and a star athlete. I'm talking about people from all different walks of life who have their worlds shattered by sexual assault.

I don't pretend to speak on behalf of victims of sexual assault. I know that every case and scenario is different, and I would never presume to understand how each individual feels. This book is not intended to hurt or upset anyone, and if it does, I am truly sorry. Becca's story does not demonstrate the way everyone would react, or perhaps it does; I don't know. I don't think you know how you'd react unless you are in that situation, and I pray that none of you are ever in that situation and are forced to find out how to deal with it.

For those of you who have read *Four Doors Down*, this book is completely different. It's much more serious and, I expect, a bit of a surprise. I think this book reflects my growth as a writer, and I also feel it is a story that needs to be told.

The idea for *Four Years Later* came to me at random. After doing some research, I realised how terrifying the statistics are and knew I had to write this book. One in five women is assaulted daily on college campuses in America. This has to change; something has to change. Nobody should be scared to come forward and report sexual assault. When they do, they shouldn't have to fear that they may not be believed and will in some way be blamed for it, and when the defendant is found guilty, they should receive a suitable, fitting sentence for their crime. It's that simple. Things have to change.

This book is for all the victims of sexual assault. You are not worthless. You are not broken. You didn't do anything wrong.

For the rape counseling helpline in the US contact:
800.656.HOPE (4673)

For rape counseling helpline in the UK contact:
0808 802 9999

For rape counseling helpline in Australia contact:
1800 211 028

For rape counselling in Canada contact:
416-597-8808

If you enjoyed this book, please consider leaving a review online or recommending to a friend.

# ABOUT THE AUTHOR

Emma loves to hear from readers.

Follow her on Facebook (Emma Doherty Author), Instagram (emma.doherty.author), and Twitter (@Em_Doh)

# ACKNOWLEDGEMENTS

This book took me longer than expected to write and whip into shape. It's a long process that I completely underestimated, and I have a bunch of people I need to thank for their help in getting me to the finish line.

First of all, thanks to Leah and Beth for being my early readers, for giving me the enthusiasm I needed to hear and being willing to reread chapters and sections. I appreciate it more than you can imagine, and Beth—I remember my promise!

Thanks to Zeia Jameson for filling me in on all the football lingo I was beyond clueless about and for all the helpful information.

Christine—thanks so much for your time and energy when beta reading. Your feedback meant the world to me. Thanks for helping me with the final few niggles and giving me your suggestions (all of which have made the book).

Sara Ney—you're wonderful as always. Thanks for helping me figure out self-publishing and never making me feel as though my endless questions are annoying (I know they can be).

Thanks to Murphy for the brilliant cover and to Holly for editing, both at Indie Solutions. You both did a wonderful job and I'm incredibly grateful.

Thanks to Caitlin with Editing by C. Marie for proofreading and her patience with me, and to Stacey at Champagne Formatting for formatting so beautifully.

Big thanks to my mum and dad. They're the best parents going and have given me so much support and encouragement this past year. I'd be lost without them.

Thanks to Laura and Danielle, the best sisters I could ask for, and to John (for all your advertising tips ☺).

Huge thanks to my brilliant friends who have been behind me a hundred percent, who are always asking about my next book and are always there to lean on and laugh with. You're the best.

To anyone who has read *Four Doors Down* and has left me a review or messaged me to tell me how much you've enjoyed it—I CANNOT tell you how much that meant to me. I was blown away by the response and I am so so grateful. You guys make me smile every day and I'm so lucky to have your support.

Finally, to anyone who has read this book, posted a review, or recommended it to a friend—thank you, thank you, thank you. It means the world to me.

Printed in Great Britain
by Amazon